BETRAYAL OF THE EVENFALL
First edition. May 31, 2023.

ISBN: 979-8-9862686-2-0
Written by Joe Field.
Cover designed by Joe Field.

BETRAYAL OF THE EVENFALL

Joe Field

Sarcastic Griffin Books

CONTENTS

Author's Note

At the end of this book are three appendices which are not necessary for the enjoyment of the novel but may be helpful if the reader develops questions. Appendix A contains a spoiler-free glossary of unfamiliar terms along with a pronunciation guide in alphabetical order. Appendix B covers details of the calendar within the world of Algendis. Finally, Appendix C provides an overview of the deities worshipped within the Gray Empire and their spheres of influence.

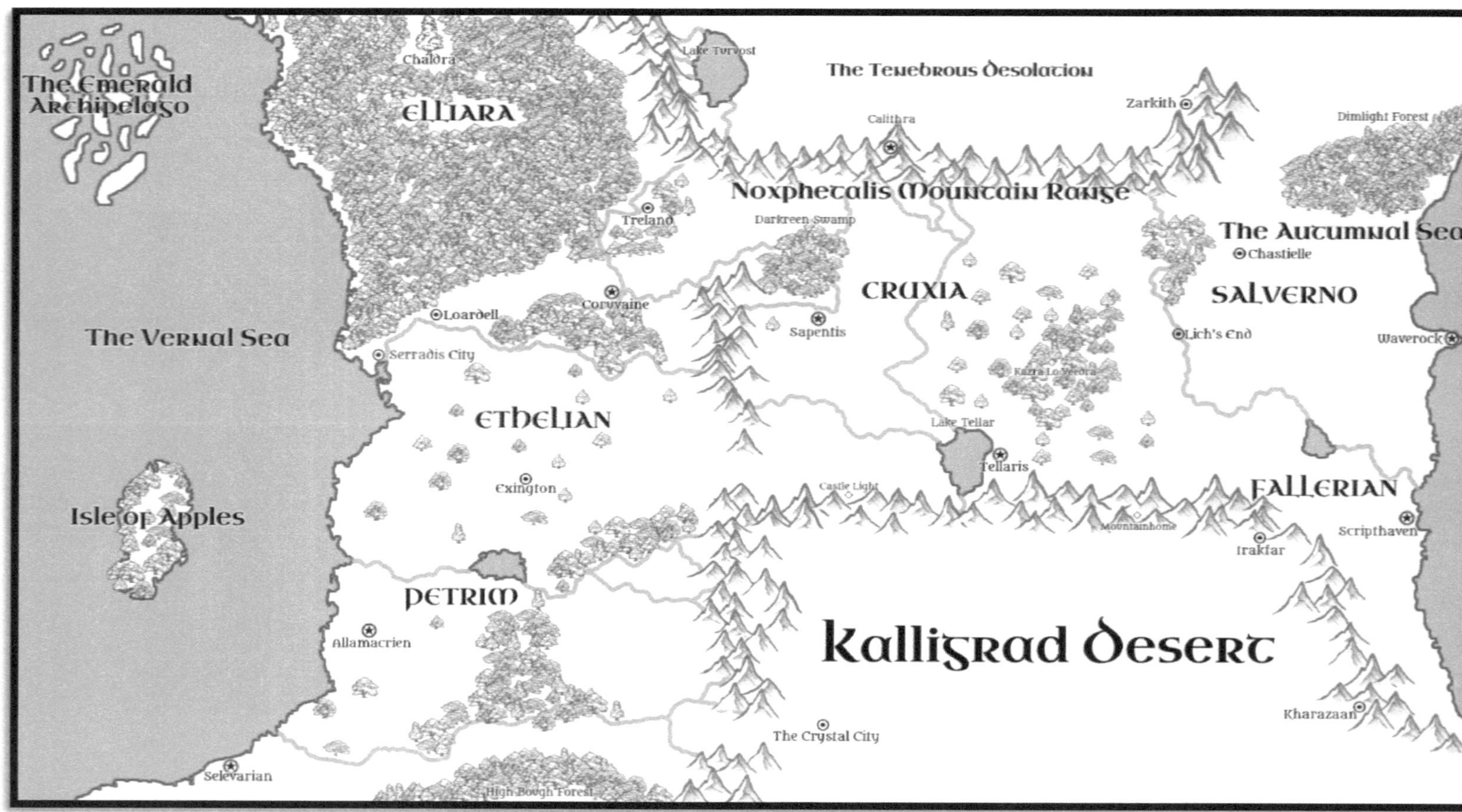

The Emerald Archipelago
Chaldra
ELLIARA
Lake Turvost
The Tenebrous Desolation
Zarkith
Calithra
Dimlight Forest
Noxphetalis Mountain Range
Treland
Darkreen Swamp
The Autumnal Sea
Chastielle
CRUXIA
SALVERNO
Coruvaine
Loardell
Sapentis
Lich's End
Waverock
The Vernal Sea
Serradis City
Kazra Lo Veora
ETHELIAN
Lake Tellar
Tellaris
Exington
Castle Light
FALLERIAN
Isle of Apples
Mountainhome
Scripthaven
Irakfar
PETRIM
Allamacrien
Kalligrad Desert
The Crystal City
Kharazaan
Selevarian
High Bough Forest

Prologue
Beginning At the End

"Told you I could do it!" Hazel shouted, grinning down from her high perch. She sat dangling her bare feet off the highest branch of the ash tree that could support her weight.

"Nicely done!" Claire called from the ground. She smirked at the boy standing beside her. "What do you think of that, Mr. I-Can-Climb-Higher-Than-Any-Girl?"

"It's not fair," Tommy complained with feigned annoyance. "Hazel is lighter than me so she can make it up to the skinnier branches without breaking them."

"You could have climbed this high if you didn't eat so many sugar rolls!" Hazel brushed a strand of brown hair from her face. "Don't blame me for your appetite, Tommy Beckinger!"

He gasped. "Hazel Enda! I think that's the rudest thing you've ever said to me! I'll have you know I'm a growing man and need my strength for when I join the palace guards! You need strength to swing a sword and catch criminals. You better hope I don't arrest you when I join."

Claire looked at him sideways. "And you better hope they have plenty of pastries."

Tommy shook his head. "It's like you both have it out to get me. I swear, dealing with you two will have prepared me more for taking down enemies of the kingdom than any official training ever could."

"Oh, yeah?" Claire said with a light laugh, tossing her blonde hair behind her. "Because we're such *dangerous criminals.*"

Tommy *was* bigger than either of the girls, but despite their jokes, much of the extra weight was muscle.

Hazel leaned back against the tree, savoring the last few hours of sunlight. She sighed contentedly, basking in the gentle warmth of the early evening sun. Summer was just emerging.

They had been friends since they were small children. All grew up in the same general area of Coruvaine, and all were educated by the same teachers. Their years spent together were filled with fun and trouble. The future, however, seemed less certain now than it had previously.

Adulthood was upon them. At sixteen, children became adults, and the schools of the capital city of Coruvaine in the Kingdom of Ethelian would bid farewell to those students who had come of age. Those with magical talent would join the arcane college, and some with non-magical interests would join the local university. Most students apprenticed with one of their parents, or a family friend.

Hazel wasn't sure what she wanted to do. Claire would turn sixteen in a couple of weeks, and Tommy's birthday was a few days after. Although both were only a month older than Hazel, they seemed much more advanced to her. They both had such well-defined plans. Hazel could also tell from the way Tommy looked at Claire and how she teased him that their plans included each other as more than just friends.

She took a deep breath of fresh air and listened to the wind rustling through the leaves and the constant murmur of the stream below her. This was what she loved. Running with her friends through the forest, holding competitions to see who could catch the biggest grass snake, having water fights in the river, climbing up the tallest trees... pretty soon, these times would end.

There wouldn't be enough days in summer.

"You two *are* criminals," Tommy said, crossing his arms. "You trespassed in the royal garden."

Claire rolled her eyes. "That wasn't *the* royal garden. Those were just some flowers growing within the first wall. They were barely inside the gate."

"That's hardly the point! It was nighttime and that's illegal!"

"And yet you came anyway," Hazel said, raising an eyebrow teasingly. "Why might that be, hmm?"

"I had to make sure you two didn't end up burning down the palace!"

"Burn down the palace?" Claire said. "By picking roses?"

"Knowing you two, anything could've happened! Besides, what's wrong with picking the roses out here, beyond the third wall?"

Claire wrinkled her nose. "These have aphids."

"So do the ones near the palace."

"Nuh-uh," Claire said, "I heard they use magic to keep the aphids away, and it helps the roses grow bigger and more beautiful. Isn't that right, Hazel?"

Hazel grinned with mock villainy. "I just wanted to break the rules."

"See!" Tommy exclaimed to no one in particular, "Criminals! The both of you. I need to be careful. Knowing both of you could hurt my chances of getting accepted into the palace guard."

"They already accepted you," Claire said.

"Well, you never know. They could take back their offer upon realizing that I have criminals for friends."

Claire playfully pushed him. "Do you think they wouldn't let you in because we're your friends, or because you couldn't have stopped us if you tried?"

He shoved her back, a twinkle in his eye. "I could've stopped you if I wanted to."

"Just like how you can climb higher than Hazel?"

They both grinned at each other, challenging each other silently.

Hazel sighed and rolled her eyes. "You two should just kiss already."

Tommy and Claire gasped in unison and stumbled back from each other. They turned their attention to the girl in the tree. "Hazel Enda!" Claire exclaimed, but couldn't think of anything else to say.

"Oh? What's this?" Hazel smiled, looking down. "I must have cast some magic spell, because both of you appear to have turned into bright red tomatoes."

Tommy stamped his foot. "Hazel! Where is your sense of prop—propry—properity—"

"—propriety?" Hazel offered.

"Yes, that! How could you suggest me and"—he waved his hand vaguely to Claire but avoided eye contact—"her would ever... I mean, I would never—"

Whap. Claire punched him in the shoulder.

"I didn't mean it like that! I mean, I wouldn't mind kiss—"

Whap! Claire hit him again, her face redder than before.

"Dammit! I think that's going to bruise! I didn't mean—"

"Please," Hazel said, grinning down, "say more. You're much better at digging yourself into holes than you are at climbing trees. Do you *want* to kiss her, or not?"

Tommy glanced between the girls, alarmed at his sudden predicament. "I, uh, you see..." He looked about wildly for a solution. He jumped suddenly with a smile. "Dinner! If we go now, it'll take at least an hour to get back home and by that time, it'll be time to eat!"

Claire sighed, but looked relieved. "Don't you ever think of anything besides your stomach?"

"Yeah, I do," Tommy said with a sudden mischievous grin. "I also think of how I'm going to beat Hazel in a race back to the third wall since she's stuck in a tree!" And with that, he took off running.

"Hey, that's not fair!" Claire ran after him. "I'll try to slow him down!"

Hazel laughed. "I'm sure you'll find *some* way to slow him down."

Claire stumbled and shot Hazel a death glare before continuing after Tommy. Hazel scurried down the branches of the tree. Tommy knew how to get a rise out of her: tell her what she couldn't do. She knew that even if she lost the race, it wouldn't be for lack of trying.

She was happy for them. They were close friends and had been for many years. In all that time, neither of them had been interested in anyone except each other. Neither would admit it, though to Hazel it was painfully obvious. She couldn't help feeling a little guilty. Did they keep themselves from being happy in order to prevent her from feeling lonely? Were they afraid she would feel cut off from them?

She couldn't help thinking the answer was *yes*. Her mother had asked if their closeness bothered her, but Hazel honestly believed Tommy and Claire belonged together. Claire was already a gifted herbalist with an excellent memory, and Tommy—for all their playful banter—had a good degree of common sense and was a natural protector. He would make an excellent soldier, and most day guards had few worries. Together, they would be a wonderful couple.

Claire occasionally asked if Hazel was interested in anyone. She poked and prodded, and even Tommy offered to introduce her to some of his friends. Romance didn't interest Hazel. The idea of it sounded wonderful—and the books she read reinforced that idea— but it seemed... confining.

Outside, in the sun and the wind—this was where she belonged. She sometimes imagined that the trees had names and were happy to see her. While she enjoyed the company of others, it couldn't compare to the serenity of the woods. Here there was freedom and clarity. In the city, there were expectations, rules, and walls. In the forest, she could do whatever she wanted. Who cared that running barefoot and climbing trees was unladylike at her age? No tree, shrub, or flower cared. There might be good reasons for the rules, but she preferred to be where those rules didn't apply.

She had descended halfway down the tree and the sounds of her two friends had faded into the distance. She took a deep breath and enjoyed the rush it gave her. The two things that made her feel most alive were being out in nature, and a challenge she could win. She had to hurry. She was a good climber and knew each branch by touch and which ones could support her weight. Her excitement mounted at the thought of racing after them. She imagined catching up to Tommy and how surprised he would be at her speed. He would probably claim she cheated somehow. She grinned at the scenario.

Her hands worked to grasp different branches to help her balance and distribute her weight. She neared the ground but was still too high to jump. She imagined she was like a squirrel running down the trunk of the tree. Her arms and legs moved instinctively with the flow of the branches. As she lowered one foot onto a bough, she shifted the weight of her left hand onto a lower branch.

Snap.

For a moment Hazel did not know what had happened. Stunned, she found herself tumbling backward, though her left hand still clutched the branch, now separated from the tree. Time slowed as she gazed through the canopy into the last hour of daylight. The beauty of it all struck her as she plummeted. She imagined someone reaching to catch her as she fell, but no one was there. A sudden cold rush enveloped her as she landed in the stream.

Thud.

The back of her head impacted against a solid rock in the creek and her vision blurred with dots of various colors against the wavering background of the water. She didn't notice any pain, just a slowed sense of confusion. Sensations slipped away, and she sank much deeper than the stream. As the last of her sight dimmed into the colored specks, she watched the sun reflecting off the trees through the rippling lens of the water. It had been such a beautiful day, but it was coming to an end. Nighttime had arrived sooner than she thought. Before Hazel could feel the sting of water as it filled her lungs, her world had completely darkened.

And that was how Hazel Enda died.

Chapter One
The Fear of Hopeless Knowledge

A massive battlefield stretched out before Hazel, strewn with corpses; some were fresh and others had long decayed. Snow was stained a deep carmine. A great army of light vied against a horde of moving corpses with gnashing teeth and gaping jaws. The roar of mighty beasts and monsters sounded overhead, and the shouts of soldiers created a deafening sense of confusion. The smell of refuse and blood suffused the air. Amid the melee, a grand estate loomed, surrounded by a cracking semi-translucent shield of dark magenta. A cold hand she hadn't noticed tightened on her shoulder and she turned to see a tall, robed aufhocker beside her, its six white eyes staring across the field.

"Behold," the creature rasped.

The earth shook with ever-increasing power. The armies ceased fighting and collapsed to the ground in disorder. Unsettling silence prevailed as green energy coalesced above the building and formed a human figure. The dark magenta shield dissolved as the figure gestured, and green magic inundated the undead. A wicked laugh rippled through their ranks as they mutated into warped monstrosities even more abhorrent than they first appeared. Then, the green shifted to deep, bloody red.

The aufhocker whispered, "All shall bow."

Soldiers fled as the undead ripped through them, scattering viscera and bodies without remorse.

"All shall weep."

Hazel stared at the hovering figure and felt herself drawn up to that height and gazed into an abyss of pain and hatred.

"All shall know the Living Lich of Half a Day."

Hazel gasped and awoke, wracked with panic as she exclaimed, " *The living lich of half a day shall rise with legions of undead that none can kill. Through betrayal of friends and oath, the living lich shall trample bodies and hearts. The world will quake as the impossible becomes the inevitable. The living lich of half a day may only be stopped by the slow progress of time. The day of the lich draws nigh.*"

It was then she noticed she floated above her bed, the same green magic swirling around her and holding her aloft. She drifted back to her bed and curled up. She was sweating, but felt cold. In the approaching gloom of her vision, she wept alone in the darkness.

What was she going to do?

Chapter Two
A Break in the Clouds

"Why don't you walk beside me?" Hazel asked over her shoulder.

Lyvaelan met her gaze with his large red eyes. "It's safer if I stay a small distance from you. I can react faster to threats."

The sixteen-year-old shook her head. "Following me from a dozen paces makes *you* look like the threat. Besides, you can use sorcery to sense people so why bother hiding?"

Lyvaelan opened his mouth to respond but then shut it. He stepped closer but still maintained some distance from her.

Hazel raised an eyebrow. "Come on, we can share my umbrella."

He looked away. "I don't mind the rain."

She raised both eyebrows and waited until he relented with a sigh. The rain that afternoon was intermittent from the time they left the library, at times a drizzle and at others nearly torrential.

After the harrowing fight the Watchers of the Evenfall endured at the hands of the Alchemist, Hazel wished to see her parents. The battle left Lara and Alistair badly injured, while Hazel and Lyvaelan sustained no visible wounds. She wondered about the toll it took on him. It was true he saved their lives and many others, but he nearly lost control. He could have destroyed the entire city and himself along with it. Strangely, Hazel didn't fear death. She hadn't, not since before she had been resurrected. Even when the cultists of Semeleme attempted to burn her alive, she wasn't afraid; she just wanted to escape the agonizing heat. Perhaps death was too big a concept to fear.

For some time after her resurrection, she experienced no emotions. She had since grown in her feelings and while they were not exactly the same as before, she now felt more human than ever—despite her green skin, ability to control plants, her healing magic, and her occupation as a supernatural guardian of the city. On further reflection, it might be more accurate to say she felt as human as she could, given her decidedly inhuman circumstances.

A sharp pain shot through her head before gradually subsiding into a dull throb, as if to remind her of one other factor separating her from most humans. Prophecy.

The headaches worsened. Her dreams grew sharper and more overpowering in their intensity and vividness.

"You had another dream last night," Lyvaelan said.

She nodded.

He sighed. "I hoped they would dissipate. Do you need to talk about it?"

"Not now, no." Hazel, in fact, *did* want to discuss the dream. The prophecy ringing in her mind demanded release. It was so close. The more she contained it, the more her headache worsened. Telling him was not enough, though. There was nothing he could do. "Lyvaelan, why did you choose to come with me to my parents' house?"

"To keep you safe," he said with quiet detachment.

"Remind me, why didn't you just put a glamour on me to keep people from noticing?"

"Glamours are less effective in large groups and during the day." He looked at her sideways. "Besides, with the Cult of Semeleme still after you, the spell would dissolve under their scrutiny. By joining you, I can directly implant sorcerous suggestions to keep others away."

They walked for a minute with nothing but the patter of rain on rooftops to fill the silence. Hazel breathed in the cold air and watched as her breath exhaled in twirling plumes of white. The world she had known was ending, and the time she had with her friends was little more than a breath dissolving in the rain.

"Will you meet my parents?" She asked.

"No."

"Not even if I asked you to?"

His jaw worked as they locked eyes. He finally averted his gaze. "I don't think they'd enjoy the experience."

Hazel stopped walking and tried to pull his eyes back to hers. "Maybe not, but that wasn't my question. Would you come with me if I asked?"

He took a deep breath before looking at her. "*Are* you asking?"

"Yes."

He searched her eyes. "Then I will."

"Why?"

Lyvaelan sighed testily and crossed his arms. "Does it matter?"

"It does to me."

"Well, you'll have to settle for disappointment, because I don't know why."

She thought back to their battle with the Alchemist. "You're not obligated to do what I want, Lyvaelan. You don't owe me anything."

His face scrunched in thought. "Whether I have an obligation to you is beside the point. I'm doing it because..." he stared off distantly, searching the horizon for the word. "... I want to. But also, I don't want to. That doesn't make sense."

Hazel smiled softly. "It's okay. So long as there isn't any guilt involved in your decision. I want you to trust me, Lyvaelan. I know you don't want to hurt me, so believe that I don't want to hurt you, either. My parents are good people, but they may be surprised by you at first. Even if it's scary, know that I will get you through it. Okay?"

He nodded, his eyes filled with an emotion Hazel couldn't identify. She smiled wider and took him down a side street, which opened into a row of city homes. The houses in Coruvaine typically had two levels. The lower level often served as a business, while the upper provided a living space. Her home hadn't required the lower level to be for business since her father was a blacksmith and did his forging outside in the yard adjacent to their home. Hazel looked at the brick and timber home she grew up in. It was strange to think she had been gone from home for so long and even stranger to find the retired Calixford University Library had taken its place. Her friends had fought alongside her. She could no more pinpoint the moment she thought of them as friends instead of colleagues than she could estimate when her feelings began to return. Perhaps they grew synchronously.

Hazel glanced to the side and nodded to a soldier who stood guard a short distance from the home. Ever since the Cult of Semeleme attempted to kill her, a sentry had been stationed to watch over the home, although there was little chance the cult would attack her parents. The living held no interest for them, only the undead.

She walked to the wooden door and knocked. Her mother's voice sounded from within when the door opened.

"Hazel!" her mother exclaimed and hugged her daughter. Lynn Enda held her close and showed no signs of relenting. Hazel sighed contentedly as she wrapped her arms around her mother.

"Hi Mom, I've missed you."

"We've missed you too." Lynn held her at arms-length and eyed her. "Are you sure it's safe coming here?"

Hazel gave half a smile. "As safe as it is anywhere."

"Well, I would have felt better if you brought someone with you."

It was then Hazel noticed Lyvaelan had disappeared.

"Is that my Daffodil I hear?" Kyle Enda barrelled down the stairs. To wrap his daughter in a crushing embrace.

"Dad," Hazel choked out, "you're making it hard to breathe."

"*I'm* making it hard to breathe?" He exclaimed. "Do you know how worried we've been? We've hardly breathed at all since you left." He put her back on the ground. "Well, come in! We haven't started dinner yet, but we'd love for you to stay or sleep over."

Hazel shook her head. "No, we can't stay for long. I just wanted to let you know that I'm doing alright."

Kyle nodded. "That's too bad. Are you sure you can't"—he blinked several times and raised an eyebrow—"'we'?"

"Yes, a friend accompanied me to protect me."

Kyle raised an eyebrow suggestively. "A friend?"

Hazel sighed testily. "Lyvaelan, come out."

A sudden gust of wind caused all of them to blink, and then Lyvaelan was there in his hood. Hazel squinted. There was something different about him.

"Lyvaelan?" Lynn said with a smile. "That's such a nice name. It's a pleasure to meet you." Hazel looked at her parents and saw both of them beaming without surprise. She knew what had happened.

"Lyvaelan," Hazel said, "no magic to hide yourself. Please."

He sighed, and Hazel sensed his facade drop as he removed his hood. Both parents gasped.

Hazel opened her mouth but was yanked back by her father, who interposed himself between her and the dark elf warlock. Lynn covered her face and backed from the door. Lyvaelan simply stood downcast and away from them. Kyle put his hand on the door to close it when Hazel grabbed the handle to keep it open.

"Stop," Hazel said. "This is my friend."

"What?" her father yelled. Her mother sank to the floor, her eyes wide.

"He's. My. Friend. Let him in!"

He shook his head. "You're crazy. You don't know—"

"I *do* know. Either he comes in or I go out!"

Kyle looked between them incredulously. "I know this is hard for you to understand, but he's dangerous. He's a monster! He's probably the reason part of the city was destroyed the other night."

Hazel winced and glanced at Lyvaelan. There was no comment her father could make that could be more painful. He was right. Lyvaelan's shoulders fell, and he wrung his hands, searching for a way to escape. But he promised Hazel he would stay. He trusted her.

Hazel closed her eyes and felt the life force of plants around her. "You're right, he is dangerous, but he's not the only one." She surrounded herself with viridescent light. The potted plants in the kitchen nearby burst from their containers, and the jasmine in front of the house grew and reached for her. She asked them to join her and they groped across the floor. The stems reached up to fan her with their leaves. Her parents gasped.

She sighed. "I'm dangerous, just like him. Will you throw me out as well? Am I a monster?"

Neither parent needed a moment to consider. "Of course not," Kyle said. "You're my daffodil."

"I could end the world." Hazel stared at her parents. "Why don't you reject me?"

"Because you're a good girl," her mother said through tears, "and that hasn't changed. It doesn't matter what was done to you, because I know you'll always be good."

Hazel wanted to disagree. The weight of the encroaching future was ready to bury her, but she couldn't tell them that. Not now. "Danger doesn't matter; goodness does. Lyvaelan is good. I've worked alongside him and he's taught me many wonderful things. He helped save me from the Cult of Semeleme. If it weren't for him, I might not be here today. I know he'll rescue me if I need saving, and I will be there for him if he ever needs me. I trust him."

Her father's grasp on the door relaxed, but he shook his head. "It's not that simple—"

"Nothing is simple," Hazel interrupted. "I know what he is. A dark elf and a warlock. I know the stories you've heard. He'd probably agree with every assessment you have of him and his race, but you'd both be mistaken. I trust him with my life. He's never disappointed me."

"Hazel," Kyle said slowly, "you can't expect us to throw away everything we know about creatures like him."

"I'm not asking you to," Hazel said. "I'm asking you to see him like I do. Don't just see *what* he is, but *who* he is. If he was as terrible as you think, do you believe he'd help me? Do you think shutting the door on his face would stop him if he wanted to get in?"

Both parents studied Lyvaelan uneasily. Lynn met Hazel's eyes. "This is a lot to spring on us."

"I know, but there was no easy way to tell you."

"We can't decide this immediately. We need time—"

"Okay." Hazel felt her headache adding to her agitation. "I'll make this easy. Either you let both of us in or I'll leave right now."

Her parents stepped back and commenced with a swift conversation. Finally, Kyle Enda sighed. "Alright Lyvaelan, can... come in." He walked toward the kitchen but stumbled. "Also, did you need to turn our home into a forest? It's impressive, but it doesn't exactly make your mother look like a model homemaker."

Her mother slapped his arm, some of the color returning to her cheeks. "With you leaving your tools everywhere, it's impossible for me to look like a model homemaker, regardless. Fortunately, guests know I'm married to you, so I can at least have their sympathy even if I don't have their respect." She looked at Hazel. "But could you do something about all of... this?"

Hazel smiled. "Sure." The green light surrounded her hand and the plants and roots crept back. "I'm not sure I can make them shrink, but that should help and they can be pruned later." She looked at Lyvaelan, who still stood outside, shifting his weight from foot to foot. "Come on, Lyvaelan." She whispered. "The only way they won't fear you is if they come to know you."

Lyvaelan ran a shaking hand through his black hair and nodded. He joined her.

As they entered the kitchen, Lynn glanced nervously between both of them and then gestured vaguely to the stove. "Do you drink tea?"

Lyvaelan cleared his throat. "Yes, I do."

"What kind?"

"Whatever you have."

They sat at the kitchen table and had the tea her mother served. As they talked, her parents gradually calmed, as did Lyvaelan. There was still uncertainty from all involved, but her parents to bore his presence better than she expected, even if her father wouldn't uncross his arms constantly glanced at a hammer he left on the kitchen counter. Her mother seemed incapable of sitting for longer than a few seconds before she needed to clean something else—a telltale sign of her uneasiness. Still, it was a step in the right direction, at least, and one which they needed to take sooner than later.

The time had come to tell them of the true nature of her work.

She told them of how they tracked down the Alchemist. She revealed that Lara and Alistair—both of whom they'd met before—were a werewolf and vampire, respectively. This surprised them, though the reaction was less pronounced than it might have been under different circumstances. She briefly mentioned their exploits, fighting aufhockers and alchemically enhanced humans. She spared some of the darkest details and kept from breaking the greater part of the confidence placed in her by the Evenfall Vigil.

When she finished, her father swept a hand over his brow and shook his head. "It's too dangerous. I don't like that you're out there risking your life."

Hazel looked at her green skin. "No matter where I go, I'll be risking my life."

"What your father means is there must be something less risky you can do. All this is too much. We worry about you, Hazel."

"I know, Mom. I know you're worried. I'm scared too. I barely know what I'm doing, but I'm trying my best. Wherever I go, trouble follows. All I can do is to be with the people best able to help me when I need it." She stood and looked at Lyvaelan. "We need to go. We have a briefing with the commander later tonight, and we still need to eat dinner."

They walked toward the door when Kyle gingerly touched Lyvaelan's shoulder. Her father's expression flickered between distrust and genuine concern. "Protect Hazel for us, will you? She means the world to us."

Lyvaelan nodded. "I feel the same." He pulled his hood over his head and strode into the rain.

Hazel embraced her parents and joined him. For some time, the two of them walked in silence.

"Why today?"

Hazel looked at Lyvaelan, his face obscured by his hood.

"Why did you want me to meet them today?"

The headache throbbed and pulsed in her temples. "Because there may be a time when they need to trust you, as I have. I should've prepared them sooner, but I didn't think to until recently."

"Why will they need to trust me?" Lyvaelan's brow knit as he turned his head to see her. "There's a haunted look in your eyes. What's going to happen?"

"Everything terrible I've seen is coming true," she said after several moments, "and there's nothing we can do to stop it."

Chapter Three
Meddling Bureaucracy

After a satisfying dinner prepared by their redcap housekeeper, Hazel set out for the Evenfall Vigil headquarters with the other three Watchers and Garo. They were less eager than the first time they defeated the individual they assumed was the Alchemist. Time had proven them wrong and they nearly died for the mistake. Despite this trepidation, they were in good cheer given the meal and conversation. Hazel noticed Alistair moved slower than usual, barely dragging his feet along the ground. Lara walked normally but was a little more reserved with her laughter. Otherwise, they had recovered swiftly from their injuries two nights ago. The vampire prince's lower spine had been broken, and he had lost a substantial quantity of blood. The werewolf had been stabbed by the vampire's enchanted sword through no fault of his own. Despite their nearly fatal injuries, both of them functioned well. Upon entering the building, they were greeted by the same soldier who filled in for Sergeant Concornus. The soldier asked them to wait as she rushed to the commander's room.

Commander Comrear exited from his room and appraised each of them silently. The bags under his eyes and his stubble revealed how little he rested in the last two days. Hazel braced herself for the verbal lashing he would undoubtedly unleash. He had little tolerance for their group.

Comrear studied them for a long moment. With a sharp voice, he shouted, "Soldiers! Attention!" All the members of the Evenfall Vigil sprang from their seats, backs straight, hands at their sides. The Watchers cast about, bewildered. "Turn!" they all turned to the five who entered. "Salute!" The soldiers put their right fists over their left breasts with their palms upwards and the index and middle fingers extended. Comrear examined the soldiers. He then turned his attention back to the Watchers and gave them a half-cocked smile. "Applaud."

The room broke out into applause and cheers. Many smiled at them. It was more than Hazel expected, and to see so many positively receive them was almost overwhelming. Comrear beckoned them to his office.

"Alright, alright, that's enough. They solved a crime they didn't kill a dragon. Back to work!" A few applauses lingered, but most soldiers sat and resumed their various tasks.

He led them into his office and sat in his chair, stroking the stubble on his chin. The group stood silently as he stared absently.

"You know," he said, chewing on his lower lip, "I've never been one to talk of the 'good old days.' I find such sentiments to be irrelevant to the needs of the present. People who spend their time wrapped in nostalgia are all too often relegated to the past themselves. Still, it's hard not to wish for simpler times." He shook his head. "When you four were thrown into my life, I thought I'd offended one or more of the gods somehow. What did I do to deserve this? The king and this magical mutt"—he gestured at Garo—"overrode my better judgment and made you members of my division. So, I made things easier for me. I gave you a simple case. Take a statement, go on multiple stakeouts, and find nothing. I've sent new soldiers on tasks like that a hundred times. Talking to the foreman was supposed to be useless. Do you know how many reports I get from citizens who claim supernatural things are happening when all they have is a rat in the wall? Too many. Riglin is a smart man, but anyone can be fooled, especially after working with magically chaotic fae."

He withdrew a bottle of dark liquor from a drawer in his desk, along with several shot glasses and began pouring. "The idea was to put you on the case and then—when you found nothing—you'd have taken care of the needs of an important individual and I wouldn't have to deal with you. Win-win. Instead, you find the *actual* culprit and follow the trail into a massive conspiracy involving a private contractor we've worked with *on numerous occasions* who's been supplying dangerous alchemical supplies to the city for over a year without opposition. You fight him, beat him, and nearly die." He looked at each of them hard. "I wish to the gods I didn't need you, but I do. I saw the damage and heard several reports from bystanders, and they were united in their praise. You beat five aufhockers and an incredibly powerful alchemist at great risk to yourselves. Thank you.

"I also owe you an apology, Ambassador. You did well in recommending them to this division."

"No apology necessary, Commander, although"—the black dog looked at the group—"some time off would be appreciated."

Comrear passed the glasses out to each of them, briefly raised his and downed it. He lifted his eyebrows at Garo. "That goes without saying. Actually, had you not arrived when you did, I was going to send soldiers to the library to take statements there." He leaned back. "You're off duty for the month. If any other soldier had taken the wounds you four sustained, I'd have them off the force for a minimum of three before beginning rehabilitation training. You all look much better, so you get a month. If by that time you still aren't feeling well, then you can take another."

Lara downed her glass of whiskey without hesitation. She then looked at Hazel expectantly. The girl frowned and pushed the glass over to the werewolf, who grinned and downed it too. Hard liquor wasn't something Hazel had developed the taste for just yet.

"With respect, Commander," Alistair said, glancing at the others for confirmation, "we only need a couple of weeks before we're ready to work again."

He smiled more warmly than Hazel had ever seen. "I appreciate your tenacity, but I won't risk putting you back in so soon after such an ordeal. Your bodies may be fine, but the emotional exhaustion weighs on all of you. Some soldiers try to start back immediately, but that's a mistake. Rest and recuperate, that's all. Even good soldiers can make terrible blunders when they've seen too much bloodshed. You four can visit and we'll fill you in on the investigation, but other than that, you won't be doing any work for the Evenfall Vigil."

"Speaking of the investigation," Lyvaelan said, shifting his gaze around the room, "are there any... casualties?" He looked uncomfortable and afraid of the answer.

Comrear poured himself another glass. "Thankfully, no. No-body inside"—he gave a meaningful look to Lyvaelan—"or outside the city were killed or suffered fatal injuries. Many citizens are rattled and there is substantial property damage, but nothing so terrible that it cannot be fixed. There were several lightning strikes within the third wall and outside it, but no one was struck and no fires ignited. In the future, try not to destroy Coruvaine when making an arrest."

Lyvaelan sighed heavily with relief. "Noted." He took the glass placed before him and downed it at once, his face momentarily con-torting at the taste.

Comrear continued. "Hazel brought a man back from the brink of death, which was impressive. He thanks you, by the way. Because of that specific act and your joint efforts protecting citizens, no one died."

"What about the rest of the report?" Lara said. She'd taken a seat in one of the nearby chairs and now rested at an odd angle, presuma-bly to lessen her discomfort.

"The rest? Well, there's about a thousand pages worth of notes I could give you on what we found. I'll give you the short version. Pax-ton Averly was—beyond any doubt—the criminal mastermind known as the Alchemist. We found everything in his laboratory. He had dozens of categorized barrels dedicated to specific parts of the bluecaps. His research focused on individual uses and interactions with bluecap body parts within alchemical solutions. The interior of that workshop was ghastly. For as awful as it was, it was equally thorough and organized. He may have been a genius but clearly misapplied his talents. Based on the largest quantity of body parts in each barrel, we believe he killed a minimum of three-hundred bluecaps over the last couple years. We didn't notice the drop in bluecap numbers partly because we don't track them but also because the aufhockers stole them from different locations each night they went out. Because their disappearances were sporadic, we didn't discover their decline in numbers. When the work on the fourth wall shifted to a single location, their absence was easier to spot.

"He created many products we are still analyzing. He had dozens of iterations of the potion he gave the man you fought before. We believe that was one of his final versions of the substance. The one he utilized was a topical variant which he theorized would grant greater speed, strength, and agility but without cognitive impairment or increased size. His research—at least what we could discern of it—contains multiple theories about the actual nature of the various bluecap parts beyond appearances. Averly appeared to take a keen interest in the preservative and temporal aspects of bluecap alchemy, but we aren't sure why. He interspersed codes within his writings we still need to decipher and so we can only speculate what he means."

"Have you questioned him?" Alistair asked.

Comrear smiled faintly. "No. He's been mostly sedated since we brought him in. I've had a few thaumaturgists and a medical wizard working on him while he's unconscious. Despite his powerful concoction, it didn't stop him from sustaining severe wounds. I wonder how that could've happened, hmm?"

Lyvaelan averted his eyes. Comrear chuckled. "I think he got what was coming to him. For the number of people he killed, I only wish he had a few more bones you could've broken. I wanted to leave him as he is so we could heal one bone at a time for each question he answered, but I've been informed that's 'unethical.' It's a damn shame."

A light knock came from the door as the soldier from the front desk entered. Comrear ushered her in. She whispered in his ear, and his expression darkened. He stood. "I'd like you five to come with me."

They walked out and saw Chief Inquisitor Thomas Eller standing in front of six others, who were dressed similarly in blue robes with a white rose on their chests.

The Inquisition.

"Good evening, Commander Comrear," Thomas Eller said.

"'Good evening' my ass," Comrear growled. "I know why you're here, and you're not welcome."

Thomas' expression remained neutral, despite the commander's threatening tone. "We're taking your prisoner, Paxton Averly, back to the Inquisition headquarters in the city to ensure his power is properly contained."

"It's properly contained *now*," Comrear said through gritted teeth. "The man can't even move, let alone make a potion. He doesn't have any power *worth* containing."

"This matter falls under the jurisdiction of the Inquisition of the Council of Archmages. You are expected to assist in this investigation to the best of your ability."

"*Assist?* We've done *all the work!*" Comrear roared. His face had flushed a deep crimson. "How is it that my soldiers work and die, then you claim it's *your* investigation?"

"We couldn't be certain the matter at hand was truly the work of spellcasters and so intervention was unnecessary," Thomas said levelly. His tone hadn't escalated with the fury of the commander. "Since we've witnessed the destructive power of Paxton Averly, we take no time in removing him so he can spend a very long time explaining himself and rotting away in Arcanathema Prison. He has done terrible things and must not be allowed to escape."

"Are you accusing my department of incompetence, Chief Inquisitor?" Marcus Comrear drew close to him, a dangerous edge to his voice.

Thomas Eller's blue eyes were icy as he stepped forward to meet the challenge. "I am. You and your department are out of your depth and range of competence. What you accomplished last night was miraculous. By rights, you should all be dead. If the Inquisition were present—"

"You weren't."

"And whose fault is that?"

"We knew as much as you did. Averly surprised us all, but the difference was *we* handled it and arrived at the scene before the sun rose. You only sent someone the morning after."

Thomas Eller sighed forcefully. "This squabbling is pointless. Bring forth Paxton Averly and complete the prisoner transfer. We will draw up the writ for your records, demonstrating our hand in this. You've done outstanding work; don't tarnish it with pointless obstinance."

Comrear locked eyes with Eller. Thomas' eyes were unreadable. Although his upright posture was unthreatening, nothing suggested he would back down. Comrear stared with a fury he struggled to contain. Hazel looked between the two as the room fell still. Finally, Comrear sighed. He gestured to the woman who alerted him. "Get Honrick. Tell her to prepare Averly for a prisoner transfer to the Inquisition along with all relevant evidence." She nodded and retreated.

Thomas inclined his head. "You made a wise decision."

"Shove it up your ass, Eller." Comrear returned to his office and slammed the door.

Thomas sighed. "The work of the Inquisition is rarely appreciated." He smiled at the group. "It's good to see you, though I hoped it would be under more pleasant circumstances. You performed in an exemplary fashion, I heard. Congratulations."

"Yeah." Lara noticed the glares from the other Evenfall Vigil soldiers. "Uh, thanks, maybe we can talk later?"

"Certainly." He followed her gaze. "This isn't the ideal place. I should return to the library later tonight after we get Averly nice and settled. You must tell me how the night went. I heard he was even more challenging than the last villain you faced. A truly triumphant conclusion to the story."

"The story isn't over yet," Garo said with a note of pride in his voice. "They have many years of solid work ahead of them."

"Of course. I meant this was a good end to their first major case, that's all. You worked hard to uncover so much and it paid off, even if the discovery was more a matter of chance than careful deduction."

"There is no luck," Hazel said suddenly, "only the providence of the gods."

He studied her curiously. "Indeed."

Ellen Honrick approached, and Thomas joined her and fell into conversation on legal matters. The group exited the building and passed a large blue cart painted with the white rose of the Inquisition.

"That was an odd thing to say, Hazel," Garo remarked. "I don't disagree, but what made you think of it?"

"I don't know. My mom used to tell me that whenever something bad happened and I felt sorry for myself. It seemed right to say it. Also"—she hesitated—"I'm not so sure this case is over."

Lyvaelan turned to her sharply. "Explain."

"The Alchemist worked with the aufhockers, right? How? Paxton Averly was just an alchemist."

Lara frowned. "Maybe he lied?"

Garo's face turned serious. "Lied? You can't lie about arcane talent. Conjuring aufhockers, especially in such numbers, would require a gifted conjurer."

"And Paxton Averly had no great magical power." Alistair's eyes widened. "I had completely forgotten with everything that happened. He couldn't have been the one conjuring the aufhockers."

"Maybe they just wanted to help for fun?" Lara ventured.

"No," Lyvaelan said. "Ignoring the fact that aufhockers see humans as food, not allies, I reached out to one of them in our battle and sensed some force manipulating it. It was definitely a conjurer, and likely a conjurer of significant talent and training."

Lara buried her face in her hands. "Ugh. NO! Does this stupid business never end?"

"It would seem not," the vampire sighed heavily. "I'm at a loss. Who should we report to, Commander Comrear or Inquisitor Eller?"

"A good question," Garo said. "I recommend telling Inquisitor Eller about this and asking him how to proceed. He knows the legal side of matters such as this. Now that the Inquisition is involved, they will probably be able to determine who he was working with quickly. There are some sorcerers within the Inquisition who could extract such information if they know what they're looking for."

They walked back to the library, discussing the matter, except for Hazel. She was bothered by this epiphany, but worried more about what lurked ahead. Could the lich of her dreams be behind this? Even now, the images and words from her dream intruded into her mind. When she spoke to Thomas Eller, it was as if she talked over a voice whispering in her ear. She felt distracted in her response, like she'd stumbled over her words, and yet what she said was astoundingly correct. Perhaps it was the guidance of the gods. She tried to shrug off the headache induced by her vision and ignore it, but she didn't know how long she could neglect the coming of the living lich.

Chapter Four
The Archmage of Sorcery

"If you keep that expression on your face, it might stay like that permanently."

The Archmage of Sorcery, Malvex Sorelle, stood in the doorway of Alvaria's office. The half dark elf wore a white cassock embroidered with swirling vaporous designs so that it resembled the whitest smoke which signified high mastery of sorcery. A sash of identical color around his waist signifying his preeminence among sorcerers as the master of high masters. A long black cloak obscured much of his body, clasped in the front with a brooch of amethyst that matched the violet color of his eyes. He leaned on his staff, which was simple—by archmage standards. It was crafted of silver wood, with a black geode containing white quartz adorning the top. Its similarity to an eye was uncanny. Popular imagination claimed that the moment one noticed the geode stare and wink was the moment the Archmage of Sorcery knew everything he needed to know. Of course, she knew better. Malvex always knew more than he let on.

Alvaria put down the pen, folded her hands, and raised an eyebrow. "If any expression will be stuck on anyone's face, it will be that smile on yours. How did you sneak past my inquisitors without getting stopped?"

He shrugged. "In the usual way. I am rarely noticed if I do not wish to be."

She nodded with mock seriousness. "They never stood a chance against not only a high master sorcerer, but the greatest of all high masters of the art."

"Careful, Alvaria, flattery will get you everywhere." He closed his eyes and shrugged. "I have little interest in wading through an ocean of well-intentioned bureaucrats to converse with a friend and former student." He glanced at the note Alvaria had been writing and beckoned with his finger. The note floated off the desk and through the air and hovered before his face. "What has you so preoccupied?"

"It's usually polite to ask before reading personal notes."

"Kazra Lo Veedra?" He read the rest before turning his attention back to her. "You still haven't settled that case?"

"Not entirely, no." She stood and strode to him. "Why don't you join me? I need to deliver the letter personally. We can discuss why you came and the business I'm working on."

"A walk to confiscations sounds enjoyable. Lead on." He gestured with a small bow.

A staff of clear glass floated to her hand. Various gems glistened along its exterior and interior. The staff spiraled up into vines that wrapped around a dark blue octahedron at the very top.

The two archmages ambled through the hallways of the Department of Inquisition. They passed several inquisitors and other administrators. Alvaria noticed many who saw them expressed momentary shock, but immediately calmed and continued past as if nothing had happened. When she said Malvex was the greatest sorcerer alive, she was not exaggerating. She had trained with him for many years before she became an archmage and found his sorcery to be almost unparalleled. While sorcery required little magic or incanting to function, the requisite mental acuity and intense creativity were challenging for many spellcasters. His abilities had grown considerably and consistently to the degree that she still used him as a consultant with the Inquisition and gave him the honorary title of Grand Interrogator. He disliked the title, but Alvaria ensured it stuck, as much to honor his contributions as to needle him. His power was nearly effortless. Many sorcerers used sorcery in this unconscious manner, but none did so with such ease or frightful giftedness. Unless one was careful and well trained in mind-shielding techniques, the Archmage of Sorcery could easily make that person forget everything they'd ever experienced or send that person to an entirely different world he created on a whim. He rarely exercised his abilities to toy with others, but sometimes used them subliminally to effect what he wanted.

His garb reflected who he was as a person. The simplicity and lack of pomp was not so much disregard or annoyance, but a genuine discomfort with being an object of attention and reverence. Many sorcerers found wealth, rituals, and customs to be tiresome and a block to mental liberty, and he felt no differently. As an archmage, he naturally attracted luxuries from his position and people who revered him. He could do little to eschew all duties, but he could avoid being noticed unnecessarily.

Alvaria witnessed these moments of recognition in others and subsequent memory loss were a product of Malvex's desire to circumvent crowds and recognition. He was a great man, but truly introverted. His power was subtle to the degree that it was a challenge even for her to notice. Sensing his consciousness was like noticing a light mist by touch alone; it was possible, but extremely difficult. He cared little for the station he was in for the fame it granted, but for the opportunities it presented. Sorcery was his passion—people were not. Alvaria understood how tiring the bows, requests, and praises could be after so many years. Archmages were both religious leaders and researchers, sworn to serve the goddess Selevara as her high priests and priestesses, with the High Archmage foremost as her beloved.

"So, Kazra Lo Veedra?" he said, turning to her. "Tell me more. That was your first major case as Grand Inquisitor, was it not?"

"It was. Almost thirty years ago to the date. I went there myself to ensure its safe capture."

He chuckled. "It's unusual for a Grand Inquisitor to enter the field except to deal with legal aspects and oversee new installations."

"Well, as you pointed out previously, I *am* unusual." She took out her key and unlocked a door just beyond the Department of Inquisition. She put a small burst of magic into the key along with her will and opened the door. They exited into another hallway nine levels down from where they had previously stood. The archmages needed to move about the massive palace swiftly, so keys that could open doors to teleport to other locations in Palace Valsidan were immensely useful. The two walked through and continued down a long and gently sloping corridor.

"True," Malvex said, "but you're also efficient, which makes me wonder why you're still sending wagons to Kazra Lo Veedra."

"Efficient and *thorough,*" she said pointedly. "Antony Larsinius was a brilliant mage. He did everything he could to ensure his lichdom came to fruition. It was by luck we discovered the estate prior to his ascendance. He did what he could to guarantee that whoever stepped foot into his home would be destroyed, or their memories erased. Fortunately, the sorcerous enchantments he placed degraded and mutated, giving anyone who came within several miles of the area severe amnesia. Some well-intentioned and spirited villagers believed a local sorcerer was responsible and contacted the local authorities, who eventually forwarded the information to me. Athelea was with us that day, I think."

"The goddess of knowledge helps us every day. Why are you sending so many wagons?"

"He possessed several oddities that are difficult to understand the origin of, and parts of the structure itself are enchanted and need to be properly dismantled outside of the property to ensure no harm befalls anyone else. It isn't enough to just lock the doors and *hope* no one else saunters in. If even a basic spellcaster were to enter and take control, the effects could be devastating. The enchantments rival those within Chateau Zarielle, which is no small feat since the chateau was designed to ward off any attack, whether from a horde of mages or from a dominion of dragons. Leaving Kazra Lo Veedra as it is could be a costly mistake."

"True. Still, I can't imagine after all these years you're still working on such distant business. Kazra Lo Veedra is on the other side of the Gray Empire, isn't it? I've never checked on a map."

She sighed. "Yes, or at least nearly. It's in the northeastern foothills of Tellaris, about a hundred miles from the edges of the imperial capital."

Malvex whistled. "That's at least two thousand miles away as the griffin flies. How long does it take to get there?"

"By laden wagon and using established paths, it would take just over three months. Using gates lowers the time to about three weeks."

He frowned. "That's still quite some time. Besides, gate travel is exhausting when done too frequently."

"Yes, which is why I instruct my inquisitors to rest a day or two about midway through such journeys. It's difficult enough for a spellcaster, but I've seen horses die instantly from a week of daily travel through gates."

He nodded gravely. "Worse has happened to greater creatures than horses. Teleportation magic is precarious business."

Alvaria inwardly shuddered. Malvex understated the matter. Teleportation came in many forms, but all were dangerous, even in their safest forms. It took absolute concentration from a powerful spellcaster to either send or travel across any distance. A momentary lapse, either from pain or fatigue, could cause an incomplete substance transfer. In the cleanest possible outcome, a spellcaster might lose a few fingers. In the more common and frightening examples, the spellcaster might arrive at every location between the place he left and his intended destination. A thin red contrail might be all that remained of a once skilled spellcaster. The gates helped prevent this by directing the magic to a specific location within a definite range.

Spellcasters could simply channel magic into the gate and step through with few worries, although the science and placement of the structures took time. If gates were placed too close, incomplete substance transfers could occur, and if they were too far, travelers could find themselves in a wholly different location, with some part of themselves missing. Even with the perfection of gates, problems still arose and their use frequently wore on users. For this reason, a receiving gate was usually not placed closer than ten miles to the next sending gate, primarily to prevent incomplete substance transfers, but also to ensure travelers rested and did not attempt journeying through more than three gates in a single day.

She looked at Malvex. "Do you know if the Department of Teleportation has installed any recent gates?"

He glanced at her, then ahead with amusement. "The last I heard, they had asked the Archmage of Crystals if they could use the Crystal City as a location from which they could send and receive travelers from a gate on the other side of the Kaligrad Desert."

She winced. "I imagine that didn't go over well."

Malvex smiled. "They probably should have gradually worked up to asking. I'm told the Archmage of Teleportation requested a pure amethyst gate for sending across the desert at the same time."

Alvaria gasped. "He asked one of the surliest archmages to open his isolationist city to immense travel *and then* requested he construct a gate of pure amethyst? What was Allan thinking?"

He chuckled. "You know Allan Dreverin. His mind is always a couple of gates away from the rest of him. Anyhow, he's now petitioning the High Archmage to override the Archmage of Crystals."

"Do you think the High Archmage will do it?"

"I think he'll develop a compromise that will placate the Archmage of Crystals while giving Archmage Dreverin what he wants. Likely he will petition the creation of an amethyst gate outside the Crystal City and at a fair distance so as not to bother the Archmage of Crystals. I don't think even the High Archmage wishes to vex the temperamental sensibilities of the Crystal King."

"A sign of the great wisdom of our leader," Alvaria said, shaking her head. "I know even Gar turns tail if the Archmage of Crystals heads in his direction, and Gar has wrestled with dragons. Do you know anyone who the High Archmage gives greater freedom to than Archmage Kalsidere?"

The Archmage of Sorcery looked at her sideways. "It's unwise to speak his name."

She rolled her eyes. "Is it really such a problem?"

"Only if he hears it. He hates any reference to life before his transformation. To answer your question, I believe the High Archmage is indulgent with all of us. We got into our positions through careful selection and professional recommendation. He doesn't need to oversee everything we do because further oversight would more likely hinder our development than augment it. How often has he visited your department or requested anything from you?"

Alvaria frowned. "He once asked me to look into a problem in Salverno. Otherwise, he's never visited or requested any documents."

"It was much the same for me when I was the Grand Inquisitor. I remember laboring over every matter in painstaking detail until I realized the freedom I actually had."

She raised an eyebrow. "Was that when you stopped writing good reports?"

He laughed. "Did I *ever* write good reports?"

She lightly nudged him with a grin. "Your reports were more on a gradient, from bad to horrendous. It was fairly clear your major interests did not lie within the white rose of the Inquisition."

They passed through a hallway decorated on both sides by a fresco depicting the War of the Gods. "True enough. I couldn't wait to leave."

"How was it you remained the Grand Inquisitor for so long? You possessed the role for almost as long as I have."

"Yes, I was Grand Inquisitor for... what, twenty-five? Twenty-seven years? Somewhere around there. I stayed because I was aided by inquisitors who cared more for the organization than I did. The High Archmage removed some of the pressure. He made me both the Archmage of the Inquisition and the Archmage of Sorcery simultaneously. Since much of the Inquisition could function on its own, I devoted more time to my true interests. Instead of my life being consumed by a single tedious chore—no offense—I could split time and remain happy while only *occasionally* being miserable."

Alvaria chuckled. "You really hated being Grand Inquisitor, didn't you?"

"You have no idea. Sorcery has been my passion since I was a child. Being at the forefront of the field is a dream come true."

"You aren't just at the forefront, though. You're the most powerful living sorcerer in existence."

He shook his head. "The High Archmage—"

"—doesn't count," she interrupted. "The High Archmage is like some higher being, surpassing the normal limits of every form of magic to an unprecedented degree. Barring the High Archmage, who is a stronger living sorcerer you know of?"

He rubbed his short black beard. "There are some who are better at specific practices than I am, but I am well-rounded, and perhaps excel in a few areas as well. Memory modification and mental probing are my unparalleled talents, but that's also the reason I was named Grand Inquisitor and ended up in the position for so long. Aside from that, I'm sure there are at least a couple mages in Arcanathema who are better in specific sorcerous disciplines than I am. The Lord of Mazes comes to mind."

"He might be a better illusionist than you, but he's also insane with arcane madness. Magic inundated his psyche irreparably. It's easy to surpass limits when one gives up everything that makes one human. Besides, you defeated him."

Malvex shook his head. "I *survived* my encounter with the Lord of Mazes, which surprised him enough to give me an advantage. Nothing more. Incidentally, I recently spoke on this subject to a group of children when I guest lectured at Selevara's Arcane Academy. There's a reason we worship Athelea and Selevara instead of Gnostrevaine and Terekmalamae. Athelea and Gnostrevaine may both be gods of knowledge, but Athelea demands effort and knowledge is the reward, whereas Gnostrevaine gives effortless knowledge and demands self-destruction as recompense."

Alvaria noticed the flow of magic changing as the hallway led underground. Fewer paintings hung along the corridor and the number of passersby had decreased. "And Selevara grants us the use of magic while separating us from the stream, whereas Terekmalamae allows the use of magic by submersion and consequent madness or immolation. Yes, I know. The archmages serve as a constant reminder to others of the unending road of knowledge and power that can be attained through merit, while warlocks serve as an example of easily gained yet volatile power that destroys itself. Although it should be said that some of us have received gifts, curses, or alterations through our studies that might outwardly appear to contradict that."

"You mean like the Archmage of Dragons?"

She nodded. "Garson *appears* as if he attained power through happenstance. He even plays it off that way. The truth is, the dragons empowered him because they thought he deserved it, not because they throw around such gifts whimsically. He gained trust, got to know them, and helped in whatever ways he could. While he might argue he could never merit such an honor, he did. He earned it every bit as much as any of us have earned our standing as archmages."

He smiled warmly at her. "How did you ever get to be so wise?"

She continued looking down the hallway as she half smiled. "I had good teachers."

They continued to curve through the perimeter of the palace and down the slope until they had reached subterranean levels. For a short while, the dark was lit by the radiant glow of magelamps, but eventually they were replaced by conventional lanterns. Despite the subterranean nature of the place, it still felt welcoming. The hall remained wide all the way down, and tall, for often carts were driven indoors to transport large confiscated materials. At the end of the slope, a slab of stone ended the corridor with only a set of large double doors of polished bronze standing before them, bearing the white rose of the Inquisition. Alvaria and Malvex opened the doors by hand. Down here, magic was scarce because of special nullification glyphs, courtesy of the Archmage of Null. It made it more difficult for magically gifted criminals to take any potentially dangerous artifacts from the vault. They stepped into an office with another stone slab behind the desk, except this one lacked any noticeable doors. A young woman sat at the desk reading a book when the two archmages entered. She jumped to attention.

"Grand Inquisitor—Grand Interrogator! Welcome! How may I serve you?"

Alvaria glanced at Malvex and noted his discomfort with amusement. "I am here to deliver a note for Inquisitor Barston. I'm sure he's busy and therefore unable to meet me in person, but I would like him to take three carts to Kazra Lo Veedra at his earliest convenience. I wrote this note for him, which you may read to ensure he gets the message even if the note is lost. He is to take four inquisitors per cart, along with whatever tools are necessary. The lich's secondary sepulcher was discovered along with an urn containing ashes of unknown origin, several time-crystals, sacrificial weapons, and a tome of the attempted lich's research. All tools for deconstruction of the lich's vault and potential phylacteries should also be brought."

She bowed. "As you command, Grand Inquisitor. I will bring this to him at once." She turned to the wall and placed her hand against its surface. She muttered a few quiet words, and the stone rippled and separated, creating a vast gap in the wall, revealing long rows of shelves containing various items and a corridor wide enough to fit a team of horses. The wall rippled back into place after she stepped through. In a few minutes, the young woman reemerged with a smile.

"I gave the note to Inquisitor Barston, and he told me to let you know he would have a team assembled and three carts on the road within the week."

"Splendid. Thank you, Emilia."

She bowed deeply with a large grin. "It is my honor to serve, Grand Inquisitor."

As they left, Malvex turned to Alvaria. "I think you made that girl's day by simply knowing her name."

"Perhaps. I'm a bit of a celebrity in this department."

"Apparently, so am I." He frowned at her. "Do you pay them to call me the Grand Interrogator?"

She looked at him innocently. "I don't pay them extra, but they have received occasional bonuses for completely unrelated reasons."

He sighed and shook his head. "You're corrupt, Alvaria. Corrupt as any I've encountered."

She laughed. "You're just frustrated you can't change every mind you come into contact with. That girl would've been much easier to affect if Avrael's magic hadn't prevented it. All of that aside, what was the reason for your visit in the first place?"

"Oh, I had almost forgotten!" he said with feigned surprise. "The High Archmage wants to speak with you at your earliest convenience."

"What?" she shouted, her voice echoing through the hall. She punched him in the arm. "Why didn't you tell me sooner? That's a *little* more important than delivering a letter!"

"Ow, that kind of hurt," he said, rubbing his arm while hiding a smile. "Must you always resort to violence? You're too worked up about this. He just wanted to see you, so he sent me to see when you're available. I spoke with him about administration and sorcery, and he asked if I wouldn't mind seeing when you're free."

"For the High Archmage? The Hierophant of Selevara? The leader of every spellcaster in existence?"

"Yes, that one." He said, his grin returning in full. "He's still just a man, Alvaria. Don't be so panicked. When would you like to see him?"

That the High Archmage would wait for *her* bordered on ludicrous. "I will see him whenever he would like."

"Good. Let's go now."

"Now? I've hardly prepared!"

He rolled his eyes. "Would you like to see him at *your* earliest convenience or *his*? You can't pick both. Besides, you look lovely today and in the height of fashion—as usual."

She frowned. "Point taken. Let's go."

They hurried back up to the surface, and Malvex withdrew a large gem-encrusted key, which shimmered at his touch. When they arrived at a door, he put the key to the lock and whispered a few words before turning it and opening. The other side of the door was a different side of the castle, much closer than they had been. Not all keys could unlock or open teleport gates to any location within the castle, but Alvaria could guess this corridor was the closest Malvex could get them to the High Archmage's office on the highest floor of the central tower, although calling it a "tower" did the structure little justice except in picturing its height. The central tower was as wide as many castle keeps and connected to other towers via lengthy and elegant bridges suspended using the same magic that allowed the entire building to exist without collapsing under its own weight.

They strode across one long bridge of white stone, with glyphs engraved on each railing's otherwise smooth surface. Along the entire bridge stood two rows of eleven guards facing each other. They dressed in ornate white armor and blue capes, each bearing various symbols and arcane glyphs. Their faces could not be seen, and they held spears topped with black ravnulium, the magic-impervious metal. They were placed ten feet apart and across from each other, and held their positions as unmoving as statues. Despite their armored appearance, these were among the deadliest mages in Selevarian. They were the Guard Unyielding, the sworn protectors of the High Archmage. Only those mages who had mastered many combative magics and physical martial arts could join them. They considered their task to be a holy mission, one granted by the Hierophant of Selevara. It was a challenging occupation and one devoid of further upward ambition. Some viewed them as nothing more than excellent servants, but Alvaria knew better. She had only seen them fight once when a roost of wyverns attacked the tower, guided by a conjurer. There was no hesitation as they leaped onto each winged monster with a grace and speed one would not expect from warriors so heavily armored. The threat had ended before the alarm could be raised. Alvaria had come at the behest of the High Archmage at that time as well.

She took in her surroundings now, faintly hoping to see a similar spectacle at this dizzying height, but there was nothing except the torrential downpour. An invisible ward protected the open walk from the elements, though she doubted even the worst blizzard would sway the determined stance of the Guard Unyielding.

They approached the door when two members of the guard crossed their spears before them. "Identify yourselves." They said in unison, their armor giving a metallic and inhuman quality to their voices.

"Malvex Sorrelle, Archmage of Sorcery."

"Alvaria Saccarra, Archmage of the Inquisition. The High Archmage expects us."

The guards simultaneously uncrossed their spears and opened both doors for them. The archmages entered a foyer with a row of chairs against the wall and an ornately carved wooden door before them. To the side of the entrance was a wide desk and a small man who stood to greet them. He appeared ancient and stooped. A long white beard hanging on a multitude of wrinkles matched his long curling eyebrows. He wore a light gray tunic and held a long and elegant wooden staff topped with many small glittering gems. Alvaria did not see the man frequently, but recognized him as the Archmage of Ceremonies. This was one of the oldest living human archmages. He crowned the new High Archmage, and supervised all religious functions, ensuring everyone followed the proper rubrics. He worked closely with the High Archmage to uphold ancient traditions and advised him whenever necessary. They were good friends, or so she had heard.

The Archmage of Ceremonies approached them with a smile. "Greetings to you, Archmage of Sorcery, and to you, Archmage of the Inquisition." His voice was soft and warm, yet worn with age. "I'm afraid the Archmage of Lights is currently with the High Archmage. If you could wait but a few moments, I'm certain she will be out shortly."

"I'm already out, Flavian dear," came a voice from the now open door. The Archmage of Lights flowed out and walked to the archmages. Her dark brown skin contrasted with her pure white hair and white eyes. Her smile—while not literally glowing—was the most radiant part of her. Her golden robes rippled into opalescent colors as light sparkled and danced off of her. A net of diamonds adorned her curly hair, and a necklace of similar make hung from her neck. A staff of pure glass reflected rainbow colors throughout and was topped with a massive opal.

"Oh!" she exclaimed upon seeing Alvaria. She rushed to her and wrapped her in an enveloping hug. "It's so good to see you!"

Alvaria almost reflexively resisted, but instead contentedly sighed into the warm embrace. She felt her worries melting away.

"It's good to see you, Archmage of Lights," Alvaria said.

"Alva," she whispered, "how many times do I need to tell you? Call me Ellia. We're friends, aren't we?"

"Mhmm," Alvaria agreed.

"That's what I thought." Ellia pulled back from Alvaria but held both her shoulders. "Alva, I swear you get more beautiful every day I see you."

"That's only because you evoke the beauty in others, Ellia."

"You are too sweet." She held Alvaria's cheek before turning to Malvex. "Mal, it's good to see you, too."

Malvex couldn't suppress a smile. "Your positivity is as infectious as ever, Elliavenra Sivenna."

She walked to him and took both his hands as they exchanged a quick kiss on the cheek. "I can't help it if I like to share the light with everyone else."

"I wouldn't have it any other way."

The Archmage of Lights was an interesting woman. Her studies ranged in the scientific and metaphorical nature of light in ways Alvaria had never thought to consider. She collaborated with the Archmage of Music each year to host a demonstration called the Orchestra of Lights. Although the performance was neither necessary nor religiously required, it had grown into an essential holiday for many who viewed it. Four hours of swirling lights and music melded perfectly to create a transcendental experience that was impossible to adequately describe. It resembled the most intimate of embraces and the kindest of words combined in a breathtaking display. No one left such a celebration without shedding tears over the sheer flood of emotions it aroused. Ellia's power made her untouchable to many of the darker creatures in the world. As a result, she occasionally helped the Inquisition deal with local threats when they arose.

"Not to prematurely end this exchange, but there is another person waiting to see both of you," Flavian Thelos—Archmage of Ceremonies—said gently. "The High Archmage has other appointments to keep."

"And so do I," said Ellia. "Mal, Alva, it was a pleasure seeing you. Take care of yourselves and take care of each other."

Malvex nodded. "We always do. I hope to see you before the next meeting."

She left the room with a spring in her step. As she departed, the room dimmed in her absence. Malvex gestured to the door. "Shall we?"

Alvaria stepped through and into the office of the High Archmage. Floors of dark cherry covered the room. Tall and intricately carved bookshelves lined the perimeter and rose to the tall ceiling. The ceiling itself was a dome with ornate and elaborate art decorating the entire surface. In the center of the piece stood Selevara holding a star aloft, and opposite her Athelea held a scroll so that the star and the scroll overlapped. This was the image spellcasters everywhere recognized as the symbol of the Council of Archmages.

Anthropomorphic representations of each of the seven arcane disciplines surrounded the goddesses. These depictions were ancient, and some historians believed they were based on actual people, but no definitive evidence existed. Candelabra mirrored both sides of the room, each bearing seven different colors of flame on unburned wicks, each with a primary or secondary color and a center white flame. Two elegant stairways behind Alvaria led to a landing with a variety of implements and special materials. Between the two staircases was a large mirror, twice as wide as a person and a few feet taller. This mirror, Alvaria knew, led to a strange room known as the Hall of Memories. While its existence was known to some, no archmage had ever been admitted into it—to Alvaria's knowledge—not even the Archmage of Ceremonies. Only the High Archmage could enter and the exact nature of the place was unclear. Neither the current High Archmage nor any of his predecessors had ever seen fit to elaborate on the finer details. Oddly, the history books mentioned its existence before the palace itself had ever been built.

Behind an ornately carved mahogany desk depicting innumerable monsters sat the High Archmage. His hair was pure white, as was his beard, which extended only a few inches from his chin. Kind gray eyes looked out from under his wrinkled brow, and a genuine smile brought a glow to his face. He was old, but somehow timeless. He exuded a youthful energy tempered by elderly restraint. He wore a pure white doublet without frills that was fashioned of a simple but strong fabric. No rings adorned his fingers, but resting on his chest was a silver amulet with a large diamond in the center with opposing pairs of various gemstones laid out around the perimeter of the circle. The silver created additional shapes and was almost unrecognizable as anything but a fine piece of jewelry, unless one was a spellcaster. The amulet formed a small but powerful conjurer's circle. Around his head, occasional twinkling lights could be seen. The Crown of Stars. The High Archmage rarely wore anything on his head, but ever-present was the sign of his preeminence among the archmages as the Beloved of Selevara, her grand hierophant. The crown he wore was not made of metal, wood, or glass, but of magic itself that could neither be dispelled nor taken by any mortal act. The brightest star shone just over his forehead, and could be seen from other angles.

He gestured before the desk, and two chairs materialized before it. The chairs turned to accommodate both of them as they approached.

Alvaria and Malvex bowed low. "Your Grand Eminence," they said in unison.

He smiled. "Come forward, Children of Selevara, with my blessing." His voice was gentle and soothing. Despite the power he undoubtedly possessed, there was something parental about his attitude.

They rose and took the chairs he summoned. When they were both seated, he turned to Alvaria. "I am glad you found time to see me, Alvaria. I hope it was no trouble."

"None at all, Grand Eminence. I only wish I had heard sooner, so I might have arrived promptly." She looked pointedly at Malvex, who avoided eye contact with a suppressed smile.

The High Archmage glanced between them with amusement. "There was no rush. Even had you delayed a few days, it would not have troubled me. I do feel I should apologize to you, however. I sadly could not attend your gala two weeks ago."

Alvaria's mind went temporarily blank when she realized what he meant. "Oh, High Archmage, there is no need for any apology! While you were missed, I did not expect you to attend and so no offense was taken."

"I know," he said, interlacing his fingers, "and yet it would have gone a fair way to validating you as an archmage." He sighed, tapping his thumbs together. "I have been troubled of late, Alvaria. Many view your position as undesirable. Among some archmages, there exists a prejudice against the Department of Inquisition. When you were appointed archmage, you were given a difficult task and already have served longer than your predecessor. He assures me you are satisfied with your position. Still, as a junior archmage, you may not feel equal to your peers. I have been chatting with Malvex and he is of one opinion while I am of another. The true wisdom of both our reasoning was found in the middle ground and so I wanted him to bring you here so you could decide for yourself."

Alvaria's brow knit. "Decide what?"

"On your promotion."

Alvaria's jaw dropped. Malvex grinned. "Promotion?"

"Indeed. The title of Archmage of the Inquisition is a title typically belonging to a junior archmage. I would like to channel your proven talents and make you the Archmage of Internal Affairs. It would be similar to the Inquisition but would oversee the Inquisition, the Council of Archmages, and practices in Arcanathema Prison. It would allow you to draft laws for practice as well as assemble a group under your leadership who would investigate such matters. You would keep all of us in check, myself included. The Inquisition has great reach in the rest of the world, but realistically does little to eliminate potential corruption within Selevarian itself. I do not blame you for this. As Grand Inquisitor, you have carried out your work with unparalleled diligence. I have appointed fourteen other Grand Inquisitors before you, and none have been so proactive. I daresay even Almar Galesti—the first Grand Inquisitor—would be impressed with what you've accomplished. You could do much good as Archmage of Internal Affairs. Malvex agrees, but seems to think you are happy where you are."

Alvaria's heart raced. She swallowed and took a deep, steadying breath. "This is an incredible honor, your Grand Eminence. I do not even know how to thank you for the opportunity alone."

He watched her. Those kind eyes stared right through her. "Do not accept the position blindly. I wish to know your innermost thoughts."

"I—" she stopped, trying hard to sort her words.

"Alva," Malvex said, gently putting his hand on hers, "don't worry about speaking perfectly. We are both on your side and wish for you to be happy with whatever choice you make."

She smiled back. "Thank you, Malvex." She looked at the High Archmage. "Your Grand Eminence, I am conflicted. Your offer is not simply enticing because it is offered by you, but also because it appeals to me on a personal level. I will admit to some frustrations as the Grand Inquisitor because of my relatively low rank among the archmages, but besides that, I am content where I am. I do not feel ready to leave the Inquisition just yet. Perhaps in the years to come I will feel differently, but for now I fear I must decline your offer."

The High Archmage nodded with a knowing smile. "Malvex thought you would say something to that effect, though I hoped I could steal you away to greater exploits immediately. Still, I am proud of you for choosing to stay with your interests and for possessing the maturity to know your limitations. That said, this new appointment needs you, so I cannot take a permanent *no* as an answer. At our next general meeting at the beginning of next year, I will initiate three new archmages. Among them will be your successor who you will share the title of Archmage of the Inquisition with until he is ready to act independently. In this way, you can continue to effect changes within your department and ensure a gradual transition. Hopefully, this change will help others to see you as a senior archmage."

"That does not bother me too much. It started as a petty annoyance that diminished with time. My work speaks for me, and any archmages who believe it is necessary to criticize me based purely on my length of association with the Council of Archmages are not worth my time."

He studied her face with an inscrutable kindness. "You know, Alvaria, your father would be proud."

She froze. A lump formed in her throat, and she did not trust herself to speak.

"I didn't know your father personally," he continued, "but I know he died when you were young. Such things are painful, even a lifetime later. Based on the early interviews with those who knew you and your family, I know he loved you and would have been beyond pleased to see what his little girl grew up to become.

"Do not let doubt drive your choices, Alvaria. An air of uncertainty has surrounded you for some time now. Even at the summit of an elite organization, we can be plagued with thoughts of worthiness. 'Do I deserve this?' or 'am I truly doing enough?' threaten the lowliest of magicians to the greatest of archmages. We are only human, with human limitations. Our control of magic may bestow us with abilities beyond that of others, but we are not gods and must one day meet our end. We can do all we may to lead meaningful lives, but part of that is making mistakes and accepting our flaws. Be at peace, Alvaria Saccarra, and be not troubled; for those who have loved you most would be the proudest of what you have become."

"Your words honor me more than I deserve, Grand Eminence," she said, a slight quiver in her voice. "Your wisdom knows no bounds, and I apologize for not accepting your offer immediately."

"No apology necessary, Alvaria. You will have a year to prepare your successor and get your new office in order starting at the beginning of this next year. Until then, I have nothing more to say. Thank you for delivering my message, Malvex, and for your wise counsel." He looked slyly at the Archmage of Sorcery. "It appears you know her better than I do."

"She was my student, Grand Eminence," Malvex said, rising to his feet and bowing, "and yet I have found there is much I have learned from her."

The High Archmage smiled. "So should it be with all teachers and students; that in teaching, one might learn and in learning, one might teach. May Selevara's blessing go with you both."

Alvaria bowed and exited with Malvex. She dropped from the rush of the experience, grateful she had a staff to lean on.

Chapter Five
Shock and Shattered Peace

Lyvaelan awoke before the others. His early appointment with the Archmage of Education made him more nervous than he wished to admit, and the conversations of the night before did little to ease his mind. Based on Lyvaelan's understanding of magic—and confirmed in part by a previous conversation with the dean of the College of Alchemy at Calixford University—Paxton Averly should have been incapable of conjuring *anything*. Conjuration required substantial charisma and Averly lacked social skills of almost any discernable form. Furthermore, the amount of magic necessary to conjure was considerable, while the quantity necessary for alchemy was negligible. Few alchemists *chose* to be alchemists only; it was usually a matter of necessity rather than desire. Paxton could have duped everyone and had much greater arcane ability than expected, but then the question remained: who taught him to skillfully conjure such dangerous creatures? A self-taught conjurer seemed like an impossible solution, even barring Averly's lack of magical ability.

The discussion with Inquisitor Eller on this subject had yielded frustrating results. The Inquisition had taken over the entire investigation and since none of the Watchers were members of the Inquisition, none had access to the information they gained. They would not learn the identity of the conjurer, though Eller assured them he would take their concerns under serious advisement. He had been apologetic about the situation, but somehow that was more aggravating than if he had been standoffish.

Lyvaelan took a breath. It was over. It may have ended without a satisfying resolution, but life was full of such disappointments. The best he could do was learn and prepare for the immediate future.

He wandered to the kitchen. Charlie, the redcap housekeeper, whistled as he swept the floor. A couple dozen biscuits cooled on one of the wracks behind him. Lyvaelan moved to enter, but the small creature whirled on him and growled, baring his needle-sharp teeth.

Lyvaelan sighed and crossed his arms. "I don't have time for a full breakfast, Charlie. I need something quick."

The redcap snorted and leaned his broom against the wall. "I can do f-fasssst. Jusssst you no, no use my kitchen." He disappeared, but the grumpy muttering about trespassing and ingratitude continued as two biscuits floated into a napkin which was tied off and drifted to him with the clomping steps of the heavy iron boots the creature wore. The redcap slowly materialized, starting with the talons that held the biscuits aloft, then down along his thin arms and over his yellow eyes and disapproving expression.

"Thank you. My apologies for trying to enter your domain without permission." Lyvaelan resisted rolling his eyes and took the bundle from him.

"Welcome." Charlie crossed his arms, which seemed a more dangerous feat with such lengthy nails. "You no do again. If hungry, I take care. Ssssee?"

"With perfect clarity, yes." Lyvaelan headed for the spiral staircase that led into the library proper. He realized how bizarre the conversation he just had would appear to any normal person. A dark elf warlock conversing with a redcap about breakfast. It was the sort of absurd situation he had grown strangely accustomed to.

As he descended the stairs, his mind drifted back to the difficult conundrum of the Alchemist. Ultimately, the truth could be divided into two general possibilities: either Paxton possessed greater arcane power than anyone realized and learned how to control the aufhockers from a secondary source, or someone else conjured them to assist him. Either way, another person lurked in the shadows who had yet to be revealed. Someone whose trail they couldn't begin to follow.

He strode into the magic section of the library, absently taking note of the organization and vast quantity of volumes. Chaldra, in the heart of the great forest of Elliara, had little use for written word, but he could appreciate the work Hazel and Alistair put into categorizing. He had only possessed a handful of books and—with little ability to obtain more—he typically reread the few he had. As a consequence, he found his interest in reading to be less than what it might have otherwise been if he had access to additional books. Still, what he read assisted him with learning the fundamentals of reading, which was better than most elves in Elliara who saw little purpose in writing beyond magical uses.

The sheer number of books in this room staggered him. Why were so many even necessary? Wouldn't a book on each subject have been enough? His eyes swept over the spines of some, reading the various titles. *I suppose these are too diverse to have in one volume,* he conceded, *though I imagine there must be* some *overlap.* He was grateful Archmage Relas had generously offered to help find the right books because some of these titles exceeded Lyvaelan's limited understanding. He sighed. Humans struggled to do what fae and warlocks could perform with relative ease, though it came at a cost. Would he rather be capable of doing whatever he desired simply by willing it, or would he rather take time to learn how to accomplish what he needed? Certainly, using magic as a warlock would be easier, but controlling his power bordered on the impossible. Easy and dangerous, or difficult and safe? Neither choice was ideal, but he supposed learning magic the human way was best. It's what Kiran would've wanted.

"You're up early."

Lyvaelan turned to see Thomas Eller smiling at him. He kept his hair back in a small ponytail that drew attention to his clean-shaven face. The mage wore his typical blue robes with a white rose emblazoned on the chest. The robes were not as loose as some mage robes, and were likely designed with a sense of utility in mind. They weren't a group of idle philosophers, after all.

"I found it hard to sleep longer than I did, though two hours after noon is hardly considered early."

"It is when you keep such long hours at night."

Lyvaelan shrugged. This bordered on small talk. Small talk was a waste of time. He returned to perusing the shelves.

"I was wondering if we could talk about what happened yesterday."

Lyvaelan struggled not to roll his eyes. "Go ahead."

"I hope you don't feel I was overreaching. My duties required me to intervene."

"Your point?" Lyvaelan flipped through a few pages of a book.

"I suppose I wanted to check in with you to ensure that we hadn't damaged our relationship."

Lyvaelan raised an eyebrow. "'Relationship'?"

"I don't want you to feel betrayed by having worked with me. You worked hard for the Evenfall Vigil—I know that. It's purely due to protocol that the Inquisition stepped in. Clearly, your commander wasn't thrilled with the arrangement, and that I can live with. You, however, I work much more closely with. I hope I haven't broken any trust."

Lyvaelan sighed with irritation and snapped the book shut, sending out a small poof of dust. "I don't understand why people make more out of relationships than they are. I couldn't care less about you, the Evenfall Vigil, or the Inquisition. My opinion has been little raised or decreased by personal association with either. I didn't join this organization because I believe in the goals of the Evenfall Vigil. I'm not from here, so what stake could I possibly have?"

Eller shrugged and crossed his arms. "Well, you could feel I stole your work or glory or something similar."

Lyvaelan eyed him. "Work? Glory? Ridiculous. The moment I defeated Paxton Averly was the moment I stopped caring about his fate beyond imprisonment. This city doesn't need to adore me. That has nothing to do with why I'm here at all."

"Then... why *are* you here?"

Lyvaelan hesitated. Why *was* he here? It wasn't the money. It wasn't because he felt inspired by the work. Was it to fulfill the desires of his deceased mentor?

"I... came here to learn." He finally said.

"Is that what keeps you in Coruvaine?"

Lyvaelan scowled. "You are extremely nosy for someone in the middle of an apology."

Thomas laughed. "Forgive me. I'm an inquisitor so asking probing questions is part of my job."

A knock on the door of the library caused Thomas to jolt upright.

"It's the archmage, isn't it?"

"Probably."

"I... I'll come out and greet him when I look more presentable. Hurry! Don't keep him waiting." Thomas hurried into his office and shut the door.

Annoying mage, Lyvaelan thought as he walked to the large double doors. He opened the door to see Archmage Relas smiling beneath a gray hood. The archmage wore a plain gray traveler's cloak over his clothes, presumably to conceal his identity.

"May I enter?" His voice was a warm baritone.

"Of course. I've been expecting you."

The archmage entered and removed his cloak, revealing his white military robes with gold trimming and dark blue epaulets on each shoulder. An ambient glow surrounded the blond archmage and lent him an otherworldly grace. A typical byproduct of possessing light elf blood. Lyvaelan showed him around the library, giving the briefest possible tour. The Archmage of Education examined the room with a broad and wistful smile, taking in a deep breath.

"I remember this library well. I have many fond memories here. Unfortunately, nostalgia isn't a good enough reason to retain an old and unused building."

"Couldn't you have kept this and built a new one?"

"Yes, but the rest of the board was more inclined to sell it and use the funds elsewhere. By the time I became the chancellor of the university, almost half of the most valuable books were removed and few students came here anymore except to study in solitude. When I realized the only one who wished to preserve it was me, I turned it over to the king. It would have been selfish for me to decide to keep it when no one else wanted it. I should congratulate you, though. It looks much cleaner than the last time I was here."

"It was a mess when we arrived. Alistair and Hazel cleaned and organized most of it. I merely charged the magelamps."

He chuckled. "I imagine a vampire *would* struggle to enjoy such a dusty nightmare. Would you show me to your magic section?"

Lyvaelan brought Archmage Relas to the books. He tied his blond hair behind him in a ponytail and set to work scanning the shelves. The archmage had an easygoing attitude. Lyvaelan had seen him in Elliara a few times before, but rarely spoke with him. Back then—and even now—he seemed legendary. He fought in the War of the Night, defeated the Warlord, destroyed a lich, killed a dragon, and ensured lasting peace between the light elves of Elliara and the humans of the Gray Empire. Despite his immense power, reputation, and many stations in life that put him above most of the population, there was no sense of superiority or condescension Although light elf blood was unmistakably in his lineage, the joyful and flippant nature of that line was balanced by the calm and temperate human side of his personality. Beyond that, Lyvaelan sensed a heaviness in the archmage. A weight he carried, but concealed well. To many, it would have been imperceptible, but Lyvaelan recognized it because he experienced the same in himself.

"Let's see... *A Basic Handbook of Thaumaturgical Meditations* is astoundingly insightful, though it is a challenge to put into practice. *1001 Alchemical Ingredients to Know* is a helpful reference book. Oh! Dullivan's *Discourses* is very insightful, though little known. It details a discussion with several great wizards that seek to understand the best way to teach others. It's a little dry at first, but their observations are still useful..." As the archmage spoke he handed books to Lyvaelan who then placed them on a nearby table. He wondered idly if Alistair would be annoyed to find the books no longer in their proper place.

A door creaked in the back of the library. Thomas Eller came out of his office at full attention. He looked the same as before, but whatever wrinkles had been present in his uniform previously were now gone.

Lyvaelan watched as Thomas strode to the archmage swiftly. "Your Eminence," he said, genuflecting and bowing his head. "You grace us with your presence."

Archmage Relas turned and smiled. "I am graced to be present in this library again. Rise, Chief Inquisitor. Archmage Saccarra speaks highly of you."

"I strive only to do her work, Eminence." He rose to his feet with a smile. "I heard you volunteered to help Lyvaelan with his studies?"

"That is correct. Lyvaelan has a creativity and drive many young spellcasters lack these days. You could say he helped to remind me of why I wanted to be an educator in the first place."

A questioning look played across the inquisitor's face. "May I have your permission to speak freely, Your Eminence?"

He raised an eyebrow but maintained his smile. "Granted."

"You are undoubtedly a busy man; you are the Archmage of Education, a colonel of the Imperial Army, an ambassador of both the Seelie Court and the Gray Empire, and Chancellor of Calixford University. Any of those tasks would be a great challenge, but you accomplish all of them. Despite this, you have decided to teach a single individual. Why? Would it not have been easier to assign someone else to the post?"

Archmage Relas glanced back at Lyvaelan with amusement. "You assume I am increasing my work by bringing on an informal apprentice when I am actually adding to my leisure. I have been working on relatively large-scale work for so long I have nearly forgotten the joys of teaching a class. Teaching was—and is—my passion. I do not loathe being archmage or any of the other things, but it was always teaching I loved. In academia, the students are often at the mercy of their professors who, occasionally, are given free rein to do and grade as they wish. I found many great potential mages were turned away for foolish reasons, so I stopped teaching and began overseeing. When I rooted out unfair practices, I realized the same could happen elsewhere. Certainly, my alma mater Calixford remained closest to my heart, but what of the schools in Scripthaven, Waverock, Chastielle, or even in Selevarian? I had to choose: do I teach a few small classes and let all the other students in the system suffer, or do I put aside my passion and fix the problems I see? One was a selfish choice, and the other was the one I chose. I don't mind being an administrator since I'm fairly good at it, but my passion will always be instruction.

"Teaching Lyvaelan is as much a help to him as it is to me. I am gifted with an intelligent student who is eager to learn, and in return, he receives an education. Ours is a perfectly symbiotic relationship."

"I see. Forgive the assumptions on my part."

"You are forgiven, though such pardon is unnecessary. If you would truly like to repent, perhaps you could help me locate a copy of Orgrum's *Musings* or Thomson's *Illusory Desires*?"

Thomas inclined his head. "It would be my honor."

The three worked together, conversing on the helpfulness of specific books. Although Lyvaelan knew little of the books they mentioned, it was fascinating hearing the two men discuss magic and authors. He imagined he could sit and listen to them for hours without speaking, and absorb more knowledge than he could imagine. It revealed to him the deep disparity between his natural talent and his ability to use it. He considered the fact that neither mentioned his near destruction of Coruvaine during his confrontation with the Alchemist as a great kindness. Before their knowledge and abilities he must have seemed like a child covered in muck throwing mud in random directions to kill a fly in an otherwise clean home. The destruction may have been impressive, but not nearly as effective as it should have been.

After half an hour, Lyvaelan heard a distant creak on the staircase. He frowned, listening. It was louder than Alistair, but quieter than Lara. Hazel? She went to bed earlier, complaining of headaches, so he supposed it made sense she was now awake. He heard her approaching and reached out mentally and immediately knew something was wrong. He glanced at the other two, who looked like they felt something similar.

"Lyvaelan," he heard her murmur from the stairs. Her voice was strained and haggard. He rushed in her direction, but she appeared in front of them before he reached her. She clutched her head with a pained expression.

"Hazel," he whispered as he walked to her, "let me help you. What can I do?"

"I'm sorry, Lyvaelan, I just... I just can't... it's too loud... I can't... hold back." Green light burst from her. Lyvaelan tried desperately to connect to her with sorcery, but her mind was cut off.

He stared at her glowing form, and it reminded him of when she was burned. "No, Hazel, please don't." He pleaded, though he knew she couldn't hear him.

She looked down at him with unseeing eyes and then gazed toward the horizon. "*In the presence of the unending shadow, a darkness shall emerge. No light shall purge it from the world, and self-sustaining shall it be. The living lich of half a day shall rise with legions of undead that none can kill. Through betrayal of friends and oath, the living lich shall trample bodies and hearts. The world will quake as the impossible becomes the inevitable. The living lich of half a day may only be stopped by the slow progress of time. The time of the lich...*" Hazel looked at them. "*... is here.*" A violent blast of green light exploded from her, sending Lyvaelan and the others sprawling. Lyvaelan regained his feet swiftly and ran to her, catching her as she fell. She looked at him with a faint smile. "Lyvaelan. I'm glad... you're alive," was all she said before closing her eyes in exhaustion. Lyvaelan turned to the archmage slowly.

Lysander Relas was pale. He had landed on his feet and still stood as if he expected another impact. His blue eyes were wide as he calculated what to do. An ornately carved wand had appeared in his hand, and he had taken a defensive battle stance. When he saw Lyvaelan had no intent of fighting and Hazel was unconscious, he spun to Thomas Eller, who had just risen to his feet.

"Did you know?" he demanded.

"Archmage, I—"

"*Did you know?*" He pointed his wand at Thomas and blue energy surged from it, surrounding the inquisitor. Truth magic. A special sorcery Lyvaelan had heard about but never seen. "Answer the question!"

"Yes, I knew about her prophecy," Thomas said, his voice slightly muffled, as if behind a thick wooden door. The magic forced him against a wall.

"Does the Grand Inquisitor know of this?"

Thomas' eyes widened, and he looked helplessly at the archmage and Lyvaelan. He resisted the magic, but it clearly pained him.

"No, she doesn't," Garo said, emerging from the shadows. "He agreed to keep silent on this matter at our request."

The archmage lowered his wand, but the blue magic surrounding Inquisitor Eller remained. "Why? Garo, what *is* she?"

"She's a girl, Lysander."

"Don't give me that!" he yelled. The whitish gold light that usually surrounded the Archmage of Education turned harsh and piercing. "Talk circles around me and I'll throw you in Arcanathema myself. *What. Is. She.*"

Garo sighed. "We don't know. We've been trying to understand that ourselves. She was dead, but came back. The magic is unclear, but she shows no typical signs of necromancy, nor does she exude the magic of the dead."

"And what would you call that prophecy of doom?"

Garo's voice was placating. "I'm telling you, we've been investigating it under the purview of Inquisitor Eller."

The blue light around Thomas faded. "I'm sorry, Excellency," Thomas said after taking several ragged breaths. "I wanted to collect additional information before sending a full report."

"Additional information? A full report? What more did you *need*—for the girl to turn into a damned lich before your eyes? This is more than a lapse in judgment, this borders on criminal negligence and insubordination!"

"Please, Lysander," Garo said, "he followed a personal request, made by myself and King Aldric. Hazel poses no threat to anyone and has saved many lives. You've talked with her. She's a good girl."

"She's an imminent disaster!"

Alistair and Lara emerged from the stairs and quickly pieced together what had happened.

"Hey, archmage," Lara said, "that could be said of anybody, but Hazel is the least harmful person I've ever met. She *heals* people, for Stezelra's sake. Caleptis himself would be envious of Hazel's healing abilities. She's saved multiple lives. You can't tell me that's wrong."

"I don't *care* what you think." He said with dark conviction. "This is a matter for the Grand Inquisitor."

"Please, Archmage Relas," Alistair said, a brief flash of white clouding his eyes, "calm yourself. Hazel is no danger. She's our friend. You've talked with her. She's safe."

Lysander Relas stared directly into Alistair's eyes. "Try one of your vampiric tricks on me again, Alistair, and I will show you why creatures of the night fear me."

"Just try it," Lara said, putting her fists up, "and I'll show you an ass-beating like you've never known."

Lysander took a breath and calmed himself. "You're out of your depth. All of you. Do you think that putting down a couple of petty thugs is comparable to fighting an archmage? You're making an error in judgment that could be fatal if I had less of a handle on my temper." He looked at Garo. "What you've done contradicts the edicts of the Gray Empire. While the greater fault lies with the inquisitor, I place much blame on you as well. I will contact Alvaria immediately. It is not my place to capture or confine any potential threat when there are inquisitors in the city. If I discover Hazel has left the city before the Grand Inquisitor sees her, then the rest of the Inquisition and the Gray Empire will crash upon Coruvaine."

He raised his wand and one of Hazel's loose hairs lifted from her head and drifted to him. It glowed sapphire blue as he held it impassively. It looped around his wand, which he twirled in the air, producing larger and larger circles of blue light until they spread beyond the walls of the library. It was a containment spell.

When he finished, Lysander walked to the door and paused. "I have placed a spell of nine bindings on her. She cannot leave and any attempt to remove the magic will alert me immediately." He turned his attention to the inquisitor. "Do not compound one mistake by making another, Eller. What you have done could warrant execution if you take further risks. Ensure she does not leave and carefully monitor the situation. Perhaps the Grand Inquisitor will show you mercy." He looked at the others. "I reiterate: she won't be leaving this building anytime soon without my express permission. Even if she did manage to escape through some miracle"—he gestured to the hair—"I will find her, and my actions then will be far more severe than they are now."

The room was quiet as the archmage left. Hazel slept in Lyvaelan's arms. He watched the girl's calm expression and realized she was the least worried of anyone at present. They couldn't keep her hidden any longer. The Grand Inquisitor was coming. His heart sank, even as he held her close. He shook his head. *I'm sorry, Hazel. I don't know what to do.*

Chapter Six
The Road Twists Long and Lonely

"No activities warranting Inquisition's attention in the southernmost section of Fallerian have occurred. Despite our low presence in the area, there has been no uptick in arcane criminal activity reported..."

Alvaria relaxed in the tub, closing her eyes as her handmaiden read the report. Nothing important from Chief Inquisitor Baylen, as usual. Fredrick Baylen was stationed in Scrillhaven, a town that had seen no major developments in nearly a century. Temperate climate, no major cities nearby, and no institutions for the arcane arts for hundreds of miles. Fae occasionally caused minor disruptions, but that was hardly worth mentioning. It was in their nature to trouble civilized people and so spellcasters planned accordingly. For these reasons, his extensive reports provided little of interest.

"... further investigation is necessary. I have extended the range of my duties in my spare time to include assisting citizens with miscellaneous requests, primarily the use of alchemical and basic conjuration to deter pests from homes and livestock. Relations with the people of Scrillhaven is considered positive for the moment. I request an extension of duties to testing the young people of Scrillhaven and nearby territories. Such an increase would exponentially..."

Will this report never end? She sighed and sank further into her bath, though it was nearly time to switch. Connected to her main suite in Chateau Zarielle was her bathing chamber. Two large, recessed baths situated beside two windows equipped with reflective magic allowed one to see out but not in—a redundant measure, given the distance they were from the ground level. The first bath—the one she currently occupied—was of alchemical silver, while the second bath was made of alchemical gold. Both were valuable in their use, but their potency was realized in uniting them. The alchemical silver bath extracted and eliminated all waste, viruses, and infirmities in a person. Even now, she felt the impurities disappearing from her. Even the minor infections would be purged, leaving her healthy. This bath could have been further enchanted to enhance this particular trait with relative ease, but too rapid an expulsion of unclean things could result in deleterious effects. It would seem that the body needed time to acclimate to healthy conditions. A metaphor, perhaps, for the human condition. How much would people cling to those things which hurt them if they were threatened with being removed? She remembered her first time using this bath, and it had initially produced overwhelming nausea and instability. Not long after, however, she had felt more clearheaded and energetic than she had in years.

Most would prefer a known evil to a hidden good. It took a certain courage to resist the comfortable and embrace change; to fly in the face of convention despite hardship and failure required ambition and a willingness to risk everything to gain more. An odd thought, perhaps, to have from the luxury of a hot bath made of silver.

She opened her eyes and looked at the white mosaic patterned on the ceiling. When she was younger she had baths, but none were of such opulence as this. Her father often bathed her in an old rain barrel. In the winter, he heated large stones in the fire before tossing them in the water so she could have a warm bath. It didn't put the water at a perfect temperature—as this bath was—but the thought-fulness and effort weren't lost on Alvaria at that age. He would jokingly say he could not survive through the winter without his daughter taking a bath. With her mother gone, her father had done his best to be both parents to her. She missed his kindness, his happy smile, his efforts to dote on her, and his little ways of teasing her. He was a simple day laborer, a builder. He liked to say he was such a good craftsman that he had to do all of them. The truth was likely that he wasn't *skilled* enough to rely on single craft exclusively, but his boasting had been in jest. He always wanted to see her smile.

She stood with a slight wobble. The silver bath still made her feel strangely ill, though never as bad as the first time. The impurities that were removed by the bath left an uncomfortable void for hours unless she used its golden counterpart. She stepped into the second bath. The first had hints of lavender and rosemary in the water, giving a relaxing scent. This second bath smelled more strongly of citrus and rose. As she inhaled, her mind sharpened. She eased into the gold bath. The water was hotter than the previous one. The warmth permeated her, energizing and strengthening her resolve. The alchemical gold fortified the body, increasing the effectiveness of every organ and repairing any defects. While it would not mend the most egregious of injuries, it would reverse the effects of aging. A normal person could easily add a year of life by simply using the bath every few months, which she used weekly. She often felt like exercising after one of these baths, but she would need to conserve energy for the trip to come.

"... initial suspicion gave way to trust, as they could ask questions and raise grievances. It is my firm belief these measures could provide us with solid grounds to establish ourselves not *above* the communities we serve, but *with* the communities we serve. A spirit of cooperation may lower the rates of arcane infractions while increasing the speed at which we are requested for aid by certain communities. The best way to contradict the rumors of the Inquisition is not to argue against them, but to demonstrate our commitment to our most important tenets. In the words of Almar Galesti..."

When did I become so unlike my father? Alvaria wondered. *He was so thoughtful, kind, self-sacrificing, simple... I struggle to see any of those traits in me.* She pondered this, but on some level, she knew. She sank deeper into the bath, enjoying the floating sensation of her hair in the water as petals and bubbles moved to accommodate her. Her transformation started long ago when time, circumstances, and decisions led her from the life he wanted for her. She wasn't cruel, but she didn't strive to be kind either. She wasn't self-sacrificing; she had to organize and command the whole Inquisition, after all. Her father's simplicity was something she couldn't emulate once she decided to become a spellcaster. Spellcasting was anything *but* simple.

She lifted a handful of water and watched it trickle through her fingers. *Would he... be proud of me?* He had spoken ill of the Inquisition many years ago, but it was the same fear many peasants had who understood little of their work. So many believed that if one spoke of magic or asked strange questions, they might be arrested, but it was an absurd exaggeration. If she explained it to him, would he be proud instead of terrified?

It was hard to say, since the life he imagined for her had been as simplistically rustic as he himself had been. He had always said he wanted her to find a good husband and have a happy life with at least a child or two. None of those things had happened. Archmages could marry and have children, but very few did so. The happiness of archmages often revolved exclusively around their work. They were truly the academics of academics. Beyond that simple truth was the problem of compatibility. She had reached an age and level of experience that meant she lacked a real equal. The archmages were equal to her station, but none had the same interests, aptitudes, or drives that were so important to her. Lysander and Garson were both sweet, but they were more like what she imagined older brothers would be than potential lovers. No, there was no love at the summit of this mountain she had climbed, and that was fine.

She had come to peace with her decisions in life, but sometimes she imagined about what could have been. If she had chosen another road, what would she be now? She could see herself as a wife—and mother—living in a cottage in the country. Her husband might be a carpenter or a fisherman. She would tend to the children, and while they might sometimes be troublemakers, they would behave if they saw their mother watching. Perhaps her father would live nearby. The kids would run out to see grandpa who spoils them rotten. They laugh and pull his beard, and she chides her father about the importance of discipline. He just laughs and tells her to let kids be kids. He inquires when the next grandchild is due, and she punches his arm for asking such personal questions. The cottage is small—no more than three rooms—but it's cozy, and it's home. The fireplace helps in the winter, and despite her husband's best efforts, he can never seem to find where that one leak in the roof comes from. It's a simple life. A happy life.

A life that would never be hers.

A light knock came from the door, interrupting her reverie.

"Enter."

The door opened. Alvaria couldn't see who it was—the bath was blocked from the door by a thin veil—but sensed her chamberlain.

"Your Eminence, pardon the intrusion, but the carriages and wagons you requested have just arrived."

"Thank you, Arlith. Have them prepared for the journey to Coruvaine." Lysander had contacted her yesterday. The business in Ethelian had nearly imploded and needed to be dealt with immediately, much to her chagrin.

"Very well, Your Eminence," he hesitated. "Might I ask how long the trip will be?"

"It will be a lengthy journey, I'm afraid. It will be some time before you see me again. Can I trust you to keep the chateau safe?"

"Of course, my lady."

"Do you recall what to do if a spellcaster comes by asking to speak with me who, for whatever reason, cannot contact me?"

"You wish me to take them to the standing communication mirror immediately."

"Excellent." She rested back into the bath with a smile. "You are dismissed, Arlith. Oh, one more thing. Ensure that everything relevant to the current endeavor is put into those wagons. It would be a shame if I needed something but could not get it due to lack of foresight."

"Indeed. Do you have any special instructions for inquisitors who come seeking you?"

"Please refer them to the main office in Selevarian. Take their names and business, but nothing more. If they ask, tell them I am on an inquiry myself and that it could take some time. Because of our work, they shouldn't question it."

"Understood. I will see to your instructions. I have laid out your traveling attire. While they are not the most fashionable, the enchantments should keep the dust of your travels off while letting you maintain energy."

"Thank you. That should be most helpful. As for the chef…"

"I have already informed him you require pies for the journey. For good measure, I instructed a surplus of cake and cookies as well."

She smiled. "If I weren't as powerful a sorceress as I am, I would think you've been reading my mind, chamberlain."

"The skill of the servant is in knowing his master's desires before she does. And—beg your pardon—such requests are common enough that anticipating your needs is hardly a challenge."

"Is it childish to appreciate sweets to such a degree?"

"No, Excellency, it is childish to let the perceptions of others drive us to be other than what we are."

"A sorcerer's sentiment wrapped in a wizard's words. Thank you again, Arlith. You are dismissed." The curtain fluttered slightly as he bowed and exited, shutting the door behind him.

"Grand Inquisitor?" The handmaid who had been reading the report looked at her. "Do you wish me to continue?"

"No, I understand the gist of his request. I would like you to compose a response simply indicating that the Inquisition is doing well without implementing drastic changes like he mentions. Our goal should be uniform to prevent confusion of identity. Plenty of magicians fulfill the roles he mentions, and such actions would come dangerously close to stepping on the toes of the Archmage of Lesser Magic. If he believes there is an arcane threat or risk of such abuse, then he may step in and claim the right to do more. His post is an exception to the rule rather than the general rule itself. To extend our responsibilities uniformly would tax many inquisitors beyond their limits. I am willing to read tailored proposals based on research, but I cannot apply such sweeping changes because a single inquisitor thinks it might be helpful." She glanced at the handmaiden, who had been furiously writing notes. "Did you get all of that?"

"Yes, Grand Inquisitor. I will draft the letter immediately." She bowed and left the room. The bath water had cooled and was creeping toward the high end of lukewarm. She stood and stretched, feeling the energy within her. Her two remaining handmaidens wrapped her in one towel while drying her off. She strode to her room as additional servants attended to her. Within a few minutes, they dressed her in the clothes Arlith selected. A gown of a burned orange color. A thin traveling cloak of midnight blue was wrapped around her shoulders, as another servant adorned her in jewelry.

Her musings on the past were pointless. She had replaced love with ambition and children with her legacy. Did she wish life was different? There was one thing she would change, but besides that, her life was so much better than the lives of others. The smallest enchanted ring on her finger cost more than her childhood home. Was she happy? Happiness had—in time—seemed more like a fleeting emotion than a solid state of being. Was something so transient worthy of pursuit? It had the permanence of written words in water. Besides, she doubted she could ever truly be happy without her father. When he died, so did his dreams for her. She strove to be the best she could and eschewed mediocrity. Love belonged to those who settled for less than what they deserved. They lowered themselves to the very standard they were once above. Love was not a height to reach but a depth to sink to. Nobody rose in love; they only fell.

She smiled faintly at her own bitter-sounding musings. If others could hear her thoughts, would they claim it was envy? Behind the emotion of disdain often hid the stronger emotion of thwarted desire. Perhaps she wanted what others had, but she could never possess.

In the end, the greatest mystery to unravel was oneself. How one could simultaneously feel superior to others and yet desire to be among them was a matter worthy of study. *Bending to the whims of loneliness keeps potential from reaching greatness,* her old master used to say. There was truth to that sentiment, and she had seen it before. A smart man who fell for a pretty face devoid of thoughts, or a clever woman settling for a musclebound idiot. Romance made fools of all who dabbled, and she was no fool. She could recognize her desires without acting on them. Alvaria's ambitions provided no fertile soil in which a romantic relationship could flourish.

She descended the stairs to the main ballroom. The Alvaria of her dreams—living a simple life of quiet joy and contentment—was nothing more than that. A fantasy as far beyond her as it was beneath her. She walked challenging roads with even more ahead of her.

The chamberlain approached and bowed, his bald head reflecting the light of the floating magelamps in the room. "All preparations are finished, Grand Inquisitor."

"Thank you, Arlith."

He raised his head with a smile. His green eyes looking slightly sad. "Your presence shall be missed, Lady Saccarra."

"It will not be *so* long an absence, I hope." She walked out the door flanked by bowing attendants. "For now, I entrust the estate to you. Hearken to my words, Arlith. While I have given you instructions, you yourself said it was your duty to know my needs even before I do. Given that, I expect you to act with my best interests in mind in any circumstance, even if it potentially countermands a previous instruction I gave you. I trust your judgment."

"I will see that I honor your wishes to the best of my abilities, Grand Inquisitor."

"I know. I chose you as chamberlain for exactly that reason."

He opened the door for her and led her to the carriage. He assisted her into it and then stepped away with a low bow. "May Komora lead you on your path."

She smiled, and the carriages pulled out, heading to Coruvaine. *Komora, hmm?* She thought. It felt oddly appropriate to her. Komora was the goddess of travelers, but also the goddess of those who were lonely or solitary. She settled into the carriage as it pulled out of the estate and onto the road. The path she traveled would be lonely indeed.

Chapter Seven
To Fight Without Hope

Lara summoned all of them. Again.

Lyvaelan failed to see how this meeting would fare any differently than the last three they had, but it was worth the effort. Lara paced in their upper living room while Alistair, Lyvaelan, and Garo watched. Hazel had slept for the majority of the last four days since she spoke those fateful words of prophecy. Her headaches had worsened, and Lyvaelan had failed to notice. What a stupid mistake.

"Okay." Lara rubbed her hands together. "What have you got?"

"The Seelie Court would take her in, I think," Garo began. "They owe me certain favors and would find her intriguing. However, Lysander bears my same designation and his father is a part of the Council of Light. It seems likely that while they would adopt her for me, they would surrender her for him. I have allies in the Emerald Archipelago who are not beholden to the laws of the Gray Empire who might help, but getting her there would be the challenge."

The werewolf bit her lip and nodded, as if formulating a plan.

"I sent a missive to my father," Alistair said, "but it is improbable that he will aid us. He will not jeopardize our reputation among the human kingdoms for the sake of one person, even at my urging. The Throne of Austerity demands that he act without the undue influence of emotion. Aldric could possibly sway him, but even then I do not find it likely that my people will intercede and risk the wrath of the Council of Archmages, especially with Lysander Relas watching over her. It was before my time, but he is known to many as the Spear of the Sun, a title won by killing many of my kind."

"Okay," Lara said slowly with raised eyebrows, "what do you have for me that we can *use?*"

Alistair crossed his arms and leaned further back into his armchair. "Precious little. Since I'm the fastest of us, I could hypothetically carry Hazel a little over halfway to Serradis City before dawn and then she could buy a horse from there and secure passage to the Emerald Archipelago. My powers will not work as effectively on the ship, however, which means I would not be able to protect her if we are taken at sea."

"Is that the fastest you could go?"

"We're almost four hundred miles from Serradis City as the griffin flies. I might be able to travel further alone but carrying her five hundred miles by the roads we'd need to take in a single night would be nearly impossible without rest for both of us."

She stopped pacing. "I suppose that could work. I doubt news of her would reach Serradis before she sailed away."

Lyvaelan heard Hazel's door open down the hall, as did Alistair. The dark elf warlock tentatively reached out to her mind and relaxed. She lacked the extreme distress she exhibited days before.

She wandered from the hallway, as disheveled as the werewolf usually was. The girl wore a white nightgown with an open chartreuse robe, the belt of which dragged unevenly on her left side. Her long brown hair was a tangled mess and sleep clustered at the corners of her eyes. He searched her face for her characteristic good cheer but was dismayed to find it utterly absent.

"Hi Haze," Lara said, her voice dropping into the most nurturing tones Lyvaelan had heard from her, "how are you feeling?"

She sniffed and curled into a corner of the couch. "Probably as good as I look. What were you talking about before I walked in?"

Lara looked at the others uncertainly. "Your escape plan."

Hazel searched Lara's face for a moment before casting her eyes down at her green hands. She said nothing in response.

"Anyhow," Lara continued, "Lyvaelan, you're up. What have you discovered?"

"The limits of my knowledge, mostly." He glanced at Hazel to gauge her reaction, but she did nothing. "I have never heard of a seal of nine bindings, but I assume that means there are multiple anchors keeping her trapped in the library. I've identified three so far, which is far from nine."

"Still, it's something," Alistair said. "Do you know how to dissolve the three you've found?"

Lyvaelan hesitated. "Possibly. The problem is that there is no way for me to undo any of them without alerting Archmage Relas."

"Well, what if you, you know..." Lara waved her hand in the air.

His eyes narrowed. "Tapped into my warlock heritage?"

Her amber eyes fixed on his. "You said it, not me."

He wrung his hand and considered the idea. "With that, and by using my dark elf abilities I might be able to break the three bindings I've found. The problem is the others. I need to be able to identify them in order to destroy them. Furthermore, there isn't a way to know if I've discovered all of them. Even empowered second sight would only do so much. At my full power, I could hypothetically teleport her to the Emerald Archipelago myself. If even one binding remained, however, the result could be fatal."

"Well, we need to figure out *something*." Lara concluded unhelpfully. She proceeded to bite her nails and paced before snapping her fingers. "Aldric," she said. "What about his Sapphire Guard? They might know about this binding stuff."

"No."

They all looked at Hazel, who continued to gaze at her hands despite her interjection.

Alistair glanced between the two women. "What do you mean, Hazel?"

She raised her eyes. "I mean what I said. No one can help me. Not now."

Lara kneeled down to her height. "Hazel, we're trying to—"

"I know," she interrupted. "You're trying to save me but I'm telling you now: there is no escape. The time to avoid this was months ago, when Hickory dug me out of my grave. It was when I got Garo's invitation. It was when I chose to join."

Lyvaelan's heart sank.

"The living lich of half a day is imminent and I will be instrumental. I know you're trying to be hopeful, but just *stop.* There's as much hope of me avoiding the lich as there is in me escaping from the Grand Inquisitor. There's nothing you can do, not when they're so much greater than us."

"Hazel," Garo said softly, "we *can't* surrender. We won't. The battle isn't over yet."

She stood. Her movement was slow and yet it caught all of them by surprise. She heaved a sigh. "This isn't a battle you can win. You need to know when to retreat. Do you think Lyvaelan and all the king's spellcasters will be able to unraveling the bindings of an archmage without him noticing? Do you think we can escape anywhere he won't be able to find me? He has my hair. He could track me all the way to the Volarim Empire. Even if he couldn't, would Alistair carry me to the sea when he can barely stand? I would be a fugitive forever, which is almost as bad as being confined."

She sniffed and turned back to her room. "I know you want to help me, but just... stop. You can't help me now. No one can." She disappeared into the hallway, leaving them in silence.

"We still have to try," Lara muttered, though her face told a different story. Alistair covered his brow with his hand, and Garo sighed on the ground.

Lyvaelan swept over their minds and sensed their frustration but also their helplessness. Hazel's words sank into each of them and even more deeply into Lyvaelan when he realized the depth to which it was true. There was no hope. She had—rightly—pointed out his ineptitude. How could he compare to an archmage, especially one as legendary as Lysander Relas? He couldn't.

I won't give up on you if you don't give up on me, she had promised. Now, she urged him to abandon hope. She was the reason he fought, the reason he never wanted to surrender. The bleakness of the world crowded in around him and his heart drifted back into the ever-present melancholy in his soul. No hope. No peace. No joy.

No Hazel.

Chapter Eight
To Drink With Memories Alone

Lara stomped through the wet streets of Coruvaine to Skilliven Tavern. She was too angry to fetch her cloak and so she was drenched by the rain. The fury energized her and filled her with a need to hit something. Fortunately, the walk was long enough that by the time she reached the wooden door of the establishment her boiling rage had cooled into a simmering moodiness.

Many wet cloaks hung on racks by the door when she entered. The smell of a roaring fire and pork seasoned with salt and garlic met her keen sense of smell first. Normally, the scent of meat would have immediately excited hunger in her but a sharp twist in her stomach spoiled her appetite.

As the water dripped from her and onto the wood floor, she slowly took in the dim interior. A young couple sat at a square table closest to the door. In the larger dining room, a group of older men sang a bar song off-tune with as many different versions of the lyrics as there were singers. At the bar, a few different groups sat in clusters. Her eyes narrowed when she spied two men sitting in the far corner of the tavern by the stairs. She clenched her fists and stormed to the table. As she got approached, she recognized two scents that almost convinced her to transform on the spot.

She set her fists on the table and stared at each of them. One was a man in his late thirties with a burly build. Hairy arms and a short black beard gave him an air of menace and challenge. His companion was a much slighter individual. Clean shaven with a short tangle of deep red hair. He was no taller than Lara.

She locked eyes with the bigger man. His eyes were a whitish-blue and met the challenge. "What do you think you're doing?" She muttered with controlled fury.

The redhead quirked a smiled and waved a hand airily. "Just having a drink, nothing too—"

"When I want your explanation, I'll ask for it, fox. Right now, I'm asking my kinsman." She leaned closer to her fellow werewolf. "You smelled me at this table. You could have chosen anywhere else to sit and yet you choose the one place another werewolf has marked. Either you have a message for me, you wanted to meet me for yourself, or you're really, *really* stupid. I'm not expecting any messages, so which is it, bright eyes? Did you just want to meet me"—her voice dropped lower and fur began to bristle from her face—"or are you really, *really* stupid?"

The werewolf's eyes twitched slightly as the tension built between them. Lara felt the werefox observing this with amusement. Gradually, the werewolf stood and slipped to the side. He coughed and averted his gaze. "Yeah, I just wanted to meet you. Don't see many of us in the city and I wanted to see you for myself. That's all."

"And are you going to take this table again in the future?"

He scratched his beard and continued to shrink away. "No, that would be rude. Let's go, Ray." Without waiting, he strode toward the entrance with what little pride he had left.

His companion rose with less hurry and more smiles. "I assure you, sitting at your table was entirely his idea," he said with a shrug. "I may never understand the big brute, but he does make for some entertainment now and again. In fact—"

"Shut up, fox. Get up and get out."

He snapped his mouth shut, but his eyes continued to study her as he sauntered to the exit.

She took several breaths and pulled a chair back but stopped short. With a halfhearted shove, she walked to the end of the bar, away from anyone else and slumped into a barstool. Digging into one of the pockets on her shorts, she pulled two silver commons and tapped them on the bar. Eustace Skilliven walked over and was about to speak when she said, "A bottle of whiskey, whatever brand. A tankard of beer, too. I'm going to be drinking a lot tonight, so consider this the down payment."

His eyebrows raised at seeing the coins, but nodded. He reached behind the bar and grabbed a brown bottle and handed it to her before disappearing into the kitchen.

She took a deep breath and opened the bottle, immediately taking a swig.

"Intriguing. You frighten away others from your table and yet refuse to sit there."

She nearly choked on the alcohol. She wheeled to her right and sitting two stools away was the werefox, looking as self-satisfied as ever. Lara glared. "What in Ryxiv do you think you're doing?"

"Sitting at a bar, mostly."

"You know, it's possible to be a smart ass and a dumb ass at the same time. You're treading a dangerous line."

He closed his eyes and held up both hands placatingly. "My apologies. Glibness is second nature to me and so I must act to suppress it. What I am doing here is wondering what *you're* doing here."

"What's it look like I'm doing?" She took a deep gulp of the whiskey which burned the back of her throat.

"Drinking your sorrows away, I would guess, although I haven't the slightest idea of what tragedy you are specifically trying to erase."

"Why should it matter to you?"

He shrugged. "I don't suppose it really does, except that you never drank like this in Treland."

Her eyes narrowed. "You're a fan, is that it? You saw me beat the shit out of some moron and now you want to know why I left."

"Well—yes, and no." He strummed his fingers on the bar. "I'm not a fan, exactly. More like an opportunist driven by curiosity. When I heard you up and left Treland I wondered what new possibility interested you enough to give up such a monumental winning streak. Surely, whatever took you away from there must be worthwhile, considering how much money you made in a single night."

Eustace put the tankard of beer in front of Lara. She looked into it sullenly. "If you're going to ask a question, then ask."

"Fine. What interesting opportunity lured you here?"

She took a long draft and set the tankard down, staring straight ahead. "A bet."

"Ah, always a gambler. Was it worth it?"

She set her head down on the bar. The alcohol was starting to affect her, but not as quickly as she wished. His question hurt in a way she didn't expect and emotions welled within her that she tried to suppress. The knot in her stomach twisted tighter as she thought of why she left and why she stayed.

"Go away," she whispered.

She heard no reply, but when she glanced to the side, he was gone. She breathed easier and put a hand on her stomach, feeling the scar where the Alchemist had pierced her. Hazel had healed the worst of it, but the silver in the sword he used meant that most mending spells would be ineffective. She rubbed the scar and bit her lip, thinking of the girl who healed her.

We have to save her. We can't let them take her.

She propped herself up on her elbow and covered her eyes. She took another drink of whiskey and tried to formulate a plan. They had maybe two weeks to come up with something, but that no longer seemed like such a long time.

Lara glanced at the table. It had only been about two weeks since they had shared drinks and laughed together here. Granted, it had ended in panic and the realization they were being watched, but besides that, it was fun. This was *their* place, and that was *their* table. If the Inquisition arrested Hazel, there would be no more meetings here. No more fun to be had together, just memories.

Maybe, if she could surprise Lysander Relas, she could defeat him and then they could break the spells he held over Hazel and she could escape the city. Granted, Lara would also be forever on the run from the Council of Archmages, but it would be worth it.

She snorted at the idea. When they visited his office, she couldn't even fight the sorcerer who manned the front desk. How could she hope to defeat someone significantly more powerful who had an established history of killing werewolves and vampires? Furthermore, she didn't know much about elves, but she suspected he would not be easy to surprise. In other words, she could do nothing.

Damn magic. Stupid spellcasters with their cheating spells.

She brawled for a living and all magic except alchemy was off-limits in the ring. The Inquisition lived by no such rules. She could knock out a troll with a single well-placed punch, but she couldn't beat the Inquisition like that. Stopping them bordered on the impossible. Perhaps if Hazel were granted amnesty from the emperor, then they would desist, but the last she checked, he wasn't on her list of acquaintances. Even if the emperor intervened, it would be too late.

He *could do it.* She took several burning gulps of whiskey. Her father could do almost anything, so long as no one cared about the mess he created in the process. He could probably even kill the archmage, but how many others would die as a result? Besides, that bastard wouldn't help her if she asked. No, he'd question why she needed help in the first place. She squeezed one of her hands into a fist. If Lara needed help, then she didn't deserve it.

She reached for the bottle and noticed it was half empty.

No matter how much she drank, it didn't give her any other great ideas. Sober or inebriated, no inspiration struck her. Who was she to challenge organizations like the Inquisition? Still, she had to think of *something.* Hazel may have given up, but that didn't mean Lara would. She had a reputation to uphold.

Chapter Nine
Moving Back to Proceed Forward

Hazel awoke, feeling calmer than she had in months. Two weeks had passed since she inadvertently revealed the prophecy to Archmage Lysander Relas. Both very little and very much had changed in that time. She could walk outside a slight distance and seemed to have as much autonomy of thought and movement as before, but Lyvaelan informed her of the magic that now surrounded the library. The archmage would know when she left the library, and attempting to leave the city would be impossible. Even descending the stairs from the entry to the library filled her with a sense of heaviness that grew with every step.

Lara had pressed Hazel to escape with her to Treland and then further into the peripheral forests near Elliara to the north, or eastward to the sea and across to the Emerald Archipelago, but Lyvaelan pointed out the impossibility of escaping the magic of the Archmage of Education. He could counteract some of the magic, but not all of it, and she guessed from his hesitancy that acting without untangling the magic completely could have devastating consequences—precisely what, he didn't say.

Beyond the practical aspects of escaping, there were still her parents to consider. And Garo. And the king. And her friends. No, there was no escaping without hurting everyone she loved and forestalling the inevitable. What would leaving accomplish except ruining the lives of those she held most dear? Would they be arrested? Even if she tried to escape, she doubted a life on the run from an organization as far-reaching and powerful as the Inquisition would last long.

She stretched and reached for her journal, committing her latest dream to its pages. This journal Aldric had given her helped more than he could have ever realized. In the few short months since she started recording dreams, she had filled it nearly halfway with notes and prophecies. The dream she had last night was the clearest she experienced. It no longer felt like a phantasm gnawing at her. She had heard that the anticipation of pain was worse than the pain itself, and the same could be said of the vision. Her dreams no longer distressed her because they were no longer dreams. They were imminent reality.

She finished writing and laid her book on the shelf among others so that it didn't stand out. That small journal might ultimately be the key to their survival. At long last, the images she beheld made sense. Everything finally had come together. The burden of helpless knowledge had lifted now that she understood. She only hoped the lessons she received from Lyvaelan in shielding her mind would keep her friends safe.

She sighed and got dressed. She wore a simple white and tan kirtle and fastened a cloak about her shoulders. It was the height of winter and although she felt little of the chill, she sensed she may not see the room again once she left it.

She exited into the sitting room where Thomas Eller, Garo, and her three friends waited. The mage hadn't been completely relieved of his duty, but the last two weeks weighed heavily upon him. Dark circles ringed his eyes and his usually prim appearance had slackened. He still wore his hair in a ponytail, but missed some strands. He had continued to shave but only occasionally, which had allowed stubble to appear. He smiled hollowly as Hazel approached.

"Good afternoon, Hazel," he said. "I'm afraid you will have to forgo breakfast until later. The Grand Inquisitor is here."

She inhaled. "Should we go see her in the palace, then?"

"When I said 'here,' I meant literally. She's downstairs."

Hazel's eyebrows rose, but she just nodded. "Lead the way."

"No leave!" At the entrance to the stairs, Charlie had appeared, holding both arms wide, barring the way. His long talons appeared larger than normal and his feline eyes bore into the inquisitor. "You no go, Hazel." He growled and bared his needle-sharp teeth.

Thomas frowned and approached the redcap but Hazel hurried in front of him. She fell to her knees and drew the demented fae into a gentle hug. Charlie sniffled and she noticed a growing wetness on her shoulder where his tears fell.

"No leave," he whimpered. "Pl-pleaaaaaase..."

"I'm sorry, Charlie," she whispered as she stroked his back. "I have to go. Thank you for being my friend."

Hazel released him and his arms fell to his sides. Every menacing aspect of him softened as tears the size of acorns rolled from his wide eyes. He staggered away from the stairs and slumped against the ground. The redcap continued to weep and watch her as he faded gradually into complete invisibility.

Thomas glanced between her and the space where the now transparent fae mourned, and strode ahead of the others, leading them down the stairs. Garo glanced to the place where Charlie was and sighed. The grim said nothing, but Hazel knew he acutely felt the small creature's pain. Garo padded silently behind the inquisitor, leaving her and Lyvaelan to take up the rear. A hand brushed against hers and she saw Lyvaelan look at her intensely. He handed her a small leather pouch with oddly sized objects within. She opened it, revealing a variety of seeds and acorns.

"I haven't given up on you, Hazel," he whispered.

"I know," she whispered back. "Lyvaelan, I had another dream."

He gave her a worried look. "I thought you would. They're getting worse, aren't they?"

They walked down the last few steps. "No, they're actually getting better. I have to tell you about the dream, but not right now. You need to—" she stopped short when she beheld the massive group of people within the library. Mages in gray wearing sapphire pendants stood to the side of King Aldric, who sat in the nicest chair in the library, tapping one arm nervously. He wore clothing embroidered with the crowned fox of the king, and a golden crown adorned his head. The king dressed better than he had the first time they met. Behind him and the mages of his Sapphire Guard paced her barely visible parents, who struggled to contain their anxiety. Standing apart from them and leaning against a tall bookshelf stood the Archmage of Education. His face was serious, but the anger he expressed before had subsided. He didn't seem like a callous person to Hazel, and even now appeared unhappy with the turn of events. Besides them and a handful of the king's guard were dozens of inquisitors in their blue robes with white flowers and several others who worked for the institution but were magically ungifted. Other administrators in the inquisition wore clothing of the same color and look, but not the robes associated with spellcasters.

Lara and Alistair waited near the bottom of the steps with grave expressions. The werewolf wore her silver-studded fingerless gloves, while the vampire kept one hand on his sword. Both had recovered from the majority of their wounds, but despite their posturing, they were still in no condition to fight.

The main doors opened, and Hazel briefly heard unintelligible, angry chanting from outside. A gray-haired inquisitor strode in and pivoted to the side with military precision.

"Her Eminence, the Archmage of the Inquisition, Protector of the People, the Grand Inquisitor, Alvaria Saccarra!"

A woman entered with methodical, ceremonial steps. A long, dark blue dress that shimmered like a lake at midnight reflecting the stars, cascaded over her with ethereal grace. She was tall and stately. Her dark hair ran in gentle waves down her back. In one hand, she held a long wooden staff, intricately carved to resemble a curling stem of a plant. At the top of the staff bloomed a large white rose—whether carved or real, it was difficult to say. From the flower, small motes of light drifted to the ground as she walked. This woman was one of the most gorgeous people Hazel had ever laid eyes on, and yet a chilling air of danger emanated from her.

The woman stopped after passing the king and the Archmage of Education and stared at Hazel. She appeared to be appraising her, although her emotions were impossible to read. The room was silent as all eyes focused on the Grand Inquisitor.

"So," she said at last. She spoke at a normal volume, but her voice pierced every corner of the room. "This is the girl I've heard so much about. Hazel Enda."

Thomas Eller fell to one knee before her. He placed both fists on the floor and bowed his head. The Grand Inquisitor watched him with the same expression. "Chief Inquisitor Thomas Eller. You are commanded to return to Selevarian to stand trial for insubordination. You are relieved of your duties here in Ethelian. You may rise."

He rose shakily to his feet, his face had lost all color. The Grand Inquisitor shook her head. "Disappointing. You had such potential, and yet squandered it like this. Through inaction, you have cast the Inquisition in a light that makes my administration appear both incompetent and complicit with necromantic activities. Shameful."

"Your Eminence," King Aldric said, rising to his feet. "some part of the blame is mine. I requested he delay his report to you. I begged before he agreed, and then it was only after allowing him to oversee her he that he compromised. Do not be harsh in your judgment."

"Your Majesty," she said, looking to Aldric, "I appreciate your candor, and your statement has been taken into consideration. This is an internal affair, however, and his actions were ultimately his own." She eyed Hazel. "The matter is much too serious to ignore. I will take Hazel Enda with me to Selevarian, where she will be studied until we can be certain that she no longer poses a threat."

"No!" Hazel's mother screamed behind the row of guards. Lynn Enda struggled through the Sapphire Guard with her husband.

"Please, please don't take away our little girl, Your Eminence, I beg you. *We* beg you. Please—"

Alvaria raised a hand, softly demanding silence. "You are the parents; is that correct?"

Kyle swallowed. "Yes, ma'am. We love her and don't want to see her go. She's a good girl and didn't ask for—"

"Stop," Alvaria interrupted softly. Somehow, the gentleness of the Grand Inquisitor added to her air of power. "You are under the impression I can be bargained with. You are mistaken. Your daughter died several months ago after falling from a tree and drowning. The moment she returned was the moment she ceased being your daughter and became something else. Reports taken from your own statements indicate that you found her substantially altered. So much so she may not have even resembled your daughter at all."

Her parents cast their eyes away. Hazel felt no anger at this revelation since she had sensed their misgivings in the early days of her revivification. No doubt their feelings had changed, but now their own words were being used against them.

"I don't claim that she is necessarily evil—unlike the protestors outside—but we cannot be certain," Alvaria continued. "She apparently possesses an unknown quantity of immense power, which could be devastating if ignored. We will perform numerous tests using implements in Selevarian that are unavailable here. This may be hard to accept, but I'm taking her regardless of your pleas."

Kyle's face grew red, and his jaw clenched. Lynn looked ready to unleash another wail when Alvaria glanced at a couple of inquisitors who closed their eyes and made a small gesture. Her parents' expressions became vacant.

"Grand Inquisitor!" Aldric cried, jumping to his feet. "You cannot go around using sorcery on my citizens with such rampant disregard for their rights! You have no authority—"

"*I* have no authority?" Alvaria interrupted, advancing toward him. Although several inches shorter than him, she still seemed to tower over the king. Her calm voice took an edge. "You are in no position to lecture me on the boundaries of my authority, King Aldric Valmore! You are King of Ethelian, but *I* am the Grand Inquisitor. By order of the Gray Emperor, the Inquisition is given ultimate authority in all cases pertaining to abuse of magic, including the spellcasters, creations, research, and victims of such abuse. You have overstepped yourself, Your Majesty. It is not for me to chastise or correct you, but I *will* remind you that the emperor will do exactly that should he hear of this. You are beloved by your people, but do you think popularity will save you from the punishments of the emperor? It would be a shame for your daughter to wear such a heavy crown at such a young age." Aldric held her gaze for several moments before sitting down again and covering his face with a hand.

"Grand Inquisitor, might I speak?" Lysander said, breaking through the tension.

She graced the Archmage of Education with a small smile. "Of course."

"It is my opinion that this girl, despite all evidence to the contrary, represents a trivial threat." Alvaria's smile dropped into a frown. "I don't mean to say she should go free, but perhaps there is some compromise that can be made. Her friends and family surround us and desire nothing more than to be with her. Wouldn't it be better to give them more time together if possible?"

The Grand Inquisitor searched his face. "What do you propose, Archmage Relas?"

"According to the precepts of your own institution, it is customary to have two separate groups when there is a creation and a creator that need to be transported."

"True, but such measures seem unnecessary," she replied coolly. "Allkirk currently presents no threat, and if we keep her in the caravan's front and him in the back, it should pose no obstacle. An archmage accompanying a caravan can counter most any situation."

"Perhaps, but what if the mage has allies who could capture him? This is a unique case that should be handled with the utmost care. I would even be willing to deliver one of them personally."

Her brow lowered. "Just a moment ago, you claimed she presented little danger."

He glanced at Hazel and she could tell he was working through a solution as he spoke. "True, but she hasn't seen Mr. Allkirk since she first returned. The results could be catastrophic if they are reunited."

She forcibly sighed. "You're making this unnecessarily difficult."

He took several steps closer to her. "Alva," Lysander muttered in hushed tones Hazel could hear only because of her close proximity. "Please. These aren't bad people, just civilians in a terrible position. Can't we afford a little generosity? I know how much you miss your father; don't you think this girl will miss hers?"

Alvaria hesitated. She gazed at Hazel's frozen parents. Finally, she sighed. "Fine. I have a solution that may work, but *do not* countermand my authority." He smiled gratefully and nodded, backing away. She spoke louder and waved to the two inquisitors who ceased their sorcery on the two parents, who briefly looked around, confused. "I have decided. Given the strange circumstances we find ourselves in, I have tempered my judgment with a modicum of mercy. My occupation is not compassionate by nature and metes out justice to those who do evil. Justice must also be done to the victims in this, however, and though it is atypical, I will bend beyond my typical range of comfort to accommodate all of you.

"There will be two separate caravans, each sent two weeks apart. The research of the mage and his creation—the girl known as Hazel Enda—will accompany me to Selevarian with my retinue, along with Inquisitor Thomas Eller and the other cases of arcane abuse requiring transport to Arcanathema. In two weeks, when we arrive and send word, the second caravan will be sent with Hickory Allkirk, who shall be guarded by the Archmage of Education." She glanced over to Lysander, who appeared ready to interject, and shook her head. "Given the strain this places upon the Enda family, I invite them to join me if they wish. They may stay in Chateau Zarielle until we come to a definite conclusion regarding Hazel, however long that may be. They will maintain the ability to see her, providing no tests are being conducted. They will be treated as honored guests, and all needs will be met for as long as they desire to stay. Would this be agreeable to you?"

Hazel's parents were beside themselves with gratitude. They simply nodded that they were happy with the arrangement. Hazel did not share her parents' enthusiasm. Her heart sank.

"Pardon me, Grand Inquisitor," Garo said, stepping forward.

She looked the grim up and down. "Yes... ambassador, was it? Do you have a concern?"

"Yes, what of these people with her?"

She glanced at Alistair, Lara, and Lyvaelan. "What about them?"

"These three are as close to her as any. One might say they are extended family. Could they accompany her as well?"

Alvaria frowned. "In other words, they are friends of no relation. I am aware of their connection—or lack thereof—and do not think it merits bringing them. I can risk the two parents because they are benign individuals with a lengthy record within the city and are directly related to the girl. These three are untested fighters capable of subduing dangerous criminals. How much more dangerous could they be should they turn on us while we are on the road? A vampire, a werewolf, and a dark elf warlock? No, I don't think your perceived close connection warrants including them as my guests."

"What if we insist?" Lara said, stepping forward.

Alvaria's expression didn't change. "Insist as much as you'd like. It changes nothing."

"Grand Inquisitor, we beseech you," Alistair said. "we have grown close to Hazel and care for her deeply. Allow us to join you and we will cause no trouble. We can even act as nocturnal sentinels."

"I don't think so."

"You *will* take us with you!" Lara growled.

"Or what?" Alvaria said coolly to Lara. "You will beat us into submission with your fists? Be rational, child. You are not permitted to join us, but perhaps—in time—I will allow you to be guests in Chateau Zarielle. Follow us or attempt anything foolish and I will see to it you are guests in Arcanathema instead."

"We won't let you take her," Lyvaelan said quietly, stepping forward.

"Damn right we won't."

"We are of one mind. Hazel will stay with us."

"No." The room turned to look at Hazel, who moved in front of them. "I will go with the Grand Inquisitor. Alone."

Lyvaelan's jaw dropped. "But... Hazel..."

She gazed kindly at Lyvaelan. "I know." She locked eyes with Alvaria. "Grand Inquisitor, please don't judge my friends severely. They want to protect me and are the best friends I could have ever asked for. I will join you. Just let me say goodbye and get my bag."

"No need to collect your things." She gestured to an inquisitor, who climbed the stairs. She turned to Lysander. "Archmage of Education, kindly remove your binding spells. It is time to leave."

He nodded to her and drew a wand from his side. With a series of cutting motions and a small flurry of purple and yellow spark, something lifted from her that she hadn't been aware of. The archmage replaced his wand and nodded to Alvaria.

Hazel moved to her parents. "Mom, dad, I love you both, but you don't need to come with me. You should stay here and enjoy life. You can't stop your lives every time something happens to me."

"Hazel," her father said, drying his eyes, "our lives only stop when you're not in them. Your mother and I are going with you. No debating or changing our minds. We're going. That's final."

Hazel bit her lip and nodded. She couldn't convince her parents to stay, even though it was safer. Pushing the issue further would only complicate matters. She turned to her friends.

"Garo, thank you for bringing me into the Evenfall Vigil. I found a sense of purpose I never had before, and I got to make such wonderful friends. Try to keep the group together and find other members, okay?"

Garo's ears drooped. "I will, Miss Enda, though there is no one in the world to replace you."

She smiled at him and turned to the vampire. "Alistair, thanks for organizing the library with me. I had a lot of fun. Try not to let Lara bother you too much while I'm gone."

He smiled and opened his mouth, but no words came out. He simply nodded, keeping his feelings concealed.

"Lara, I'm going to miss you barging into my room without knocking. Thank you for protecting me when you did."

"This isn't right," she muttered. "You shouldn't have to go. We should've found a way."

Hazel tried to meet her eyes. "Be strong. Stay together. We're a team, remember?"

She approached Lyvaelan. His wide, red eyes stared at her in confusion and disbelief.

"Lyvaelan, I'm going to miss you. Thank you for teaching me to trust myself and my visions. I've grown so much because of what you taught me. Thank you for never giving up on me and know I still haven't given up on you. I want you to have the books in my room. I know you don't read much, but I think you'll like them, and I hope they will remind you of me."

"How could they not?" he whispered. "Everything I see, or hear, or touch reminds me of you. How can I move forward when all I see are moments of the past frozen in time?"

She opened her mouth to speak but shut it again. It was too hard to respond. She smiled at him through tears. "Take care of my books, Lyvaelan, and read them soon."

The inquisitor descended the stairs with her suitcase and passed the Grand Inquisitor.

Alvaria beckoned to her. "Hazel, it's time to go."

She nodded and walked forward. Before she stepped outside, she turned to the group. "I hope to see you again soon." And she left.

Outside the library, two rows of guards bearing tower shields on the outside stood with a row of inquisitors facing inward. The inquisitors waited at attention with their hands clasped behind their backs. A multitude of citizens had gathered, shouting at Hazel. *Abomination! Monster! Unholy creation!* the people cried. Through the teeming crowd, a single figure moved, and the masses parted. High Priestess Caeli Relinon of the Cult of Semeleme interposed herself between the carriage and the Grand Inquisitor. The woman wore her typically austere black dress and veil. Although she was only a few years older than Hazel, her seriousness and displeasure undercut her otherwise youthful appearance. These people appeared to be here on her behalf, though the High Priestess showed no joy or satisfaction. Her scowl moved from Hazel to the Grand Inquisitor, who continued forward while Hazel was held back by two inquisitors.

"High Priestess Relinon, I assume?"

"Correct." The High Priestess's tone was icy. "You have in your possession a thing which ought to be destroyed."

The corner of Alvaria's mouth twitched up. "Oh? And what might that be?"

A darkness swirled and grew around the High Priestess as a chilling sound like a hive of angry bees filled the air. "You know very well of what I speak. I will not waste words with the Inquisition."

"Then you should have stayed home, priestess," The Grand Inquisitor replied. She stepped closer and into the tangle of twirling smoke. Alvaria shivered momentarily but then smiled. "Your magic may be as infinite as the goddess of death, but you may find its range of application lacking compared to mine."

"You underestimate the goddess," Caeli replied through gritted teeth. The tendrils writhed with increasing fury and extended in all directions. Others who came in contact with the strange magic paled and shrank away. "Even you must feel the overwhelming sense of mortality and all that means to you."

"Indeed, I do." Alvaria's demeanor drew visible confusion from the High Priestess. "Step aside, or I will show you a different kind of magic that you will enjoy far less than I have enjoyed yours."

The High Priestess held Alvaria's gaze for what seemed like ages. Several guards approached from behind the Grand Inquisitor and waited for her command. Caeli's eyes flicked to the men and then back at Alvaria. The dark magic receded until it was no more.

With a slow step, she turned back to the crowd. "I will leave you with your ambition, Alvaria Saccarra," Caeli said as she walked backward into the crowd. She glanced at Hazel, then back at the Grand Inquisitor. "May it throttle you when you least expect it." With that, she disappeared into the citizens and walked away without turning back.

"What a charming woman," Alvaria remarked dryly. "Come, Hazel. This carriage is for us."

The row of guards led to a line of wagons and carriages. A few inquisitors rode on individual horses and kept watch. Hazel stepped into the carriage emblazoned with the white rose that Alvaria indicated and her parents soon followed. Archmage Saccarra took time to detail plans with a few inquisitors before getting in a few minutes later. In a short time, the caravan had moved beyond the crowd and into the southern part of the city. An additional wagon joined them as they left Coruvaine. After just an hour in the carriage, they were further south than Hazel had ever been from the city.

Her mom sidled up to her. "I know this seems bad, Hazel, but think of it as a vacation! I've never been to Selevarian before."

Hazel smiled halfheartedly at her mother but looked across at the Grand Inquisitor, who gazed out of the window.

Hazel kept her eyes fixed on Alvaria.

The Grand Inquisitor smiled faintly at her but said nothing as the carriage moved south and away from Coruvaine.

Hazel had never seen Selevarian before either. She doubted she ever would.

Chapter Ten
The Wall Crumbles

No one spoke as they supped in the library. The food consisted of leftovers thrown haphazardly over uncut fruit and bread. The redcap chef didn't seem to have it in him to make a meal worthy of appreciation, nor were the remaining members of the Evenfall Vigil capable of appreciating it even if he had. Garo joined them in silence. He lay dejected on the floor, his eyes unfocused. Lyvaelan assumed the grim would make some saccharine speech about remaining a team or letting Hazel go, but he was as morose as the others.

It hadn't been six hours, but already they would be far away. Lyvaelan knew little about traveling by gates, but the Inquisition had turned two months' worth of travel into just under two weeks by using them. He had considered using farsight to see her, but what good would that do? Would it soothe the ache of her absence? Would the Inquisition even allow his sight to find them? It was pointless. An idle fancy born from vain hopes.

She was gone.

"We should have stopped them," Lara muttered. She dropped a half-eaten chicken leg onto her plate and pushed it away.

Alistair slouched in his chair, his hand cupping his chin and covering his mouth. An unusually relaxed position for the vampire. "How?" His voice was tired.

"I don't know." She leaned back, shaking her head. "But we should've done something."

"Like what?"

"I said, 'I don't *know!*'" she shouted, slamming her fist down and sending splintering cracks through the table. "We're her friends, aren't we? We dashed in when aufhockers tried to cut her in two, we rushed her to safety when cultists wanted her dead, we defended her against everything but the moment a bunch of white rose assholes show up we let them walk over us. By the gods, we should've done something." Tears of fury welled in her eyes. "We should've tried."

"We would have failed," Alistair said. His eyes were vacant.

"Oh, and you're trying so hard to come up with excuses," she hissed. "You're the idea guy, the one with smart plans and thinking ahead. Where were you, huh?"

Alistair's hand slowly balled into a fist. "There were a hundred things we could have done, but none of them would've worked."

"So what, this is your big plan? This is how we're going to protect Hazel?"

He gritted his teeth but maintained his tone. "There is no plan."

"I guess it wouldn't have been polite to stick up for your friend. I'll bet your people would be proud."

He slammed his fist down, shattering the wood and sending a chunk of the table clattering to the ground. His eyes glowed icy blue and his fangs extended as he stood to confront her. "Enough! There is nothing I wouldn't do for her if I thought it would help. I'm as new to this as you! Maybe I'm the oldest, but I don't know about fighting, war, or the Inquisition! Do you know what I *do* know? If we fought them, we would've died. We'd be fighting against *two* of the most dangerous archmages alive. We know how dangerous the Inquisition is, but do you know about the Archmage of Education? Among my people, he's called the Spear of the Sun. I studied battles and learned about the War of the Night. He's killed more vampires than I've ever *met*. That doesn't even cover the number of were-wolves, warlocks, or dark elves he's defeated either. Do you think we could really fight him or hope to escape? We'd be lucky to be blood smears on the floor before he'd broken a sweat. Is that what you desired—or all of us to die pointlessly while Hazel watched?"

"Friends help each other." She leaned toward him. "What we did wasn't helping, it was giving up."

"Damn you! What do you *want* from me? I'm just one person who barely knows what he's doing."

"I want you to *do better*," she screamed, tears were now pouring from her eyes. "I'm not good at strategizing, so you have to be!"

"Enough," Garo growled. He hadn't risen from his spot. "Neither of you could do anything. The Inquisition—"

"Yeah, what about you?" Lara sniffed, rubbing her arm over her nose. "You seemed easy enough to talk down. One feeble attempt to persuade the Grand Inquisitor and you show your belly like a good doggy?"

"I'm an ambassador to the fae. Nothing more." His voice was quiet. "This matter doesn't concern my sphere of influence."

"This doesn't concern you? *Hazel* doesn't concern you?"

"Of course she does!" He snapped, leaping to his feet. "I'm as worried as any of you, but fighting about it now accomplishes nothing useful. You could no more have vanquished them than I could have persuaded them not to take her."

"Couldn't Aldric have done anything?" Alistair asked, falling back into his seat. "Was he truly as helpless as the rest of us?"

"If he intervened, it would've meant breaking international law. Since Ethelian is part of the Gray Empire, it must abide by the rules set by the Gray Emperor. The law would side with the Inquisition, which could cause his deposition and Hazel being taken, regardless. He has to think of all his people, not just her."

"Damn the laws!" Lara yelled. "Why should we follow these stupid rules if they hurt someone like her?"

"You mean the laws you've all sworn to protect?" Garo asked.

"I don't care. I don't care about the laws, you, the king, or this stupid building! I came because I thought it might be fun and, guess what? I'm not having fun."

"That's what it's all about?" Alistair said, shaking his head. "It's all about fun? Do you think Hazel would see it that way?"

"Well, let's ask her! Oh, wait, we can't. We were too cowardly to do anything!"

Alistair bared his fangs and hissed. His nails had extended into sharp points, which bit into the table. Lara faced him with a deep growl. Fur had started to grow on her arms and neck.

"Stop it! All of you!" The room shook, and darkness choked out the light from the windows and candles. The world distorted as if the library were suddenly a boat cast onto stormy waters. A howl whipped through the air and then gradually subsided. Lyvaelan stood, shaking. His pupils were dilated to complete black, and veins of the same color spread from his eyes. His voice took on a tenebrous and ethereal tone. "Hazel is gone!" Tears streamed from his black eyes. "She's gone." The darkness receded and his eyes regained their blood-red color. "It's my fault. It's my fault they took her. I decided to take lessons from the archmage. If I had just said no, or postponed our meeting or done *something*, then she'd still be here. Instead, she's being carted off by the Inquisition. She'll be vivisected and examined. There's no point in waiting for her when she's never coming back. Why bother hoping for better tomorrows when there are none? I made a selfish choice, and it hurt her. It hurt all of us. This is as bad a cataclysm as any, and I didn't even see it coming."

Garo sighed. "It isn't your fault, Lyvaelan. She wouldn't blame you for this calamity."

"She isn't always right."

"I think she would be, in this case. She told you—all of you— that she would go alone. She made a choice."

Lyvaelan shook his head. "What kind of choice is it when threatened with the death of friends? She's the most unselfish person I know, and I—we—couldn't even take care of her. We all failed, but I failed first."

Garo shook his head. "You're all so quick to forget. Do you remember what she said to you? To each of us? We should strive to be worthy of her words, not stuck in our own melancholy. This should bind us together instead of breaking us apart."

Lara scoffed. "It's already broken us apart. Without Hazel... what's the point?" She pushed her chair over and stomped toward the stairs. "I'm going out."

Garo looked at her. "When will you be coming back?"

"Don't know. Maybe later, maybe never. Who cares?" She left the room without another word.

Alistair stood. He sighed and walked to his room. Garo lay back on the ground in silence. Lyvaelan wandered to his room. He paused and gazed down the hallway to Hazel's room. *Take care of my books, Lyvaelan, and read them soon*, she'd said. *I'm sorry Hazel*, he thought, *but I can't. You should be here to enjoy your books, but you're not. How can I find happiness in your books when you can't?* He entered his room and sat on the floor. The way they talked about Hazel was like she was dead. She wasn't, but it felt that way. How long could they stay together without her? It didn't matter. Maybe nothing mattered after all. She was gone and there was nothing he could do to change that. He curled up in his bed and let the shadows coalesce around him as he fell asleep.

Chapter Eleven
Fox and Wolf

Lara awoke to a sudden shout followed by peals of laughter at the end of the alleyway. She groaned and sat up, wiping the sleep from her eyes and the drool from the side of her mouth. The bottom of her hand and her entire side was slathered with mud, and the rest of her clothes were damp where they weren't soaked through. She scraped some mud from her hair and stood.

The rain had started to fall again and the magelamps dotting the streets had started to glow in the early night. She picked up a bottle that had been tipped over when she fell asleep. Sniffing it she determined there was little whisky left and that the majority of its contents was now rainwater. She cast it aside and stumbled out of the alley. While her werewolf blood made her impervious to many of the negative effects of alcohol, she still felt off. She hadn't eaten all day yesterday and the sheer amount of whisky she consumed would have killed a troll. Lara rubbed her face with her hands, not caring about the dirt. Which bar had she been thrown out of yesterday? Was she banned from more than one? The last one tossed her out because it neared four in the morning and she showed no signs of leaving. She recalled wandering for some indeterminate amount of time before settling here with her bottle of booze.

The werewolf blinked and swore when she realized where she stood. This was the alley near Skilliven Tavern, where Hazel had been shot.

She shook her head and staggered away from the alley and the memories. Sniffing the air, she detected the smell of roasted pork. Her stomach grumbled and she decided to obey. Following the scent, she came to the familiar establishment of Skilliven Tavern. She hesitated a few paces away but eventually stepped in.

Few patrons paid her any mind, intent on their dinners. She glanced back at *their* table and sat at the bar. Eustace Skilliven eyed her but made no mention of her appearance. He took her order and walked back to the kitchen to get her food. A few minutes later, a plate of roasted pork and mashed potatoes appeared before her. She stared down into it, watching the steam rise and enjoying the savory fragrance.

"It's polite to thank your server, you know."

She looked up sharply to the grinning face of the redheaded werefox across the counter. He wore a brown apron over a white shirt but otherwise appeared like he had the first night she met him.

Lara groaned. "Don't tell me you're working here."

"Fine then, I won't."

She sniffed at her food. "Did you do something to my food?"

The werefox assumed an injured expression. "Lara, you wound me! And after all we've been through."

"We haven't been through shit, Foxy."

"Fair point." He shrugged. "I didn't do anything to your meal, though. You would've smelled that something was off. Even if you didn't, the worst I could probably do would be wolf's bane, but that would probably just give you a nasty tummy ache."

She closed her eyes momentarily and pinched the bridge of her nose. When she opened them, the werefox sat beside her without his apron. She was about to reprimand him when Eustace Skilliven approached and set down a plate with roasted pork, garlic mashed potatoes, and a few sprigs of parsley. From the aroma, she guessed it also had rosemary and black pepper.

"Here's your dinner, Miss Lara," he said, "and I'll be getting your beer shortly."

She scanned the bar, but the original plate of food the fox set down was nowhere to be found. Finally, she lifted her eyes to the werefox's. "I'll bet you think you're really clever."

He shrugged with a nonchalant smile. "A wolf needs to eat, and a fox needs to play. A minor deception that caused no one any harm." His green eyes met hers momentarily, and she got the impression that he somehow knew more about her than he let on.

She began to eat with her hands. "What's your name?"

"You don't remember? Shocking," he said dryly. "I am Raynard, though my friends call me Ray. You, I have a feeling, will call me whatever you like."

"True enough." She continued to eat in silence while the werefox studied her. After a full minute, she stopped with a grunt and glared. "What?"

"Hmm." Raynard's eyes flicked over the ceiling as if considering several things at once. "I'm considering how to move the conversation along to where I want without upsetting you."

"Just get to the point," she growled. She had no interest in whatever games he wanted to play.

"Very well." He folded his hands on the bar. "You lost something. What, precisely, I do not know. A battle, perhaps, but not the kind you can fight with fists. In the last week and a half you have wandered around drunkenly, incapable of facing that loss, so you face the bottle instead. That's such a waste of what you're capable of. Perhaps more than that, you and I both know that a werewolf suffers when he—or she—is alone. You were made for community and whatever pack you thought you'd build here has evidently crumbled. No one is looking for you."

"So? I don't want them to look for me. I chose to leave."

He offered a sad smile. "It's sweet you think that, but it isn't true. You mask yourself with zealous independence to trick yourself into thinking you don't need friends. The ache of needing others hurts less when you can rebel against it and reject them first. It's a way of asserting control that really only hurts you." Upon observing her mounting aggression, he held up both hands placatingly. "That's not really my point, though. I want you to join me."

She snorted. "Why would I ever do that?"

"For adventure, friendship, fun"—he raised his eyebrows suggestively—"romance?" She gave him a flat look. "Or just those first three things. That's fine too. I have wanted to see the world for some time, but such an excursion would be better in the company of another."

"Why me? What about your other werewolf friend?"

"Because you're the strongest, of course! Werefoxes aren't exactly weak, but compared to other therianthropes, our abilities are nothing impressive. My friend wasn't even willing to *try* fighting you, and he was almost a foot taller. You're a scrappy one. Besides, you seem to have a sense of humor and care enough about others that you're drinking yourself into the gutter. Join me. Travel the world and maybe we'll meet others. Coruvaine is nothing special. Leave."

Lara searched his eyes and found an unexpected earnestness. She took a long drink from the tankard Eustace had left a minute ago. What would it be like to travel the world? So much of her life had been spent training and fighting. What would it be like to just... leave?

"Why do you care?" she asked.

"I don't. Not yet, at least." He eyed her thoughtfully. "It would be terribly disingenuous of me to claim you mean the world to me when we only met a handful of weeks ago and spoke briefly. Rather, I smell an opportunity. Despite the mud, the heavy drinking, and the soiled clothes, you're something special, Lara. Meeting you by chance allowed me to see the hand of Fal Inderva at play. You don't owe your talents to anyone, but you do owe it to yourself to live a life you can enjoy and be proud of. Leave the criminals to the guards. Join me, and we'll become fast friends."

She shifted in the stool and bit her lip. Was she actually considering the offer? Guilt and grief swirled inside, but part of the offer excited her.

"I... can't decide yet."

Raynard smiled. "Nor would I expect you to." He rose and smoothed his shirt. "You have my scent, so you should be able to find me without issue. I'll be returning to Treland in a week or so. If you can't find me here, then I'm probably there." He turned to leave but looked at her over his shoulder. "The world is a big place, Lara. There's no reason you should ever feel trapped, least of all by an empty table." He departed with a small skip in his step.

She drank from her tankard. Alone, again, but she didn't need to be. Lara drained her beer and ordered another. Maybe it was worth losing her bet with Aldric.

The werefox was right. There was no reason she should feel trapped by an empty table and the memories that sat around it.

Chapter Twelve
Empty Room and Rumination

Alistair gazed at the city below from his high window. A light mist had settled between the streets, creating a halo around each lamp. From this tower, he could almost see the fourth wall in the west. Many long years ago, this room would have been used to house prisoners. When Alistair had first been welcomed into the castle by Aldric, he entreated the king to allow him to stay in this place. Aldric granted the request on the condition that he was given time to alter the room into something suitable for an honored guest. In so many ways, the king had welcomed Alistair into his home.

Why did Hazel give Lyvaelan her books?

He shook his head, warding off the thought, and yet it remained. They spent so much time together organizing books and talking. Why would she bequeath her treasures to someone who cared little for reading at all? Her words echoed in his mind with the singular question endlessly. He gritted his teeth and focused his attention elsewhere.

Footsteps sounded distantly at the bottom of the stairs. Whoever approached now came to see him, since the stairs led to no other places worthy of note. The vampire allowed his eyes to wander around the room. Thick embroidered rugs of red, blue, and gold covered the floor. Heavy drapes to block out the sun were tied off with tasseled golden ropes. A massive four-poster bed overlaid with blankets and twenty different pillows of various sizes and shapes took up the center. The room itself was large enough for a fencing match to take place in and still have space for a few dozen spectators. A series of large mirrors outlined in gold trim ringed the room, which made its already considerable size appear enormous. Alistair could never see his reflection and so the room forever seemed massive and empty.

The footsteps neared, and he could tell from the gait that it was Aldric. Another set of steps he was less familiar with. Bare feet touched the floor gently and a faint rustle of fabric hinted that the individual was of a slight statue.

"You may enter," Alistair said moments before the knock.

The king entered the room with a soft smile. He wore a burgundy half-cape favoring his right side. An ornate dagger with a hilt of carved bone was fastened to his waist by a leather belt. His doublet matched his cape but featured additional swirling designs of gold.

"Good evening, Alistair."

"And to you, Your Majesty. Apologies for not rising but I'm..." he trailed off, losing the motivation to finish the sentiment.

Aldric pursed his lips. "I have a problem you might be able to help resolve."

Alistair glanced behind the king and caught sight of Canneva, the silkie. Her skin was pale as snow, with hair and irises to match. Although she was older than both Aldric and Alistair combined, she appeared no older than a ten-year old girl. Her large eyes and gently pointed ears combined with the surreal grace of her movements left no doubt in anyone's mind that she was a fae. She wore a thick silken dress of white that had little more to it than an unadorned nightgown. Alistair had never heard her speak and only seen her a handful of times. While Aldric may have been the king of the castle, Canneva managed each minute aspect. Several brownies had placed themselves under her command, though Alistair doubted their help was even necessary.

"Canneva tells me that a small quantity of grain has gone missing. I don't want to jump to any conclusions, but—"

"It's by the foot of the bed," Alistair interrupted quietly. "It's all there. Five-thousand, seven-hundred, and ninety-two grains of wheat." He looked back out the window. "I've counted it six times. My apologies, Mistress Canneva. By all means, take them back."

From the reflection in the mirror, he saw the silkie tilt her head curiously but showed no other emotions. She extended her hand, and a multitude of gossamer threads fell from the ceiling and attached to the bag of wheat. It lifted off the ground and moved toward her as small strands attached and detached as necessary. She gave Aldric a curt nod and left the room with the bag trailing behind her.

The king sighed and took a chair next to the door. "Alistair, I know you're not alright."

"My problems are my own, Your Majesty, and nothing you should concern yourself with."

"I disagree. How long has she been gone?"

"One week, four days, six hours, and twenty-seven minutes."

Aldric rubbed the arm of his chair. "I am happy to have you here, at the castle. You're family, to me. Still, I cannot help but wonder if you are here because you're avoiding the library."

"Was there really nothing I could do?" Alistair looked up at him. "Could I have stopped them from taking her? What if I struck the two archmages first, right after she was released? Maybe I just claimed that I would have failed because it meant I didn't have to contradict figures of authority. Did I choose the law over the life of a friend?"

Aldric's eyes turned stern. "We've talked about this, Alistair. You are not to blame. Hazel made her own choices. All these counterfactual thoughts do nothing to help you. If you attacked either of them, it would create an international incident. Besides, it was daytime. Maybe you could have taken her to the top of the library but then what? No, Alistair, there was nothing you could do." He shifted in his chair. "I sent an appeal to the Gray Emperor the moment I learned the Grand Inquisitor would arrive, but I've received no word. The request is likely buried under a mountain of other letters deemed more important. I sent pigeons and a messenger but... nothing."

Aldric stood. "I offered Hazel the ability to go into hiding. I told her I could make her and her family disappear, but she declined the offer." He shook his head. "Whatever awaits her is out of our hands now and in the hands of the gods. We did all that we could." He walked to the door and stopped. "I hope you will come to see that in time. You did all that you could. Be at peace."

The king left, leaving Alistair in his vast and vacuous room alone with thoughts he could not banish from his mind.

Chapter Thirteen
The Final Entry

Three weeks had passed since Hazel rode away in the carriage of the Grand Inquisitor. Garo had departed on other work, leaving the three remaining Watchers alone. Given their fractured state, Commander Comrear doubled their time off—not that it made a difference. To Lyvaelan, the pain of losing her had not dimmed in the slightest. Each day started with the sharp pang of knowing she was gone and ended with the ache of knowing sleep would provide only a temporary reprieve.

Alistair and Lara had ceased arguing. They had stopped talking altogether. All of them grieved, but grieved alone. Lara went out every night to drink. Some nights she came back with blood on her clothes, though she had no visible wounds. Often she would not return at all. A slew of violent emotions bubbled within her, which Lyvaelan avoided comprehending. Alistair spent his nights flying above the city or in the castle. His physical wounds had healed, but others remained. He berated himself for the smallest of mistakes and had taken to recounting the grain in their stores. Everything was cleaned twice a day, down to the most minute detail.

Lyvaelan stayed to himself. An easy thing, given how absent the others were from the library. He occasionally searched for Hazel, using farsight, but her location was blocked, as he anticipated. He sent his mind flying down the path to Selevarian, through Ethelian and south into Petrim. Despite hours of searching, he found no trace of her. He should have expected it. Using farsight to see those who were cloaked amounted to nothing more than a waste of time. He asked Garo if he could find her, but informed Lyvaelan that traveling through shadows required knowledge of where one traveled to. Since he did not know where Hazel might be along the road, it would be impossible for him to find her quickly.

Lyvaelan was lost. Hazel had changed something in him, though he wasn't sure what. She had brought a small measure of what life could be; a tiny parting in an overcast sky that admitted the sun. How quickly that break in the clouds had disappeared.

Part of what hurt, he came to realize, was how nonchalant she had been. She smiled as she left and seemed calmer and more confident than normal. Using techniques he had shown her, she closed off her mind to him. How could she be okay when all of them were hurting? Did she know how much her absence would hurt them? Did she really care about them? He tried to shake the thought, but his mind drifted back and he couldn't help but think if she didn't care about him, it made perfect sense. Why should she care? She was wonderful, sweet, and warm. He was... none of those things. He was terrible, bitter, and cold. They should have taken him instead. *There is no justice in life except for what we bring to it,* his old mentor used to say. Kiran had forgotten to mention that often it didn't matter *what* a person tried to do; justice would fail regardless of the effort exerted.

He walked into the hallway. The library felt lifeless. It was early evening and the other two were not in the building. Apart from the sounds of Charlie quietly cleaning the kitchen, the library was silent. Lyvaelan moved into the kitchen to find the water in the kettle already hot. Lyvaelan was fairly consistent in his desires. The redcap appeared briefly and placed a teacup with dried lavender leaves in it.

He poured the steaming water over it and disappeared again. Lyvaelan picked up the cup and inhaled the aroma. He smiled bitterly. Hazel hated the smell of lavender. Such an odd scent to dislike. He walked into the hallway and gazed toward her room. He hadn't been in there since she left. He felt conflicted, but some part of him had worn down. Why did it matter? Maybe it didn't. He absently snapped his fingers and surrounded his whole body in a blue sphere of Elchoran. The library was quiet, but he preferred silence.

He dragged himself to her room, plodding noiselessly down the hallway. Her room maintained a cleanly simplicity. The best lit room in the library. He studied the plants on her balcony. *Curious,* he thought. *I would have expected the jasmine to invade the daffodils.*

Moving away from the window, he sat on her bed, taking in the room. He had spent much time in this room watching over her after she was burned. His eyes gradually drifted to her little bookshelf. He set his tea on the floor to peruse the books.

A Collection of Fairytales, Princess's Bounty, The Pirate Queen, the titles read. He shook his head. *How useless,* he thought. *How could she possibly expect me to* want *to read these?*

He was about to leave the shelf when something slightly different caught his eye. A thin book with no discernable title, with a piece of paper poking out from the top, sat wedged between two larger novels, nearly concealing it. It was the same color as the bed and partially obscured by a pillow. He took the book out and unfolded the page. It was a letter addressed to Hazel. *Ah,* he thought, *this must be the journal she kept. Aldric gave it to her.* He sat down.

I'm not sure how to begin this book, the first entry read. *Beginnings are always the hardest. They're awkward and you don't know what's going on. I don't know why I should feel awkward writing, though, since I'm the only one who will read this.*

He raised an eyebrow. "Not *entirely* true. I guess you don't always know the future."

I'm not sure I know what to make of the others. Alistair is nice, and I feel the closest to him. We both like books, and he helped move me in. Lara is funny and kind of rude, but not bad. Lyvaelan is strange. It sounds like he's powerful and knows a lot about magic. Maybe I can learn from him.

Lyvaelan sighed. He flipped through the book, skimming through the majority, reading only enough to get a sense of the content. It was interesting to see her writing get livelier as she wrote. It was also intriguing to see her dreams gain additional details over time. Occasionally, she wrote entries on daily life, but mostly it focused on her visions. A lump formed in his throat. This was a part of her. Reading it was almost like she was here. He had flipped almost halfway through when he came across her most recent dreams. He frowned. She wrote the same vision, sometimes multiple times in a day. He knew they were getting stronger, but he didn't realize *how* strong. He flipped through and then stopped. The journal entry was dated the eighth of Athelia. The day they took her.

Lyvaelan, she wrote, *I hope you read this soon. It will be hard, but I need you to be very careful and not do anything brash. Today, I will be taken by the Grand Inquisitor. You cannot stop this; I have foreseen it. That doesn't make you helpless, though. I saw it last night, and it filled me with calm. I think it's because it's happening right now. It isn't the future anymore—it's the present.*

I dreamed that, surrounded by a field of corpses, the living lich rose. I could see the place distinctly, though I've never been there. There was a massive estate, though not quite a castle. There were no gardens or trees, just a flat plane where creatures came to die. The green light surrounding her seemed to fuel her and it came from me. I am the reason the lich will come to power, but I am not the lich. I thought I was, but I was wrong. This time I saw the living lich clearly. It was a beautiful woman with wavy dark hair and incredible power. I heard those same words of the prophecy before, except instead of saying "the day of the lich draws nigh," it said: "Behold! The living lich shall rise, and her name is Alvaria Saccarra."

Lyvaelan dropped the book. A shiver ran through him. With trembling hands, he picked up the book and continued.

I know who the living lich is, and I know who Alvaria Saccarra is. If she's the living lich, then I don't know who to trust, except for you. I don't know if any mages are safe. I hope and pray to Hemericanth that at least one spellcaster in Selevarian is not corrupt. You need to save me. If you can't find me quickly, then the world will be in danger. You know more about magic than I do. I trust you, and know you believe in me, just like I believe in you. You're the last hope I have. Please help me.

Lyvaelan stood. That was the last thing she wrote. He gritted his teeth. She was terrified. She walked knowingly into the mouth of a monster with a smile. This was the only way she could think of to help without making the Grand Inquisitor suspicious.

He snapped his fingers and a blue wisp of smoke floated up, and the sphere of Elchoran popped. "Stupid!" He yelled, storming from her room. He banged repeatedly on Lara's door. "Up werewolf! Now!" he moved to the other side. He touched his throat and felt the light tingle of magic along his vocal cords. "Alistair! Get out here!" his voice boomed, shaking the library. He paused momentarily, remembering that neither had been here for days. Immediately, he sat where he was and reached out to them mentally. Lara stooped over a bowl of stew in a grungy tavern a mile from the library. She drank from it while glaring at the wall.

Lara! He shouted telepathically. She jolted, spilling half of the contents of the meal in her hair and over her shoulder. *Come to the library immediately! It's an emergency.*

She looked equally flustered and annoyed. "What emergen—" she began to ask out loud, but Lyvaelan severed the connection and searched for the vampire. While he could guess Alistair currently occupied the castle, the fortress itself had various enchantments that made farsight difficult. Nonetheless, Lyvaelan began to call out with his memory of Alistair. He remembered different traits and thoughts and sent these images through the barrier to establish a link. After several minutes, Lyvaelan beheld Alistair sitting by a large circular window in a fancy room filled with mirrors.

Alistair! Come to the library immediately. It's urgent.

Alistair didn't bother responding but his cape and sword before dashing out. The message had been delivered.

Lyvaelan paced the floor when both arrived at nearly the same time. "Stupid! Careless!" he muttered to himself.

The two glanced at each other. "What? Who's stupid and careless?" Lara asked.

His red eyes burned with fury. "I am, but that's unimportant at the moment."

"Lyvaelan, what is this about?" Alistair asked cautiously.

"Hazel. We have to save her. She's in danger."

Lara leaned against a wall. "I thought we'd already established that."

"Yes, what makes this different?"

Lyvaelan continued pacing. How much should he tell them? It was a difficult balance. "I can't tell you more except that she's in danger. Your minds are basically open to any sorcerer who wants to look. I know more, but can't say more. If I did, then we might as well be carrying around banners with the information. I don't know who I can trust."

"You're saying you don't trust us," Lara stated, folding her arms.

"Yes, exactly," Lyvaelan replied. "Neither of you are trained to block sorcery from your minds. Even I'm at risk and, of the three of us, I'm the least susceptible to its effects. I need you two to trust me." He glanced between them and his heart dropped. Despite the danger she was in, neither could put aside the painful weeks they experienced without her. Neither wanted to be in the room with the other. Calling an emergency with nothing to back it up would not suffice. He needed to disclose something important but nothing that could damage the mission.

Lyvaelan sank into a chair. "It's not enough," he whispered. "I'm sorry that I can't tell you everything. I wouldn't trust me either, if I were where you two are standing. In order to move this along, I need to be open with both of you. I can't share the details of what's happening with Hazel, but... I can tell you a story. A story about a time I lost control."

He licked his lips and wrung his hands. Their minds revealed confusion, but their impatience had waned.

"Twelve years ago Kiran—my mentor—showed me how rudimentary enchantments worked. He took me through the process, which is generally laborious compared to what elves and fae can accomplish. He was like a father to me. I asked him about my parents, but he knew little except that my father was a warlock and my mother was a dark elf. I think a combination of the tedious work we did, coupled with loneliness, drove me to secretly try to expand my abilities further with farsight. Progress by conventional means had frustrated me and, driven by a desire to know who my parents were and if they still lived, I drew on my warlock heritage. I pulled magic through myself and saw an image swimming before my eyes, indistinctly. I did not know it then, but the great tree of Chaldra itself—in whose branches I lived—vied against my power. I pushed harder against the image, yet it remained out of reach.

"Kiran burst in. The whole room had been thrown apart. He shouted at me to contain it, and it was only then that I realized what I had done. Kiran pushed against the storm, but the magic had grown too great. I reached out my hand to him and he dissolved into nothing." Lyvaelan took a deep, shuddering breath. "I'm a monster. I know that. I killed the closest thing I had to a family for a selfish desire. That's why... I wanted you to kill me."

Both Lara and Alistair stepped back. They tried to mask their emotions, although they did a poor job of it.

"It's funny," Lyvaelan continued softly. "I asked Hazel to kill me if I ever lost control around the same time both of you first talked about the same thing. Of course, it wasn't until after she was burned that you both agreed to do what must be done." He looked both of them in the eyes. "You may not believe me, but I took great comfort in knowing that not everyone would die because of me. I no longer needed Hazel's promise because I had both of yours. I apologize if you think reading your surface thoughts was an invasion of privacy. The elves predominantly communicate telepathically. The guilt in both of you is unnecessary. I arrived at the same conclusion. It was something I hoped a friend would do for me." He shook his head. "Hazel found a way none of us did. That's why we need her. She grounds us in a different reality than the one we've all come to accept for ourselves—a reality where we aren't monsters, but heroes."

Lyvaelan stood. If this failed, he didn't know what else to do. "I will tell you everything, eventually. I swear it by all that I hold dear. For now, we need to reach Selevarian."

They relaxed and looked at each other. Their eyes held hurt, worry, and uncertainty. Despite this, something else moved within them.

Lara sighed. "You're a crazy bastard, Lyvie, but I'll trust you. It's not the dumbest thing I've done in the last year."

"I trust you as well," Alistair said. "The mind-reading notwithstanding. What is your plan? Selevarian is almost two months of travel away on foot. How are we supposed to reach her swiftly if time is against us?"

Lyvaelan's eyes darted back and forth, searching for a plan. He snapped his fingers. "We use the gates."

"What?" Alistair exchanged an alarmed look with Lara. "I thought only mages could use them."

"You're right." He nodded. "That's why we'll join the Archmage of Education on his trip back to Selevarian. He's supposed to transfer Hickory Allkirk as soon as he hears from the Grand Inquisitor. The trip shouldn't have taken them over two weeks. It's been almost three, and he hasn't left yet. He mentioned he'd stop by to deliver any messages we had personally before he left. Tonight, our mission is easy: speak to the archmage. Get him to take us on the trip down to Selevarian. Then we save Hazel."

The other two rushed to gather a couple of things. Lara put on her gloves, laced with steel and alchemical silver. Alistair donned a long black cape, different from the one he had arrived in. The three of them informed Charlie they might be gone for a while before leaving the library.

We're coming, Hazel, Lyvaelan thought. *We just have to trick an archmage into helping us.*

They entered the study of the Archmage of Education. The sorcerer at the front desk eyed them curiously, but admitted them, sensing the severity of the situation. The archmage was reading some papers on his desk when the group arrived. He looked up and smiled.

"Greetings—"

"No time," Lara interrupted, putting her hand on the desk and leaning over. "Hazel is in trouble."

"The Grand Inquisitor is also in trouble," Lyvaelan added. It wasn't a lie, but it certainly wasn't the same trouble Hazel was in.

He raised an eyebrow. "Really? What proof do you have?"

Lyvaelan hesitated. "Archmage, you must believe us. We have our sources, but I fear you would discredit them without a second thought. Instead, I would ask: doesn't it seem strange that you haven't received word from them? It's been almost three weeks and we've heard nothing."

He leaned back. "A few days' delay could mean a broken wagon wheel or a malfunctioning gate. It isn't enough to worry over."

So, he hasn't heard from them? Lyvaelan thought. "If either of those were the case, wouldn't they contact you?"

"Hmm." He considered it. "They should. It isn't enough cause for apprehension, but perhaps you're right." He drew a golden mirror out of his desk with inlaid emeralds. He gazed at the mirror. "Alvaria Saccarra." The surface shimmered and warped, but then returned to its usual reflective surface. He frowned. "Alvaria Saccarra, Grand Inquisitor." Again, the mirror shimmered and returned to its previous form. "Odd," he said. "She carries a scry mirror everywhere.

Malvex Sorrelle!" The mirror shimmered and turned dark blue. After a few moments, the blue cleared and revealed the face of a half dark elf man with a short black beard.

"The Archmage of Education. To what do I owe the pleasure?"

"Archmage of Sorcery, it is good to see you, but I fear I must cut to the point. Have you seen the Grand Inquisitor in the last week?"

"No, I haven't. In fact"—the man closed his eyes briefly—"she isn't in Selevarian or at Chateau Zarielle."

"Are you certain of that?"

The man raised an eyebrow. "You're asking if the Archmage of Sorcery knows how to perform basic sorcery?"

"My apologies, I'm concerned for Alvaria. She left Coruvaine and took longer to reach Selevarian than expected."

"I assume you already attempted communication using your scry mirror. Maybe her mirror is broken. I doubt there's much cause to worry."

"Indeed. Well, thank you for helping, Malvex. I'll see you again soon." The image faded from the mirror. Lysander strummed his fingers on the desk absently. "This is troubling."

"So, you agree?" Lara asked. "You think they're in danger?"

He met her eyes. "Not necessarily. However, wars are won and lost because of effective communication or its absence. If we don't have that, then we're in trouble. Simply because I *hope* they're not in danger doesn't mean they *aren't.*"

He stood and threw a white cloak over his shoulders. "Let's collect Hickory Allkirk. You three may join me on my way to Selevarian, though it may be a quicker route than you'd normally enjoy."

They arrived in the dungeon beneath the palace. A larger prison was built outside the first wall, but the subterranean levels of the castle housed more dangerous criminals, especially those apprehended by the Sapphire Guard. Hickory, who had been in the custody of the Inquisition, was turned over to the Sapphire Guard since they possessed better facilities for containing dangerous criminals long-term. They hurried down the steps in silence until they came upon a spellcaster of the Sapphire Guard, a young woman with brown hair who snapped to attention upon seeing the archmage.

"Sir! We are honored to have you here!"

"At ease. We're here to collect a prisoner for the Inquisition."

"Which prisoner?"

"Hickory Allkirk."

"Certainly, sir, right this way." She led them into the chamber. Several lamps hung with candles within. Using magelamps could be dangerous if someone in here needed an extra boost of magic to get free. The young mage glanced back at them. "I'm glad you came by to pick him up. He's been acting strange lately."

"Strange, how?" Lysander asked.

"Well, Eminence," she said, continuing through the dark hallway, "a couple weeks ago, he stopped eating. He just sits in his cell meditating most of the time."

His brow creased. "Really? Is that all he does?"

"No, my lord. He sometimes stands and stretches, but besides that, he doesn't do much else." She stopped when they entered a larger space. A single cell with metal bars took up half the room while benches lined the wall on the opposite side for visitors. "Here's his room. Be careful, his most recent meal is probably still on the floor. When you take him, I'll have some papers ready for you to sign." She took out a key and unlocked the door.

Dust and filth covered the floor. It reeked of sweat and feces. The archmage waved his hand, and the odor disappeared with a small gust of wind. He squinted into the dark to see the wizened figure of Hickory Allkirk sitting against a wall with a look of intense concentration. Two books sat forgotten on his mat, and two different trays with food on them remained close to the door.

"Hickory Allkirk?" The archmage said.

The imprisoned mage opened his eyes to look at him, but then closed them again. Lysander frowned. He rubbed his hands together, creating a small ball of light. He released it into the air.

"Something is wrong," the archmage muttered. "I sense a small trace of magic that shouldn't be here."

Lyvaelan nodded. He couldn't pinpoint the cause, but something was off.

Lysander's eyes narrowed. "Hickory Allkirk?" The man opened his eyes to look at the archmage, but closed them again. Lysander frowned. "Hickory Allkirk." The man did the same thing. The archmage pulled back the air with his hand and pushed it at the sitting man. He didn't move. Not a single hair on his head shifted.

"An illusion!" Lysander exclaimed. A black vortex appeared in the archmage's palm, draining magic from the room. The man sitting against the wall distorted and dissolved into the whirlpool. The emaciated form of Hickory Allkirk, lying unconscious on the ground, replaced it.

Lysander closed his eyes and leaned over him. "Sorcery. Someone searched through his memories and he tried to resist. Whoever it was evidently possessed more power and skill. His memories and consciousness have been scrambled. He's essentially comatose."

"Can you do anything to help him?" Alistair asked.

"Very little at the moment. His mind will reorganize on its own. My assistance would only reduce his recovery time by a few days, while potentially requiring weeks of work. We don't have that time." He laid a hand on Hickory and his palm glowed. "I can revitalize him. Fortunately, in this state, he conserves a substantial amount of energy. Still, without receiving sustenance in the next few days, he would have perished." The boney frame filled somewhat as light poured from Lysander's palm. After a few minutes, Hickory no longer appeared starved so much as sleeping. The archmage rose and exited, with the others following.

"Are you not taking the prisoner?" The Sapphire Guard asked when they reached her.

"No. Someone placed an illusion in his cell. Who was the last person to see him as he normally was? When did he last eat?"

The guard was taken aback. She drew out a large book and flipped through it. "It must have been a couple of weeks ago. The archmage wanted to see him—"

"—*Which* archmage?"

She showed him the page. "The Archmage of the Inquisition."

Lysander's expression darkened. "Impossible." He strode swiftly up the stairs and out of the dungeon.

"Are we not leaving for Selevarian?" Alistair asked.

"Oh, we *are*," he said, "but we're leaving Mr. Allkirk behind. It will probably be a month before he can talk again, let alone pose any credible threat."

"Then are we going to get a wagon?"

"No, we'll be riding individual horses. It will only be the four of us. We leave tonight. If we hurry, we can reach Selevarian in four days."

"Four days!" Lara said. "I thought it was supposed to take two weeks when traveling by gate!"

"It does when you're dragging a wagon or carriage. If you travel light and you're willing to go through multiple gates rapidly, then it's only four days. The horses won't like it, but I will soothe them and keep them alive. You may not enjoy it either, but I can't help feeling pressed for time. Something strange is going on and I need to find out what."

"Are archmages supposed to destroy the minds of people they talk to?" Lara asked.

He looked at her sharply, but then averted his gaze, his expression dark. "No. No, they are not."

As they sped into the night, Lyvaelan's heart beat faster. *We're coming, Hazel. We're on our way. We will find you and prevent the living lich of half a day from rising. Just hold on.*

Chapter Fourteen
Ambitions Thinly Veiled

Alvaria stared over the frigid plain. They had finally arrived. After teleporting through the gate south of Coruvaine, they exited on the opposite side of the city and were nearly a hundred miles from the northern gate. A misconception held by the commoners was that teleportation occurred in the same direction that one faced when entering a gate. On the contrary, they could link to any other within a specified range regardless of the individual's position. It was for this reason that no one who watched them depart would realize they traveled in the opposite direction. The gates existed several miles from any major city in the unlikely case they malfunctioned. For this reason, the two parents of Hazel Enda appeared unaware of the difference in scenery. As far as they knew, they were on their way south to Selevarian and the estate they approached was Chateau Zarielle. There was little reason to believe anything was amiss. Hazel, on the other hand, appeared cognizant of the situation, though she remained calm. What little training the girl received in sorcery served her well in keeping Alvaria from reading her surface thoughts. The girl understood more than what she admitted.

The ground surrounding Kazra Lo Veedra was desolate. In the cold of winter, covered with snow, it appeared to exist in the middle of a wasteland of ice, but even in the height of summer, it remained a miserable and stark place. No plants grew, and no birds sang. The area surrounding the building had magic designed for a specific purpose: it drew creatures there to die. The enchantment was odd and oddly effective. Creatures approaching death found the plain soothing and peaceful. Humans, animals, fae, and even daimon had chosen this area to die in. The dead ring around the estate called to all beings approaching death and provided them with some last few moments of meaningless pleasure before their demise. None of the dying could refuse the bewitching call of Kazra Lo Veedra. The enchantment had worked, but poisoned the earth to living things. Not even the heartiest weed would lay roots in the soil where the enchantment held power. Those bodies that fell within the circle decomposed slowly, and even flies refused to infest the fallen with maggots. Nearby villages found the area suspicious, and many avoided talking about it for fear of bringing bad luck. In many cases, the superstitions of uneducated peasants were annoying and challenging to deal with, but in this case, it provided freedom for the Grand Inquisitor to work and alter the area to her needs.

The impressive size and shape of the estate owed to its sole purpose: raising a lich and providing a defensible position for that lich to rule from. The building had a single level above ground, but its high roof made it taller than most buildings with three. While the architecture appeared bizarre, the meaning of each geometric choice would not be lost to a conjurer. A series of triangles, squares, pentagons, and circles connected by various hallways created arcane connections built from stone in a labyrinthine mess of walkways and largely unusable rooms. From the outside, it was impressive but appeared no more significant than any other building, but upon traversing the halls and viewing it aerially, one could see a giant conjurer's circle. While rudimentary, at this size, it hardly mattered. Even a novice conjurer could wield enormous power with safety from the interior of the estate.

Alvaria descended from her carriage, waving away an attendant who offered help. She stretched, popping her back and neck in several places. They had rested on the road at several points, but she finally felt capable of relaxing, despite the urgency of her mission. Rushing to complete her work after a tiring journey would do no good. As she exhaled, she watched her breath curl into a fluttering cloud of white.

She turned to a nearby attendant. "Please show Mr. and Mrs. Enda to their room on the lower level. Ensure they are fed but request they remain in their accommodations for the present." The attendant nodded and signaled to a couple of other inquisitors, who rushed to pick up the bags of the Enda family and ushered them away. The two seemed grateful for the help, with no sense of how to properly react. It was faintly humorous to see them bumbling over how to treat serv-ants. Hazel paid them little attention and instead focused her attention on Alvaria. The feeling behind those eyes—so appropriately hazel-colored—was challenging to read. This girl differed from others Alvaria had known. Then again, Alvaria had been far from ordinary at sixteen as well.

"Hazel, would you walk with me for a little while?"

Hazel nodded and joined her. Alvaria waved the inquisitors back. They walked several paces behind them as they ascended the dozen long steps to the door.

They entered through the bronze doors of Kazra Lo Veedra. "I imagine you have questions, Hazel. I know this all seems strange, but it will be over soon."

"I know you're the living lich of half a day." Hazel remarked quietly.

Alvaria continued silently. Only the sounds of their steps and her staff on the ground echoed off the marble floors. "And how do you know that?"

Hazel glanced at her. "I saw you in my vision the day you came. I've dreamed of the living lich before, but that night it was you."

They passed through the antechamber and into a hallway lit with magelamps. A series of silver and gold patterns and lines wrapped through the interior of the estate like veins of a long dead titan.

Alvaria smiled. "Then I have manifested the prophecy. Good. Hazel, I don't think you're fully aware of what you've stumbled into simply by coming back to life."

Hazel stared at her sharply, her voice taking an edge. "You mean I don't realize that the Inquisition, who are supposed to destroy corruption and undead, are actually trying to create the most powerful undead creature in existence? Is that what I don't realize?"

Alvaria chuckled. "You have a sharp tongue, child. You understand much more than those beyond my organization, but still grasp only the outline of the situation while utterly missing its repercussions. Do you understand what a prophecy is?"

"A vision of the future."

"It can be, yes, but that's only how it's commonly understood. The truth is far more... nuanced." She gestured with her hand and smoky wisps of blue light trailed from her fingers. "Magic surrounds us. It permeates the world and all living things. Even those with no magical aptitude—such as your parents—possess and produce vast quantities of magic. Magic is much like water in that some areas have more or less of it. For this reason, many liken it to a vast network of streams running through the world.

"Magic does not flow simply like a stream, however. Water naturally runs downhill. Magic moves in all directions simultaneously; up, down, left, right, and in every imaginable configuration. It also moves temporally. When we speak of wells of magic, we mean areas possessing vast quantities of magic that attract mages and creatures who thrive on it. Wells of magic are not only spatial locations; they are also events. Most are mundane enough that wells go unrecognized, but occasionally—very rarely—a person sees that future arcane well. It isn't *created* by anyone, but they are usually a *symptom* of someone's direct involvement. You were likely not born when it happened, but when King Mael of Salverno came to power at a young age, the event was the subject of a large magic well.

"You might wonder what the use of these wells is. What purpose do they serve? The patterns mages have observed show that they predict important historical events that are unavoidable, to some extent. Even a simple person can understand the importance of knowing the future. Using such an event is much more interesting, however. Temporal wells only appear within a limited time, as one might expect. If one were to take advantage of such powerful magic and use it all at once, it would be possible to work miracles."

"Isn't that what magic is? Miracles?"

Alvaria sighed as she led Hazel through the labyrinthian hallways of the estate. "I can see how it might seem that way, but no. Sadly, magic has rules and limitations. More frustrating, however, is when magic seems to break its own rules for no apparent reason."

"Like me."

"Smart girl," Alvaria said dryly. "Yes, you are an anomaly. I actually spoke with your alleged creator."

Hazel turned to her. "You spoke to Hickory? What did he say?"

"Very little." She shrugged. "He wasn't explicitly helpful, unfortunately. I had to pry the information I needed from him, though he struggled spectacularly. He was truly mad to resist the efforts of a mage so far beyond his abilities."

Hazel stopped walking. Her eyes widened. "What did you do?"

"Oh, he'll be alright. Eventually. His mind was as cluttered as his notes, but the gist of what I understood was that what he did shouldn't have worked. Similar experiments have occurred countless times and yielded no fruits whatsoever. The idiot thought he stumbled on some special combination of magics to bring you back. That's what the Sapphire Guard focused on when discerning your nature. I've read the notes. I searched his mind. Given that, I can definitively conclude that your return was not the work of mortal hands."

"What do you mean?"

Alvaria chuckled. "You're sweet, Hazel, and you don't realize how powerful you are. You're the product of divine intervention."

Hazel eyes widened.

"Yes, divine intervention," Alvaria said with slight frustration as she led Hazel further in, "I don't mean fae, daimon, or even the distant yokai. I mean the gods."

"How?" Hazel caught up with her.

"You recall that damnable high priestess? Relinon, I think?"

"Yes, the High Priestess of Semeleme."

"You are basically identical to her, though the god is different." Alvaria eyed Hazel. "You know, it really is frustrating as a woman of science to deal with beings such as yourself. You break the rules. Necromancy may be abhorrent, but it *uses* the rules to accomplish wondrous horrors. You? You're nothing more than a product of divine meddling."

Hazel studied the archmage. "It isn't just that I break the rules, is it? You hate me for some other reason."

Alvaria stopped walking. While the archmage felt no special affection for the girl, she found the accusation of hatred to be too strong. "You misunderstand. It is not *you* I hate. You had nothing to do with any of this. It would be unreasonable for me to despise you for existing beyond your control. It's the gods I loathe."

Hazel gasped. "You shouldn't say things like that!"

"Or what? They will decide to *not* bring me back from the dead?" She scoffed. "Come with me." She led Hazel through the maze of hallways and rooms to the center of the structure. A huge, round room with six arches leading to separate hallways along the perimeter. The floor sloped into a spherical shape but bottomed out into a flat surface. In the middle of the floor, a magnificent sarcophagus inlaid with many gems rested. It belonged to the deceased owner of Kazra Lo Veedra, Antony Larsinius. He reposed within. Waiting. Sleeping.

She studied Hazel, who marveled at the strange architecture and lush use of metals and precious gems. The room was impressive, but Alvaria couldn't help finding flaws with the execution. Certain lines were not carved as distinctly as they could be, while several circles were placed oddly. The mage had miscalculated a few measurements for what would be *most* effective. An imperfect execution of an otherwise impressive room. Even Chateau Zarielle hadn't featured as much arcane utility as this, but she still found it mildly irritating to see someone do this much work unnecessarily.

"Here he will return from the grave," Alvaria announced.

"Who?"

"A mage of middling ability but unquestionable ambition," she said, resting in a chair near a work table. She gestured for Hazel to sit as well, but she remained standing. "His name was Antony Larsinius, a citizen of the Gray Empire proper. His father acquired great wealth and land akin to a baron, though the title does not exist in the Tellarian outskirts. Antony had amassed quite a fortune himself, which he used to construct this place. He didn't rely on the gods; he relied on himself. Through time, effort, and my mercy, he will return from the dead."

"You're going to turn him into a lich?"

"Not at all. I'm simply going to let him become one. Having a lich on retainer should be helpful given the dangerous waters I'm wading into."

Hazel stared at the sarcophagus. "Wouldn't he just kill you?"

"He might, but he wouldn't dare. I have his phylactery."

"His what?"

"His phylactery. Many liches choose to have one, mostly because of paranoia. All humans possess both a spirit and a soul. The spirit is simply the animating force, or that which keeps one alive and from decay. The soul is the memories, thoughts, feelings, and so on. When a person dies, the two are separated. The spirit goes to Semeleme, and the soul goes to whatever afterlife it deserves. Liches bring back their souls, but their spirits are tainted. Spirits keep one alive, so what happens when the spirit goes to the underworld? Well, the spirit instead strives to preserve its death instead. This is why liches and other undead are destroyed by healing magics. The spirit reacts aversely to such magics and flees back to Semeleme. For a lich to exist, both spirit and soul must remain in the world. The soul is impossible to really send, but the spirit is temperamental. The solution is to hide the spirit somewhere outside the body, usually in a vessel. While this does not negate the physical damage such being suffer, it does preserve them from permanent destruction."

Hazel shook her head in disbelief. "How is that possible? If the spirit lets us move and live, how can it exist outside the body?"

"The soul," Alvaria replied. "It's ingenious, really. Liches' magic is so powerful that—by sheer force of will—their bodies move, talk, and exist. They do not need the animating force of the spirit to keep their bodies together, since they maintain the innate power of their souls, which serve as the locus of arcane power. The body is then little more than an advanced puppet to them. For that reason, if the body is destroyed, it can be rebuilt through sheer force of will, though I've heard the process is challenging and intensely unpleasant."

"That sounds ghastly and... wrong."

"On that point, Hazel Enda, I agree with you."

"What? Aren't you trying to become a lich?"

"Yes," Alvaria said, a distant smile on her face, "but with your help, I will become a lich unlike any other. A *living* lich. My body will serve as a vessel to both spirit and soul."

"Why would I help you do that?"

"Because my goal is ultimately the same as yours. I want to keep others from dying."

"By becoming a lich?"

"Exactly. You know of the seven arcane disciplines? Wizardry, sorcery, enchantment, alchemy, conjuration, thaumaturgy, and lesser magic. These designations are helpful from a scientific perspective, but useless in terms of true boundaries. Lesser Magic, for example, is a mere smattering of all the other disciplines to achieve a desired effect. We create these separations because they are easier to understand and focus on. It's like a person who says you can study eagles, falcons, kites, hawks, ospreys, or harriers, when all of those are simply birds of prey. Liches have access to a different magic that is accessible only when one has gone to the grave and returned. In the previous example, normal spellcasters may study birds of prey but liches study reptiles." She hesitated a moment. "It's a clunky analogy. Liches gain access to Eldritch Magic. It's capable of many wonders, but more than anything, it is the direct manipulation of life and death."

Alvaria stood and placed a hand on the ornate coffin, tracing the figures with her fingers. "Has it never struck you as unfair that humans live such brief lives? We are given eighty years while dwarves live triple that, and elves live triple that of the dwarves. Vampires are virtually ageless and therianthropes live a couple of hundred years as well. Even the most gifted human mages rarely live longer than three-hundred years, and those who do usually have assistance from some other source. Your three friends, for example, would all outlive you by a span of centuries. Is that really fair?"

Hazel shrugged. "That's just the way it is."

"And who decided that? The gods, in their infinite wisdom." Alvaria's grip on her staff tightened. "Why? Why are we so frail? Look at your friends and what *they've* survived. The vampire's lower back was torn out, and the werewolf was stabbed through the stomach and beaten into a bloody pulp. A week later and they are almost completely recovered. You, when you were normal, died from falling out of a tree. Not toppling from a mountain, not falling from a cloud, you dropped from a tree only twenty feet high to drown in less than two feet of water. Pathetic." She glanced at Hazel. "I'm not saying that you're innately pathetic, but that the human condition—*our* condition—is laughable. Why shouldn't we have longer lifespans and be more durable? It's insulting. For all our potential, we can get killed by falling from a tree or getting kicked by a horse.

"The gods made a mistake. I plan to rectify that. If I become a lich, I will be capable of keeping people alive if they desire. No wound would be too grievous for me to heal, nor would any life be cut prematurely short." She put a hand on Hazel's shoulder. "I want to give others the same opportunity that you've had. Is that so wrong?"

Hazel looked away. Alvaria was right, the girl just didn't want to admit it. The Grand Inquisitor smiled. Finally, Hazel met Alvaria's gaze. "I don't believe you."

Alvaria frowned, and her blood froze. "What?"

"I don't believe you. Maybe you want to do something good, I'm not sure, but regardless of your intentions, you will crush anyone who doesn't agree. You've hurt people in the past, haven't you?"

"Great endeavors require great sacrifice," Alvaria stated coolly.

Hazel shook her head. "They weren't your sacrifices to make. I won't help you. I don't even know how I *could*. Even if I did, I still wouldn't. You betrayed your own friends. The way you treated those who tried to do good things, like Thomas Eller, was terrible."

Alvaria took a deep breath. She tapped her fingers on the lid of the sarcophagus. "There is still time for you to change your mind. I have many preparations to take care of in the upcoming weeks. Consider my words, and perhaps you will find my motivations more compelling. Until then, you raise a valid point. I haven't treated Chief Inquisitor Eller justly." She turned to one of her attendants. "Bring me Eller. We'll be in the southeastern sitting room." The attendant rushed off while Alvaria led Hazel through a different hallway and into a red carpeted room with a fireplace and surrounding magelamps. The sweet aroma of frankincense permeated the air. They had just sat in a couple of large leather chairs when Thomas Eller appeared.

"Eller, come here."

"Yes, Grand Inquisitor." He genuflected before her.

"Hazel believes I have treated you unfairly. I will admit I was initially annoyed by the situation, but you should be commended for your service. Rise." He stood. "You performed everything to the best of your capabilities. Did Averly complete his special salve?"

"He did, Eminence, though he will likely require a few more days of preparation before it is up to your desired specifications."

"And is he on the mend?"

"He is," he hesitated, "though the psychological toll is harder to estimate. His work drives him, however, so his psychological state shouldn't impede his research."

Hazel looked at them with a growing expression of realization.

"Perhaps I should introduce you to Chief Inquisitor Thomas Eller? It would appear you two haven't truly met. Thomas, why don't you explain your specific assignment in Coruvaine?"

"The official, or the actual?"

Alvaria watched Hazel. "I think she knows the former, but the latter is likely unknown to her."

He nodded. "I was the Grand Inquisitor's hand in Coruvaine. All cases of arcane abuse, when they could be replicated or proven, were sent to me. From there, I informed the Grand Inquisitor and did as she commanded. We have been aware of Paxton Averly for many years now and decided to... increase his research funding. When you were discovered, the king's reticence at relinquishing you gave me the perfect opportunity to both control the situation surrounding Averly's eventual capture, and to take notes on what sort of creature you were. Thus, we put you under various stress tests. I knew where you were, thanks to my aufhockers, and since you all gave such excellent reports, it was easy for me to collect data. After the cult attacked you, I was frustrated—less because you kept a secret from me, than because I didn't want you to think I knew about it as it could lead to suspicions. When you told your friends about your dream in Skilliven Tavern, one of my shadowy assistants remained close and listening. I would report to the archmage whenever it seemed appropriate."

"You lied to us." Hazel balled her hands into fists. "You controlled the aufhockers and had them capturing bluecaps!"

"Yes," he replied impassively. "A necessary sequence of deceptions to serve my true mission."

"You betrayed everyone. Even the Inquisition."

"The Inquisition?" Alvaria scoffed. "Do you know why the Inquisition even came to exist? It resulted from a man driven by vengeance to eradicate knowledge and individuals who he deemed 'dangerous.' Do you realize how much we lost in the Great Purge? The knowledge we have now is sanitized to the point of obsolescence and efforts to move beyond that result in prayers and supplications to Gnostrevaine. We are in the right; we simply lack the power and authority to publicly claim as much. Eller knows my mission and why I wish to achieve it. Not every inquisitor knows or agrees, but there are many I trust who have worked to achieve my goal. They understand the ideal for what it is: the promise of a painless, better world."

Eller cleared his throat. "If I may, archmage?" She nodded her assent. "I betrayed nothing. I have been consistent in my labors and sacrificed relationships with others to bring about Lady Saccarra's vision. There were difficult times, and I didn't savor lying or hurting any of you, but make no mistake: if I needed to act a second time to make the Grand Inquisitor a living lich, then I would."

Alvaria smiled. Eller had been in the Inquisition for almost twenty years, and she knew him even before then. He lusted for greatness and practically worshipped her. Perhaps more than his ambition, she enjoyed his unwavering dedication to her.

"What could she possibly promise you to make it all okay?"

"Whatever they wish," Alvaria answered. "As a lich, I can alter them into whatever form they desire. Once I ascend, I will have unfathomable power. To those inquisitors who help the most, I will bestow the gift of empowered immortality without decay."

"Is that even possible?"

"It is, for one of sufficient power. I cannot make them more powerful than myself, since such a thing is typically impossible, but their abilities will increase exponentially. The only price is working for me. More important than riches or ability is the mission itself. These mages will fight and die because they believe in what I am trying to accomplish. This is a war, Hazel, and we will not lose. You should consider which side of history you would like to be on."

Hazel shook her head in disgust. "History can think what it wants about me. If it means hurting others, I want no part of it."

Alvaria stood and grabbed her staff. She gestured for a couple of inquisitors to lead Hazel away. "I think the chance of being ignored by history disappeared the moment you came back to life. The living lich of half a day shall rise, and you will be instrumental, whether you desire it or not."

Chapter Fifteen
Hospitality Somewhat Lacking

Lyvaelan dismounted from his horse, dumbfounded by the magnificence of the city. He breathed the briny sea air of Selevarian, the city of mages. Carriages held aloft by magic flew past, drawn by pegasi, griffins, and hippogriffs. Some buildings floated off the ground, suspended by a current of living wind. Winged ships of varying sizes journeyed ponderously through the sky. The city sprawled on endlessly. Coruvaine had been a large city, yet was dwarfed by comparison. The most prominent feature of Selevarian that formed both the heart and the head of the city towered above all else: Palace Valsidan, home of the High Archmage. The structure and its grounds were as vast as a city, and as tall as some mountains.

The Archmage of Education led them through the main gate, and Lyvaelan gasped as he beheld the statue of Selevara. The sculpture—beautifully depicting the goddess of magic—stood well over a hundred feet tall. Her austere expression and the stairs she guarded challenged Lyvaelan to climb them only if he dared.

He roused from his reverie when Lara nudged him with her elbow. "Hey, she's almost as serious as you."

He gave her a flat look and followed Lysander. He could tell Lara was also astounded by the place. She walked uneasily past all the robed mages, and likely felt underdressed. The archmage paid no mind as he climbed the steps and retrieved an ornate key from his pocket. He approached a large wooden door and unlocked it. He ushered them in and they stood in a hallway overlooking the statue of Selevara on the far northern side of the building, facing a different direction than they had expected.

Without having the chance to ask about the magic, the group rushed ahead, with Lysander moving swiftly before them. Lyvaelan tried to stretch his aching legs after the long journey. Lara and Alistair maintained their formidable stamina while Lyvaelan used magic to ease his muscles somewhat, but with the limited sleep they had over the last few days, he wanted to use as little magic as possible to keep himself from overexerting. They completed the ride in four days using teleportation gates without sleeping and arrived in the late afternoon. The archmage kept their horses alive, although in the last stretch Lyvaelan wondered if even a spellcaster as great as Lysander could keep their mounts from collapsing.

Lyvaelan recognized the danger of pressing forward too strongly, but knew how necessary it was. While his darkest moods came when he had little sleep, Hazel's safety was his overwhelming priority. He would prevent himself from causing an arcane cataclysm. He had to.

Fortunately, Archmage Relas negated the adverse effects of sunlight on Alistair, using the very complex spell he had demonstrated a few weeks prior. The magic remained too difficult for Lyvaelan to fully grasp, but the archmage cast it without a second thought. He desired—as much as any of them—to understand the situation, and refused to let sunlight slow their progress, though the nausea and disorientation from passing through multiple gates each day tested their resolve, even with the archmage's enchantments protecting them from the worst of the adverse effects of teleportation.

People bowed as Lysander passed, but he ignored them. After crossing a bridge into a nearby tower, Lyvaelan noticed the white rose of the Inquisition. Lysander approached a desk where a brown-haired male inquisitor sat. The man jumped to attention when the group approached.

"Archmage Relas! It's an unexpected pleasure to see you! How can I—"

"Where is the Archmage of the Inquisition?" he demanded.

"Eminence, I haven't seen her today—"

"When did you see her last?"

The man glanced about, bewildered. "Not since she went on her latest mission to Coruvaine."

"Hmm. Very well. I would like to use her office, if you don't mind."

"Actually, Eminence"—the inquisitor fidgeted with his robe nervously—"you aren't supposed to go up there unless the Grand Inquisitor herself is present. Protocol, set by the Archmage of the Inquisition herself."

Lysander forcibly sighed. "What if it were an emergency? I fear the Grand Inquisitor is in trouble. She should have arrived here over a week ago, but I've heard no word from her. There may be something in her office that could help."

"That may be true, but I cannot break this rule. My apologies. Perhaps there is another way..." He drew a mirror from the desk.

"I already attempted to contact her via scry mirror," Lysander interrupted testily. "Multiple times. It didn't work."

"I see." He appeared crestfallen. "Did you try the estate?"

"You mean the chateau? No, why?"

"Well, the Grand Inquisitor trusts much to her chamberlain. I believe if anything was amiss, she would contact him first. Technically, he outranks me within the Inquisition and is the highest-ranking officer we have in Selevarian, even though he isn't in the city proper. If you want permission to enter her office, speak with him. He may also have documents that could assist you."

"That may be a good lead." The archmage nodded curtly. "Thank you for your time."

"I'm sorry I couldn't be more helpful."

Lysander walked the group to the door closest to them and unlocked it. They exited out where they first entered and hurried to the stables.

"Wait," Lara said, "why didn't we just teleport to that door in the first place?"

"Security," He responded without turning around. "If an enemy of the Inquisition got my key, they would still struggle to find the correct area without being spotted. The general design of the palace is to make travel easier without being *too* easy. This is still supposed to be a defensible position. Convenience comes second."

"Who'd be dumb enough to attack a palace full of mages?"

Alistair smiled. "The Knights of Petrim."

"How do you know about that?" Lara asked.

Alistair shrugged. "I'm an avid reader. The Knights thought they should reclaim Selevarian, since it was originally gifted by the Kingdom of Petrim before it reformed into an aristocracy. The Knights attacked when the High Archmage refused to relinquish the city."

"How did that go?"

"About as well as you'd expect. The Knights are a skilled collection of warriors, but they couldn't even breach the gate of the palace before retreating. Their siege lasted only about five days, from what I heard."

"Really?" Lara said with surprise. "I heard they were a tenacious bunch. Guess I was wrong."

"They were, and still are," Lysander said as he descended the steps. "Some like to paint the Knights in a humorous light, but they do so at the risk of underestimating their considerable power. In this case, they weren't expecting the specific tactics my predecessors employed. They prepared to deal with wizardry, and any magical creature our conjurers could throw at them. They also had armor resistant to most alchemical tricks. Indeed, the Knights are accomplished spellcasters and armed themselves accordingly. They hadn't counted on sorcery as a means of defeat."

Alistair's eyes widened. "The sources I had were vague on the specific reasons they left. How did sorcery drove them away?"

"A young and powerful high master sorcerer named Malvex Sorrelle enlisted the help of many sorcerers to infect the dreams of the soldiers with nightmares. Because of history too long to explain, the Knights view sorcery and enchantment as the feminine side of magic while the others disciplines are properly masculine. Since none of the warriors or Knights are women, they brought only a handful of sorceresses to prevent mental assaults. While defending against a psychic attack is easier than taking the offense, they should have gathered a stronger defense. For the entire siege, not one of them slept more than a few minutes before waking and screaming in terror. What many don't realize about war is the actual fighting often contributes less than other factors when determining victory or defeat. Sleep is one of them. Imagine spending an entire day exercising and not being able to rest. Then imagine another day like that. Then another. And another. Our journey here might make it easier for you to comprehend. The exhaustion alone would be crippling, but after a few days without sleep, the personalities of the combatants change. Paranoia and hallucinations may occur. Emotions run high. Imagine an entire army beleaguered by enemies such as these. Generals who need to think clearly are incapable of forming halfway coherent sentences. Soldiers who need skill in combat can't even maintain a grip on their swords. It's one of the few wars where not a single citizen of Selevarian was killed. There were casualties on the other side, but the losses remained negligible."

"I can imagine that working," Lara said, "but why wouldn't they come back after they slept?"

"After they retreated, the Grand Knights planned on invading again. Malvex went among them as a diplomat. When they refused to relent and threatened to seize him as a hostage, he vanished from their sight but remained among them. The Grand Knights didn't have a single night's rest until they signed the peace treaty. Malvex informed them that if they ever attacked Selevarian again, he would return and ensure none of them would sleep until death took them. Apparently, they believed him and we've had peace ever since."

Lara whistled. "Wow. I hope Malvex got a medal or something for that. Sounds like he deserved it."

"He eventually became Archmage of Sorcery as a result, so I think he gained proper recognition in time for his efforts."

Lysander gestured to a stable hand and led the group beyond the last wall of the palace, waving to a nearby carriage. "We can continue these discussions as we move. For now, we must be away to Chateau Zarielle. We shall leave our horses to rest here and take a swift carriage out of the city and hopefully discover exactly what is going on."

They traveled swiftly through the countryside. Lyvaelan silently thanked the gods that he now sat on a cushion instead of a horse. While the need to hurry to their destination had not lessened, the exhaustion of the trip wore on him. The other two appeared mostly unhindered, but he felt certain they must be tiring. He still hadn't told them what Hazel had written. Occasionally he sensed the mind of the archmage brush over him and felt relief knowing the other two could only speculate on what had transpired rather than actually knowing. He wondered if this was the right decision, given what they might be walking into.

He closed his eyes. Now was not the time to second guess himself. If the archmage was truly good friends with the Grand Inquisitor, he would be reluctant to believe the prophecy, or them. Perhaps even worse, he might suspect them of some nefarious plot, making finding Hazel impossible.

Lyvaelan doubted the archmage allied himself with the Grand Inquisitor's hidden agenda. At any point in their travels, he could have killed all three of them with little trouble. Waiting until they arrived in a major city to destroy them made little tactical sense. Before they left Coruvaine, he had pondered the possibility that they could all die, but realized it was a risk all three would willingly make for Hazel.

Lyvaelan didn't doubt that the archmages would discover her betrayal eventually, but speed was important. Alvaria Saccarra could be torturing Hazel, for all he knew. Trusting Lysander to believe them would be unnecessarily dangerous. Then again, it could be the dark elf side of his heritage that inclined him to distrust the affable archmage.

Fortunately, the Archmage of Education appeared wrapped in his own thoughts for much of the carriage ride. He gazed out the window, his eyes troubled. What might he be thinking? The business with Hickory bothered him to an unexpected degree. Lyvaelan knew sorcery could destroy or badly damage minds, but he wasn't sure if such methods were off-limits to the Grand Inquisitor. Did necromancers *have* rights? If a necromancer refused to reveal pertinent information, did that justify having his mind temporarily shattered? Moral answers to these questions existed, but the legal answers were harder to guess. This was more than simply confining a common criminal; this was subduing a dangerous mage who was amoral at best and might have placed harmful contingencies on his creation. Extreme methods could be justified or excused, but perhaps the Council of Archmages frowned on that.

They arrived at the chateau in just under three hours, driving at a quick pace. The final embers of sunset lit the distant horizon, which highlighted the estate. Lyvaelan stepped out of the carriage to view their surroundings. Chateau Zarielle was impressive in its size and architecture, though after witnessing Palace Valsidan, any other building appeared subpar by comparison. Even so, the artistry of the estate was undeniable. Where Palace Valsidan was overwhelming in scale and overt in its construction, the chateau maintained a subtle and detailed beauty. It was the difference between the grandest of eagles and the prettiest of songbirds. The gardens favored a naturally wild design, although Lyvaelan saw through the conceit that gave the building a sense of naturalness, despite its glowing facade.

They climbed the steps behind Lysander as two attendants opened the doors to the antechamber. Marble floors with silver and gold lines inlaid in complex designs spread out before them. Lysander muttered a few words to one servant, who nodded and hurried off into the main hall. Lara flopped onto an expensive couch and Alistair sat nearby, taking in the surroundings. Doubt gnawed at Lyvaelan again, but he shoved it down. These two were likely more confused than anyone. They had traveled over a thousand miles in only a few days and had gone from one magic building into another with no opportunities to ask questions. Lyvaelan found it disorienting too, but at least had the conviction of the mission. The others only had vague hunches with no clear idea of what purpose any of this served.

"The chamberlain will see you now," the servant said, opening the door to the hall. They walked through and into a magnificent ballroom. A single wide staircase split into two symmetrical loops that met, creating a circle of steps to a second landing. This, in turn, had another wide staircase leading to the upper level. Coming from the left staircase was a bald man roughly middle aged, dressed in a gold and black robe covered over with a half-length cape that obscured his upper torso. A large and ornate amulet of gold hung from his neck, resembling a spiked star or sun.

He smiled and bowed as he approached. "Greetings, esteemed Archmage of Education. To what do I owe the supreme pleasure of your visit?"

"Hello, Arlith. We seek information about your master."

His brow wrinkled. "The Grand Inquisitor? Might I ask what this is regarding?"

"We have lost contact with her. She was supposed to arrive in Selevarian almost a week ago, but there has been no word from her."

He frowned. "I could see why that would be troubling, but I'm sure you needn't worry over her safety. My lady is quite a capable individual."

"That may be true, but even the canniest are not immune to the perils of the road. To compound these fears, she hasn't been answering her scry mirror."

Arlith stroked his chin. "You will pardon my skepticism, but she is a busy woman. She may simply have misplaced it. As for her arrival, maybe they are simply taking their time or making repairs."

"An excellent conjecture, however, we traveled the same route and found no trace of them, despite their large caravan. I need your permission to examine her records and determine the exact route they followed."

Arlith nodded slowly and then noticed the others. "May I ask who these individuals are?"

"They accompanied me from Coruvaine. Arlith, this is important. We may not have much time."

He sighed. "Very well. Since you didn't find her on the path and contacted her with both scry mirrors, I suppose the only other option would be—"

"What?" Lysander interrupted. "*Both* scry mirrors?"

"Of course. The Grand Inquisitor wouldn't rely on only one method, though the secondary one is kept confidential." He paused. "I apologize. I assumed you knew."

"No, I was unaware."

"Oh. Well, that would be the fastest way to get ahold of her. I spoke with her only a week ago myself."

"Why did you not mention this?"

"Forgive me, Excellency. When you said she was not answering, I assumed you meant either scry mirror. Since I spoke with her recently, I naturally was not overly concerned about her safety."

Lysander sighed. "I suppose that makes sense. Do you have a connected mirror here?"

"I do, my lord. I can lead you to it while your... companions wait here."

"Very well." He turned to them. "Hopefully, this won't take long."

The chamberlain clapped his hands and two servants came from under the staircase. "Please see that these fine people are brought refreshments. Show them the hospitality of Chateau Zarielle." The two servants nodded curtly and hurried back to the hallway under the stairs. He gave the guests a polite smile. "If you would kindly wait here, the servants should be able to attend to you. Ask them for anything, and I'm sure they will happily oblige."

Lyvaelan watched as they ascended the steps out of sight. What would happen if the Grand Inquisitor answered the call and everything appeared fine? His mood darkened. He hadn't thought of that. He had no doubts she was guilty of everything Hazel accused her of, but that didn't make her any less devious or threatening.

"Waiting around isn't so bad," Lara said, walking to a long side table that had just been set by a servant. She flopped into a chair. "This place is pretty incredible. I've seen more crazy things in the last day than I have in my entire life."

"It is impressive," Alistair agreed, gazing at the walls, "but I still feel a little lost about why we're here."

"We're here to help Hazel," Lyvaelan said.

"Yeah, we get that, but I think me and the vampire are still lacking details."

"I will reveal the information soon. For now, you're better off not knowing."

She frowned. "Is it really that bad?"

Lyvaelan crossed his arms and leaned against the wall. "No, it's worse."

"Great. Another exercise in trust. I hate trusting people."

"I don't blame you," Lyvaelan sighed. "I don't know that I would trust me if I were in your place."

"I don't think the problem is that we distrust you," Alistair said, "but that we cannot be trusted ourselves. We both understand the necessity for secrecy, and after seeing what happened to Hickory Allkirk, the need for caution cannot be overstated. The frustrating thing is knowing that while we can trust you, you cannot trust us."

"Perhaps... one day," Lyvaelan hesitated, "I can show you how to shield your minds from sorcery. There just wasn't enough time. Or—if there was—I was too stupid to realize it needed to be done."

They fell silent as four servants approached, carrying plates of fruit, cold meat, bread, and cheeses. They arranged the dishes before them and bowed. They exited quietly, leaving the three alone.

"You're not stupid." Lara picked up a bread roll. "We could've asked for help anytime, but we didn't. Even after getting mind-tricked by that bastard at the college, I *still* didn't ask for help shielding myself. I might have rejected it even if you *had* asked."

"Lara is right. We are responsible for ourselves. You cannot take all the blame for yourself. Beyond that, the last few weeks have been more hectic than most."

"No kidding," she mumbled through a mouthful.

Lyvaelan nodded. Still, he felt foolish. He grabbed a bunch of grapes and began eating.

"Anyway," Lara said, "how long do you think this will take?"

"Hard to say." Lyvaelan shrugged. "I wouldn't expect it to take longer than fifteen minutes, but depending on the conversation, it could take longer. Also"—he dropped his voice—"there's a chance we will need to fight soon. Be ready."

Lara grinned. "You mean we might finally get some action? It's about damn time."

"Who would we be fighting in this scenario?"

"I'm not sure. Just be ready and don't let anyone catch you off-guard. It probably won't be any of us, though."

"Well, *that's* comforting."

"I know you're joking," Lyvaelan said, "but that fact should be anything *but* comforting. I'd much rather fight either of you than the people we'll likely be facing."

"Ya know, you're terrible at inspiring us."

"I'm just stating a fact."

They sat in silence for the next twenty minutes, picking through the food. Alistair seemed paler than usual. Having no access to blood wine over the previous few days left the vampire drained and lethargic. He talked less than normal, but didn't complain. They should have prepared, but there hadn't been time. Was rushing in like this a bad idea or did delaying give the enemy the upper hand?

Alistair looked at the top of the stairs. He heard something. Moments later, Lyvaelan also heard the soft footfalls of the chamberlain. He stood at the top of the staircase and looked down at them.

"I hope you have enjoyed yourselves," he said. Although he stood far from them, his voice carried without needing to shout. "The Archmage of Education has spoken with the Grand Inquisitor this entire time and is trying to understand the specifics of the circumstance. He regrets to inform you he will be busy for several hours in conversation and examining documents. He has arranged lodging for you within the city and urges you to go and wait until he is done."

"Thank you for your hospitality and message, chamberlain," Alistair said. "I think we are content to wait until he has finished. We are eager to hear whatever additional news he may bring."

Arlith smiled thinly. "Of course. He mentioned you might be unwilling to depart. I want to urge, however, that it would be best for you to retire to the inn. You need rest. You can find information regarding your friend later. He should be along in only a day or so. Wait, sleep, and then speak with him again."

Alistair nodded. "Yes... that makes sense."

"Yeah, alright." Lara got up, stretching. "Guess it's back to the city we go."

Lyvaelan cocked his head at the vampire and werewolf questioningly when something nudged his mind. He held against it and it pressed more insistently before yielding. Lyvaelan gazed up at Arlith, whose expression darkened. He glanced at his companions, who had reached the door. Lyvaelan contacted them mentally. Some external psychic force influenced them, like strings pulling puppets in a specific direction. He snapped the mental strings.

Arlith is the enemy! Lyvaelan shouted into their minds. *Be ready to attack!* The two jumped and shook themselves.

"How unfortunate," Arlith said, "that you didn't simply *leave.*" A ball of purple flames erupted from his hand, exploding between them. Lyvaelan leaped to the side and rolled behind the table. He focused on hiding and gathering shadows around him. Lara and Alistair avoided most of the blast, but the shock threw her against the wall. She growled and stood as Alistair drew his longsword.

Arlith smiled humorlessly and traced symbols with his hands around himself. "You should have left, but instead you choose this folly. I do not know what challenges you've faced, but you are severely outmatched."

"Funny"—Lara rose to her feet—"I was about to say the same thing to you." She dashed to the stairs as Alistair floated up and toward Arlith.

The chamberlain closed his eyes and spread his arms apart. "Come forth, great dark one! From beyond the touch of the Otherworld, encircled in the mantle of Semeleme, I call to you across the dreaded abyss of Ryxiv! Rise!"

A loud tearing sound split the air upon the first landing as a purple crack of wavering electricity appeared and opened. Lara halted halfway up the steps as a cacophonous screech blared from the conjuring portal. Dozens of long, pale arms humanoid arms a full foot thick wriggled from the opening, each coated with a viscous purple slime. Hands much bigger than anything human scraped and trembled with emaciated fingers. From the dark of the portal, a howl issued that filled Lyvaelan with inexplicable dread. The piercing shriek cut him to the heart. The other two appeared dumbstruck by the cry. Each long arm flopped and wrapped around the banisters with a multitude of elbows which seemed to break and change direction randomly. With great effort, the arms pulled through a smoking ball of white and purple sludge. Along its doughy surface, human faces emerged with eyeless sockets. Each time one of these arose, a mouth opened and a new voice added to the scream. Agonized visages appeared and disappeared without apparent reason along the arms, as thick mucus splashed from them with every motion.

"Impressed?" Arlith asked with wide-eyed elation, though he looked pale as the others. "Few have witnessed these creatures among the living. I'm afraid he cannot fully manifest in our world, but I assure you, he is just as dangerous here as anywhere."

Alistair shook his head and flew toward Arlith, rising above the creature's grasp. The monster shuddered and three searching hands shot from its body toward Alistair far longer than the others. He attempted to dodge, but one grabbed his arm and held him with white-knuckled determination. The others grasped his legs and torso. He struck with his sword and cut one hand off, provoking more screams. Purple sludge oozed onto the ground, forming puddles of the creature's blood. Lara cursed and nimbly dodged several of the arms.

Although the visible portion of the creature's body was only thirty feet in diameter, the arms of the thing appeared to grow to virtually any length. Lyvaelan would have been fascinated if it weren't trying to kill them. Lara punched at one arm as it missed her, only to find her fist stuck within the pallid flesh. She tried to push it off, but was stuck fast. She finally pulled away and staggered back into a puddle of its blood. A boney hand emerged from the blood and seized her leg. She groaned and gritted her teeth, struggling against it.

Alistair fared no better. He kept slashing, but each swing grew increasingly labored. Lyvaelan realized the creature wasn't simply wearing them down, it actively sapped their strength.

During this battle, Arlith hadn't stopped declaiming in loud, confident tones. "I don't envy your position. This creature is dreaded among the souls of the dead. Its power here is undoubtedly different, but even now you likely feel it draining you of stamina while the creature grows ever greater. Were you simple humans, you would each be dead by now, but apparently your power protects you from the swift death it grants others. No matter. It will drain you shortly. You only prolong the inevitable with your struggles. There was never any hope of succeeding against so great a being..."

Lyvaelan watched the mage and then the beast. From what he knew of conjuration, the relationship between servant and master could be disrupted if the links were severed. There was something in the way Arlith talked that was unusual. He barely took the time to pause or even breathe. The mage lauded the creature effusively, but there was something else at play.

Lyvaelan's eyes widened. The long string of compliments and observations kept the creature under his control. There were no promises he could make, no food to offer such a monster, nor vast stores of magic to entice it to do his bidding. Instead, he talked to it. Arlith likely shielded himself from overt attacks, both physical and magical, which made stopping him a major obstacle. How could Lyvaelan prevent him from...

He looked up at Lara and Alistair, and a thought occurred.

A dark smile crept across his lips. Lifting his hand, he tapped into the flow of magic around him. He sent his consciousness to the mage and sensed a bubble shielding him, as expected. Lyvaelan moved his hand in a circle. This was going to be bigger than any he had done before, but it should work. He was an expert at this technique. Thanks to his bickering friends, he had practice.

"Your time is at an end, my guests. The powerful being before you will draw your souls through the void and into the next world. It is unfortunate you will never learn the great secrets of this world. No, instead—" Arlith's speech was cut off as Lyvaelan snapped his fingers. Small tendrils of light blue smoke wafted from his hand and a bubble the same color manifested around Arlith. The chamberlain's mouth continued moving, but no sound came out.

Lyvaelan smiled. *I've always loved the spheres of Elchoran. What better way is there to get someone loud and obnoxious to shut up?*

Arlith retreated a step in confusion and terror. The creature stuttered and wriggled along its entire body. Several faces along its bulk pivoted toward the mage. Arlith threw his hand out, and the sphere shattered, but it was too late. A hammer-fisted arm crashed down inches from Arlith's head as it slammed into an invisible barrier. The mage sputtered to regain his speech, but Lyvaelan snapped his fingers again and another sphere appeared.

The creature released another scream, but this one sounded angrier than before. All its arms turned and smashed down on Arlith. The mage shielded his head, blocking with an invisible magic as countless slimy hands pummeled it. Lyvaelan broke from his cover and scaled the wall up to the stairs. *Crack.* Lyvaelan spotted a thin line in the air above the chamberlain. The barrier was breaking. The creature, denied of its quarry, redoubled its efforts. The banister shattered and the entire building shook with the fury of these flailing arms and the screams of the monster. With each hit, the cracks grew in number and magnitude.

"No! No, you damnable beast! Back! Begone!" He cried, breaking through another sphere of Elchoran. The creature paid no heed. With the echoing sound of shattering glass, the barrier broke. The monster screamed triumphantly. Arlith dropped his hands, paling before the creeping mass of hands reaching toward him. The fingers wrapped around him as a giant face opened up along the middle of the creature. The monster lurched forward, dragging the portal that summoned it up the stairs. Rows of brilliant white teeth opened the way to an endless void as the arms brought Arlith down.

Lyvaelan vaulted from the top of the stairs over the beast and a few steps from the lower landing. The creature would ignore him until it killed its former master. Lyvaelan extended one hand out and held himself high. Conjuration required charisma as much as magic.

"Creature of the void!" Lyvaelan yelled with fanatical zeal. "How *dare* you enter our world? I command you, in the name of Selevara and Semeleme, to return to the realm from which you were called. Begone! I banish you. Return never and be drawn back to the abyss where you belong!" The portal pulled the creature back. Its arms whipped about frantically as it pulled banisters apart in an effort to remain. Lyvaelan stood with his hand outstretched without fear. Disgust rose within him from seeing this creature writhe, fueling his imperious rage.

"Go! I condemn you! Be damned to the blackest pit of Ryxiv! I demand it!" The creature, with a final, frenzied screech, was sucked into the portal along with its thick blood. The arm holding Arlith slapped him onto the ground before withdrawing. Arlith lay on the ground, unmoving. The hall fell silent. Lara and Alistair staggered up. Both appeared haggard.

"Pretty smart thinking, Lyvie."

Lyvaelan sighed and relaxed. "Are both of you alright?"

Alistair smiled weakly. "I've seen better days, but that could've gone worse." He looked at the still body of the mage and then closed his eyes for a moment. "He's still alive; I can hear his heart beat. What should we do with him?"

"Both of you are injured," Lyvaelan said. "You should stay and guard him. I will search for the Archmage of Education."

"You don't think he killed him, do you?" Alistair asked.

"Doubtful, but possible," Lyvaelan said. "I imagine killing an archmage would alert someone and bring more attention, but I don't know for certain." He got up to leave.

"Wait, don't you want one of us to help?" Lara asked.

He paused. "I appreciate the thought, but it's likely there are traps. He expected to defeat us, so there probably wasn't time to set many of them. If he did, it would be easy for one of you to get hurt. I can sense the magic in the area, so I should be able to avoid them. I won't fall prey to the same trap as the archmage, if only because I fully expect it. If something happens to me, return to Selevarian and get help. Hopefully, it won't come to that."

He ascended the steps as Lara and Alistair dragged the unconscious chamberlain toward the table. Lyvaelan walked in the same direction he saw the archmage go in earlier. He breathed in and exhaled a long, even breath. A faint glow in the shape of footprints appeared. Two tracks journeyed further into the chateau, while one set—that glowed the brightest—exited out.

He frowned. Tracking spells were normally easier to use and see, but on marble in a mansion so filled with magic, it made the tracks disappear quicker than would have been convenient. Fortunately, they were just visible enough to give him some direction. He approached slowly and placed a web of magic around himself to help him sense potential traps. The magic in the magelamps that hung in the corridor he chose to ignore, though that presented a small risk. He ascended a flight of stairs and continued down a long curve. Upon turning right, he sensed resistance to his web. He frowned and tried to walk around it, but its presence extended along the length of the hallway. Lyvaelan retreated several paces and ducked around a corner. He imagined expanding his web to press against the magic and then sent a pulse of energy into it. A sudden blast of air nearly threw him from his feet as a concussive force exploded through the hallway. Lyvaelan shook his head and noticed gashes in the marble near where he had first sensed the magic.

Lyvaelan scoffed. *"Hospitality" indeed!*

The tracks faded as he moved down the hallway and entered a large bedroom. They led through a small antechamber and into a study. He walked to the antechamber, but the tingle of energy along the web alerted him to the presence of strange magic. Backing into the hallway, he sent a surge out, but nothing happened. He sent out another. Nothing.

Cautiously leaving his shelter, he sent a pulse of anti-magic toward it, but still no response. He approached the symmetrical antechamber and studied it. Nothing appeared out of the ordinary, but something was there. He hesitantly extended a hand and touched an invisible surface. The barrier slowly yielded to his hand. When he tried to withdraw his hand, it clung to him. He pulled his hand free with effort. No residue remained on him despite feeling stuck. He glanced at his hand and at the antechamber, then at the tracks within the barrier. They were far fresher than any he had encountered so far.

He cocked his head. What was going on here?

He searched the room and picked up a pen. He approached the antechamber and pushed the pen into the invisible wall of force and stood back, watching it for the next few minutes. The pen moved, but with exaggerated slowness. This started to make sense. He scrutinized the room from outside the barrier and discovered a small crystal bottle with its stopper removed next to it. He closed his eyes and lifted the stopper. It floated up painfully slow and closed itself over the bottle. The bottle glowed, and the pen fell faster and faster until it finally hit the floor.

Lyvaelan smiled to himself. Temporal magic. The bottle contained the time, and when the time was released, it filled the antechamber that acted as a means of containment. The stickiness of it was due to the surface of his hand moving slower than the rest of his body. He stepped into the space and through to the room beyond. There he found the Archmage of Education staring blankly at a standing mirror. Lyvaelan approached, careful to avoid it. The archmage was evidently insensible to the world around him.

This provided a special challenge. Breaking the mirror could hurt Lysander and potentially render him comatose. Using sorcery could be dangerous for both of them. Perhaps a spell of blindness? Could that work? He crossed his arms at the archmage. *This would be so much easier if you had actually* taught *me something,* Lyvaelan thought. He pushed lightly against Lysander's mind but felt nothing in response.

He shrugged. Breaking visual contact with the mirror *might* work. There would be little harm in trying. He imagined a thick smoke rising around the mirror. He remembered smoke as a result of combustion and shifted the air into mimicking that specific look using wizardry. Black smoke rose from the bottom of the mirror and rolled over its surface. He watched the archmage, who still appeared unresponsive. He probed lightly with sorcery and received a slight nudge back.

Break it, a voice in his head said. Lyvaelan shrugged and pushed the mirror over. The mirror shattered and, as if waking from sleep upon hearing a loud noise, the archmage jumped and looked around.

"Lyvaelan?" His eyes darkened. "Where is the chamberlain?"

"He's with the others. He isn't a threat, for now."

"Let's make sure of that, shall we?" He stormed from the room with Lyvaelan in tow.

"I would caution you," Lyvaelan said, "he placed traps—"

"I'm well aware." The archmage slammed his staff on the ground and a surge of light burst around. In the distance, Lyvaelan heard another explosion, and the sound of something shattering. "There, we've set off all the traps. Now, let's deal with the treacherous chamberlain."

They rushed through the corridor to the main hall. Alistair and Lara sat eating while the chamberlain was laid over a chair in an undignified position.

"Hey, archmage!" Lara called. "How was your talk?"

"I was... deceived." He sat on the last few steps. "I don't understand. Why did this happen? What was the purpose of all this?"

Lyvaelan walked around to face him, trying to meet his downcast eyes. "Archmage, I have something you need to see." He held out Hazel's journal. "If you flip to the last few pages, it will have the relevant information." He turned to his friends. "I'm sorry I couldn't tell you all sooner, but Hazel has been kidnapped by the Grand Inquisitor. Alvaria Saccarra is the living lich of half a day."

Silence.

Lysander held the book, unmoving. His eyes searched Lyvaelan unreadably. He finally opened the book. After a minute of examining the journal, he closed and set it aside. His eyes stared distantly.

"I'm sorry I didn't say something sooner," Lyvaelan said, "but you wouldn't have believed me."

"It can't be," Lysander said, running his fingers through his hair.

"It *is* true," Lara exclaimed. "It *must* be! Hazel has never been wrong. And now *your* Inquisition holds her prisoner."

The three members of the Evenfall Vigil silently watched the archmage. He sat with his hands covering his face. Lyvaelan almost feared to move lest he evoke Lysander's ire. The room fell still. Slowly, he rose to his feet. He looked at each of them before settling his gaze on the unconscious chamberlain. The archmage strode to him, grabbed him by his foot and dragged him toward the stairs.

"Follow me. We don't have much time."

The three glanced at each other and hurried to match his pace.

"Pardon my asking," Alistair said, "but where are we going?"

"We are returning to Palace Valsidan," he replied, taking two steps at a time.

"Uh, yeah, about that. Isn't our carriage out there?"

"It is, but we must move swiftly. We have no time to dally. There are carriages on the roof that should be faster." Lara looked confused as she attempted to understand what he meant.

"Should we place some spell on the chamberlain to prevent him from waking up?" Lyvaelan asked.

"Unnecessary. If he is unwise enough to awaken, then he will have me to answer to and I *am not happy.*"

Lyvaelan shivered slightly. Lysander could be kind, but there was no doubting the genuine threat in his voice. As the archmage walked up the stairs, he hauled the limp chamberlain without effort or ceremony.

"Uh, new question," Lara said. "Do you want me to carry him? He doesn't look that heavy."

"He isn't. I wanted the satisfaction of dragging this bastard up a few stairs."

Lara grinned wolfishly. Evidently, that was the sort of response that increased her appreciation for a person.

He led them through the hallways and up another flight until they exited the building onto a large patio. Chateau Zarielle's summit was only a dozen feet higher than their current position. The patio itself was wide and long and led to a smaller building on the roof that resembled a large stable.

A stable hand rushed out. "Archmage Relas! It's good to—" he trailed off when he saw the body Lysander dragged.

"Listen carefully, and don't speak," the archmage said. "I need to return to the city as swiftly as possible, and I require a carriage. I need it ready within a minute. If you attempt to leave or attack, then I *will* fight back, and you *will* lose, and I will be on my way, regardless. Nod if you understand."

The wide-eyed stable hand nodded vigorously.

"Good. Now *GO!*"

The young man scrambled away in a sprint toward the stable. Lysander followed more slowly and opened a large pair of doors, revealing an ornate carriage. It was a dark cherry with motifs of the white rose all around it. Gold and silver filigree lined its wooden frame with encrusted jewels of diamond, opal, and amber. Dark gray stones were polished and placed around the edges and near the bottom of the carriage that Lyvaelan did not recognize. Oddly, the carriage had no wheels.

"I recognize the gemstones, but what is the gray rock? What purpose does it serve?"

The Archmage of Education looked at Lyvaelan and his features relaxed slightly. "That is alchemical and enchanted lodestone." Lysander put his hand on the carriage and Lyvaelan felt a small arcane pulse. A wave of light surged through the vehicle as it lifted a few inches off the ground. Archmage Relas grabbed the carriage and pulled it forward with little effort. "Lodestone is especially helpful for levitation. The stones on the sides and even near the top help to ensure it doesn't twist or topple and it naturally rights itself."

"Is this how we're getting to the city so fast?" Lara asked with wonder. "Can this really fly on its own?"

"No, it would be much too slow that way. Slower than a conventional carriage. We need something to pull it. Something faster."

Lara and Alistair gasped as a large eagle head appeared behind them. The creature—a hippogriff—stood no less than three feet taller than the biggest horse Lyvaelan had ever seen. Dark gray—almost blue—feathers tapered down its back and to its powerful forelimbs, which ended in intimidating, muscular talons. The feathers eventually gave way halfway down its back to a dappled gray horse's hindquarters with a silky white tail. Two long triangular ears covered with short feathers flicked about, listening. The creature looked them over as they gaped. Something in its aquiline face seemed pleased or amused.

"Whoa," Lara said, "I've never seen one of these things up close before... do they bite?"

"Only when we want, two-legs."

Lara jumped back as the hippogriff cackled and stamped one of its hooves. The creature's voice was remarkably clear. Lyvaelan had heard of birds that could imitate speech, but transcended such simple mimicry.

The archmage smiled and approached the hippogriff, scratching behind an ear as the stable hand fixed a harness to it. The creature trilled and closed its eyes contentedly. "Hippogriffs are remarkably intelligent creatures, as are griffins, their cousins. They can learn human speech and even read if they wish. They make for loyal friends and swift mounts."

"If they are as intelligent as you say," Alistair said, approaching cautiously. "Is it really ethical to keep them as beasts of burden?"

The hippogriff opened one eye at him. "Do you think the scrawny two-legs could stop me if I wanted to leave?" Its voice had a creaking quality to it, but it was deeper than expected.

The archmage chuckled softly. "She has a point. Hippogriffs are smarter than dogs, but just as loyal and friendly. They bond especially well with spellcasters and thrive in metropolitan areas. They aren't as fierce or independent as griffins and they get along well with horses, which is another reason they are favored over their ferocious cousins. By the way, I haven't introduced you properly. Alistair, Lara, Lyvaelan, meet Terava. She's fifteen years old and a good friend." He turned to the stable hand. "Is she properly harnessed?"

"Yes, sir!"

"Good, then we should be on our way." He turned back to Terava. "Can you take us to the palace? Land directly in the courtyard and get us there with all haste, please."

"Sure, Lysander, you may have my speed. Why else would you use me?"

He cracked a smile. "Why, for the pleasure of your company, of course!"

The hippogriff cackled again and moved forward slowly, bring-ing the hovering carriage with her.

Lysander opened the door and ushered them in. When the three were seated, he tossed in the chamberlain's body and got in after. He slapped the side of the carriage twice and shut the door. The carriage lurched as the hippogriff took off.

"I hope you don't mind me questioning this choice," Alistair said, "but it took us close to fifteen minutes to get up here and depart when we could have left immediately from the horse-drawn carriage. Is this really so much faster?"

"Significantly faster. It took us nearly two hours to reach the chateau by horse. To return to the city this way will take no more than five minutes." He gazed out the window at the dark sky. "I fear we have no time to waste."

Chapter Sixteen
To Trample Hearts

Peace within the violence.

Silence within the scream.

Stillness within the storm.

Malvex allowed his consciousness to be swept into the magic stream. In the vastness of the unbounded field of pure sensations, he was but a speck. Tranquility could be found here, as could confusion. Music and cacophony. Silence and noise. The infinite power flooded through and around him. Although he sat on a wide pillow, he couldn't feel it beneath him.

Peace within the violence.

Silence within the scream.

Stillness within the storm.

Through magic, all things were possible; and in magic, all things could be found. If one sought chaos, then he would find it. If one sought peace, then he would find it. It was the mark of a full-fledged sorcerer to control meditation within the stream of magic. To direct one's sight required diligence, creativity, and a developed sense of self. What separated the sorcerer from the high master of sorcery was the ability to build an unshakeable sense of self and willpower and then to let it all go. To allow the stream to carry oneself wherever it willed, permitting the magic to push or pull without attempting to resist it, frightened even the most stalwart. The long, deep breaths one took to begin meditation reflected the dual necessity to be indomitable and yet submissive. To inhale was to demand control, and to exhale was to relinquish it—a simple truth easier to teach than to adopt. Viewing the magic field for the first time reduced many to tears. It immediately impressed upon all who experienced it the immediate sense of how little one knows compared to how much there is to learn. Some described it as an unending fall from a great height, with every moment bringing one closer to an ever-expanding surface. Many stood on the precipice and turned aside, never pursuing the core truths.

Peace within the violence.

Silence within the scream.

Stillness within the storm.

Through roiling darkness and blinding light, his mind traversed the tumult, a leaf upon the back of a hurricane. Magic did not speak with a voice one could recognize in a language one could know. Even so, he listened. Each random string that pulled him indicated something that the flow of magic sought to teach. This experience filled many with the terror of losing themselves to the torrent of unstable, living energy. To maintain one's identity in such a potentially dangerous place required three things held simultaneously.

Peace within the violence.

Silence within the scream.

Stillness within the storm.

Something approached. The stream was agitated, more so than normal. A storm had been brewing in recent years, but now it spread upon the horizon. Many times, Malvex sought to understand it, but his sight remained impeded. Few things escaped his notice, but the obfuscation altered each time he observed it. None of his colleagues noted this, or, if they did, it took on such a different form as to be unrecognizable. When he informed the High Archmage, his superior took the news seriously and urged Malvex to continue investigating. He had, but with no significant success. Part of its presence felt intentional, as if someone deliberately blocked him from viewing what existed within the looming clouds of the kaireidonic fog. Despite the impending danger it exuded, it remained muted, subdued. No crash of thunder or howl of wind heralded the oncoming storm. It disguised itself without hiding. He examined it curiously.

A sharp pang burst in his chest. A powerful emotion shot through him that was not his own. He reached to the magic and it sucked him deeper into the of anger and pain. No, not anger. Sorrow. A deep and crushing hurt that wrapped itself in the mantle of fury to prevent it from being overwhelming. He had seen it countless times before; the natural alchemy of the heart often transformed the worst feelings into the most acceptable ones. He sought the source of these emotions as they drew closer.

Pulling himself from the stream with a deep inhale, he returned to his faculties in his quiet room. Focusing his will, he released a mental pulse and brushed over the thoughts of those in the city. The warm gleam of Lysander Relas caught his attention. Strange. He had noticed his presence in the palace a few hours earlier but could not greet him in person before the Archmage of Education departed. Now he returned? Curious.

Lysander, old friend, he said telepathically, *why do you hurry to the palace?*

Get Gar. Meet us by the High Archmage's office. This is urgent. Do not delay.

Malvex floated to his feet. He cast his mind throughout the building. Most of it had anti-scrying technology, but few could block out the Archmage of Sorcery entirely. Garson Varaldan debated on one of the lower levels over the taxonomy of wyverns.

Garson. Lysander wants us to meet him by the High Archmage's quarters immediately. It sounds important.

Garson didn't reply, but moved to a door to take him closer to the High Archmage. Malvex strode to his door and put in his key. He stepped out as close to the High Archmage's tower as he could. Looking down the hallway, he saw the tall, golden scaled archmage just a few paces behind him, exiting from a different aperture.

"This better be good, Mal," Garson grumbled, small plumes of smoke trailing from his nostrils. "I was enjoying an invigorating discussion when you called to me and you know I hate missing those."

"Don't blame me," Malvex said, hurrying to keep pace with Garson's long stride. "I merely relayed the information. I must admit, however, that I have my own concerns as well."

"Do you know what this is about?"

"Not a clue, though I felt his emotions and thoughts. Whatever it is has Lysander severely distressed."

The golden brow of the Archmage of Dragons furrowed as much as his scales would allow. "Hmph. He's levelheaded most of the time, so it's fair to assume he didn't summon us frivolously. We'll have to wait and see."

They walked to the arch before the bridge and waited. Soon he approached with four other people, one of whom was being carried. They were odd characters: a handsome young vampire, a shabbily dressed young woman with amber eyes—who carried the body over her shoulder—, and a slender dark elf. No, *half*-dark elf. Guessing from the aura Malvex sensed around him, this young man was also powerful magically.

His eyebrow shot up when he noticed the garb of the man being carried. Was that the chamberlain of Chateau Zarielle?

"What's going on, Lysander?" Garson demanded. The newcomers appeared shocked by the Archmage of Dragons.

"No time, Gar, we have to see the High Archmage immediately." Lysander continued without pausing, and the two archmages followed. They knew Lysander better than to question him when he was this driven. Malvex considered what could upset Lysander like this. He shivered slightly and moved forward.

They entered the main office after vouching for the other guests to the Guard Unyielding. The wizened Archmage of Ceremonies stood in protest. "What are you doing? This is highly irregular! You cannot—"

"—We must see the High Archmage. Now."

"But who are—"

"*Now.*"

The Archmage of Ceremonies' expression darkened.

Something is going on, Malvex communicated telepathically. *There is nothing more urgent than this. Please hurry.*

The mental speech transmitted faster than normal words, and the Archmage of Ceremonies' expression melted into mild annoyance as he opened the doors.

The group entered the study. The High Archmage sat at his desk, reading through a book. He frowned as they entered and stood. Reading their expressions, he swiftly circled to the front of his desk, waving into existence multiple chairs and a chaise lounge. The Archmage of Ceremonies entered after them.

"Grand Eminence," the Archmage of Ceremonies began. The High Archmage waved him off.

"Dispense with the formalities. What's going on?"

"My lord," Lysander said, "I believe a great treachery is on our doorstep. These three people saved me from the chamberlain of Chateau Zarielle, who sought to imprison me through ocular transfixion. I suspect the Grand Inquisitor has betrayed us."

"What!" Garson exclaimed. "You accuse Alvaria? Are you *mad,* Lysander?"

The High Archmage held a hand to silence Garson. "I assume you have evidence of such an egregious accusation."

"I do, and in plentiful supply. First, I submit the journal of Hazel Enda, a girl who returned from the dead with precognitive visions. Her dreams have proven true on multiple occasions, but the latest one involves the ascension of what she calls 'the living lich of half a day.' In the last entry—written mere moments before the Inquisition took her—she wrote a perfect description of this ascendant lich and named it: Alvaria Saccarra."

Malvex staggered back. He felt like he had just been smacked in the face. Alva? No, never. A lich? How was it possible? He trained her, mentored her. They were *friends.* Lysander handed the book to the High Archmage, who scanned through it grimly before looking at Malvex helplessly. It *was* true.

"For my second piece of evidence, I submit the treacherous chamberlain, Arlith Kovak, trusted by Alvaria to maintain the estate and keep her affairs in order. I was directed there after seeking information regarding why her caravan had not arrived in Selevarian, despite leaving Coruvaine three weeks ago. He trapped me but my allies—members of Ethelian's Evenfall Vigil—fought him, almost to their deaths, and rescued me. We need to search his mind to determine what he knows."

The Archmage of Ceremonies glanced at the High Archmage. "Authorization for such an interrogation could take some time, unless—"

The High Archmage nodded. "By my right as High Archmage, I forgo the requisite investigation due to credible witnesses and the urgency of the matter at hand. Malvex, can you interrogate him?"

Malvex looked at the mage lying down. He was just beginning to stir. "Yes, my lord, but I'll need to wake him up first."

"Do whatever you must."

Malvex nodded. He hated doing this, but it *was* his specialty. He walked to Arlith and tapped his forehead, sending a zap of energy into him. The mage jumped and looked about, suddenly alert.

"What? Where?" Arlith stuttered, looking around. It was disorienting waking up, though the pounding in his head didn't help. He quickly appraised the situation. He was surrounded by archmages, including the one he subdued. Before him sat the calm and amiable Archmage of Sorcery.

Malvex smiled. "Hello Arlith, welcome back to the world of the wakeful."

"No." Arlith paled, shaking his head. "I know you, Archmage of Sorcery—or should I say Grand Interrogator?"

Malvex frowned. "I don't like that name. I never have. I'm not here to torture you, Arlith. There's no need."

"You're not?" Arlith's head felt thick and heavy.

"Of course not. I'm the Archmage of Sorcery. Alvaria herself called me the greatest sorcerer of our time; do you really think you can conceal the truth from me? Sorcery is a subtle and beautiful art when used by a master. So subtle, in fact, that you don't even realize you've already told me everything."

He bolted upright. "What?"

"Oh, yes," Malvex Sorrell said calmly. "You know it's impossible to keep secrets from me. Your thoughts are as loud and obvious as an energetic child at play. I know all about Alvaria and her... ambitions."

"No," he whispered, "you're lying."

"Why would I lie? I have nothing to gain. I know why she went to Coruvaine herself. I know the instructions she left in case someone came to investigate prematurely. All those deep, dark secrets. Everything she trusted you with... I already know it all. She desires to become the living lich of half a day and the Enda girl will help her accomplish it."

"That's... no... it can't... how?"

Malvex leaned forward. "You know it's true. I'm not lying."

Arlith concentrated before crying out. "No, my lady! I'm sorry! How could I have been so weak? I've betrayed you! I'm so sorry!"

Malvex sighed. "Not as sorry as I am."

Malvex stood not two seconds after he woke Arlith. The chamberlain had said nothing out loud, but to the lachrymose mage on the couch, it seemed like he had carried on an entire conversation. Arlith wasn't aware he was in a fabricated environment. That was part of what made it so effective. The illusion convinced Arlith he had already failed before he even tried to oppose him. By causing a nightmare and forcing him to think he had relinquished all he knew, the mage had actually yielded his secrets. It was like telling a man his greatest treasures were stolen and then following that man to discover their location and nature. This was the gentlest method of interrogation Malvex had developed. It was the kindest way he could extract information from someone noncompliant. If it had failed, there were other methods, though each hurt the individual more than the last. Even so, he hated it. The fear, the paranoia, the questioning of reality the man would experience over the next few weeks was hardly debilitating, but it still hurt Malvex to do it. He would occasionally use the same method in reverse to eliminate paranoia, but it seldom worked. Bad memories were always the hardest to forget.

He searched all the chamberlain's thoughts in an instant, sorting through memories and opinions effortlessly the moment Arlith examined his own. His suggestion that the deepest, darkest secrets were already revealed brought those to the forefront and made the task significantly easier. When he finished, he calmed Arlith's mind, soothing away the unpleasant emotions and suggesting exhaustion, which the mage readily accepted. Arlith immediately fell unconscious once more. Malvex took a breath and faced everyone who waited expectantly.

"It's all true."

Garson roared, and the room shook. The three individuals who accompanied Lysander crouched into fighting stances reflexively. Malvex stood numb. The Archmage of Dragons clamped a scaled hand on his shoulder and shook.

"You must check again! He could be lying, or—"

"It's the truth, Gar." Malvex looked up at his friend. He could see the draconic archmage searching desperately for a truth that wasn't there. Malvex wanted to see it too, but there was no comfort in the truths he found. He placed his hand over the large claw on his shoulder. "I'm sorry," he whispered.

Garson staggered back and fell weakly into a chair. His eyes unfocused as he ran a hand over the horns on his head. Malvex forced down the lump in his throat, both from his own inner turmoil and the immense pain that emanated from Gar.

"We've been betrayed," he continued softly. "Alvaria intends to use the magic well of this prophecy to become a lich and raise an army of undead more powerful than any that has come before."

The High Archmage nodded. "Do you know where she is?"

"Kazra Lo Veedra."

The High Archmage leaned back, his expression troubled. Lysander slammed his fist into the arm of his chair. The three who were with him looked about confused.

"What is Kazra Lo Veedra?" the vampire asked.

The High Archmage continued to stare at his desk. "It is a site designed to be a heavily fortified fortress for a lich to rule from. It was built over an area where a great battle took place. From there, raising an army of the undead would be simple." He looked up, a fire in his eyes. "But we will not let that happen." He rose to his feet. "Alvaria has betrayed us. That much is clear. This conspiracy runs deeper than any of us know. We were fooled. As of this moment, the entire Department of Inquisition is under suspicion of treason. I will require each of you to take on additional roles. Malvex"—he moved forward and genuflected shakily before the High Archmage—"you are still the Archmage of Sorcery, but I now bestow upon you an additional title: Archmage of the Counter-Inquisition. You are to investigate the Inquisition and interrogate every member without exemption. Your authority supersedes that of the Grand Inquisitor. You may appoint officers to assist you in this matter at your discretion." Malvex felt magic flow into him as the new title manifested. Some of his grief transformed into determination before it returned, though not as poignant. Others would now recognize him by his new title, even if the title had never been mentioned in conversation.

"Lysander, step forward." The Archmage of Education kneeled before the High Archmage. The High Archmage hesitated. Malvex knew what needed to happen and a pang of deep struck him. "Lysander, I am truly sorry it has come to this. It is not enough that a dear friend to us all—and to you especially—should betray us, but now I must place a burden upon your shoulders I never wished to bestow again. Would that these were happier times when the necessity for such things were relegated to distant memory, but to remove this tumor we must open old wounds."

"I understand, my lord, and I accept this pain if it means putting an end to this treachery." He spoke bravely, but the agony of what he embraced shadowed his face.

The High Archmage nodded sadly. "Lysander Relas, though you remain the Archmage of Education, I now charge you with another mission, born of necessity. On this day, I invest you with the power and title of the Archmage of War. You are granted control and authority over the guards and standing army of Selevarian. Even now, those who have sworn their service will feel you rise to the highest point of the hierarchy as the fist of the High Archmage. These are grim times, but if Alvaria Saccarra raises the undead, many will perish. You will lead my army to war."

Lysander rose. He seemed taller, stronger somehow. Still, as he backed away from the High Archmage, Malvex noticed a tear.

"To you three," he said, addressed the newcomers who obviously felt out of place, "I can only offer my sincerest apologies. We have failed you. *I* have failed you. The web of deceit woven by Alvaria Saccarra blinded me, and now your friend has been abducted. I trusted her too much. Her transgressions are her own, but my mission is to protect others from the possible harm that may come from the Council of Archmages, and I have failed in that." He bowed to them and held the stance for several seconds before rising. "You have done more than you realize in helping us, and yet I must ask for an additional favor. Alvaria has tricked and manipulated the entire Council of Archmages to a shameful degree. She has anticipated our every move. I ask that you accompany the army of Selevara to Kazra Lo Veedra to prevent the living lich from rising and to save Hazel Enda."

"Of *course,* we're going!" The shabbily dressed woman blurted out. "Why else would we be here?"

"She speaks for all of us," the vampire said. The dark elf nodded in silent agreement.

The High Archmage smiled. "You have my earnest and perpetual thanks. You are friends of the Council of Archmages. Wherever you go, you will have my blessing. The city of Selevarian is open to you, as are the halls of Palace Valsidan." His face fell as he turned to the others. "This is a matter of haste, and you all have your orders. I want the army ready to move out with supplies in three hours, no more. You are to take eighty percent of the mages we have on staff and all but twelve of the Guard Unyielding. They know you well, Archmage of War, and will unerringly follow your command. In addition, you are to take a thousand brave soldiers. I know that isn't many, but if we should fail, we cannot risk having the soldiery fall in battle to become undead servants of a lich. We do not have many, but I can spare a dozen hippogriffs to serve as a scouting party. I would also like a minimum of three other archmages to accompany you and lead the charge. I know you have destroyed a lich alone in the past, Lysander, but if Alvaria succeeds, she will be much stronger than any lich that has ascended in millennia."

"I volunteer to go."

The High Archmage turned to Garson Varaldan. "Are you certain?"

"Not at all, my lord, but that won't stop me. I need answers. I trust you and everybody else, but I can't believe Alva would do this. I need to see it for myself."

"And what will you do if you see her become a lich?"

"I will hold nothing back." The anger in Garson's voice was undercut by the sorrow and hurt Malvex sensed in him.

"I shall go! Me! Me!" The group turned to the newcomer's voice. The tall, willowy form of the Green Archmage filled the doorway. The man was nearly ten feet tall and slender as a reed. He walked haltingly and searched the room with wide eyes. A long and unruly brown beard stuck with twigs and leaves flowed from his viridescent chin. Moss covered his worn robes, and a wildness swam in his green eyes.

Many—even among the archmages—believed the Archmage of the Green to have arcane madness, but his power, which had never been used selfishly as far as Malvex knew, was as considerable as his knowledge of growing things. He rarely came to Selevarian, and many would not see him for decades before he'd suddenly reappear.

"You wish to go, Bertrand?" the High Archmage asked.

"Oh yes, Lyle, I must go"—*Lyle* was the first name of the High Archmage, though none ever used it so casually—"the trees spoke to me and the moss whispered: 'Go! She needs you! Green as springtime ferns and sweet as apricots but spoiling for lack of sun and the choking dark that would make her into jam rather than let her grow. Find the sweet lady who knows the whispers of the grass and the discourse of the branches. The autumn is over and winter's cold could freeze the natural lady not yet harvested.' So I hurried here, to stop Foul Lady Winter's creeping cold."

The High Archmage smiled. The others were perplexed. "I've missed you, Bertrand. You may join them."

He nodded and let out a soft creaking groan as he stared at nothing, swaying gently to an invisible breeze.

"I would also like the Archmage of Lights to go with you," the High Archmage continued. "The Archmage of Crystals could also be helpful, if he consents. In the meantime, I will contact the Paladin Order of Kalendril. The Mountainhome is close to Kazra Lo Veedra, and they could be a great aid in the coming battle. The Gray Emperor should also know of what has transpired, but I will advise him to tell no one of the Inquisition's betrayal. We will send out a recall to all members of the Inquisition and order them to return to Selevarian immediately for an emergency redeployment. We can discuss these details at greater length, Malvex. I will assist you with the Counter-

Inquisition. For now, I need to plan with the Archmage of War and those embarking on the journey. Could you take the three members of the Evenfall Vigil somewhere they can rest?"

"We don't need to rest!" The woman jumped up. "We can go whenever—"

"My dear," the High Archmage said soothingly, "you've all done incredible work, but your exhaustion is palpable. We need you healthy and ready to fight. Vampire, when was the last time you consumed blood or blood wine? You could all do with some sleep. I assure you, with my word as High Archmage, you will not be left behind. You may be the key to our success. I can't have you falling asleep in the middle of a battle. Go. Rest."

Malvex forced a smile and brought them through the door and out of the High Archmage's office. The young dark elf studied him closely but remained silent. He led them through a door and into a room that appeared to be made of pillows. Malvex gestured, and a table rose from under the sea of cushions to float just above the floor. Food materialized on the plates along with chalices of alchemical silver and mercury.

"The goblets will look empty, but they are filled with whatever liquid you most desire. This is not an illusion, but the truth, so I would advise against drinking too much hard liquor. The plates are similar. Time moves faster in this room than outside, which should allow you to have a full nine hours of sleep after you've supped, if not more. You are, of course, free to leave this room whenever you would like, but I recommend taking the High Archmage's advice seriously and resting before the expedition. I'm sure it won't be easy." He nodded to them and walked to the door.

"*Through betrayal of friends and oath the living lich shall trample bodies and hearts.*" Malvex turned. It was the young dark elf who spoke. "You were one of those friends, weren't you?"

Malvex sighed and allowed a heaviness to settle into his chest as he left the room. "Yes. I was."

Chapter Seventeen
Allies of Necessity

"Show him in." Alvaria stood before the sarcophagus of Antony Larsinius as inquisitors bustled about making notes and preparing for the lich's emergence. Two glowing crystal bottles rested upon the lid, working their magic for the previous two nights. If all went well, he would emerge soon. She stared at the gold amulet, destined to contain the spirit of the lich. The phylactery had been easy to find, relatively speaking. A spirit jar needed to be close to the body at the moment of return as a matter of necessity, so Alvaria could hardly fault him that they discovered it within weeks of the Inquisition capturing Kazra Lo Veedra.

She clenched her fist around it, and half smiled. This small piece of jewelry was the key to her success.

A small, spectacled man stepped in, observing the room with open admiration. She had never met him personally, but she knew him through her constituents.

"Greetings, Mr. Averly. Are your accommodations satisfactory?"

"Quite so, Your Eminence," he said, continuing to take in his surroundings. "This place is quite a marvel." He met her eyes and bowed with a smile. "I should also thank you, Lady Alvaria, for funding my research. I would never have gotten as far as I did if not for your generous patronage."

She gestured for him to sit. "Indeed. Tell me about your research. As your sole investor, I have great interest in knowing if I can immediately apply your findings."

He continued to search the room, though it was difficult to determine if his interest was born of fascination or fear. A nervous energy surrounded him that differed from what she expected. He blinked several times at her. "Of course. I should start by saying I truly believe my research had only really hit its stride when I was arrested. There is so much more to explore and learn about fae anatomy and alchemical properties that remain untouched. Now, if I could get ahold of some pixies, or maybe a couple hundred sprites—"

"Paxton. Contain yourself." Alvaria saw the Alchemist getting a hungry look in his eyes as he licked his lips.

"Of course, forgive me. My point is that for all the work I did, I fear it is not nearly enough to repay your kindness. If I had more time, I might have provided a better return on your investment."

She sighed. "I know what you mean. My own plans have been rushed beyond what I desired, but such is the way of things. Another year, or another decade, and we would likely feel no more ready than we presently do. I recognize your trepidation in thinking you have failed, but money was no object to me in the slightest. What I needed were conclusive results with scientific backing, which is why I chose you instead of an unscrupulous spellcaster who desired money and not knowledge." This was only half true. She had hired through various sources other spellcasters to attempt similar experiments, but none had yielded significant results relevant to her needs. Many were arrested before additional work could be done, despite her inquisitors' legal tampering. Averly was, regrettably, her last fail-safe.

A little coldness entered her tone. "Though I will say the manner in which you were apprehended was... disappointing. Leaving a door unlocked like that was careless."

He flinched. "Apologies, my lady."

"Accepted." She leaned forward with both elbows on the desk and met his eyes. "Tell me about your most recent research on the bluecaps."

"Certainly." He brightened. "Based on over five hundred bluecaps I've dissected and processed in various compounds; I have concluded that a handful of their internal organs perform a variety of effects within an oddly narrow range. For whatever reason, bluecap components specifically alter time. For example, the liver of the bluecap hastens the rate of toxin elimination. This includes conventional bodily waste through urine and feces, but also administered poisons. Rats injected with lethal levels of deadly nightshade after consuming a small quantity of the liver would immediately eject the poison from wherever it was administered. It didn't *neutralize* the poison; it rather quickened its expulsion from the body."

She nodded slowly. "The liver of many other animals would have flushed the poison, but the bluecap's nature sped up the process."

"That's right. Interestingly, the temporal effect was not uniform for each body part. Crushed bone, for example, slows one's physical state. When I consumed some of the bone, I found my digestion had nearly halted while my energy level remained constant throughout the day, with no exhaustion. At first, I thought it was an energetic effect, but upon further inspection, it turned out to extend or prolong the state any creature is in when it is taken.

"I found the skin helped with physical speed and allowed one to perceive the world slower, which turned out to have significant—"

"Paxton," Alvaria interrupted, "using these bones, can you theoretically create a salve that preserves a body for a hundred years?"

He looked toward the ceiling, making several mental calculations. "I... I think such a thing should be possible. I never tested the outer limits, but with enough crushed bones from bluecaps along with a few other augments, I might create an effect that lasts that long. It wouldn't be capable of keeping a person alive for a century, since the effect burns faster with increased physical activity. What do you wish to prolong?"

"Physical preservation. I want to know if you can keep a corpse from decaying."

He frowned. "I think so. It's an unusual request, but I can make something that works. Are you"—he jumped at a nearby shadow, but there was nothing there—"ah, are you sure that's all you want? I found many other interesting things—"

"I'm sure you did, but my primary interest was in delaying the passage of time while simultaneously accelerating it."

He gave her a puzzled looked.

She regarded the Alchemist for several moments. His nervousness was not of her, but of something else. It was interesting to see a full-grown man literally jumping at shadows. "Do you know what this is?" She held out her hand.

He adjusted his glasses, peering at it. "It's an amulet, but there's more to it than that, I assume."

"Indeed. It belongs to the gentleman reclining before you."

"It—what?" He searched the room until his eyes settled on the sarcophagus. "What? No. You mean that's a—" his face paled, and he shrank from the coffin. "Liches don't take kindly to strangers threatening their phylacteries." His eyes darted around the room.

"You would normally be correct, but I suspect this one may feel differently. In fact, let's ask him." She stood and gestured to the nearby inquisitors, who placed five additional small crystal bottles across the surface of the sarcophagus, one at each corner and one in the center between the two active ones. She walked to the foot of the sarcophagus and examined their work. "Antony Larsinius was a mage of middling power and greater strategy, but we discovered his resting site only forty years after he died. It takes a lich no less than one hundred years to rise from the grave, though many choose to remain dead longer, presumably to gather greater power or knowledge. Poor Antony would never ascend if another Grand Inquisitor had found him, but another Grand Inquisitor *didn't* find him. I did." She extended her hand and the crystal bottles glowed white as thin wisps of smoke flowed from the sarcophagus into each of them. "He has been entombed for almost seventy years, but I think it's time he saw the land of living. So, we're going to speed up his ascension by about thirty years." As the crystals gathered the smoke, they glowed. After several minutes, Alvaria nodded to the inquisitors, and they removed all but the center crystal bottle. They withdrew to the corners of the room as she advanced, extending her hand.

She could feel it. Time passed differently within the confines of the sarcophagus than outside it. The glorified stone coffin provided an arcane field similar to the room they stood in, from which time could be drawn with some minor adjustments. Time passed rapidly within, but more than that, magic flowed into the space in abundance from elsewhere, heralding something incredible about to occur.

The lich stirred.

She summoned the bottle to her hand, and it floated over, the flow of time cut off at the last instant. She gave it to an attendant and watched as the sarcophagus trembled with increasing violence and then stopped. The room was still. The magelamps dimmed, and shadows grew long and jagged. Paxton Averly whimpered and recoiled from the dark. Black fingers of smoke reached around the perimeter of the lid and lifted it softly and slid it to the side. A sigh reverberated through the spherical chamber as a desiccated corpse levitated from the tomb. Its garments had dissolved, but jeweled rings adorned its fingers. Some preservation magic had kept the skin and bones intact to a degree Alvaria did not expect. The corpse righted itself and reached a hand toward the sarcophagus, where it had lain on a bed of many precious gems. Two yellow cymophane gemstones, perfectly polished into spheres, shot into its vacant eye sockets. A pearlescent gem—likely moonstone—flew into the lich's mouth as the skin of the lich grew and stretched over its frame. It did not heal from its death, but strangely, it returned to a facsimile of its living self. The yellow-brown skin slid over its bones as more of the gems lodged themselves throughout the corpse. A diamond in each hand, three amethysts in its forehead, a ruby in its chest, and one sapphire in each foot. Various tiny gems, almost too small to see, entered various parts of the lich's body in a swirling display of glittering death.

The others shrank before the morbid display as the lich paid them little mind assembling itself. Paxton cried in a fetal position by the desk. Alvaria could not look away. Far from fear, her heart filled with awe. This was a being of sheer power. The others were too scared to notice each gem simultaneously undergoing an alchemical change and a further enchantment as they were picked up by the lich. It was not only a beautiful display of power, but seamless artistry without effort. The rotten corpse before her—this perversion of magic—was the most beautiful thing she had ever seen. She glanced at the amulet, which now pulsed faintly with the lich's contained spirit.

The glowing yellow gemstones in its sockets, resembling cat's eyes, observed them, its expression impossible to read.

"Welcome back to Algendis, Antony Larsinius," Alvaria said.

The lich noticed her but continued to take in the room. He maintained his hovering position above the ground but moved off of the sarcophagus and down to about two feet off the ground. He looked into the air and sniffed—as much as a creature without a nose could—and then gazed at his hands, flexing each finger and examining himself. Finally, he turned to Alvaria. "How?" though he spoke softly, that quiet voice echoed through the room, sending chills down Alvaria's spine. The being's tongue and vocal cords had long since withered away. He spoke now through the moonstone in his mouth.

"Temporal magic," Alvaria said. "You no doubt guessed this is not as long as it should have been."

"Indeed." His voice chilled her, less for its otherworldly tone than for the magic that spoke to her soul.

He clasped his hands behind his back. "You are the Grand Inquisitor," he observed.

"Yes."

"And yet"—he studied her with a tilted head—"I am not destroyed. Why?"

She held up the phylactery. "I have a favor to ask."

His emotions were nearly nonexistent. She had expected an extreme reaction, but instead he watched her.

He sighed, sending a chill through the room. "You wish me to impart the secrets of lichdom?"

"No," she said, eliciting another expression of curiosity from the skeletal figure.

"Then what?"

"I have my own methods for becoming a lich. I merely require two things from you. The first is that you to defend me until I ascend to lichdom."

"Hmm…" A deep rumble came from its chest as it considered. "To ascend takes much time. You would have me wait a century for my immortal freedom?"

"Yes—and no." She held aloft one of the crystal bottles. "In a matter of days, I will possess a particularly well-crafted temporal container. It will enable a hundred and twenty years to pass in approximately twelve hours within a contained area."

His eyes gleamed. "You also wish to use my tomb."

"Yes, which brings me to my second demand. I wish for complete access to Kazra Lo Veedra and all its resources, magic, and…" She stared at the lich. "Corpses. When I rise to lichdom, I will maintain that permission and power while you no longer need to defend me. You will also do nothing to actively harm me or my constituents before or after my ascendance to lichdom."

For nearly a minute, the lich gazed at her impassively. She mentally prepared for an assault on her mind while formulating a spell to break the phylactery. No such assault came, however.

He drifted closer to the ground. "Done." With an emaciated finger, he drew a shape in the air and a semi-translucent document floated to Alvaria. She read it and noted that it included all the terms as she had agreed to. The lich required the safe return of the phylactery and the disappearance of the phylactery itself into a pocket dimension until her ascension. She further noted that the lich had placed the proviso that although the corpses could be used by Alvaria, the corpse of Antony Larsinius remained his own and would not be included in the arrangement. She smiled faintly, wondering if she could have held him to the contract for longer without that stipulation, but it was impossible to say now. She read through it another three times to ensure it was to her liking before she reached her hand onto the paper and pushed magic into it, linking herself to the contract. Geas magic was dangerous, powerful, and often vague, but the lich had no apparent ulterior motive. She expected this.

The phylactery disappeared with the contract.

"It is done," the lich said.

"Excellent. I suppose we skipped introductions. I am Alvaria Saccarra, the Archmage of the Inquisition. I know a little of you, such as your name."

"Do you?" The lich almost sounded amused.

"Antony Larsinius. You built this place."

"Ah." The lich gazed off wistfully. "That name belonged to a different man. In another lifetime, I built Kazra Lo Veedra, but it holds no place for me anymore."

"What name would you prefer to be called, then?"

"Zylit." When he said that word, dark magenta threads wove a garment around his body. It swiftly became an ornate robe of maroon and dark magenta, as elegant and kingly as any. He looked back at her. "You will forgive my lack of manners regarding clothing. I suppose such things matter to the living."

She raised an eyebrow. "Very well... Zylit." The name sounded familiar to her, but she couldn't place it. It was some obscure technical magic term, she was sure. "I will execute my plan in the coming weeks. Until then, you are free to do as you wish."

"So long as I protect you."

"True, though the geas may not reflect it, I only need your help when I enter the tomb. I only said I needed your protection before that time in order to secure your promise no harm would come to me."

"Do you think I would kill you in revenge?"

She studied the creature whose most extreme emotions were mild in anyone else. "I don't, but liches can be unpredictable."

"Rarely," Zylit said, his gaze passing over the frightened people around him. "Liches are little different from humans—mere collections of established patterns and behaviors."

"Humans can be unpredictable as well."

"Rarely." Zylit looked back at her and held her gaze. He drifted toward her. "I'm curious. How did you deceive the Council of Archmages? Such a feat is not easily accomplished."

She smiled. She saw the point he was making. "I know them well and planned for years—"

"Based on patterns and behaviors." The cymophane eyes bore into her. "You calculated, and you answered correctly. Humans and liches are predictable more often than not. If they were unpredictable, you would not have been capable of this. Behaviors only maintain the illusion of whimsy when one does not properly understand motivation." He drifted closer. "What motivates you, Alvaria Saccarra?"

She waved to the others to continue working while she spoke. "Is lichdom not motivation enough?"

"No, it is not." Zylit leaned in to inspect her. "Lichdom comes only from great sacrifice. What must be sacrificed, you might wonder? Everything."

"Then why did you become a lich?"

"Antony Larsinius became a lich because he grew frustrated with his lack of skill"—Zylit said impassively. As he spoke, the room changed. There was less dust and the signs of the Inquisition were gone. A young man in gray robes with graying hair moved to fit the narrative Zylit spun—"*skill* spoken of generally. He was mediocre in almost every pursuit." The image of Antony Larsinius shifted. He worked minor spells while others ignored him. Where he conjured a dove, a younger peer summoned a giant eagle. Something glowed in his eyes when he watched other spellcasters. She watched him slam his fists into a table and throw books in fury as he pulled his hair. "Even the effort he expended was mediocre, which prevented him from rising above his station. He desired to stand among scholars and archmages, sharing grand ideas and groundbreaking discoveries. He was a fool.

"He exhibited ordinary skill in magic, barely specializing in more than lesser magic. What was he willing to sacrifice?" A dangerous glow entered the eyes of the man again as he a lifted jagged knife to the throat of a weeping child who dissolved in blood and smoke. "Everything. Why? Because he desired to be anything other than what he was. More than anything in this world, Antony Larsinius desired to be anyone but Antony Larsinius. In this, he was successful" When he said this, the man's face burned away, leaving Zylit's skull in its place.

She crossed her arms. "Do you still feel that way?"

The lich paused, floating silently. "I feel nothing," he finally said. The illusion faded and Alvaria noticed the Inquisition continuing to work, oblivious to what he showed her. "Antony would be overjoyed by this accomplishment, but in ceasing to be himself, he also robbed himself of the joy of his eventual success. I am not happy, nor am I sad. I simply am. I am greater than I previously was, but it means little. It is all I have, however, so I shall maintain my existence if only to circumvent the void." He drifted down to her level. His presence brushed against her mind, and she shivered. She kept her thoughts shielded, but there was no telling how much the lich gleaned before he was detected. "Whatever you seek in lichdom, you will not find."

She stared into his cymophane eyes. "Are you also trying to dissuade me from becoming a lich?"

"No," he shook his head. "It would not benefit me to keep you from that path. Many seek lichdom, few obtain it, and none enjoy it—or so it is said. You may feel differently. Regardless, you never said why you wished to become a lich."

"I'm aware."

"If you cannot speak your desire out loud, how do you expect to coax it from the arms of eternity?"

She smiled humorlessly. "I wish to be a master of life and death. That's all I need to tell you."

"Very well." He drifted up and away from her. "At least you will become master of *one* of those."

A day had passed since Zylit ascended and Alvaria stood gazing at his empty tomb. Desiring time to herself to consider the best time to begin working, she instructed the inquisitors to leave the chamber and dismissed her other attendants. The lich hovered beside a distant wall. He hadn't spoken or moved in over an hour. While he did not seem to study her, he was not unconscious either. None of the literature she read indicated liches needed rest or sleep. Rather, the act of returning from the dead turned them into magic wells with tremendous power that replenished faster than most. She felt a brush of wind and a quiet growl from the edge of the room.

"Youuuu arrrre reckless," whispered a voice from the shadows. She knew who it was but was less than excited.

"I made a choice. The opportunity to fulfill a prophecy does not occur every day."

The creature shifted from his place in the dark. He had a form somewhere between feline and human, though he obscured his body with two large batlike wings. His black fur made seeing his precise shape difficult, for the darkness clung to him magnetically. Hundreds of tiny sharp teeth reflected white and his yellow feline eyes glowed through the shadows. A long, sinuous tail, ending in a dagger-like point, whipped about in agitation. "You make problemssss for the master." He spoke intelligibly, but lingered on certain words.

Alvaria rolled her eyes. "I doubt that very much. Did you come just to aggravate me, or did he send you?"

"Some of both." The creature stalked around the perimeter on all fours like a lion circling its prey.

Alvaria didn't conceal her disdain for the monster. "I would turn you into a frog if I didn't respect your master as much as I do, Shadarqiir."

"He is *your* master, too."

"He has never required that I refer to him as such."

"He is generoussss." Shadarqiir raked the razor-sharp claws on his hands along the ground to punctuate the hiss of the last word.

"Or he doesn't care." She crossed her arms. "Try existing a thousand years and see if you care about titles."

"I intend to." The creature continued to circle the edge of the room, keeping just out of the light with its eyes locked on her. "You might be able to as well if you didn't act so rashlyyy." His voice was surprisingly smooth and soft for such a monster.

"Is it careless to strike when opportunities arise?"

"It is when the opportunity is rushed."

"I had little—"

"Choice? Yes, I know. The master tells me much. Still, you could have waited and risked passing the prophecy. It was uncertain it meant you until you forced it."

She sighed. "What is the message you came to bring?"

"The master bids you early congratulations"—the creature grinned and his eyes narrowed—"and early condolences."

Her eyes narrowed. "What?"

Shadarqiir glanced at the lich as if noticing him for the first time. The dark monster eyed him for a minute before releasing a derisive snort and returning his attention to Alvaria. "There is much the master knows."

"And little enough does he share."

"Not so. The god of secrets has spoken. Gnostrevaine, the Lord of Eyes, has imparted knowledge to him of your future."

Alvaria's eyes widened. She approached the monster. Under the best of circumstances, Gnostrevaine was a devious entity. He was the god of djinn and the keeper of forbidden and dangerous knowledge. He stood in opposition to Athelea, one of the two goddesses sacred to spellcasters. Folklore told of him giving just enough knowledge to destroy the person asking for it, but the reality was more complex.

"Shadarqiir," Alvaria said, "tell me *exactly* what he said."

"Gladly." His tail swished in amusement, the dagger spike on the end producing small sparks as it struck the stone. "The message was simple. Nothing too... exciting. My lord wished you to know that the god predicted your success should you fail, and your failure should you succeed. That is all. Simple words are all it wassss. It should be easy for someone as sssssmart as you, Alvaria."

She ignored him. The message was less prophetic than it was a mutually exclusive eventuality. Either way, there would be disappointment. Still, she strove for many things, so the exact nature of the statement remained impossible to accurately decipher. It was of greater significance that a god took an interest in what she did, especially Gnostrevaine. *That* was worth noting.

"Intriguing. Was that the entire message?"

"One more thing," Shadarqiir said, raising a long, sharp finger. "He said that even though he sympathizes with your mission that he will not aid you any further. He will not openly oppose Selevarian at this time."

"Indeed. I hoped he could assist me, but I hardly expected it. He has already done much that I am grateful for. In all likelihood, I will not need his help."

The creature grinned. "Oh, I think you will. The army has already assembled to destroy you."

Alvaria stared hard at him. "What?"

His toothy grin widened. "The master saw this and informed me as I flew here. An old title has been revived, and a new one is created. The Archmage of War assembles an army, and the Archmage of the Counter-Inquisition destroys your legacy."

"When did you receive this information?"

"Three hours ago."

"Damn," she muttered, turning back to the sarcophagus. "I had hoped for more time. Still, I can work within these constraints so long as those damned cultists arrive soon." She looked up. "Thank you for bringing this to my attention. Though you meant to antagonize me, you conveyed useful information. When I ascend to lichdom, I will keep your assistance in mind."

"*Ifffff* you ascend. I suspect you will—"

Thomas Eller walked out of one of the hallways. "Archmage, we—"

Shadarqiir hissed and, in a rush of wind, disappeared.

Eller staggered several steps back. "What *was* that?"

"That's a hard question to answer," Alvaria said, musing on what had happened. "He is one of a kind, so you could say that *what* he is could be answered by saying *who* he is." Eller appeared genuinely perplexed as Alvaria smiled at him. "He is sent from an ally of mine. Nothing more than that. I have learned that we will receive no reinforcements from that ally, but I anticipated as much. The creature also informed me that we have been discovered sooner than I hoped. All that means is that our plans must be advanced."

"I see. Is that why you summoned me?"

"No, it isn't. I sent several inquisitors to destroy or dismantle the nearest gates to impede the progress of our enemies yesterday. Doing more would yield no greater chance of success, at this point. Walk with me." The inquisitor stepped behind her as she led the way through the labyrinthine halls of stone. "I had some questions for you regarding your time in Coruvaine. To get right to the point, will Paxton Averly be able to deliver what he claims he can?"

"I personally vouch for him, Lady Saccarra. Paxton has his eccentricities, but is ultimately a capable alchemist with a firm foundation in research. Why do you ask?"

"He seems... skittish. Nervous. I grant that what we are doing would frighten many, but the man jumped at nothing more than a shadow earlier."

"Ah, that." Eller looked less certain. "I had hoped he'd recover from what happened in Coruvaine. One of Hazel Enda's friends allegedly cursed him."

"Oh? Say more."

He sighed. "When he was discovered, one of them, a dark elf warlock named Lyvaelan, unleashed a considerable amount of power that broke most of Paxton's bones and nearly shattered his mind as well. From what I gather, Lyvaelan used illusions to affect Paxton beyond the actual physical damage to produce a psychological effect."

She nodded. "By causing physical pain and showing terrifying images, he came to associate one with the other. Is there any evidence an actual curse may have been placed?"

"None, my lady, though it was inflicted by a dark elf, so it's possible we wouldn't find it even if we looked. Since Lyvaelan is part warlock, we considered the possibility of a hex, but can't know for certain. I find it unlikely he could actually create a true curse with his limited knowledge, but determining if Lyvaelan actually hexed the Alchemist will take time. Despite his insistence that he's been cursed, Paxton refuses to submit to our sorcerers for psychological evaluation and claims his anxiety will do nothing to adversely affect his work."

"Has he been sleeping?"

"Yes, though it is only through the use of low-doses of alchemical deadly nightshade and chamomile."

Her eyebrows shot up. "Deadly nightshade? Is he trying to sleep for a night or for a decade?"

"He uses a small dose. He mixes some bluecap component to speed up the effects to prevent oversleeping."

She thought about it. "Likely the blood or pituitary gland, if I had to guess. Has the use of this concoction affected him adversely?"

"Not that I can tell. I've made sure his room is lit on all sides by magelamps, which seem to maintain his mental state. Once he starts working, he forgets all else, even basic necessities."

"I've noticed his drive. That was the most of what I wished to discuss on this subject. The next question is far more important." She looked at him seriously. "Can Hazel Enda do what we need her to do?"

"Well, her visions suggest—"

"I don't want to know what they *suggest.* I want to know if you've observed her. Does she have enough power to fuel the sarcophagus?"

Thomas shifted his gaze away from her. "If she truly has the backing of a god, then she should be capable of—"

Alvaria suddenly gripped his shoulder and leaned closer, her voice dangerous. "I understand what she is, but even the conduits of the gods have limits. Gods may be infinite, but humans are not. Even if we were granted access to the power of a god, it would be limited by the channel of that power. Answer me concretely. *Can she do it?*"

Thomas paled. "I—I don't know, Excellency. She has shown an increase of skill and a similar increase of power, but the amount of magic you need is tremendous. I think that, with a few sessions of leeching her power, we should be able to energize the tomb."

She sighed and let go. "No. We don't have that kind of time. I fear I must resort to a tactic I'm not fond of. Prepare the chamber for our guests tomorrow and affix the arcane magnetism spell to the sarcophagus. It is already engraved with the proper diagrams and stones. All it requires is the enchantment, and any magic used in that chamber will flood into it."

"You wish to drain her power in the morning?"

"As early as possible. Time is not our ally."

Chapter Eighteen
For My Father

Hazel awoke from a sound sleep. Her dreams had receded, due to the impending fulfillment of everything she had envisioned. She hadn't tried to escape, nor had she warned her parents, although they knew something was wrong. What could she do? She didn't fear for herself; she never did. Her parents had been dragged into this only because they were good people. Her father was strong and might fight and defeat one guard individually, but in a fortress filled with mages and unfathomable magic? There was no chance. Different inquisitors brushed over her mind with sorcery, but she could resist them. Her parents had no such training.

She sighed and stretched. Oddly, she was relieved. She wasn't the living lich. Hazel would not betray her friends or crush hearts. She didn't cause the emerging evil, even if she would play some part in it.

Alvaria had given her much to think about in the last two weeks since they arrived at Kazra Lo Veedra. The answer to the mystery of her creation both made sense and didn't. She was brought back from the dead because of a god? What had Hickory done, then? Why did a god care about a random teenage girl who died in a stupid accident?

There were still many questions and not enough answers. She supposed Alvaria *could* be wrong, though it was unlikely. The Grand Inquisitor possessed considerable knowledge, and some of it wasn't what she would have expected a spellcaster to know. Based on what she learned in school, the Inquisition had been destroying information regarding liches since the beginning and maintained the practice all the way until the present. For her to have been above suspicion from the other archmages must have meant she not only tricked them with her personality but also with the degree to which she understood the possibility of becoming a lich.

Hazel sat on the edge of her bed. Her mind drifted to her friends. She hoped they would listen to Lyvaelan—so much rested on him. Had he read her journal? Had she hinted enough? She remembered the expression he had when she left, and it crushed her inside. He looked so hurt. Seeing that pain in him felt like a knife in her heart. Had they really become that close? It wasn't long ago she merely acted in a caring way, but now she couldn't help but feel concern for her friends. Garo was right; she had regained many of the feelings that she'd lost. She hadn't noticed them returning, but they did. It was strange, though. She felt all the same emotions, but they were tempered and yet more powerful in some ways. She understood the value of those feelings that others kindled within her. It gave her a new sense of perspective.

Her family, her friends, and those who helped her all did so, expecting nothing in return. They grew close and helped a girl who had the potential to be some evil creature. They believed in her. Not one of the Evenfall Vigil Watchers had ever rejected her or feared she might hurt them.

Determination surged within her. She wouldn't let this be the end. She would fight to live happily with all of them. She had loved being alive before, but now she was dedicated to it. Life could be terrible, but even at its worst, it was still worth living. She would make others feel that same joy she experienced. She would help the people of Ethelian sleep soundly and live peacefully. More than that, she would make Lyvaelan a happier person, too. She looked at the small satchel of seeds and acorns he had given to her. He had done so much to help her. She would repay him.

For the dozenth time she studied her room. It was close to how she imagined a prison would look, though not as dank. There were no windows and only one door. The room contained a dresser, a bed, a desk, and a chair. Beyond the furniture, there were rugs and two magelamps. It was drab and disorienting without the sun.

She left occasionally to wander the halls or use the latrine, with no one stopping her. The Grand Inquisitor knew her location at all times, Hazel suspected, though she couldn't say for sure. Even if Hazel escaped, it was the height of winter and wherever Kazra Lo Veedra was located, it was far colder than Coruvaine. Her parents and she had dressed for the warmer weather they expected further south in Selevarian. They wouldn't make it far.

She didn't leave her room often, despite her partial freedom. Something terrible lurked nearby that made her uneasy. While her room couldn't protect her, she felt better staying here than exploring.

A knock came from the door. A few moments later, Thomas Eller poked his head in. Hazel picked up her shoe and threw it at him. It bounced off the wall just to the side. He glanced at the shoe on the ground, then at her. "I suppose I deserved that."

She scowled. "No, you didn't. It missed."

He smiled. "True. I need you to come with me immediately. The Grand Inquisitor wishes to see you." He exited while Hazel switched out of her nightgown and into a yellow dress. She usually favored wearing white, but ever since she saw the white rose of the Inquisition everywhere, the color was tainted. A minute later, she exited into the hallway, where Thomas waited.

"Ready?"

She shrugged and followed him. They walked in silence and ascended a single flight of stairs to reach the main level. She hadn't seen him since the day Alvaria revealed he worked for her. Her gaze wandered to his garb. His disheveled appearance in Coruvaine had disappeared into perfect order. "Is it really appropriate to be wearing the white rose? Are you even an inquisitor anymore?"

He glanced at her. "I am an inquisitor to the core, Hazel. You just weren't aware this was what it meant."

"I think you've corrupted its meaning. Do you believe the founder of the order would agree with what you're doing?"

"Almar Galesti is dead," he said dispassionately. "He based the Inquisition on faulty principles which are antithetical to the pursuit of knowledge. He halted spellcasting developments a thousand years by placing arbitrary limitations on research and outlawing necromancy based on the traumatic experience of losing his friends to Dranderis the Mad. While his agony was understandable, his reaction was inexcusable. His entire life's work amounted to nothing more than revenge against a being who was already destroyed. Alvaria betrays the organization to correct the misstep of a zealot. She won't be praised or idolized for it, but doing the right thing is rarely easy."

"And sometimes doing the wrong thing is hard."

He rolled his eyes. "I wouldn't expect you to understand."

"Good, because I don't. Was it so easy acting friendly with us? You toyed with us the entire time. We almost *died* because of you."

He sighed. "Hazel, nothing was easy for me. In fact, it was quite painful. I enjoyed being with all of you and there were a few times I felt guilty. I took no pleasure in deceiving you."

"I'm sure you didn't. You know, I had a dream of an aufhocker shaped like a man who brought me to the living lich. That was you. How many did you trick and betray? Besides all of us, Commander Comrear, and King Aldric, you also tried to frame an innocent woman to take the fall for the murder of numerous innocent people. How do you live with yourself?"

He continued walking. "Sacrifices are sometimes necessary."

"That's easy to say when you aren't the one making them."

"True enough. We're here."

He led her into the large spherical chamber at the heart of the estate. Her eyes widened at the sight of the floating skeletal figure on the opposite side of the room. He remained as far from her as possible without leaving the area. Alvaria wore a beautiful gray dress that appeared more functional compared to the other dresses Hazel had seen her wear. The Grand Inquisitor gestured to a couple of mages, who bowed and exited. She turned to Hazel.

"Today is an important day," she said. "Today will be the first big step in my ascendance to lichdom and I need your help."

Hazel crossed her arms. "We've talked about this. I won't help you."

"You haven't reconsidered? How unfortunate. Perhaps I can persuade you with a little additional information. As an old teacher of mine used to say, where rhetoric fails, knowledge prevails. Do you know how a lich is created?"

Hazel searched her intense expression. "You said a lot about liches, but not that."

She took a deep breath and strode to the tomb. She held her hands clasped behind her back. "It is popular knowledge that liches are born from great sacrifice. This sacrifice entails a substantial sum of arcane energy and one's own life. A lich cannot die naturally. Some believe it is a simple suicide, but truthfully, a specific concoction of alchemical ingredients that forms a deadly poison must be used. The death is not painful, though I imagine it could be terrifying."

She studied Hazel. "Do you remember dying? Do you remember your last moments of life before death took you and the light faded from your eyes? Did your brief existence flicker before your vision as the world slowed around you?"

Hazel remembered. The feeling of endlessly sinking, the sunset deteriorating into night. It should have been frightening, but it felt like falling asleep.

Alvaria placed her hand on the sarcophagus. "One who becomes a lich must die in such a way and be laid to rest in a specialized tomb. Ideally, such a resting place would prevent parasites from entering and preserve the body against decay. As you can see from Antony Larsinius over there—or Zylit, as he prefers to be called—there is no living regeneration from death. Maintaining one's body is paramount to ensure the lich requires only limited magic to function physically.

"I mentioned before the necessity for great magic. Preserving the dead and reuniting the soul with the body requires tremendous energy. The longer a soul rests, the deeper it becomes entrenched in the afterlife. Traditionally, the magic is stored within gems on the sarcophagus, since gemstones are much better at containing magic than precious metals or glass. The gemstones can also be jewelry worn by the future lich, but they risk being stolen, whereas gemstones on a sarcophagus can be inlaid and harder to remove, or else be hidden.

"Spells require energy as magic in order to function. There is no precise way to measure magic and convert it into discrete units. Part of the problem rests in the inconsistency of energy necessary to cast any spell. For example, transforming a slug into a snail requires more magic than shooting a bolt of lightning from one's hand. Depending on the time of day, day of the year, weather, and location, the same spell cast by the same mage in the same manner may change significantly. In fact, when magic is observed, it requires more energy than when it is done individually, and when the observation is done in a spirit of research, it requires *even more* magic. It resists attempts to be measured in a strictly scientific way.

"Despite the inconsistencies, magic functions the same for most people. A spell that works for one will typically work for another. That is why lichdom is both possible and why information about it is so carefully expunged."

"Why are you telling me all this?" Hazel studied the archmage and the room. What was she driving at?

Alvaria smiled thinly. "I'm getting to that. The power of a lich requires a hundred years of death, if not more. The magic required to fuel the process—as I said—is monumental. I could live a dozen lifetimes and pour all my stored magic in daily and still have less than half of what would be necessary. It would be tiring and fruitless. The way around this has been through ritual sacrifice. *Human* sacrifice."

Hazel felt a twist in her stomach.

"Sacrificial magic is abhorrent, but effective. At the instant of death, a person releases a large quantity of magic. The moment happens so quickly that even the most skilled can rarely capitalize on it unless they did so intentionally. Killing a person in battle doesn't have the same surge of power a true sacrifice does. Something about cutting off a person's potentiality prematurely seems to be responsible, but that's an untested hypothesis.

"The question you might then ask is: how many must be killed for a lich to rise? Well—I might answer—assuming that the implements are correct and sufficient, a hundred human sacrifices would be enough to bring about the dream of a potential lich."

Alvaria watched Hazel, who had backed away. "Don't look so worried. I have another method I would much prefer over killing one-hundred innocent people, because that *is* the alternative." She laid a hand on the smooth marble of the sarcophagus. "Sacrificial magic is powerful, but so is living magic. I believe sacrificial magic is tainted by the deaths of those who fuel it, which is why liches are so horribly injured by living magic, such as what thaumaturgy is capable of. Imagine, instead, that a lich was entirely fueled by living magic. What would happen? No one has ever tried, to my knowledge. If a lich should return to life with soul and spirit intact, then it is possible such a being would be utterly invulnerable to all things by conquering both life and death.

"That's what I want, Hazel: to become a living lich. Even before I had heard of you, I researched this and found claims and sources to back it. Unfortunately, the amount of life magic would have to be truly staggering. All the paladins in the world working to produce it ceaselessly would still take years."

She walked to Hazel and put a hand on her shoulder. There was fire in her eyes and excitement in her touch. "Together, we can make history. You can bring about the first lich who didn't need to murder the innocent in order to exist."

Hazel met her eyes. "Tell that to the bluecaps you killed."

Alvaria withdrew her hand and frowned.

Hazel set her jaw. "How many others have you killed, Grand Inquisitor? How many people died because they got too close to your secrets or made themselves a nuisance? No, I couldn't help you become the first lich who didn't murder innocent people. You've made that impossible. There's so much blood on your hands it drips a trail wherever you walk that others will follow."

"My patience *thins,* Hazel Enda." Her voice had cooled. "Will you power these gems or will I have to sacrifice a hundred people to appease your stubbornness?"

Hazel stepped forward. "There aren't a hundred innocent people here. I couldn't feel any. The nearest village must be half a day away by horse and transporting that many people will be slow. You're going to fail."

Alvaria composed herself. "You are half right. There is no village in the immediate vicinity and it would be inconvenient for me to transport so many here, though hardly impossible." She waved at someone down a corridor. "Fortunately, I don't need to kill all one-hundred at the same time. Just two."

Hazel's heart sank.

The three guards that rushed off had returned with her parents between them.

"Hazel!" Lynn cried as they approached. "What is this place?"

Kyle looked around and his eyes widened. He may not have understood what everything meant, but he sensed the immediate danger. He paled even further upon noticing the lich hovering on the other side of the room.

Alvaria kept her eyes on Hazel as the guards brought her parents in front of the sarcophagus. "You see, Hazel, in some ways, I am the monster you think I am, though I take no pleasure in it. I'm still human—*painfully* human—and that will make what I have to do all the more terrible."

"Wait—wait!" Hazel cried, throwing up her hands. "I still don't understand how it works, I—let them go! I just, I don't know how to do what you want, please just—"

"Daffy," Kyle said softly, using the familiar pet name he had for her. "It's okay. Don't give her what she wants. I—" a guard punched him in the stomach, causing him to break off coughing. Alvaria held up a hand for the guard to let him be. She gestured to the man holding Lynn, and she was ushered off to the side despite her mounting protests.

"What did you call her?" Alvaria asked. Several conflicting emotions played over her face that Hazel didn't understand.

"Daffy..." he struggled to say, "because she's like a daffodil."

"That's sweet," Alvaria said, her voice softened. "You know, you remind me a little of my father. He was a good man, too." Her eyes burned with equal amounts of pain and conviction as she looked back at Hazel. "I guess we'll both have to learn to live without our fathers." With a swift motion, she drew a dagger from a guard's hip with one hand, pulled back Kyle Enda's head with the other, and dragged the dagger across his throat.

Lynn screamed.

Hazel's vision blurred. Her father's eyes bulged as deep crimson blood gushed from his neck.

Alvaria dropped the bloody dagger with a clatter. "I will do what I must, no matter the cost."

Hazel screamed and reached for her father. A green halo of light surrounded her body as she willed with her entire soul for her father to live. She remembered them laughing as he carried her piggyback. She remembered wrestling him and how he'd let her win. She remembered how lovingly infuriating he could be.

Two guards kept her back from him, even as one prevented Kyle Enda from falling to the ground. A green blast erupted from her hands. The same power that healed her, Lyvaelan, and others concentrated as it extended to him.

He continued to bleed.

She pushed back more ferociously, willing the power to reach him as many others stood back. Lynn, tears streaming down her face, stared in awe.

Kyle blinked, still bleeding.

Alvaria yelled instructions to the others, who did as she ordered, several moving to examine the sarcophagus. The lich retreated.

Hazel gritted her teeth. It wasn't enough. A tear fell from her eye as she watched her father dying. She couldn't let him die. She *wouldn't* let him die. She thought of how hard he tried to make her happy, even when she wasn't able to feel anything. He teased her, and she teased back. She would see him smile again.

He would live.

The green energy whipped around her, making her almost invisible amid the green maelstrom. The green current reached her father.

He will live.

She thought she heard a voice reassuring her, but she couldn't be distracted now. Others shouted over the roar of her power, but she continued fighting. She felt exhausted, like she was falling unconscious, but she pushed against it.

Slowly, Kyle's wound knit together.

With a last surge, her father gasped as the wound closed and he sprang back, eyes wide, not comprehending what happened.

Hazel teetered. The guards holding her had released her minutes ago. Her vision slipped and faded as she fell. Arms caught her before she hit the ground and a voice comforted her.

Her vision momentarily cleared, and she saw Alvaria supporting her. She had Hazel's arm over her shoulder and supported her.

"You've done well, Hazel, so well. I'm... so glad." Alvaria's voice held no pride, no joy in what she said, only relief and exhaustion. Others came to relieve the archmage, but she waved them off.

Hazel stared with faltering vision at the Grand Inquisitor. Tall, beautiful, and usually serene, but right now she looked scared. Why? As she helped Hazel back to her room, she noticed tears in her eyes.

She had lost her father, too, except Alvaria couldn't do anything about it. As Hazel blinked in and out of consciousness, she wept.

Hazel shed tears for who Alvaria was, for who she could have been, and for the helpless girl who lost her father.

Chapter Nineteen
The End of the Harvest

Lysander studied himself in the mirror. How many decades had passed since he last assumed the mantle of the Archmage of War? Memories flooded in of previous battles and those who never returned home.

Before they departed, he had time to rest and prepare. After issuing orders and deciding a plan of attack with the High Archmage, he returned to his private chamber to rest. Every day on the road without sleep had caught up to him and dulled his senses so that he had been tricked with embarrassing ease by Arlith. Sleep and a bath had rejuvenated him. The title he now bore sharpened his senses, granting clarity while suppressing emotions. It enabled him to make difficult and wise decisions without hesitation.

He frowned at his reflection and touched the blond ponytail he usually kept tied behind him. Long hair was ill-suited to the demands of war. He brought a knife up to it and paused. In that instant, he heard a knock at his door.

Lysander put down the knife and mentally commanded the door to open. "I'm in here."

The Archmage of Sorcery—and of the Counter-Inquisition—
swept silently into the bedchamber, his characteristic smile absent.
Malvex glanced over at Lysander briefly. It was unusual to see another archmage in an informal setting such as this. Lysander had not yet
donned a shirt and wore only breeches currently. The Grand Sorcerer's eyes moved to the knife in his hand.

He sighed and sank into a chair. "How did it come to this?"

Lysander stared hard into the mirror. "All that matters is that it
must be dealt with."

"I suppose you're right, though I can't help but wonder if that is
you or your title speaking."

"It makes no difference."

Malvex nodded tiredly. "Then it is your title. Understood." He
gestured to Lysander. "Are you going to cut it off?"

"My hair is too long for combat. If it's long enough for an op-
ponent to grab, then it's an unnecessary risk. A luxury unsuited for
the battlefield."

Malvex's eyes unfocused somewhat. "It reminds me of some
lines from a song they used to sing. "The Season of Harvest," I think
it was called." He hummed and softly sang:

In springtime, the wheat is planted to grow,

In summer, it rises up high

In autumn, the harvest is cut and brought low

Because winter is when it will die, aye,

Winter is when it will die.

"Do you remember that song, Lysander?"

"I do," he whispered. "Though I've not heard it in many years."

"Do you think they still sing it?"

"I don't know."

Malvex shook his head after several seconds. "Regardless, I
should tell you why I came. I don't know how helpful this information will be but it is better that you be the judge than me.

"For the last few years, I have observed a great tempest in the magic stream, concealed by a kaireidonic fog I could not penetrate despite my best efforts. Granted, it required the use of foresight, which is perhaps the weakest sorcerous tool to wield effectively, even so, it should not have remained as insurmountable as it was. I believe it related to the current events. Despite her betrayal, Alvaria remains one of the most competent mages I have ever come across, but her skill cannot account for what I beheld. Furthermore, the effort necessary to maintain such a thing would far exceed the power that any single individual could accomplish."

"You suspect allies from outside the Inquisition?"

"I do. Powerful individuals with the ability to cast spells capable of blocking the vision of all sorcerers within our organization. Why did Hazel Enda alone prophesy this? If the prophecy is as powerful as we suspect, a much larger number should have recognized it."

Lysander put aside the knife and pinched his chin between his thumb and forefinger. "She may be the easiest part to determine in the equation. Her prophetic abilities may not stem from the same source as a normal sorcerer and thus may have fallen beneath the notice of whoever attempted to block the rest of us. The question is who possesses the resources to deny a prophecy from the minds of all spellcasters?"

"Perhaps the Dark Order, or the fabled Council of Liches? I do not think this bears the mark of any Fae Nobles, though they could do so if they desired. Regardless, my point is that you may not be fighting just inquisitors when you arrive. Alvaria might be as high as the conspiracy goes in our organization, but that does not mean there are not others she answers to."

"You were right to bring this to me," Lysander said. "I will incorporate this into my general strategy."

Malvex stood and walked to him. "One more thing. Bring Alvaria home. Her life has been difficult, and we were blind not to see it. I do not want to make your task more complicated than it already is, but please. Help her. Return her to Selevarian and we will find some way to reconcile what she has done. She may tread dark paths, but it is not too late to turn around."

"I will do all that I must," Lysander replied. He ran his hand through his hair and sighed. "If I can, then I shall save her. The chief hope of war is eventual peace. If there is a way to spare the bloodshed and bring her to justice, then that shall be the route we take."

Malvex stepped back. He nodded sadly. "You do not think she will accept."

Lysander half smiled at a memory. "You should know better than anyone how strong-willed she is. It is not us she needs to overcome but herself."

"Then I will pray to Veratheragan for peace, and to Caleptis for healing."

"I fear your prayers will only be answered after the war."

"Will you bring your sword?"

Lysander looked to where the weapon was mounted upon the wall. Bizarre by most accounts, the weapon was a combined sword, shield, and gauntlet. Its reflective sheen hinted at its high silver content, which would normally be impossible to mix perfectly with steel if not for the arcane smiths who forged it. He had not touched the weapon in decades and even now the only reason it gathered no dust was the servants who regularly cleaned the apartments.

"No," he replied finally. "I will bring my marinom, but the sword shall remain. What I must battle will not be better affected by the blade than anything else. It represents a time long past I will not revisit. I would have melted it down but—" he clutched at his chest and his vision swam for a moment. He struggled to continue what he was saying, but the words refused, despite the flattening effect of his title.

"You wish to remember her," Malvex whispered. "The last one to fall to that blade."

Lysander gasped as tears scattered from his eyes. He stood straight and regained his composure. "Yes. And to remember what the Archmage of War is capable of without love, mercy, or joy."

Lysander picked up the knife once again. He cut off his ponytail and placed it aside as he trimmed the rest of his head. As he worked, the Archmage of Sorcery softly sang the end of the song:

> Because winter is when it will die, aye,
> Winter is when it will die.

The army of Selevara had been assembled. The total number of soldiers rose just over six thousand. A thousand were part of the brave soldiery—those ungifted with magic. Each was outfitted with weaponry that would work better against the undead than most. Another thousand represented soldiers trained in amplified fighting techniques which utilized schools of magic to better combat magic. About seven hundred wizards, most trained in war magic, went with them. Five hundred thaumaturgists joined, as did two hundred conjurers and a few dozen sorcerers. Sorcery as an art was powerful but less than effective against the undead. The remainder were mages of mixed ability, including magicians, to attend to basic needs and repairs. Each of the archmages brought their research assistants and attendants as well, though they hadn't factored into Lysander's headcount. Beyond these, close to a thousand represented cooks, messengers, smiths, farriers, and other laborers to ensure the soldiers remained in peak physical condition during the march.

He watched scores of wagons wheel into the courtyard. Most were filled with supplies, weapons, and tools for spellcasters. They could have mustered additional forces, but there was too little time.

Hippogriff riders strode over to the main courtyard, just before the statue of Selevara, which was perfectly visible at night. Lysander wondered what the Lady of Magic thought of this. She represented knowledge and wisdom. How would she handle this situation? He shook his head.

"Sometimes I wonder if we have it all right."

Lysander glanced at Garson, who stood beside him, gazing at the statue. He had gathered himself considerably since the meeting, but Lysander still sensed the emotion in his friend.

"We are supposed to gather knowledge and magic, but who is to say our way of ethics is ultimately right? Magic doesn't have any innate morals, correct?"

"You're asking the wrong man."

Garson raised an eyebrow. "Because you're the Archmage of War, not the Archmage of Education?"

"I am both, but until this battle is won, I am less archmage than I am Master General of the Army of Selevara."

Garson studied him quietly for a moment. "Then I will not ask her to guide you. May Veratheragan guide you in strategy and help you bring an end to this conflict."

Lysander nodded. He glanced at four high master conjurers who stood a little way off. Two men and two women.

"Friends of yours?" Lysander asked, tilting his head at them.

He followed his eyes. "They agreed to join me. They also sit on the Board of Conjuration, representing the four elementals. I convinced them to come as a personal favor."

He knew them more by reputation than by association. They had mastered conjuring the primary elementals, which was no easy feat. Some of them appeared to have paid for it.

"I heard," Garson said, "the Archmage of Crystals will join us."

"You heard correctly."

"That is unusual."

"These are unusual times." The three members of the Evenfall Vigil headed in his direction from the palace. They appeared sufficiently refreshed.

Good, he thought, *I'll need them well-rested for the battle. They might be useful.* He shook his head. His title had taken root in him. More than he wanted.

"Archmage Relas!" Alistair called. "Are we ready to depart?"

Lysander searched his surroundings. Everything appeared to be in order. "I believe so. We await the High Archmage's blessing before we leave."

They didn't wait long. A few minutes later, the High Archmage descended the stairs to the front of Selevara. All those in the courtyard fell on one knee as the High Archmage appeared, wearing a long white cape and holding a gold and orichalcum staff studded with diamonds and topped with a massive octagonal amethyst. The Crown of Stars shone brightly around his head.

He stopped a few steps down from the statue of Selevara. "Fellow servants of the Lady of Magic," he said, his voice projecting over the crowd, "a great perversion has entered our ranks which cannot be allowed to persist. There is a threat of unknown magnitude and we will answer it. I would not ask you to fight were it unnecessary, but I must. The Grand Inquisitor has betrayed the cause and must be brought in for questioning. March to Kazra Lo Veedra and go with the Lady's blessing." He turned to Lysander, his voice at a normal level. "I consulted the gates and it appears that both the northern and southern gates closest to Kazra Lo Veedra have been dismantled."

Lysander pursed his lips. Alvaria had really thought of everything. "Understood, High Archmage. It will make the arduous journey a little more difficult, but we will manage. At that rate, it will take us six weeks if we move quickly."

"No, it will not."

The High Archmage turned away and raised his staff. Lysander gasped as he felt a large swell of magic in the area. Purple, swirling smoke coalesced around the staff of the High Archmage with a pulsing hum. He slammed it into the ground at the feet of the statue with a resounding *boom*. The magic spread and stretched out forty feet around in a semicircle. Purple smoke continued to waft from the top amethyst as the High Archmage looked back at the gathered masses.

"I have said these are dire times! I will not sit idly back and do nothing while all of you risk your lives. Enter! I bring you as close to Kazra Lo Veedra as I can, in the middle of the Gray Empire."

Lysander's eyes widened. "Soldiers! March!" As the soldiers moved into the swirling portal, he stared with awe at the High Archmage. He had created a gate right in the middle of Selevarian with no physical gate present. Furthermore, he claimed this gate opened up two thousand miles northeast.

"High Archmage, is it... safe?"

"Yes, quite safe." He gave a wry smile. "Why? Do you not trust me, Lysander?"

"I do, but something like this borders on the impossible."

"Few things are truly impossible, sadly." The High Archmage gazed into the gate, maintaining his pose. "Today I am doing all I can to prevent Alvaria from succeeding. This is serious, Lysander. If she wins, she may kill millions, and we'd be no closer to defeating her. I have asked you to take on onerous responsibilities. I, too, must do all I can and no less."

He placed a hand on Lysander's shoulder and dropped his voice. "Stop her, Lysander. Kill her if you must, but stop Alvaria Saccarra."

Lysander bowed low. "I swear that if it is within my power, she shall be stopped at all costs."

"Not at *all* costs," the High Archmage corrected. "Only a lich will sacrifice that which is not his to achieve his desired end. Fight, win, and return with a clean conscience."

"It shall be done, my lord." Lysander rose and watched as the forces finished entering the portal. Only he, Garson, and the Evenfall Vigil remained. With a deep breath, he stepped through the portal.

Chapter Twenty
Strategy and Patience

Alistair peered from the front of the wagon. The hippogriffs had left an hour ago and should return within the next few minutes. He wasn't certain how well the creatures could see in darkness, but he supposed that factored into this specific scouting strategy. It was early in the morning—an hour before dawn—and eight hours since they walked through the gate.

The air was colder here. Selevarian maintained a warm and breezy climate consistent with its southern coastal location, but this far inland and north afforded no such comforts. A blanket of snow covered the paved road and quieted their movement, save for the slushing of the wheels and the crunch of walking soldiers. It reminded him of winters back home in the Noxphetalis Mountains, though the storms there were worse than the current gentle snowfall.

He focused his hearing on the hippogriffs. It wasn't easy to sustain singular focus, but he had practice from living with older siblings for most of his life. Learning to shut out certain sounds while hearkening to others required time and patience, but he possessed an ample supply of both, especially since he had moved to Coruvaine.

Distantly, he heard the heavy flap of multiple wings. He brought his head back into the wagon.

"They should return in two minutes," he said to his companions. "They are still a few miles off but given their speed, we should see them soon."

"I don't suppose you heard if they found anything?" Lara asked. The werewolf acted oblivious to the cold, though a few goosebumps appeared on her exposed arms and legs. She sat on the floor, legs extended with ankles crossed—much too relaxed, given the situation.

"No, I didn't. Besides, the riders are focused on flying here, so I doubt they'd say much. I'll listen when they relay the report and see if anything interesting came of their mission."

"Doubtful," Lyvaelan muttered. He rested with his back against a crate. "It took them almost an hour to leave and return, which means we're another few days out at least. The Archmage of War stated as much."

"You might be right." Lara scratched her neck absently. "Isn't it weird we all know him as the Archmage of War now? It even seems like the guy himself has changed."

It was strange. Alistair found that particular magic disconcerting. How did it function? In the past day, he had seen more magic than he had in his entire life. It was awe-inspiring, but also terrifying. How much did he witness that he didn't realize was magical? Sorcerers seemed to know when he attempted to persuade them, which wasn't supposed to happen. He mentally promised himself to research more when they returned to Coruvaine.

If they returned to Coruvaine.

He dismissed the thought. It was a strong possibility he would die, but it wouldn't be without causing some consternation in the process. They had fought aufhockers, an alchemist, a mage, and a many-armed shadow monster from the world of the dead. They wouldn't die. Not on this mission.

He clenched a fist. "*Take care of my daughter,*" Kyle Enda had once said. Alistair gritted his teeth. He'd done a terrible job in *that* regard. He tried not to dwell on it, but his innumerable failures piled up. How many times had Hazel been injured when he could have prevented it? Too many. He had failed this time, too.

They all had.

"They've landed," he said, closing his eyes. He listened as they spoke. They were close enough that even Lara could hear if she focused.

"What are they saying?"

"Hmm." He opened his eyes. "I'll wait for the archmage to tell us. He's heading this direction."

A few moments later, the flap of the wagon opened and Lysander stepped through. He sat on a nearby crate.

"You may have already heard. The scouts arrived just now."

"Any good news?" Lyvaelan asked.

"Not precisely," Lysander said. His voice was direct and lacked its usual warmth. "It would be more accurate to say we have helpful information than that I have any 'good news.'

"In the first place, the hippogriff scouts have located Kazra Lo Veedra. We are heading in that direction as we speak, but at a slow pace. They estimate it should take us four days to get there.

"Second, they apprehended and killed a peryton which acted as a familiar to someone inside."

"Truly?" Lyvaelan asked. "They actually killed it?"

Lysander clenched a fist. "That one of the Inquisition formed a bond with such a creature is disgraceful, but yes, it was destroyed to the extent a familiar can be. Against a single hippogriff it may have provided a challenge, but facing three with mages riding them, it stood little to no chance."

Alistair had seen perytons at a distance when he lived in Noxphetalis. Half-bird and half stag, the creatures flew in violent, carnivorous flocks. Occasionally, they attacked vampires, mistaking them for humans. The result was usually much bloodshed on both sides, without casualties. Some dark magic made them impervious to weapons crafted by humans. While nosferatu could not kill them entirely, the perytons were not immune to the claws and fangs of the vampires. They were hardy creatures of unbridled malice and hate.

Lysander interlaced his fingers and rested his chin on them. "While killing it was the right decision, the mage it belonged to will notice its demise, which means they know we're close. They will probably continue to monitor our movements but will conclude the advance scouts are almost a week ahead of us."

"Four days gives them ample time to prepare," Alistair said, rubbing his chin.

"I agree," Lysander said. "That's why we'll make it there in two and a half."

"What?" Lara looked up. "How is that possible?"

"The estimate comes from the fact that we are only as fast as the slowest among us. The foot soldiers and wagons travel at about the same pace, but we must eventually travel four miles east of the road. That area is difficult ground and will impede the progress of our wheeled transportation. The terrain adds an extra half a day to their estimates. We will leave the wagons on the road and the non-military personnel will drive them behind us. The soldiers will carry their own rations for the next day after that and then we will fight."

"I'm not the best at math," Lara said, "but that still means there's an extra day uncounted for."

"You're right. That's why we'll be moving at high speed while we can. Rest for food will be done at a normal pace, and we shall eat as we walk. Besides, the evaluations of scouts err on the side of overestimation."

"I hate to mention it," Alistair said, "but I won't be at my best in two-and-a-half days. Even if the day is overcast, I'll be weaker than usual. Your magic negates the deleterious aspects of sunlight, but I'll still lack my optimal speed and strength."

"Your own strengths and weaknesses factored into the calculation. That's why I've pushed it to two-and-a-half days. When we arrive within a mile of Kazra Lo Veedra, we will encamp in the surrounding tree line to strategize further and allow the soldiers to rest before the assault. We will attack under cover of nightfall. Not only will you be at your strongest, but we will need the edge of stealth that night can give us to enter Kazra Lo Veedra. The estate is essentially a fortress, so a frontal attack is unwise, at least as our primary plan."

"What is your plan, if I may ask?"

"Evolving by the moment, but I have the gist." He took a wand from his side and drew glowing patterns in the air that remained where he placed them. "Kazra Lo Veedra is symmetrical and circular, with four entrances in each cardinal direction. I will enter with some of the Guard Unyielding in the back. If we sneak in, we might take the estate from the inside without worrying about opposition. If we defeat Alvaria, then the rest will submit."

"Where do we factor in?" Lara asked.

Lysander continued to draw the battlefield in glowing yellow lines. "The bulk of the force will attack the western gate, which is the main entrance to the estate. It makes the most sense since the opening is widest and also the least defensible. The army will wrap around the sides, drawing attention to the northern and southern entrances as well. I will lead the eastern incursion with my small group while the main assault draws the attention of the defenders. I need you three to attack either the north or the south."

"Why either of those? Wouldn't we be more effective in the main army or with you?" Lyvaelan asked.

"No, I don't think so. Most of their spellcasters and guards will defend the front, which will make it a challenge to beat. They will still suspect an attack on one of the other sides, and will most distrust the eastern entrance. If you punch a hole through their southern or northern defenses, it will divert soldiers and spellcasters from both the west and the east, which benefits the main army and my mission."

"You say we need to 'punch a hole' like there will be a massive horde opposing us," Lara said. "There's no way there are *that* many inquisitors."

"You are correct." Lysander leaned back, his voice grave. "But there are thousands upon thousands of dead bodies surrounding

Kazra Lo Veedra. If she becomes a lich, she will summon them and possess an army easily numbering in the tens of thousands. It likely will not be an extremely *powerful* force, but the sheer quantity could create a wall of protection around more valuable mages. That's why I need you ready to be the tip of the spear instead of the head of the hammer. If you can cut through the lines swiftly and treat it less like a battle and more like a race, you will call reinforcements to your position, which will benefit our cause. It will also give you the ability to rescue Hazel and her parents."

Alistair looked at the archmage sharply. Lysander met his gaze and nodded.

"I didn't want you to come in order to fight our war and deal with our systemic corruption," Lysander sighed. "I wanted you to join us so you could find your friend. You three benefit us tremendously, but I don't want you to think I merely want to use you. Hazel was dragged into this, and it's largely my fault. I allowed friendship to blind me to the facts. Alvaria was always ambitious and secretive. I never pried and now pay for my negligence.

"The High Archmage already apologized, but I must do so as well. I failed horribly, miserably, and completely. The best I can do is attempt to repair this evil and reunite you with Hazel."

The three were silent. None wanted to speak for the others. Alistair finally spoke, "We appreciate your efforts. It is more than some would do. There's another problem we are reticent to broach, however."

"And what's that?"

"We've been beaten repeatedly by spellcasters," Lara said. "Only Lyvaelan stood a chance in our battle with the chamberlain and the Alchemist, so I'm not confident we can win against these guys."

Lysander nodded, and a small smile crept across his face. "Well then, I'll have to teach you how to fight and kill inquisitors."

"Really?" Lara said. "You think you can help us?"

"Of course." He folded his hands. "I know all the combat tricks of inquisitors—I invented half of them. You can take the information

I give and do with it what you will. Alvaria is crafty, but I am unparalleled in combat and offensive magic. I redeveloped the training program of the Inquisition before she became an archmage. Let me show you how to defeat any inquisitor you cross paths with."

Lara grinned wolfishly. " *This* is how you make amends. Teach us how to destroy the Inquisition. We only have a couple of days, so you better give us the accelerated class."

"I'll do my best, but time is limited and I must still lead the soldiers, so it will have to be accelerated indeed." He faced Alistair and Lara. "The inquisitors were specifically trained to hunt and subdue other mages and their undead creations. Alvaria likely had them do additional training, but the bulk of their education will surround those issues. While Lyvaelan may be more powerful as a partial warlock, they are trained to handle any bombardment of spells and so it would be more dangerous relying on him to defeat the inquisitors. For that reason, Lyvaelan should seek to support and defend both of you from their spells. Speed is your ally. Spellcasters and undead are not exceptionally fast, so if you can break through their defenses quickly, it will make it harder for them to counter. Arcane shields can be shattered through either acute or aggregate damage. In other words, you can break through a shield with one big hit or with numerous small ones. Most will expect their shields to endure for some time before anyone smashes through, but with your exceptional abilities, fragmenting their defenses instantly will induce panic, which will make defeating them easy. Such shields can be repaired so the faster and harder you hit, the better.

"Lyvaelan, they usually employ sorcery when dealing with non-spellcasters, as this is the easiest and swiftest method to end any confrontation. From what you've said, the chamberlain initially used sorcery to get all of you to leave peacefully. That will be their preferred method, although they may not use such kind techniques. If you can defend the minds of your friends from mental assault, then they will be forced to use methods other than sorcery. They will default to either combat wizardry or conjuration."

He leaned close to Lyvaelan, his voice grave. "Do you remember how you defeated the chamberlain?"

"Yes, I disrupted his confidence and concentration."

He nodded. "It was fortunate he used a creature he lacked significant rapport with. Do not expect such luck again. He was uncertain of your abilities and thought it better to kill you with a wildly unpredictable power rather than give you the chance of attaining victory. The others will not be so bold and will attempt to reassert influence over the being they summoned. At the moment they lose control, you can take the reins of the creatures they summon and turn them against their conjurers."

Lara gasped. "You can *do* that?"

"It's possible"—he glanced at Lara—"but difficult. You must be ready immediately or the opportunity is lost. The most reliable way to cause them to loosen their grasp is through pain. There are other ways, but for you, that should be the main avenue. In that split second you take over a creature, the mage will be too surprised to act and realize what is happening. Capitalize on that moment. This is not a technique broadly used because conjuring or controlling any being usually takes several seconds. You, Lyvaelan, cast spells much faster because of your lineage. For that reason, this strategy may work."

He turned back to Alistair and Lara. "You must fight the mages, not their conjured beings, if you can help it. They may summon powerful beasts that are hard to ignore, but by engaging them, you play into the inquisitors' hands. The only exception would be if they focus on Lyvaelan or are too close to overlook. Otherwise, attack the inquisitors. Go for the throat."

He sighed. "I had hoped to return to the field of education, and now that I get my chance, it is to advise others in how to win battles. It is an irony I deserve. Do you have questions?"

"There is something that has been bothering me," Alistair said, "though it is off-topic. Shouldn't we let King Aldric know?"

"The thought occurred to me," the archmage said, rising, "which is why I told the High Archmage to contact him. He will instruct all the kingdoms in the Gray Empire to watch over members of the Inquisition but nothing more. The only exception was King Aldric, who he told the entire story to, including your part in it."

Alistair winced. "Including our random disappearance and working outside our jurisdiction?"

"You might be more concerned about that than he was. We requested Garo join us near Kazra Lo Veedra for the assault as soon as possible. He has been to Tellaris in the past and explored much of the area, so he should be capable of traveling through a shadow close by. The only issue is he may not visit Aldric in time to join us unless there is a little additional intervention. I've already contacted my allies in Elliara, who will alert him if he is there. I may need to do something a little more drastic to ensure he receives the message."

He waved a hand, dispelling the magic lines in the air and sat on the floor, drawing a piece of chalk from his pocket. He traced out a small conjuration circle on the wood and exited the wagon. After a moment, he returned with a candle and a handful of clean, white snow. He muttered words Alistair didn't recognize as the snow melted in his hand. Holding the candle above the circle, he created a brief arc with the water in his hand. To Alistair's surprise, the water remained suspended in place, as did the candle, when Archmage Relas withdrew his hand. The fire thinned and wavered as the candle glowed brighter. The water reflected the light with an opalescent sheen and wavered in place. It twisted into a spiral and spun around the candle, sending off a multitude of colors in rapid succession until the water all at once dropped. Standing in the middle of the circle was a small, winged humanoid.

The creature was only a foot or so tall, barely larger than a pixie. Its wings resembled feathered bird wings, and although its naked body appeared androgynous, there was something in the creature's mannerisms and appearance that gave Alistair the sense that it was female. Its body was slender and youthful, while its large eyes gave it a childlike face. The entire body was an ever-shifting array of glowing colors. The wings, too, emitted light and glittered like they were dust-ed with a million microscopic diamonds. The creature's long hair floated around it as if the creature swam through water. Its eyes—most striking of all—had an iris similar to any normal human's, except it was every color of the rainbow.

The creature glanced at the others but seemed to intentionally ignore them as she turned to Lysander. "Well?" she said. Her voice was high and musical. "You called for me. Don't you know it's rude to keep a girl waiting?"

Lysander smiled and bowed. "Of course, lady of light, please forgive me. I was struck silent by your beauty."

The creature rippled into bright shades of yellow and pink. "Yes, I could imagine that, but you have called me before and still answered just as slowly. Are you not used to me?" There was a sense of mischief and mock drama in this creature.

"Child of rainbows, one never tires of the beauty of irids. The body may desire food but the soul longs for beauty. It is only in your presence, fair Lexia, that my heart is satisfied."

A series of bright colors flashed across its skin: indigo, blue, green, purple, and a blazing yellow. Her smile widened into a huge grin. "You always know what to say, Lysander. That's why I keep coming back." She turned from him and looked over her shoulder with her hands clasped behind her and below her wings. "You're attractive yourself, for not being one of us. Though"—she tilted her head and frowned—"I don't like what you've done with your hair."

Alistair raised an eyebrow. Was she... flirting?

Lysander smiled. "A sad but necessary sacrifice. Regardless, I receive your compliment joyfully. Praise from an irid is among the greatest of treasures; for who best to judge beauty, but those who possess it in greatest supply? Oh!" His eyes widened in realization. "I just remembered! There was something I needed to tell you about. A... secret message."

Blue and teal washed over her body in waves as she turned back to him with curiosity. "Secret message?"

"I just heard about it today, so you must keep it a secret."

The irid leaned in close with wide eyes as her skin sought darker shades of conspiratorial blue.

"I heard"—Lysander glanced back and forth—"that Garo, the black dog, ambassador to the Seelie Court, has a secret admirer."

A flash of ecstatic pink rippled across her skin before returning to dark purple and blue as she gasped. "Who?"

"The King of Ethelian!"

She gasped again, leaping back as yellow and pink raced through her body like shooting stars.

"It's true. The King of Ethelian *loves* Garo and wants to be with him as soon as he can, even though the king is already married. This love is a matter of life and death."

"Oh!" The irid shivered with excitement and her feathers ruffled.

"I'm telling you this because it's important Garo hears about this as soon as possible. He's a friend of mine, but he shouldn't know this information came from *me*. That would be *bad*."

The irid nodded, flashing a little green before shifting to purple.

"Telling your siblings about this would be dangerous, since so many of them struggle to keep secrets. So, don't tell anybody else. This could be a problem of monumental proportions if others heard about it. My name can't be connected to this or else the king will be furious. Do you understand, Lexia?"

"Yes, I understand." There was an eagerness in her eyes Alistair didn't find exactly trustworthy.

"Good. Now fly! Quickly, or the king may die of sadness!"

The words no sooner escaped his lips when she disappeared in a flash of light. If not for Alistair's heightened senses, he would have thought she teleported with how quickly she moved. She flew far faster than any creature he had ever witnessed.

"What in Stezelra's name was that?" Lara exclaimed. Lyvaelan looked equally confused.

Lysander settled down again with a sigh. "That was an irid. They are devious little daimons in a similar class as nymphs, although most claim they are technically a kind of lesser nymph, though they don't take kindly to that."

"Okay, but what what was all that nonsense about the king being in love with Garo?"

"It's necessary to be a little deceptive when working with irids. They are the fastest, most dedicated messengers in existence. They will travel a thousand miles within minutes if they believe it's worthwhile. Their character flaws make them... difficult to control, however. They thrive on gossip and will contort any story they hear to make it more interesting. They are also terrible at keeping secrets and will spread the news to the rest of their kind which means that although the message will be heard by its intended recipient, it will also be heard by hundreds or thousands of people who were *not* the intended recipient. People don't use them for that reason. If you are especially clever, then you can get them to do as you wish.

"By telling Lexia it was a matter of life and death, she will increase the gravity of it tenfold, making the message seem adequately dire. Demanding secrecy will ensure she is incapable of doing so and will inform other irids who will disseminate the information to any black dog they can find. Finally, the coded message that the king loves him tells Garo that the king needs to speak to him about a matter of great importance. Since I also told her *not* to tell anyone I was responsible for the message, she will feel compelled to tell everyone that I told her. Thus, the message that Garo will receive soon is the king needs to speak with him urgently and that Archmage Lysander Relas wished that information to be relayed."

Alistair frowned. It seemed needlessly convoluted. "But... will that really work?"

"Oh yes, I've used them on multiple occasions. The other advantage is the very act of using an irid is usually an act of desperation. Garo will recognize this and take their message to heart. Irids do not require rest or food for survival. They are also extremely perceptive, and the magic I used to summon her connected us in such a way that she knows exactly who Garo is, as if he were an old acquaintance.

They can communicate and share images telepathically, so other irids shouldn't struggle with this either." He smiled. "They are gossiping flirts, filled with vanity and mischief. What isn't there to love?"

"I've never heard of them." Lyvaelan mused. "Though I know of nymphs such as dryads, meliae, and nereids."

"They don't really make themselves known. They prefer to spread gossip invisibly. Sometimes, when you have an intrusive thought about someone, or a strange idea comes to mind, it is the work of an irid. They hunt secrets and then spread those secrets as quickly as possible. For that reason—among humans—they are considered pests and are mistaken for mischievous fae. Most cities employ deterrents to keep them from wandering in or staying. It's unlikely you would have known about them in Elliara, simply because light elves don't really keep secrets and wood elves typically communicate telepathically with each other and with beasts. If there is no drama to uncover, then the irid wants no part in it."

Alistair tapped his sword absently. "I hope this works. Garo would be a great help to us."

"He'll come." Lysander stood and readied to hop off the wagon. "He wouldn't miss this for anything. I've worked for him for many years and he's grown attached to your friend who was taken. I don't know if he'll forgive me, but he certainly won't forgive Alvaria." He shook his head. "I wouldn't want to be the one who stands between him and saving Hazel."

He hopped from the wagon and strode toward the front of the army. Alistair heard him talking with the other mages about their plans. Soon after, the wagons picked up pace.

"Ya know, how he said he wouldn't want to stand between Garo and Hazel?" Lara clenched her fists. "Well, I that goes double for us. I'm aching for a battle. I really need to beat the shit out of someone."

"I think you'll get the chance soon," Alistair said, "and it won't just be *one* person you fight, but likely dozens."

"Or thousands," Lyvaelan said, "if the Grand Inquisitor summons an army of the undead like Hazel predicted."

Lara grinned. "Good."

They both looked at her.

"What? It's not like *I'm* summoning a bunch of undead punching bags for us to fight. I just get to enjoy it."

"Let's hope you live *through* enjoying it. I doubt Hazel would want any of us to die or be gravely injured in the course of her rescue."

Lyvaelan nodded. "Agreed. We must take this seriously. The time for playing is over. If her parents still live, then we need to find them first."

"Much as I want to save our girl, Hazel, you're right. If she really can't die, then it's her parents who are in the most danger. We'll save them, then get her."

Alistair nodded. They were in agreement. He looked at his allies—friends—and saw the fire of determination in their eyes and knew he mirrored it. Garo might be formidable in his own right, but he was nowhere near as dangerous as these three Watchers of the Evenfall Vigil. They would save Hazel, and no threat from the grave or beyond would stop them.

Chapter Twenty-One
Life and Death

The warmth of summer mocked the cold of her grief. There, in a plain wooden box, reclined the last person she cared about.

A heavy hand rested on her shoulder. "He was a good man, your poppa," said Galvius. The grizzled old man wore work clothes to the funeral, though he had washed beforehand. He sniffed and wiped his nose with the back of his other hand, which also held his cap. "We'll all miss him."

She continued to stare at the box. A priest in dark robes with a shovel spoke quiet prayers over the body, asking the earth to welcome him home. It was all a lie. How could the earth be his home when he belonged with her?

"Y'know, he would've stayed with you forever," Galvius continued. "He loved you more than anything in the world. I'll bet he's trying to dig his way back out of the underworld just to be with you."

How did this happen? Only a few days ago, he had been smiling and teasing her about how tall she'd grown. He laughed when she punched his arm. Now... there would be no more teasing. No more smiles. No more laughter.

"'Course I'll help you however I can. He'd have wanted that. The owner of the horse offered some recompense, so you'll be set for a little while, at least."

She hated the man speaking prayers over her father. What right did he have to lay him to rest? Why should this priest be the one to say he lived a good life or did his best? He didn't even know her father. He only cared because her poppa was dead.

Galvius sniffed again. "Well, child, it's time to say your good-byes." He gently guided her to the open casket where her father reposed. Nothing of him looked right. His serious expression and the cold, waxen skin made him seem like another person. Life had left him. Her eyes drifted to his face where the concealed marks of a bruise were. Killed by the kick of a horse—

She blinked. Her father didn't die that way. She blinked again and saw his throat cut, bleeding into the casket. Her breathing quickened, and the knife dragged across his neck with a scream. The image flashed between this and the man in the casket, and her head swam with the image and sound until—

"Dad!" Hazel cried, jolting up.

She panted. For a moment she forgot where she was and it took several seconds for her to recognize her subterranean room at Kazra Lo Veedra. How long had it been? How long had she slept?

She exhaled and buried her face in her hands. He was alive. That was all that mattered. What was that strange dream about? She leaned back in bed when something in her periphery caught her attention. Turning her head, she saw the desiccated form of the lich sitting in the far corner of her room. She jolted upright. The lich observed her in silence.

A slight dark magenta light shimmered around him, matching the robes he wore. The being was grotesque, but also oddly fascinating. She had heard so much about liches over the years, and now she shared a room with one. It wasn't what she expected.

In the stories she read, and the poetry she heard sung by bards regarding the Seven Companions, liches were dangerous, bloodthirsty creatures who murdered for no other reason than because they enjoyed it. They were beings of near-infinite power who wished to drown the world in horrors. The one in front of her was placid and seemed content to simply sit there.

Hazel closed her eyes. She mentally pushed out, seeking living things around her. Was the lich alive? What would she feel when she reached out to sense him? She noticed something dark and sick for a moment before the presence retreated. There was something living about it, and yet... not. It was like a problem that needed to be fixed, or an open wound that needed healing.

"Do not touch me, child," the lich said in his strange, ubiquitous voice.

She opened her eyes and blinked at him. "What?"

"You reached out with sorcery to sense me. I am here, in this room, with you. Refrain from using such magics in my presence." His tone was not angry, but spoken with a level and didactic tone.

She shook her head. "Why are you here? Aren't you supposed to be guarding Alvaria?"

He cocked his head. "The geas stated I must protect her from anything that could thwart her ascension. At present, you are the greatest threat and so I am watching you."

"That seems like a pretty loose way to interpret it," Hazel said carefully. "She still has my parents, so trying to escape would be pointless."

"An astute observation. You are correct. A geas is powerful due to how vaguely it can be interpreted. It is rarely necessary to break a geas contract since workarounds are usually ample. I gave you my justification for being here according to the magic that binds me. My reason for interpreting it in such a way is because I wished to study you further." He inclined his head to her. "You had a dream, didn't you?"

"Yeah, I'm kind of famous for having those." She frowned. "It wasn't like anything I've seen before, though."

"I wouldn't expect it to be."

She quirked her head. "Did you do something to me?"

"Some gentle suggestions is all."

"But... why?"

"So that you could see the truth. What you heard before were merely words, but now you can see the veracity that lies behind them. A truth she may not want you to realize."

Hazel sat up. "What truth?"

The lich's gemstone eyes flashed in the light. "That is for you to discover."

This was going nowhere. She moved to get out of bed, but Zylit raised his hand. "Stay where you are."

She studied him curiously. His movements were immediate. So different from his previously calm demeanor. Was he...?

"Are you afraid of me?"

The lich didn't answer for a long stretch. "Not precisely."

"What do you mean?"

"I am incapable of most emotions. Joy, fear, hate, love, I no longer feel any of them. Is it possible to fear anything when emotions are nonexistent?"

Hazel remembered when she had recently risen from the grave. "I used to feel that way, too, when I rose from the dead. Maybe you'll feel emotions again in the future."

"Improbable."

"Why is that?"

He leaned back. "Because I am dead, and the dead are insensible to the passions of the living."

"But... I felt nothing before, and now I do. Couldn't it be the same for you?"

A deep chuckle echoed through the room. "You assume we are the same kind of being, but we are not. I returned from the dead, still dead, but you returned very much alive."

Hazel's eyes widened. She *was* alive. She wasn't some dead or undead creature. She was really, truly alive. "Are you sure? About me, I mean?"

"Child," the lich said, his chilling voice speaking in even tones, "I am as certain that you live as I am that I am a lich. You ask for certainty? Understand, then, that you are the most dangerous thing in this world to me. You are alive, yes, but more than that, you exude life itself, which makes you poisonous to me and all the undead."

"Is that what the magic surrounding you is for?"

"It is. It prevents living magic from entering, though I doubt it could withstand a barrage like you unleashed to power my sarcophagus."

She drew her knees up to her chest. "Then why risk being here?"

"You don't wish to kill me, and I was curious. Your existence is riddled with strange magics grown out of control. Besides, without my phylactery, destroying me would be temporary. I would still return, although it would be excruciating and time-consuming."

"Alvaria said I was brought back by a god who is now responsible for my power."

"That is only partially true. While a specific aspect of your power is divine, there is much that is altered. You are a combination of confusing—or at least confused—magic and chimerical parts."

She smiled. "I could have told you that." She considered his words. "Is it so difficult to understand what I am? Aren't liches supposed to be masters of magic?"

"We are, but consider this: a master chef leaves a small child with a plethora of food items. The child makes some mashed concoction of random ingredients and stirs them together in imitation of a great master chef. When the chef returns an hour later, do you think he will easily identify the ingredients in the child's absurd creation?"

She squinted at him. "That is an unexpectedly human metaphor."

"I was human once."

Zylit's expression had hardly changed at all from the beginning. His brownish yellow skin, nearly translucent, showed bones underneath. The eyes she looked into were gemstones which only gave the semblance of actual eyes, though they appeared feline.

"Was it worth it?" she asked.

"What do you mean?"

"Becoming a lich. Was it worth it?"

Zylit leaned back. "Your question is unclear. Elaborate."

"Was it worth becoming a lich if you would just end up losing your emotions? Was it worth killing a hundred people? Was it worth building this place so it could be stolen from you while you became a servant in its walls?"

"When I was human, I would have answered yes."

"What about now?"

"I cannot say," he replied, his ethereal voice a whisper. He lifted a hand and watched as a flicker of dark magenta slithered through his fingers. "I have lost my emotions, and regret was one of them. Without the emotional draw—or aversion—to alternatives, it is difficult to say whether lichdom is worthwhile. My existence may be one of the most wretched in the world, or the most blessed. It is impossible for me to say. I lack the capacity to feel joy or misery like I once did, so it is impossible to find value in anything save my existence."

"If you find no reason to exist, then why bother existing? Why not just... die?"

"O child, were that it was so simple," he said, leaning forward. His countenance suddenly darkened. "Though emotions are denied me, I have much knowledge of this world and of the world that comes after. The price of lichdom is not merely the deaths of oneself and others, but a complete refusal of the afterlife—of *any* afterlife, but one. What do you know of the afterlife, child?"

"Well, I've heard that there are as many afterlifes—lives? After-lives?—as there are gods. Depending on the god you worship when you die, you go to the one that matches you the most."

"That is a simplistic and largely incorrect understanding, though it aligns with what I recall being taught when I was human. There is but one afterlife. The beings within it are blessed or hindered by the gods who loved or despised them. The afterlife remains the same, but the perceptions of the dead turn it into a paradise or a prison. Despite the intervention of these deities, there is still but one god of the dead and she is not prone to forgiveness."

"So, what happens?" Hazel asked. Zylit had fallen silent, and she waited almost a minute before filling the silence herself.

"Semeleme is a goddess of chaos, though she permits more order than her kin. Those who rise as liches lose all access to the mercies of the gods. There is no intercession, no generosity that can reach us.

"As I returned to the land of the living, the Dark Lady spoke to me. *Return to my realm and I will bless you with my eternal judgment.* I then beheld the afterlife as she willed it to be. It was a place of monsters and torment, where no division exists between reason and madness, and the only certainty is a rising pain and fear. Every day in the land of the dead, liches die and are brought back by the Dark Lady. There is no end to it—there is no sense to it. The liches in that plane are stripped of their ability to reason and are granted only the knowledge that this has been taken from them."

He looked at Hazel, who sat stunned. "Maybe this life grants me no joy, but it preserves me from oblivion. For that reason alone, I strive to continue my existence at any cost."

She shivered. It sounded horrible. "Will that happen to me?"

"What do you mean?"

"I was brought back from the dead. Will she also make me suffer like that when I die?"

The lich mused on this. "I do not think so, but I cannot say for certain. The intractable goddess of death is difficult to predict for such finite minds as ours. I suspect that the return experienced by a lich differs from the resurrection you were granted. If there was some god involved in your revivification, then it seems probable you have that god to advocate for you. Some liches have attempted to appease other gods, but I doubt it availed them upon their demise."

"That isn't comforting."

"Liches are not known for their ability to put the living at ease."

A sudden thought occurred to Hazel. "Earlier, you said I was using sorcery. What did you mean?"

"I do not think that statement requires elaboration."

"Okay, but only a sorcerer or sorceress can use sorcery, right?"

"Only as a matter of definition. What humans call sorcery is the practice of sorcerers and sorceresses. The specific powers and uses are found in other creatures, though it is not termed as such. Why do you pursue this line of questioning?"

"Because I'm not a sorceress! I thought I could only talk with plants."

"That is a curious talent, but not related to the sorcery you used in trying to sense me. Were you not instructed by someone in the use of sorcery?"

"Yes, but only to help with my ability to see the future."

"He neglected to mention you could use sorcery. You are still but a neophyte in the lengthy practice of the art, but in time and with training you could hypothetically become a full sorceress."

Hazel scratched her head. "It's strange he didn't mention that."

"It is possible with the confusion of magics within you that sorcery seemed an insignificant thing. Perhaps the necromancer who summoned you altered your body in such a way as to give you the potential to learn sorcery."

"Maybe you're right. I suppose the ability to come back from the dead, heal things, and control plants eclipses the novelty of sorcery." She looked the lich up and down. "You've been very open with me. Why?"

He turned away. "I owe no allegiance to Alvaria, save what I am contractually obligated to fulfill. I speak with you because it is more intellectually stimulating than waiting in the sanctuary while she barks orders at her underlings."

"How long have I been unconscious?"

"Three days."

She nodded. How much could she trust this thing? "How go her preparations?"

He looked sideways at her. "According to plan. She awaits one final piece, but has contingencies in place if those who come to deliver it are delayed. I believe she will use a crystal temporal containment vessel to speed her ascension—most probably one of substantial power and delicacy. A clever contrivance made possible by the funding she possessed and alliances she forged."

"When is the latest she will start?"

"Tomorrow morning."

"What!" she exclaimed. "Why so soon?"

"The army of Selevara marches against her. She does not have time to waste waiting for a device that may be superfluous."

"They're coming." Hazel felt a smile grow on her face as a chill of excitement ran down her spine. "They got the message."

"Your plan was successful."

Hazel searched the lich's face with confusion and apprehension.

"I examined your mind as you slept and noticed your scheme. It was a risk, but it has reaped substantial rewards."

"You're going to tell Alvaria, aren't you?"

"To what end?" he asked. "She is aware they are coming. A familiar belonging to one inquisitor was killed by an advance scout two days ago. Four days prior to that, a messenger from some other individual came bearing news that an army marched against her. It is unnecessary for her to know of your involvement. I am tasked with protecting her, nothing more."

"I appreciate you keeping it a secret, but you shouldn't look into people's minds when they're sleeping, or even at all! That's terrible."

He tilted his head. "For perspective, you are talking to someone who has killed over a hundred innocent people to become a master of raising undead abominations. Looking through a person's memories is among the most innocent activities I've engaged in."

He had a point.

Zylit lifted his head as if noticing something. "I should depart." He glided off his chair and toward the door.

"Wait," Hazel said. "Why did you *actually* come here? I don't believe that you were just interested in me. Why did you give me the vision of Alvaria as a child?"

The lich paused. "My bond requires me to protect Alvaria Saccarra until she ascends to lichdom. What happens after is irrelevant. Remember what I've told you. Perhaps in time you will comprehend." He looked back at her. "Utilize your powers sparingly. By extending yourself to the point of exhaustion, your abilities have far outstripped anything you were previously capable of. Who knows what you might accomplish if you set your heart to it?"

The door opened from the other side to reveal Thomas standing outside. "The Grand Inquisitor demands your presence," he said to Zylit.

"Of course. It was pleasant conversing with you, Hazel Enda. Enjoy your captivity for the time you have it."

Chapter Twenty-Two
When the Dead Laugh

The inquisitor and the lich strode through the hall in silence, though the lich's feet never touched the ground. Thomas's skin crawled in the presence of this creature. For so many years, he'd been told that the undead were evil, disgusting beings, and upon coming into contact with one of the greatest examples of the undead, he understood. This lich was an abomination.

Thomas was no stranger to aberrant magic. He had, over the course of years, witnessed many uses for magic that contradicted the codes of the Inquisition. He beheld research delving into sacrificial magic, arcane grafts, curses, mental manipulation, and permanent transmutation. Some results had been grotesque, while others had been devoid of ethical judgment.

He looked at Zylit. This was the worst affront to the arcane arts he had ever beheld.

It wasn't a rational response, and he recognized it. The matter of sacrifices didn't bother him. He'd killed several people to get where he was, so it struck him as a natural progression for those who pursued great ambitions. The appearance of the being wasn't even what he found so odious, though it was unnerving. It was... difficult to understand.

"Something troubles you, Inquisitor Eller."

Thomas glanced at the lich. "More than one thing. These days there are many concerns."

"True though that may be, you are attempting to misdirect. When I noticed your discomfort, it was not the multitude of petty troubles hovering at the edges of your consciousness. It was me."

Thomas suppressed a shiver. The thought of Zylit touching his consciousness was appalling.

"You are the most revolting being I have ever encountered."

Zylit hovered in silence. "And...?"

"Does anything else *need* to be said? I have never encountered anything half as repulsive as you. Everything about you flies in the face of the natural world. It's as if I have the personification of corruption before me."

Zylit nodded slowly. "That is natural."

"Is that all you have to say?"

"What more is necessary? Your statements are less opinions than observations. You could as well walk outside and say, 'there is snow on the ground,' as state that a lich is aberrant. Little more needs to be said."

"It was new to me," Thomas grumbled.

The yellow cymophane eyes flashed at him. "Does it bother you that your leader strives to become one of us?"

"The Archmage of the Inquisition is *not* like you."

"She wishes to become a lich."

"And yet she will use living magic instead of sacrificial magic. She will rest in the afterlife for a century, but it will be only a day in our time. If a lich is exceptional, then Archmage Saccarra is extraordinary."

"She is more skilled than many who have ascended, but she is still resorting to the same fundamental magics. Perhaps there is some other problem that gnaws at you. What bothers you, Thomas Eller?"

Thomas shivered as the lich said his name. He looked at the lich. Zylit asked many questions. Probing questions. For a creature that was supposed to lack emotions, he demonstrated exceptional curiosity. "I don't trust you," he finally admitted.

"You do not trust me, though I have signed a geas contract?"

"Geas contracts are untrustworthy enough. You signed it without giving it half a thought, from what I heard."

"I deliberated, but ultimately found myself without leverage. The requests of Alvaria were reasonable enough. I wrote up a contract as agreeable to me as possible. She signed as quickly as I did without seeking any major amendments. Perhaps it is not me you do not trust rather than the judgment of your superior." He stared at Thomas. "Do you question Alvaria? Perhaps it is not Hazel Enda who poses a threat to her ascension but you."

"Don't be absurd." Thomas paled significantly but otherwise maintained composure. "My loyalty is not in question. I have worked for her for years, fully aware of her intentions."

"And just what *are* her intentions?"

"She wishes to rid the world of death for humanity. She wants to extend the lives of all beyond what they are currently capable of."

The eerie, reverberating laugh of the lich echoed in the halls. "Is that what you think?"

"It's what I think because it's *true.*"

"And that's *all* she wants? Her intentions are entirely selfless?"

Thomas hesitated. "Yes, mostly."

"Forgive me for thinking you would pose any threat to your master. You pose absolutely no threat whatsoever." The unnerving laugh echoed again through the halls.

Thomas looked the lich up and down. "If you lack emotions, how is it you have a sense of humor?"

Zylit floated ahead with his hands behind his back. "Some things are so absurd that even the dead may laugh."

Chapter Twenty-Three
Vision of the New World

The sun would rise in the next hour. Alvaria hadn't slept in the last couple of days in order to prepare for her day of ascendance. Exhaustion wore on her, but through magic and her own rising excitement, the lack of sleep became a minor inconvenience. The enemy was nearly upon them. Time had run out.

She stood in the central chamber, contemplating the sarcophagus. This room worked perfectly as a containment field. The magic that would be released by fulfilling the prophecy would fill this area and enter several enchanted diamonds she had arranged. They would attract and absorb much of the released energy within a certain distance, but given the sheer quantity that could be produced by a prophecy, she could triple the number of diamonds and still get less than half of the magic that would be released.

Hazel had finally awoken. A twinge of guilt remained in Alvaria when she remembered the girl crying out to her dying father. It was a necessary move, but a desperate one. The greater part of her guilt dissolved when Hazel succeeded in keeping her father alive. She inwardly thanked the girl for saving him, not just for the sake of powering the sarcophagus, but for keeping Alvaria from killing a parent who loved his daughter. It had taken courage to kill him and restraint to keep herself from saving him. Others had died over the years in her quest for ascendance, and it was justifying those deaths that spurred her on. She had come too far and done too much to relent before she completed her mission.

"Grand Inquisitor." One of her inquisitors genuflected before her. "Seven nosferatu vampires just arrived."

"Good. Show them in." She turned to another inquisitor. "Bring the urn from my study."

A few minutes later, she had the urn in hand, and not long after, the seven vampires approached. All were pale and dressed in black, save for short cloaks of small white feathers with various symmetrical patterns in black, brown, and yellow resembling eyes. Three of the vampires appeared to be leaders, while the other four who trailed were presumably for security.

"Greetings, Alvaria Saccarra," said one of the male vampires. He was the tallest and had the most apparent muscles. From his attitude, it wasn't hard to guess he considered himself their leader. "We have come, as you requested, both to deliver an item of great importance to you and to retrieve a relic of ours unjustly taken by the Inquisition many centuries ago."

Alvaria studied him and the others. Another male stood behind him. He was shorter and slighter than the leader and betrayed no emotions. A woman waited with arms crossed. She inspected the room critically, as if appraising potential threats. She was beautiful, but evoked a sense of fear from those who she looked at.

"We welcome you, Transcendent Society of the Moth," Alvaria said, "though we did not expect you so late."

"We were delayed by... research." The leader glared at the shorter vampire, who shrugged. "Forgive us for our late arrival, and for not introducing ourselves sooner. I am Orson zar Aeneus, the seneschal of our absent king. I am joined by the captain of our guard, Aviana za Serus, and our librarian and historian Mikhail zar Alacris."

"You are forgiven. It is a pleasure to meet all of you. Admittedly, the mission I had for you was one which required immediate action, so though you are later than I desired, it is natural. Fortunately, you are not *so* late that the trade cannot take place. Did you retrieve the item I requested?"

"We did, Lady Alvaria," Orson said. "We acquired the item from the Clandestine Society of Independent Researchers and Academics. The Oblate of Shadows especially wished us to express his excitement over your nearing ascension. Director Alson told us this was the extent to which they would help. They will not risk direct confrontation at this time."

"That is to be expected. I am honored the Oblate would wish me well. May I see what you brought?"

Orson nodded and waved a guard to come forward. The guard approached, carrying a small wooden crate. He handed it to an inquisitor, who opened it and dug through several thick blankets before revealing a large crystal jar. The cut of the crystal reflected rainbows across the room, even with only the dim magelamps and candles to illuminate it. Tiny diamonds were etched into the corners, which made the entire vessel difficult to look at. Alvaria stifled a grin. This was the most perfect time containment vessel she had ever seen. The miniscule diamonds would increase the rate of temporal suction, while the crystal would absorb the time into itself. This kind of craftsmanship was beyond the skill of many, even in Selevarian. The cost alone would have nearly bankrupted her department. Fortunately, she had connections that made obtaining such items a little easier.

"I am pleased," she said at last. "I don't suppose they responded to my request for magic in a bottle?"

"I'm afraid not. They appeared annoyed when we pressed the question, but they would only say was it was *unnecessary*."

"It was worth a try, regardless." *Magic in a bottle* was a phrase used by the Clandestine Society of Independent Researchers and Academics to denote any kind of subjugated djinn. She had spent her entire life as a spellcaster trying to locate a djinn she could control, but to no avail. The Clandestine Society likely possessed a djinn, but the chances were slim to none they would let her even know about it, let alone use it. She may have sat on their high council, but they still viewed her more as an asset than a leader. Both the Society and the Council of Archmages had treated her similarly, and both had made her current circumstances possible.

She held up the gold encrusted pot. "Are you certain you want the urn as recompense? You are, of course, welcome to it, but it seems a small price to pay for such excellent service."

"We are certain," Orson replied. "Our task was no less difficult or easy than your own. Were our roles reversed, I think it would have been easier for you to obtain that vessel than for us to steal into the Inquisition's vaults."

"True enough," she said, extending the urn to them. Before Orson could take it, Alvaria withdrew her hand and motioned for him to wait. "Before I give it to you, I should provide some additional information. I do not know what this urn is supposed to be used for, but the original purpose may no longer be feasible. When it was confiscated by the Inquisition, my predecessor thought it would be wise to discover its contents. There was a spell that sealed it and rendered the urn impervious to external damage. That enchantment has been dispelled. The contents at the time were simply dust—presumably the ashes of some long-deceased creature—but there was nothing magical about it. As it presently stands, neither the container nor the ashes are magical. Is that a problem?"

Orson and Aviana glanced nervously at Mikhail, who stood as emotionless as before. "May I see it?" he asked calmly.

"Certainly."

The vampire stepped forward and examined the urn. His eyes darted over its surface and he murmured observations to himself as he studied it. He opened the lid briefly before replacing it and giving it back to Alvaria. "It should be fine. The enchantments were to preserve its contents. If the ashes are still contained, then—according to *The Histories* and *Memoirs*—we will still be capable of using it." The other vampires heaved a sigh of relief. Orson stepped forward to take the urn, but Alvaria raised a hand to stop him.

"I wonder," she said, "what a group of vampires from the Transcendent Society of the Moth would want with ashes? It is strange to me. This odd scenario leads me to ponder another question I have not yet found the answer to: to whom to do the ashes belong?"

The other vampires glanced at each other. Orson's face tightened as he met her eyes. They stood in tense silence for a long moment.

"It was just a matter of curiosity," Alvaria said with a casual shrug, handing the urn to Orson. "As a token of goodwill, perhaps I can have that re-enchanted? It will take about a day, but it should make the urn safer to transport."

"It's fine as it is," Orson said. The vampire maintained the barest air of civility with her. Perhaps she'd struck a nerve?

Mikhail looked between them. "It might be wise to—"

"It's *fine*," Orson growled. Mikhail stepped back, and the larger vampire returned his attention to Alvaria. "We appreciate the offer, but our mission calls for speed and any delay would ultimately be problematic."

"Very well. You seven are free to use the lower rooms to rest in, if you wish. I must apologize, however. War looms on the horizon and we may be besieged by the next sunset. For vampires of your considerable talent, you should be able to move past the enemy unscathed. Given that, I offer my hospitality, flawed though it is."

Orson frowned. "Your hospitality is unnecessary."

"Do you have a better place for us to rest, Orson?" Aviana asked. Her voice was sharp. "I'd love to hear about it."

Orson glared at her, and she glared back. Mikhail cleared his throat. "I think the offer from the Grand Inquisitor is generous and fortuitous. We can depart after resting and avoid the sun. We would be incapable of swift travel in the sunlight and in our weakened state we would be unable to provide sufficient protection for the reliquary."

"Very well," Orson grumbled. "We shall accept your offer."

"Excellent," Alvaria said, "I will have my servants show you to your chambers and bring blood wine with them in case you require a refreshment—though I've heard you may object to its consumption."

"You heard right," Orson replied, showing his fangs as he spoke. He lingered a moment and then turned to follow Alvaria's servants. Aviana rolled her eyes and made to follow him along with the others.

Alvaria smiled as they turned to leave. "Oh, and say hello to your master for me when you see him, won't you?"

The vampires turned sharply. She felt someone trying to read her mind. The touch was subtle, but she was a skilled sorceress. She looked at Mikhail. "Trying to read the mind of your host? That's a little rude, don't you think?"

Orson shot Mikhail a look, but the vampire just shrugged.

"No matter, you are forgiven. Give your master my best and good luck with your mission. Accomplishing what you have in mind will be far more challenging than what I'm about to do."

Orson nodded warily and walked out with the others.

"Is it wise to antagonize the vampires?"

She looked at Zylit, who had been hovering quietly nearby. "They won't do anything to jeopardize my mission. It would be counterproductive."

"Their leader appeared ready to do something counterproductive on his own before his two lieutenants intervened."

"True. It's strange that *he* was the leader. Regardless, we now have the item we need. Zylit, as my guardian, I need you to protect the sarcophagus and temporal vessel. Once the time has elapsed, teleport it somewhere safe. You alone will oversee my ascension."

"It shall be done."

"Grand Inquisitor, forgive me for disagreeing," Thomas said. He stood close at hand for anything she might need. "I think a detachment of inquisitors should guard you instead."

"What is your reasoning?" she asked.

"The inquisitors are better suited to obey and attend to your every need."

"Really?" she said, approaching the inquisitor, who suddenly looked uncomfortable. "Do you think you could protect me better than Zylit? He is contractually obligated to work for me until my ascendance. Can you be more loyal than one compelled by magic, or more powerful than a lich?"

"Lady Alvaria, we can do much to assist you—"

"I agree. That is why I need you and the others to guard Kazra Lo Veedra with your lives. Zylit is simultaneously the most powerful and most temperamental agent I have. If he is destroyed by fighting with the army, then we stand no chance against the forces which oppose us. If he remains here, the undead will shield us long enough that the inquisitors should suffer few casualties."

"That makes sense, but—"

"No, Thomas, you *will* listen." She drew herself up. She had slept little and grown tired of his micromanagement and excessive worries. "I spent the last fifty years strategizing, planning, and working to reach this moment. I examined every outcome and created contingencies for every failure. *I* am the strategist. You are mistaken to doubt me. Continuing to question this will bring into doubt your belief in my competence, which I *will not allow.*"

Thomas stiffened. "Of course, archmage, forgive me. We will aid you by defending the estate to our last."

"That is what I want to hear. You will be rewarded for your loyalty. Now fetch the Alchemist. It is time to begin."

Zylit watched as Thomas left. "He wishes to live forever and believes you are his only hope. That is why he questions."

She crossed her arms and leaned against the tomb. "Loyalty can be won through many means—love, fear, or respect—but in my experience, greed commands the greatest devotion."

"Mercenaries are easily bought and sold."

"True. Ordinary people seeking riches and all that money can afford are inconsistent. I don't speak of the uneducated rabble whose lowest desires fuel their decisions. I refer to those who seek the impossible. Those are the ones I've attracted to my cause. I offer them the one thing in the world they want, and they cannot get it from anyone else. Complex men have complex desires. It is a human flaw that can be useful in the right circumstances."

"Your alleged mission is a hoax, then?"

She smiled. "I am quite sincere in bringing immortality to humanity. Whether they care about my goals is secondary to their belief that I can bring it about. Some may be altruistic in their views and convince themselves they are part of a greater movement, but in the end, they work because they will be paid."

"And yet you ask them to risk their lives."

"Yes, I do." She met the lich's eyes. "This drives fanaticism: the belief that one is unquestionably right, that one will be rewarded for their work, and that an enemy exists who would deprive them of that reward. The Inquisition has ever been the department of zealots and the self-righteous. Those who joined me had that drive—I merely redirected it. They will die because they know when I become a lich, I will raise them from the dead. They have murdered, lied, and labored tirelessly to uphold my mission. In their minds, there is little distinction between who I am and what I do. Thomas wishes to protect me, not because of love or friendship, but because I am his future. I am the one who will grant life eternal and justify all his evils."

Zylit's face was unreadable. "You need not convince me, Alvaria. I am not one of your sycophants begging for scraps from your table. Especially since all that begging will come to naught."

She waved dismissively. "You are too pessimistic. I *will* ascend."

"That is correct. I have no doubts in that regard."

"Then you question the promises I've made?"

Zylit hovered away, his arms behind his back. "I remember a young mage who sacrificed everything to escape mediocrity. He wanted to become a lich and killed many. He didn't enjoy it, and silently—within himself—he promised each one that they would return to their previously happy lives. It comforted him."

Alvaria raised an eyebrow. "You could still revive them."

"I could, yes, but Antony Larsinius never will."

"Even if you have changed, you are still who you were."

"That is incorrect. My soul is historically the same, but is not identical to that of my former self."

She rubbed her temples. "I understand what you mean, but fail to see how it applies. I am not the exact person I was a minute ago, but I am still mostly the same. When I was a little girl, I hated celery, and I *still* hate celery to this day. The ephemera of our lives wax and wane, but our deeply held convictions remain. You may now lack the drive to fulfill the promises you once held dear, but that does not justify breaking your word."

"Have you never promised wonders to a lover, only to later end things between you?"

She rolled her eyes. "I was never one for romance."

"Then perhaps you made promises to someone else you loved." He leaned in closer. "Promises you couldn't keep."

Alvaria's blood ran cold. "Tread carefully, Zylit."

"Very well. Have you ever come to a conclusion that later proved false, although you were certain it was correct?"

"Of course."

"That is the nature of promises. When you die, they die with you. Returning from the grave does nothing to alter that singular fact. Antony Larsinius cannot bring those people back to life because Antony Larsinius no longer exists. I could honor the sentiment, but it would amount to nothing more than vacuous homage."

"I doubt the dead would see it that way."

His eyes shined. "And how *do* you think they would see it? Would they bless me for correcting an evil? No. Even if they were granted new life, it has been nearly seventy years since their sacrifice. No one lives who would remember their names or care that they had returned. Their revival would do nothing to amend the lives they lost. No, to bring them back would be a mockery of their deaths. If I brought them to life, they would exist forever with the toothless misery of returning from the dead to a world that neither cares nor appreciates what they've lost."

"Not all the dead must feel that way," Alvaria said, resting a hand on a small wooden box a servant had brought in. "Some might be grateful to return."

"Name one."

"Hazel Enda."

Zylit chuckled. "You would base your argument on a divinely powered anomaly?"

"If it happened once, it can happen again."

Zylit drifted away. "All but one, and one is all. Your speculation does not hinge on her but on your assumptions about one of the dead."

"What?"

"Remember, Grand Inquisitor, you can contrive the same circumstances and do everything perfectly and still yield different results."

Alvaria was about to respond when Thomas reentered the room with Paxton Averly in tow. The alchemist had several bottles in his hands as his eyes flicked around the room nervously.

"Thank you, Thomas. I would also like you to collect Miss Enda, if you don't mind. I would like her to be here to witness history. She deserves to, given her contribution."

She turned to Zylit. "Nothing will prevent me from becoming a lich. I will uphold my promises and bring life to the world."

Zylit bowed and hovered backward. The lich was evidently unconvinced, but Alvaria would soon be a lich unlike any other. The living lich of half a day. She would bring life to those around her and save all she cared about from death. The world was about to change forever.

Chapter Twenty-Four
Where Creatures Go to Die

Finding the path to Kazra Lo Veedra hadn't been difficult. Lara occasionally jogged ahead to plot a route to the destination, but even without her heightened sense of smell and excellent tracking abilities, it would have been evident. The snow, which had fallen after the Inquisition had passed through, made discovering the tracks annoying but not impossible. Years of travel by carriage and wagon had carved a path not only into the ground but through the surrounding foliage. Beyond that, the hippogriff scouts had confirmed the location they had on their maps.

Despite the redundancy of her mission, Lara continued to track. It gave her time to think. Out here, she was in her element. Lyvaelan and Alistair were both exceptionally smart guys. They were also in the company of mages. Somehow, life had thrown her in with a crowd substantially better educated than her. She didn't mind not receiving much in the way of a formal education; she was confident in her own abilities. Still, the endless strategy talks exhausted her. She understood the importance of a basic plan, but until they knew what they were fighting, what was the point of calculating the minutia?

The enemy could be exactly as they predicted or completely different. Given how much Alvaria had hoodwinked everyone, she suspected another trap would be coming soon.

The rest of the group trailed a few hours behind her, and the estate itself should be less than an hour from her current position. In her half-wolf form she could sprint for hours without tiring. She had eventually returned to human form to maintain stealth, but running wild for the time she did had been immensely freeing, even if it meant being mostly nude in the snow.

The army had brought along several wagons but prioritized the soldiers and mages, only bringing a few important carts along with the main group. Getting through the snow was initially challenging, but being in an army full of spellcasters made the situation much easier than it could have been. Pack animals needed less rest and food while the road before them cleared of snow and hardened, allowing the wagons to progress unimpeded. The mages accomplished this as if it was rudimentary.

Stupid spellcasters with their stupid magic, Lara thought. *They always have it so easy.*

She grudgingly thanked her father mentally. He may have been the biggest bastard she'd ever known, but he was an excellent tracker. She may have possessed better senses than any human, but those skills were useless if she didn't hone them properly. He taught her to recognize various tracks, how to smell the differences in the blood of various creatures, or how to determine the age of a corpse. She learned of the hidden warrens of rabbits and the lofty dreys of squirrels. More than once, he led her into the deepest woods and abandoned her to find her own way back home. He had been utterly useless as a father, but was a damn good survivalist and raised her to follow in his footsteps—literally and figuratively. The man tolerated no weakness, and her stubbornness meant she consistently rose to the challenge.

She rubbed her arms for warmth. When she moved, she could endure frigid weather without a problem, but the moment she slowed down was when the cold crept up on her, especially when she went without shoes or sleeves. Her normal clothes hung in rags from her transformation, except for a thick cloak that remained unaffected by her shapeshifting. Her breath curled around her as she waited. She knew the direction to go in, but needed to tread carefully. This close to Kazra Lo Veedra, she believed greater caution was called for than usual.

Lara sniffed the air as a wind whispered past from the southwest. Her sense of smell was better than even some dogs, but the winter months brought annoying challenges. Most smells didn't carry as far as they normally would, which meant she couldn't track all the nearby changes in location. On the other hand, the limited number of scents made noticing those that *did* appear substantially easier. As she smelled the breeze, the faintest aroma of sweat and blood wafted from the south.

A faint stumbling crash sounded through bushes some distance away in the smell's direction. She stealthily crept to the sound, occasionally sniffing to confirm the direction. The creature cried out. *A deer?* Lara saw the animal leaning against a tree. Its steaming breath filled the air with ragged pants. Gashes along its flank and a deep bleeding wound revealed the animal didn't have long to live. That, and the trail of dripped blood behind it. Whether this was the work of an animal or man was unclear from Lara's perspective, but whatever had hunted it no longer did so now. It likely outran its pursuers with a brief surge of energy before succumbing to the gravity of its wounds.

Lara stepped out toward the deer and faced it. It was a doe, middle-aged or older, but not elderly. The animal noticed Lara but made no motion to flee.

"Poor hunted animal," Lara sighed. "What happened? Did a hunter get you with a bow but wasn't able to finish the job? Maybe you outran a wolf or two? I know I'm one to talk given that I'm—"

The deer staggered toward Lara. She backed up slightly, confused that the animal would approach a stranger, but the deer didn't react. Lara wondered if the deer was rabid, but noticed no signs of it. The werewolf stepped aside, and the deer lurched past her. Curious, Lara followed. The doe continued to stumble forward, occasionally stopping to lean on a tree and pant. Still, she trudged on.

Over the course of the next hour, Lara tracked the injured doe. Several times she fell, and it seemed to Lara the animal would not rise, only for the creature to pick herself up and continue forward. Where was she going? Why had she completely ignored the werewolf? After an hour, the doe gained greater energy despite heavy blood loss and let out a desperate bleat. The creature jump-staggered out of the tree line almost ten feet and collapsed to the ground. Lara rushed up. The doe's eyes were open, and vacant. She was dead. Lara looked up and about half a mile away stood a wide building in the middle of the clearing. She stared at the deer. The animal died excited. Happy, even. Lara sniffed the air.

She froze. She sniffed again. The smell of decay surrounded her. It was faint, covered by the light blanket of snow, but she knew it was there. This deer hadn't come here to survive.

She came to die.

Lara viewed the expanse in the predawn light and backed into the forest. She knew what this place was.

She had arrived at Kazra Lo Veedra.

Chapter Twenty-Five
To Die is to Dream of Tomorrow

Alvaria had stripped down into a linen body wrap that left less to the imagination than she would have normally desired. Liches commonly wore such wrappings before their ascendance. Whether the partial mummification aided in bodily preservation or acted as part of the arcane process was unclear, but it was an easy step to take and she would leave nothing to chance. She needed to be dressed minimally for this ceremony regardless, but she didn't relish the thought of being practically nude before so many of her subordinates.

"Paxton, do you have the concoctions I requested?"

The Alchemist shuffled forward with a bowl in one hand and a red liquid with purple flecks in a glass bottle. He made an effort to only look her in the eyes but then quickly cast his gaze elsewhere nervously. "I have done as you asked, my lady, though I can only vouch for the ointment. This other potion is unknown to me. If I may, I fear this may be dangerous to ingest—"

"I should hope so. It's supposed to kill me."

His eyes widened. "I—but why?"

"Because in order to live again, I must first die. It will be a temporary death, thankfully." She took the bottle and set it aside. Her gaze drifted to Hazel, who stood between two guards. The girl kept her emotions in check, but anger burned within her. It was better than Alvaria expected. If she had been in Hazel's place, she would've leaped at any opportunity to kill her. As it stood, she merely appeared to disapprove of the proceedings.

"I would like to announce," Alvaria said, "that once I have become a lich, Hazel Enda and her family are free to go immediately. If they should choose to leave, no one is to impede their travel. If they seek provisions for their journey, they are welcome to them. When I have ascended, I will place them under my personal protection. Until that time, they will remain my involuntary guests. They will be confined to their rooms once I have been placed in the sarcophagus." The servants nodded in acknowledgement. Alvaria strode up to the girl, her bare feet lighting on the cold, stone floor. She spoke a little more quietly to Hazel, "I'm sorry that this is the best thanks I can give you for the tremendous work you've done for me. I know I cannot thank you for helping without sounding exceptionally conceited or cruel, but please believe my gratitude is genuine. You have saved a hundred people from dying by assisting me, and you've saved me from having to kill them myself, which I am doubly grateful for. You may not see it this way now, but one day you may be proud of how you contributed to today's events."

Hazel stood defiantly before her. There was so much courage in this young woman surrounded by enemies. "*In the presence of the unending shadow, a darkness shall rise. No light shall purge it from the world, and self-sustaining shall it be. The living lich of half a day shall rise with legions of undead that none can kill. Through betrayal of friends and oath, the living lich shall trample bodies and hearts. The world will quake as the impossible becomes the inevitable. The living lich of half a day may only be stopped by the slow progress of time. The time of the lich is here.*" Hazel shook her head. "You *will* be stopped, even if it takes forever. I will stop you."

Alvaria shook her head. The girl could not be swayed. It would be admirable if it weren't so misplaced. She walked back to the sarcophagus and held up the red potion. *Lich's Tea,* it was sometimes called, though it was neither brewed nor served hot. *So beautiful and strange. Like droplets of blood suspended in blood. How appropriate that a lich should perish by such a liquid after killing so many.*

She looked to her constituents. All was prepared, they only awaited her word. "On this day, I transcend humanity. On this day, death itself shall die. Immortality lies within our grasp. Many of you have toiled for this outcome, and now the time is here. Soon we shall rejoice, and our tears will be for joy and not for sorrow.

"I will not extoll the virtues you have exemplified heretofore, though they are many. Nor will I remind you of my promises to you, for they are known to us all. I have ever been a woman of action and now is not the time for honeyed words to those who have no need for them. Instead, I want you all to bear witness to an event that will shake the world to its foundations and cause even gods to tremble in fear and anger as they behold the rise of the living lich of half a day!" Alvaria downed the contents of the bottle, ignoring its pungency and bitter taste. She set the bottle down and looked at Paxton. "Bring me the ointment." She gestured at nearby attendants. "Apply it."

The ointment was likely unnecessary. A redundancy in case Hazel's magic was insufficient to keep her body intact, even in death. After witnessing her display of power, it indeed seemed superfluous but if one had many resources, it was wise to make use of them.

The room fell silent as her attendants hurried to apply the alchemical ointment. She felt a tingling numbness in her fingers. The Lich's Tea was taking effect. The ointment was cold, but the creeping numbness had spread over her skin. Within minutes of ingesting the poison, sluggishness and exhaustion weighed upon her. After they applied the ointment, she got into the sarcophagus and took one last look around. She wondered if she hadn't just killed herself without reason. Others came forward to help her, but she dismissed them. Who could understand the gravity of all she had done?

"I stand on the precipice of eternity," she whispered to no one in particular. "In whose company shall I belong? Without peer and without equal, I tread alone to the summit of high mountains. Who will meet me there? Now that I see the end and feel it reaching for me, I find myself afraid. What awaits me in the dark beyond?"

The room faded, and everyone but Zylit disappeared. The lich hovered on the opposite side of the sarcophagus. If the skull and gemstones could express anything gentle, she beheld it now. "You will find all that you have dreamed and dreaded. You cannot turn aside from the path you have chosen."

"I know. It is a road I found and claimed many years ago. Through meticulous planning and so much blood, I have become master of this destiny. Am I wrong, now, to fear it? Is it wrong for me to fear the end of my life?"

The lich slowly drifted up and away. "You have chosen the path that rejects the dichotomy of right and wrong. Sleep, Alvaria Saccarra, and dream the dreams of those who will wake at the end of time."

The room returned, and the others gave no sign of noticing anything she said to Zylit. The poison moved into her face and all movements came with great effort. He was right. She stood beyond the edicts of good and evil. All that remained was her will to forge a new reality. With a small surge of magic to ameliorate the numbness in her tongue, she proclaimed, "I do not die so much as I dream of tomorrow when the world will be made new!" She pulled herself into the tomb and laid back. Whether it was the lid sliding over her or death finally taking her, Alvaria fell into total darkness.

Chapter Twenty-Six
The Archmage of War

They established camp by midmorning along the fringes of the forest west of Kazra Lo Veedra. Sorcerers created static illusions that the forest remained undisturbed by their presence, but it likely did little good. Alvaria had shown forethought enough to create a contingency plan in case Lysander visited Chateau Zarielle. He doubted she would be caught unawares in the stronghold of a lich. The familiar killed by hippogriffs would've alerted her. No, there was no point in masking their presence. She knew they approached.

He surveyed the soldiers, taking stock of their current resources. They had no war machines to speak of besides a few small battering rams, but against a small estate, such measures were unnecessary. With the arcane defenses that likely surrounded the building, it was improbable catapults would have helped. The soldiers were prepared for battle, though tired from the swift march he had ordered over the last couple of days. He crossed his arms and gazed across the future battlefield. The pure white of the snow would soon be stained by the blood of many. Men and women who trusted him with their lives would inevitably die in this assault. People who had families, dreams, and varied interests would die in the next twelve hours. Those soldiers without magic were called "brave," to differentiate them from the magically "gifted." A well-intentioned contrivance to boost morale in the face of often insurmountable odds, though Lysander found the irony sickening. What good was courage against magic?

He briefly contemplated starting the assault sooner than later, but decided against it. Not only did these soldiers need rest, but he sensed a trap waiting to be sprung. This open area was too inviting and calm to be natural. Animals had not appeared in the woods for almost a mile around. What few tracks they found led to the clearing and ended with corpses. The carrion remained untouched by buzzards or crows, and other creatures avoided the area altogether. This wasn't an innocent field; this was a graveyard with Kazra Lo Veedra as its church of unnatural death. Lara mentioned feeling uneasy, and he experienced the same discomfort that couldn't be attributed to pre-battle nerves. This place evoked a primal disgust.

Perhaps more than that, something sinister lurked within Kazra Lo Veedra that made his skin crawl. That ominous presence was connected to the sensation here, though its exact nature remained hidden. Many records of Kazra Lo Veedra had been expunged by the Inquisition prior to Alvaria's departure. He obtained information from Malvex, which was useful, but likely outdated and incomplete. He knew Kazra Lo Veedra had been built in the middle of an old battlefield and many dead now rested around its perimeter. The surrounding magic attracted dying creatures. This perverse method of collecting the dead was intended for one purpose: creating an army.

He turned and entered the war tent they had erected for the archmages. Using sorcery, he summoned them. A table of molded earth stood in the middle. It had hardened into a fine gloss and left no particles when leaned on. The temperature inside was comfortably warm, and the ground was dry. One by one, the archmages arrived, and he mentally appraised their skills and uses in war.

Garson Varaldan, the Archmage of Dragons, stepped in first. Conjuration and wizardry were his areas of expertise. He could main-

tain calm determination in situations that commanded it. Throughout his long life, he fought many abusers of magic, some of whom
possessed power beyond the average spellcaster. Despite his carefree
attitude, he was a proficient strategist and a reliable ally. Amplified by
the gift of dragons, his magic reservoir surpassed many archmages
while his scaled skin put the strongest chain mail to shame.

Elliavenra Sivenna, the Archmage of Lights, entered next. She
was not a fighter, but *was* a protector. Her magic focused on using
light similar to the kind emitted by thaumaturgy. While the light was
not as effective at healing as close-range thaumaturgy, it still filled
good men with hope while inflicting pain and fear on the undead.
She was kind and generous to everyone and would not tolerate cruelty. Alvaria's betrayal hurt all of them and filled her with grim resolve.

Corrim Kalsidere entered after, although he refused to be called
by his name. Rather, he named himself the Crystal King, or the
Archmage of Crystals. Various gemstones comprised his body, with
the majority resembling quartz and diamond. Harsh, sapphire eyes
darted about the room. Quartz spikes protruded from his shoulders
and glasslike spikes made for his hair. He appeared more monster
than man, though he had not always been this way. Research had
twisted him into something both more and less than human. His
body of animated gemstones would be difficult for any enemy to destroy. Ferocious in the friendliest of interactions, in serious conflicts,
he entered a frenzy. The arcane conduction of the crystals around his
body could easily extend thaumaturgical effects far beyond himself.
His ability to create gemstones of any size with little effort provided
them with much-needed versatility.

Bumbling through the tent flap, looking lost, came the
Archmage of the Green, Bertrand Rollodore. This archmage was
largely unknown to Lysander, despite being one of the oldest. Some
natural magic blessed him, that rendered him permanently green and
mentally unstable with arcane madness. When he was lucid enough
to speak, it was more than half nonsense. Still, he had desired to be
there, and the High Archmage believed he would help. That he vol-

unteered may have been the strings of fate at play. Perhaps his natural magic would help deter the unnatural undead.

Besides these archmages were two of the highest members of the Guard Unyielding. These mages possessed ample ability with magic and the sword. Their serious eyes spoke of the intense experiences they had endured to reach their current rank. Lysander knew firsthand their training was the best of all combat education. He had experienced it once, and changed the program when he was first appointed Archmage of War to include training in unarmed combat and improvised magic and alchemy. In wartimes the Guard Unyielding provided a small group of elites to carry out missions requiring high adaptability and power. They upheld efficiency and tenacity as virtues beyond most spellcasters.

With all his generals gathered, it was time for the Archmage of War to lay out the strategy. He laid both hands on the earthen table and eased magic into it, creating a detailed map of the area along its surface. "All of us are here for one reason: to stop Alvaria Saccarra. She has betrayed all she stood for. Still, I would prefer to take her in to stand trial than to execute her here. This book"—he held aloft Hazel's journal—"details a prophecy that states a legion of undead will rise that cannot be killed. The source of these undead should be clear. We all feel the death in this place. With that in mind, I have a basic plan that we shall follow.

"Garson, you will act as general of the outside forces. I know you care little for leadership, but you're our best option. Commander Castus will assist you." He looked to one of the Guard Unyielding, who nodded. "I cannot predict every move of the enemy, so I need you to adapt to the situation in my absence. You will lead the assault on the western front."

"And where will you be, Archmage of War?" The Crystal King asked, his voice characteristically cold and cutting.

"I will lead a covert group of the Guard Unyielding into Kazra Lo Veedra from the eastern side. Our goal will be to strike hard without raising the alarm. Whatever lich controls the undead, it will be our job to destroy and give you the opportunity to lead the forces unimpeded into the estate."

"'Whatever lich'?" the Archmage of Lights said. "What do you mean? I thought it was known that Alvaria would be the lich."

"That is true," Lysander said, "but we should work under the assumption there are two liches to contend with instead of one."

"On what grounds?" growled the Archmage of Crystals. "Egotistical monsters such as them rarely collaborate. What makes you speculate two would act with a common goal?"

"Kazra Lo Veedra once belonged to a man who sought lichdom. We had confirmation he was destroyed, but neither his tomb nor his body were ever brought into Palace Valsidan. Given Alvaria's involvement, I think it's likely she sent false information to Selevarian while preserving the future lich's existence. I pondered this possibility as we traveled here, but now I feel certain she woke the lich before its time." He held a hand to objections. "I know this is difficult to accept, so I do not demand you accept it as fact. I would love for our battle to be as simple as walking up to the doors, but she has outwitted us at every step. Knowing that archmages would come to prevent her ascension, she would use only the most powerful beings at her disposal to ensure her success. I think it's *likely* she would enlist the aid of a lich, especially one who knows the grounds. Given her complete control over the estate, it would make sense she could control a lich who would protect her until she could protect herself. There may not be one, but I cannot deny the possibility."

He gestured at the map on the table. "I would like the Archmage of Crystals to be in the northernmost edge of the assault. If our force is in danger of being surrounded, I know you can thin their army and protect the northern flank. The Archmage of Lights should be with the bulk of the army, preferably wherever the highest density of soldiers and undead are located. Garson will lead the western assault with a preference to the south."

"What about me?" The Archmage of Green asked as he stared off into the distance. "The trees do not whisper for fear of being heard, nor grass that slumbers deep, but in the ground only dead things wait which leaves will not speak of. No flower has given me direction and so I must be planted where the soil will take me."

The Crystal King scoffed. "What nonsense!"

Lysander smiled at the Archmage of the Green kindly. "I would like you to assist with the false southern assault and make certain the southernmost flank is not encircled."

"False southern assault?" the Archmage of Crystals said. "What southern assault?"

"I am sending the Evenfall Vigil in through the south to do as much damage as possible and divide their attention."

"What makes you think they will be as unexpected as you say?"

"Because it's possibly their most defining characteristic," said a voice from the corner. A black dog emerged from the shadows. The Guard Unyielding advanced, but Lysander waved them back.

"Ambassador Garo. Will you join us in the siege?"

He barked a laugh. "You couldn't stop me if you tried." His green eyes gleamed dangerously.

Lysander nodded. "Garo will lead the Evenfall Vigil in the southern assault with the Archmage of the Green providing support. It's settled."

"As to the specifics of your strategy," Garson said, "how long do you want us to press the attack?"

"Until my team has destroyed the puppeteer of the undead, or until the army has entered the estate and secured it."

Garson hesitated. "And if you should fail in that?"

The tent was silent. It was a question no one wanted to ask but still needed to be addressed.

Lysander tapped the table absently. "It's likely Kazra Lo Veedra is shielded from sorcery, so I won't be able to contact you directly. As such, from the moment I leave, I want you to push the attack for the next two hours at least. If our forces are doing well but the undead remain, continue to cut them down. If our casualties rise and the tide turns, I want you to immediately order an organized retreat."

"To where?" The Archmage of Lights asked. "The undead are tireless and will not stop attacking simply because we flee."

"That's true. In such a case, I would like the Archmage of Crystals to create a crystalline perimeter the soldiers can retreat to. Something that will amplify and spread thaumaturgy. As part of our preparations, I would like you, Crystal King, to erect an amethyst gate that can send soldiers as close to Tellaris as possible."

"What?" the Crystal King roared. "Never! Such a thing is—"

"Necessary," Lysander said firmly. "Make it strong enough to transport soldiers, but weak enough to be destroyed. Obliterate it without entering it yourself, if you wish, but do not allow my men to die. If none of us survives to spread the news of Alvaria's ascension, then the whole Gray Empire will be in trouble and the Council of Archmages will surrender all credibility and many innocent lives will be lost. This is not my first choice of action, so understand this is only for the direst of circumstances. In fact, I want the amethyst gate created immediately following this meeting. If we are routed, then we cannot waste time waiting for it to be built and enchanted.

"I hope the Paladin Order of Kalendril will find their way north to us shortly, but I have no way of contacting them, and their main house is hundreds of miles south. We can hope they arrive in time, but we cannot trust that as a certainty. Are there questions?"

"Yes," Garson said, "I'm no master of military strategy. How am I supposed to lead these soldiers?"

"To the best of your abilities. Besides that, I have specific formations in mind, given the likely presence of undead.

"I want the soldiers in front to protect the mages. Brave tower shields should form the perimeter of the army with thaumaturgically gifted spearmen and pikemen behind them. When the dead are raised, they will likely be zombies, so chopping them down should be easy so long as you hold formation. We will not use archers, since enchanted arrows are in limited supply and would do little to deter the undead. Wizards should primarily focus on arcane shields against whatever ranged attacks the inquisitors may hurl at the main force and should be stationed toward the middle of the force behind gifted soldiers. Conjurers will prepare countermeasures to the summoned creatures of the Inquisition from the trees where they will mostly go unnoticed. A small company of brave soldiers, thaumaturgists, and sorcerers will protect them from any undead that may unexpectedly stumble upon them. All gifted soldiers should remain with the body of the army and placed according to specialization."

"If the zombies are easily counteracted," the Crystal King said, "then why speak of retreat? We are some of the greatest mages in the world. Why consider withdrawing at all?"

"Fighting individual zombies is usually not problematic," Lysander replied. "In larger groups on the field of battle, however, they can be a challenge for multiple reasons. Unlike human soldiers, they are immune to any psychological tactics that may be leveled against them. They feel no fear, remorse, pain, or sense of self-preservation. We exploit this by chopping through a flood of creatures who do nothing to defend themselves, but that relentlessness can take a toll on our army. The grotesque nature of the undead also psychologically affects us adversely. If soldiers die, the lich will control them, and then the soldiers will fight their own friends and siblings in combat, which can quickly cause a break in rank and morale.

"As many of you know, the undead require little to remain in existence. To kill a zombie requires either an extreme quantity of fire, thaumaturgy, living magic, decapitation and destruction of the head, or dismemberment in flowing water. All other methods do nothing but hamper them. These are the methods we must employ. If we do not, then the risk arises that they will seem unkillable to our soldiers, which will demoralize them."

"You speak excessively on matters of psychology," the Crystal King growled as a cluster of sharpened crystals emerged from his back.

Lysander shook his head. "Not excessively, Your Majesty. Realistically. Entire battles have been won and lost by morale and perceptions. Even the best warrior can succumb to the hopeless dread of the battlefield when confronted with the living embodiment of death itself.

"We must also remember we are fighting the inquisitors as well. While I estimate their numbers are less than two hundred, they are in a defensible position that will make hurting them from out here challenging. Fortunately, whatever spells they use will likely need to traverse a great distance. Wizardry should be easy to counter if we watch for it. Sorcery against the brave soldiers will be prevented by our few sorcerers. Conjuration may provide the greatest challenge and will likely be used to cause a break in rank. Be aware of that and ensure soldiers reform the line if they break through.

"We should post guards near the camps to ensure no undead from the forest surprise us. I suspect the lich will only reach out within the empty field around Kazra Lo Veedra, but I could be mistaken. There may be corpses within the forest that didn't make the trek to the plains surrounding the estate. Any further questions?"

The generals shook their heads.

"Good. We attack after sunset. We have eight hours to make the necessary preparations and rest. Meeting adjourned."

He watched all of them leave except Garo, who sat near him.

"I'm glad you got my message."

Garo raised an eyebrow. "I probably wouldn't have if you hadn't resorted to desperate measures."

Lysander sat down. "These are desperate times."

Garo shook his head. "This is a mess, Lysander."

The archmage sat and wiped a hand over his face. "I know."

"If Hazel Enda is hurt, I will hold all of you responsible. The High Archmage himself will hear from me."

"That is... expected," he said tiredly.

"One more thing"—the dog glared at him with smoldering green eyes—"stay away from the Evenfall Vigil. They are not yours to command, Archmage of War. When your people unlawfully took citizens of Ethelian hostage, this became an international affair and now falls under the jurisdiction of Ethelian. Since there are no available commanding officers here, I have been vested with the full rights of leadership by King Aldric Valmore of Ethelian to lead his soldiers into battle in whatever way I see fit." A piece of parchment wafted from the shadows and landed on the earthen table. It was an official writ signed by the king. "We will follow your plan of external assault because it is a good strategy, but you do not control us. The moment Hazel and her family are safe, we will cease to intervene. This is your disaster, not ours, and I will be damned before I let you turn us into your pawns."

"Understood." Garo plodded to the entrance of the tent when Lysander called out to him, "I'm sorry, Garo. I had no way of knowing about any of this. I swear by Selevara herself I will do all I can to make it right. Don't think of me as your enemy. We were friends before this—before all this strange and terrible business."

Garo didn't turn around. "I know why you did what you did, but ignorance of a committed wrong does nothing to make it disappear. We may have been friends once, but I can barely say that word without wanting to bite my tongue. The only reason I haven't unleashed my fury on you is because Alvaria Saccarra awaits us inside. Until this is over, we are allies and nothing more." Garo exited quietly and headed to where the three friends of Hazel Enda waited.

Lysander sank to the ground with his head in his hands. Pain washed over him, but receded before the weight of duty. Remorse was an emotion for those in times of peace. He was the Archmage of War. Implacable, relentless, and ever with an eye on the best strategy. The emotions of civilians were a luxury he could not now afford. All those feelings were pushed down unbidden by the magic of his title.

He rose again, less Lysander Relas than the Master General of the Army of Selevara. His eyes gleamed with determination for the coming battle.

He clenched his fists. *We're coming, Alvaria. Today I will show you the full power of the Archmage of War.*

Chapter Twenty-Seven
To Be Master and Servant

"What do you *mean* they're here?" Thomas Eller demanded. The lich, in his typically placid demeanor, regarded the inquisitor with those inhuman eyes and unreadable expression.

"I shall reiterate, to appease your disbelief. The enemy has arrived. I noticed a scout at the outer perimeter of the plain an hour or so before dawn. The army has settled and is currently resting in the trees, though they use sorcery to mask their camp."

"How do you know this? Aren't the walls shielded against sorcery?"

"They are"—his eyes flashed—"but I am the master of Kazra Lo Veedra. The enchantments bear my mark, and so I ignore them as I please. The grounds are enchanted, so I am aware of all that transpires within two miles of the estate."

"If you knew they were here, why didn't you inform the Grand Inquisitor?"

"It was unnecessary. Her plans would not have changed in the slightest. Alvaria Saccarra is prophecy-driven now. The intractable pull of magic has propelled her to fulfill the prediction of the girl, likely beyond her control."

"That is irrelevant. You should have told her! We have no time to prepare! They could attack at any moment and yet you act like nothing has happened?" Thomas shook his head in disgust. "Useless."

Zylit hovered and studied him. "You will never achieve greatness."

The inquisitor narrowed his eyes. "What is that supposed to mean?"

Instantly, the lich teleported inches from his face as dark magenta swirls slithered around him. Zylit's voice cut through Thomas, cold and quiet: "You lack perspective." The magenta smoke held Thomas aloft as he paled before the skeletal grin of the lich. "You are too small-minded to comprehend the necessity behind the actions of your betters. You know the rules of the game but not the means to win, choosing to follow orders without understanding their purpose. Alvaria is more than blind aspiration; she is what occurs when great ambition marries great effort with intelligence. While she relentlessly pursued her goal, the closest you could get was doggedly following behind her. You are a blind sycophant who does not approach the outer limits of understanding the person he supports.

"We are willing to risk everything to become a lich, even our own souls. I have traversed the unending abyss of Ryxiv and beheld indescribable horrors beyond your meager ability to imagine. You refuse to risk even the possibility of displeasing her. You believe we are equal servants of the same master, but we don't even exist in the same hierarchy. Though I serve under compulsion, I shall be free when she rises while you will remain her perpetual slave. She cannot free one who clings to his own chains. All humanity are masters or slaves but requires neither to possess the traits of either. Even if she was enslaved, she would be a master, and even if you wore the most resplendent of crowns, you would be but a slave. Such is your existence."

The world darkened around them, and strange voices whispered from the corners of the room. "Cry, weep, and fret over how you've displeased her while I contemplate the deepest powers of eldritch magic that will unmake the fundamental laws of the universe. Your vision is only for her, but even that vision is clouded by your base mortal idea of who she is." He leaned closer, the dark magenta swirling and twitching with anticipation. "Perhaps I can *give* you perspective and show you what it means to be Alvaria Saccarra and what secrets the afterlife has for people like us." Thomas Eller's feet rose further off the floor and his face neared that of the undead mage. Those eyes of stone reflected the horrors of the eternal pit and the long, unrelenting scream of the damned. Thomas's nostrils filled with the iron scent of blood as the air thickened with the murders committed by this monster of necromancy's apotheotic magic.

"No," Thomas whimpered, averting his eyes.

Zylit tilted his head. "What?"

"No," Eller gasped. "Please. I—I—"

The magic relaxed, and he drifted to the ground. Zylit floated away, his hands clasped behind his back.

"Run along and make preparations for war," the lich said. "They will use the cover of nightfall to obscure their assault. Rest, and make ready for the upcoming battle, little inquisitor. Provide the midrange defense of the estate while I serve as both the strongest shield and the sharpest spear. I may not like your master, but I am bound to protect her and have respect for the methods she has employed and her ingenuity. She shall become a lich, as I have promised. Do not speak to me of her supposed aspirations and unspoken commands when you cannot fathom even her shallowest depths."

The lich stroked his chin. "I recommend your inquisitors use the ladders within the antechambers to reach the roof and provide additional support to my zombies. They will merely supplement my forces as necessary. Conjure additional horrors for the enemy to fight and we shall see how they fare. Wizardry should be superfluous, since I have defensive measures already installed that will bombard them with greater force and require less expended energy than what most humans are capable of. Your magically talentless soldiers should guard the doors and stand in reserve in the unlikely case they break through. I will maintain communication with each group of inquisitors and guide them to the best locations. Should any breach the doors, I have several traps I can activate that were not dismantled by your fastidious organization."

Zylit waved a hand airily. "You may go."

Thomas stumbled backward, sweat dripping from his forehead as he adjusted his uniform, smoothing out the white rose. He opened his mouth, but no sound came out as he remembered what he beheld in the lich's eyes. He rushed from the room to alert his fellow inquisitors. What did that damnable lich know about Alvaria that he didn't? Nothing. It was all bluster.

The aufhocker within his shadow stirred. A wash of disgust emanated from the creature which Thomas felt through their bond as master and familiar. He exerted his will on the monster, quieting its disapproval at his perceived cowardice. What did it know about confronting a lich? Nothing. Thomas refused to be bullied by such a lesser being.

The real threat waited outside. It was unexpected that they would arrive so soon, but Zylit gained nothing by lying about the presence of an army, especially when the news of hippogriff scouts only a few days earlier proved they were on the march. The inquisitors would do their job, like they always did.

He just hoped that monstrous abomination would do his.

Chapter Twenty-Eight
The Nature of Strength

Lara rested against a tree. She had slept for a few hours in the morning, but her uneasiness wouldn't permit her any more than that. It was midafternoon, but the camp was quiet. It was strange to think of so many humans adopting her sleep schedule, but small sacrifices needed to be made in wartimes. She settled further into her blanket. They were protected from much of the cold weather and the spellcasters had melted the snow in the nearby area. The blanket was less for warmth than comfort.

It was easy to get lost in her own bravado, but not today. In fact, these past couple months showed how far out of her depth she was. The first battle against the aufhockers demonstrated how—under specific chance circumstances—she could be completely useless. Her later battles helped rebuild her confidence, while the fight against Paxton Averly had been a complete disaster for multiple reasons. She'd never been so close to death, and it wouldn't have been a glorious dramatic death either. That stupid little alchemist could make himself stronger and faster than her. She'd been overpowered. Then, fighting against the chamberlain, she'd been overtaken by a monster she couldn't kill and had no hope of defeating on her own. Not to mention if it wasn't for Lyvaelan, she wouldn't have even fought the chamberlain's monster. It was laughable how quickly she'd been willing to leave Chateau Zarielle because of a little magic trick.

She realized, as she studied the camp, she hadn't simply lost battles. She was a loser.

For so long, she believed she was one of the best—one of the strongest people alive. The audience in Treland represented the entire world in her mind, but coming to Coruvaine changed all that. There were enemies she couldn't stand against, even if she tried. Before, she thought fighting a dragon or a giant might be fun, or even easy. Now, she wasn't so sure.

"Lara, you seem troubled," Garo said softly. The grim hadn't walked through shadows like usual but approached from the main camp. "What's going on?"

"What do you *think* is going on?" she snapped.

Garo cocked his head slightly and waited.

She sighed. "I'm not mad at you—I'm mad at myself. I feel so useless. All this time I thought I had it figured out, but I don't. Fal Inderva keeps showing me the futility of trying when I'm bound to fail."

"Do you really feel that way?"

She nodded and bit her lip to keep from crying.

Garo settled next to her and watched the rest of the camp. "Others feel similarly, but I know this is different for you. You're recognized by so many as a strong person, both physically and emotionally. The others depend on that strength, whether or not you want them to. When you can't protect them, or your power can't assist them, it feels worse than simply being helpless; you feel you've disappointed them."

Lara buried her face in her blanket to mask her sobs.

Garo kept his gaze averted. "It's hard to feel that way," he said after a long pause, "and I think the hardest thing about it is knowing what to do in order to get through it."

"How *do* you get through it?" she asked, her voice muffled through the blanket.

"I wish I knew. I suspect it varies between people. This may be a problem overcome in the next hour or it could take many years. What I do know is you love your friends. You only feel this hurt because of how much you care about them, and I know the feeling is mutual. I can also say all four of you—five, if you include me—are weak in your own ways."

"How can I protect them when we're all so flawed? I can't even shield myself from stupid sorcery."

"Exactly who protected you from sorcery in the past?"

She lifted her head a little to look at him. "Lyvaelan."

"And who defeated the thug that nearly killed Lyvaelan?"

"Me and Alistair."

"Yes, though he followed your lead on tactics. The point I'm driving at is you cover each other's deficits. You can't always be strong, but you can be strong when they can't. The reverse is also true. You can be weak while they are strong. I know it's hard to allow someone to support you when you need help, but if you accept that, then you can develop a different strength—a purer strength, in my opinion. When that happens, and you pool your collective talents, then my Watchers of the Evenfall will be unstoppable."

"You're assuming we'll survive."

His tail wagged slightly as he returned his attention to her. "You will. It might hurt or be terrifying, but you will live through this harrowing ordeal and through many others."

"Do you know that through your shadowseeing?"

He shook his head. "No, I don't need the shadows to tell me that—I believe it with all my heart. I will fight alongside you to ensure that happens. Consider me an honorary member of the team."

She sniffed. "Thanks, mutt. I guess dogs and wolves can get along alright after all."

"That we can." He turned his attention to the mansion. "It may sound selfish of me to say, but I'm grateful this happened. Not that

Hazel was taken, nor that something evil may yet occur. I believe through the crucible of adversity, we are strengthened and progress into the best versions of ourselves. We may all suffer because of it, but when we emerge on the other side, we will appreciate each other more and withstand greater obstacles than we could have imagined."

"That's twisted, but I get it." She studied him more seriously. "Do you really think we'll be able to get into that place to save her?"

Garo's eyes glowed green. "I'd like to see anyone try to stop us."

"Well, I'm sure you'll get your wish"—she stared across the expanse to Kazra Lo Veedra—"and you won't have to wait much longer to get it."

Chapter Twenty-Nine
Prelude to the Conflict

Garson watched the sunset. Lysander had taken his company deeper into the perimeter of the forest and layered a plethora of spells for stealth that would disguise their movements both physically and magically. Lysander believed those within the building were aware of their presence, and Garson agreed. Knowledge of their presence provided them the opportunity to give them a false sense of comfort, at least in theory. That they hadn't sent out scouts or established visible sentries confirmed this. The walls were impervious to sorcerous exploration, which made gaging the number inside difficult, but no battle could be totally determined by numbers.

The Evenfall Vigil began to stir and move into position. They were an odd group, but he wasn't one to judge. They were dedicated to the mission, and he didn't need to command them, so they concerned him little. Dense clouds of steam puffed from his nostrils as he breathed. It was cold. The snow was thick enough to keep troops from slipping, but light enough to make a full charge possible. With the massive number of dead things around them, he was reluctant to lead a rushed charge, since the easiest way for their soldiers to be killed would be for them to be surrounded. They were to approach slowly—cautiously—and see how the enemy reacted. If they responded slowly, then a full charge would commence to overwhelm the mages within. If the undead were raised, however... a more defensive strategy would be implemented.

This plan was primarily Lysander's, of course. Garson was many things, but he hated the idea of being a war strategist. It wasn't the puzzle of war he struggled with. In games of strategy, he was no fool, but the possibility of his plan causing the deaths of those he commanded threatened to crush him. Many accepted that loss in war was necessary, but how did those who gave their lives feel? Perhaps some believed in their mission, but surely some were here simply because they were paid. How many realized that today could be their last day alive? If they knew, would they willingly choose to be here?

"You're easy to read, Your Eminence."

He glanced at Commander Selevia Castus, one of the two leaders of the Guard Unrelenting that had accompanied them, who stood just behind him and to the side. Her dark brown hair was tied behind her in an efficient ponytail that fell over her bright white armor. She leaned against her spear with her helmet beneath an arm and smiled wryly at Garson.

"Oh? And just what am I thinking?"

"You're thinking, 'how can I keep all these people alive? I'm a scholar, not a warrior!' or something similar."

He snorted. "You see much."

"I do."

Garson studied her. The woman would have been considered conventionally beautiful, save for two large scars along the left side of her face. Several smaller scars, almost imperceptible, lay parallel to the two larger ones, one of which went through her left eye. The wounds—a repercussion of fighting and killing a wyvern single-handedly—had left her without an eye until the Archmage of Magomechanics offered to create one. The eye he constructed was predominantly the coppery gold of orichalcum with a circular piece of iolite where the pupil would be. Miniscule glyphs and geometric shapes were etched into the metal and behind the iolite. Within the eye itself was a small diamond attached by thin wires to her socket. Garson had read the research paper the Archmage of Magomechanics published after successfully creating it, and it was truly astounding. He based the design on what he studied during his visits with the infamous Warlord of Sarth, Corbin Parstasia, in Arcanathema and then replicated aspects of the artificial eyes of the tyrant. Her magical eye gave an alien appearance to the woman that was hard to overlook.

All that said, she still *was* beautiful, but it had taken a different form. The scars added a character to her face that spoke of experience and successful trials. They gave her an air of respectability that didn't need to be earned or questioned. She knew what she was doing, even if it cost her something dear.

"What do you see out there?" Garson asked. The magic eye allowed her to see directly into the stream of magic, as well as various other things that were invisible to human vision. By losing one eye, she had gained unparalleled sight.

"Just what I've mentioned before," she said. "There's magic tied to the ground but also to that place," she nodded at the building. "There are loose strings spilling out of it in all directions that run on for miles. It resembles a loose net of sorts for creatures dying of a terminal malady, which explains the number of dead. There are invisible arcane shields around the estate that *can* be destroyed but would take some time. Beyond that, there's the overwhelming aura of death and conjuring in this place that we've already noticed. The hippogriff scouts noted the layout of the estate is a giant conjurer's circle and I can confirm the magic is present in quantities that rival Selevarian's."

Garson nodded. A circle of that size would allow a conjurer to summon virtually anything with relative ease without fear of the spell rebounding and the creature fighting back. With these dimensions, the distance the conjurer could control something, the strength of the entity being controlled, and the safety of the conjurer would all be drastically increased. If the circle were broken, then the spell would be too, but there were hardly any promises of *that* happening, and the rebound would be relatively minimal.

"You're doing it again."

"Doing what?" Garson folded his arms testily.

"Worrying about what hasn't happened yet."

"So? It's a common human experience."

She chuckled. "True, but these soldiers depend on you. They need to think you know what you're doing, even if you don't. If you can't muster that much, give orders to those you *do* know who need to prepare. If the spellcasters and soldiers see that, it'll put them at ease. Superior officers who don't bark orders on the eve of battle inspire no confidence."

He glanced around the camp as soldiers moved cautiously to their posts. Officers gave quiet directions with some hesitation. Garson grumbled. The Archmage of War should have been giving them orders, not the Archmage of Dragons. Still, Selevia was right. He knew little of war or command, but he knew about conjurers.

He turned to her. "Commander Castus, I leave the organization of the troops to you. In thirty minutes, we march on Kazra Lo Veedra. Ensure they are prepared with all necessary spells and send a runner to check on the progress of the amethyst gate. We are only to march once the gate is completed and the Crystal King is in position."

She saluted with her ravnulium-tipped spear. "Yes, sir!"

He turned. "Elimerita's Chosen Conjurers, to the front!"

Four conjurers stepped forward. The name of their group had been a joke made long ago, but now carried substantial prestige. These four were the experts on the four prime elementals and sat on the Council of Conjuration with Garson. They were close friends of his, though their interests in conjuration varied considerably.

Each drew a conjurer's circle on the hard earth. The circle with all its components could take several minutes, even with perfect procedural memory, but among Elimerita's Chosen Conjurers, the variation was even more pronounced. The geometrical designs required precision for the beings they were to summon.

Mark Annokest, the eldest of them, finished the first circle. He had sketched within the innermost circle the two-dimensional tetrahedron and placed at each of its points a single gemstone: ruby, garnet, tourmaline, and carnelian. The conjurer took a deep breath and smiled. Short gray hair peppered the top and right side of his head, but the left side bore the marks of a horrible burn that had healed over long ago.

Mark extended his hands with a flint in one and a piece of steel in the other, his voice calm. "I request the aid of the great elemental of fire, the burning salamander Sakirikas, if he should desire to appear." He struck the flint and steel together as a tiny spark flew out and transformed into a massive, roaring flame. The fire shifted, forming a humanoid shape from flames of various colors: yellow, orange, red, blue, green, and magenta. A head, face, eyes, and even hair formed along the creature into sharp, harsh, yet elegant features. Its eyes shone out as a menacing gout of blue flame as it towered over him.

"You dare to summon me, mortal? What audacity have you to call upon a great salamander?"

"Well, Sakirikas, mostly I just wanted to see you. If it's too much trouble, you don't have to stay. I just have some enemies I'd like to burn, and I figured you'd appreciate the invitation."

The salamander leaned closer. *"What enemy is worthy of my attention?"* the voice sounded like the hiss and crackle of logs in a flame. *"I do not enjoy wasting time."*

"I know, I know," Mark said, holding up his hands placatingly, "you're going to have to trust me on this. We're going to be fighting undead."

"Undead?" Sakirikas's eyes narrowed into two burning white slits. *"You summon* me *to fight against lowly reanimated corpses? My fire will burn through them unimpeded, without effort! You want me to act as some base funeral pyre?"*

"Well, yeah."

Sakirikas drew close to Mark, reaching out a long and slender hand of fire to the mage's already burned side. *"You mock me? You would use my power to destroy such useless things? Should I remind you why I gave you those scars...?"*

Mark smiled and closed his eyes. "No need to remind me, I remember. You gave them to me so I'd always remember your friendship and kindness."

The salamander's hand dropped as a wave of confusion washed over his face. He leaped backward into violent laughter. The fire flared brighter than before. *"You, Mark, are indeed my friend. I'm sorry I scarred you back then. Had I known how hilarious you are, I never would have done it. Ah, regrets. So useless."* He looked up at the conjurer. *"So, are these enemies I am to immolate behind you?"*

"No, they're in the building behind you and scattered across these plains. Most of them are buried, though."

The elemental raised a fiery eyebrow, searching the nearby plain. *"There is no fuel on this battlefield and you summon me during the season of my elemental opposite. You will need much magic to satisfy me during this fight."*

"Yes, I considered that. Fortunately, I brought along some magic I was filling in containers for just such an occasion. I'm not risking you running out of fuel before we've won the battle. For now, though, it might be best if you rested on that fallen branch over there." He gestured back to the tree line. "I know you hate waiting, but think of this time as preparation."

The salamander crackled with annoyance as it shrank and landed on the tree branch Mark indicated, assuming a vaguely lizardlike shape. *"You're too easygoing, Mark Annokest."*

Mark shrugged and glanced to his left, where the next conjurer had just finished her circle.

The second circle belonged to Felicia Durhost, who hummed to herself as she drew. She was many years younger than Mark, but had shown remarkable talent that demonstrated her prowess was equal to the older conjurer, with the potential to exceed it in time. She finished inscribing the two-dimensional hexahedron and placed gems at each point: emerald, onyx, agate, malachite, lodestone, smoky quartz, epidote, and jet. With a bounce in her step, she smiled at her finished work and bounded out of the circle, her blond ponytail swishing behind her. She picked up a handful of dirt from the ground and returned to the middle.

She cast the dirt around her and cried enthusiastically, "I ask for Darundar, the strong gnome of the earth, to join me! Come on! It'll be fun!" She released the remainder of the dirt and the ground quaked. Jagged points of rock and loose earth broke from the surface of the snow with a series of groans and sighs. A small, vaguely humanoid shape rose from the dirt and ice. Gemstones dotted its surface, giving it a full range of expressions as it turned two emerald eyes to Felicia. Its heavy arms nearly touched the ground, and every movement was slow and labored.

"The ground is filled with those who once lived, now forgotten. They rot away with the memories loved ones once had for them. The world continues on and leaves them behind."

"What?" Felicia said. "Darundar, you always say the saddest things. Cheer up!"

"To what purpose?" the gnome sighed. *"Each joy is tainted by its inevitable end."*

"That's true, but every sorrow is also brightened by the joy that one day, things will get better."

Darundar tilted his head, not comprehending.

"Think of it like this: right now, it's winter and there are no flowers, but I can still find the snow and scenery beautiful. Even if I don't like it as much as spring, I know that in a month or two spring with return with greener leaves and brighter flowers than before."

"But even those will die."

"It's their temporary beauty that makes them worthwhile."

"And what..." Darundar hesitated, *"what if there is a flower that you* don't *want to see disappear?"*

She kneeled down to the gnome and smiled. "Then I protect it for as long as I can. I look at it, enjoy being with it, and when it's time for it to die, I thank it for being with me for as long as I had it."

"And that doesn't sadden you—having to say goodbye?"

"Of course it does, but I know there are other beautiful things to enjoy and if I stay sad and withdraw, I might miss something even better."

"What if you found something so wonderful that nothing could compare?"

"Then I enjoy it for as long as I can and when it's time to part ways, I thank the gods for the opportunity I had to enjoy something so perfect."

The gnome gazed at the ground, considering. The earth shifted around him and he grew in size. When he first appeared, he was about a third Felicia's height but now stood three times her own. He met her eyes, his deep and cavernous voice reverberating, *"I do not know if I will be capable of expressing gratitude when you depart from this world, Felicia, but I will protect you against any threat without exception."*

She smiled and touched the rough stone of the gnome. "Thank you, Darundar. I know I can always rely on you."

Zelim Thain finished the third circle and completed the inscribed octahedron with a sigh. He placed the stones of air at each point: amethyst, peridot, jade, moonstone, clear quartz, and kunzite. With this done, he took an ocarina from his bag and sat in the middle of the circle. Although younger than Felicia by several years, many thought he seemed old for his age.

"Veliyana, joy of the airy sylphs, hear my song and come to me." He played the ocarina softly. The sweet tones of the instrument carried a melancholy that was hard to ignore. After a minute of playing, Zelim drew the ocarina from his lips. The ocarina continued to make music, but the song had shifted into something light, fun, and sweet. In the air, barely visible but for the swirling snowflakes, was the form of a young woman made of wind. She took the ocarina from Zelim's hand and danced with it through the air. She changed shape many times as the wind whipped around with surprising warmth. The ocarina drifted back to Zelim.

"You're so good at playing, but why do you always play such sad songs? You can't dance to sad songs."

"Why would I ever want to dance?"

"Why wouldn't *you want to dance?"* Veliyana exclaimed. *"Look at all these trees! Don't you want to twirl through them as you walk?"*

"No, I mostly try to avoid tripping on hidden roots. That aside, I need your help. In a few minutes, this clearing will be filled with undead who seek to kill us. Many will die whether or not I intervene, but I must do what I can, even if it isn't enough."

Her expression softened. *"You always do your best, and today will be no exception. Think of the lives you save and not the ones you can't."*

He sighed. "Easier said than done, Veliyana."

"Don't worry," she said, wrapping her arms around him in a hug, *"we'll get through this together."*

Garson directed his attention to the final conjurer, who sat furiously scribbling on the ground. Cassiana Sommura was the youngest of them, but her ambition had served her as the preeminent conjurer of water. She finished inscribing the complex two-dimensional figure of the icosahedron and placed at each point one of the stones of water: pearl, sapphire, aquamarine, alexandrite, topaz, chrysocolla, azurite, iolite, chalcedony, lapis lazuli, hematite, and turquoise. She swiped a handful of snow and returned to the center of the circle.

"By my power, I summon the great elemental of water, the undine, Abalia! Come forth!" The snow in her hand melted and reformed into a trickling swirl of water, which gently floated out of the circle and into the snow. The snow coalesced and took shape as a woman of water, with wavy hair and a rippling dress.

The undine approached Cassiana and held the conjurer's brown hair in her hand. *"Why would you cut your hair so short, Cassiana? Wouldn't you prefer something long and flowing?"*

"That's stupid," Cassiana said with a frown. "My hair is the perfect length. Long enough for most styles and short enough to stay out of my way. It's efficient."

Abalia tilted her head. *"Is human hair* supposed *to be efficient?"*

"Mine is. Besides, that isn't why I called you here. Enemies are going to attack soon, and I need you to crush them for me."

"Must I?" the undine asked frowning, *"I don't really enjoy fighting; it's a lot of work and I don't like conflict—it's draining."*

"I know, that's why you won't be fighting so much as cleaning out the filth that others have created. We're fighting undead and they're nothing more than garbage that requires disposal. You're good at cleaning, right? Think of it like that. Besides, it's winter. This is when you're strongest. I'll tell you what to do when the time comes. It'll be easy."

"If you say so. You seem to know what you're doing."

Garson studied the four assembled. Each elemental was powerful on its own, but all elementals together were a formidable force.

Not as impressive as dragons, of course, but elementals were good in their own way.

"Sir!" Garson turned to the messenger. "The Crystal King has constructed the amethyst gate as requested. He awaits further orders."

"Thank you. Tell him to assume formation and we will commence the assault. He should create a wall of glass in the north to protect our soldiers as soon as we begin the march. After you speak with him, alert the other commanders in the front lines and have them ready to move within the next three minutes."

"Yes, sir!"

The final embers of daylight had nearly extinguished. He waited until the sky was fully dark blue and the Evenfall Vigil members assumed a position near the Archmage of the Green. The elementals awaited orders.

Garson took a deep breath and reached out mentally to the commanders in the army with sorcery.

Maintain rank and move with caution. We march to war. Now.

Chapter Thirty
The Siege of Kazra Lo Veedra

The army crept forward. Soldiers in plate armed with tower shields stood in front with pikemen immediately behind, and mages backing them. Lyvaelan watched some conjurers summon various creatures and remembered the advice Lysander had given them regarding conflicts with the Inquisition. His stomach hurt thinking about the battle to come. He had tried his breathing exercises but failed to calm himself. What was this emotion? Fear? Anticipation? Excitement? Perhaps it was more than one.

On the one hand, the likelihood that they would die could not be overstated. They were laying siege to the fortress of a lich with scores of proficient spellcasters defending it. The magic in the area was so strong, he wondered if even those with no arcane leanings might sense it. Their prospects of success were slim.

Yet with Hazel trapped inside, there was no option except to succeed.

His light footfalls made no sound on the snow as he walked, nor did they leave an imprint. Despite the sylph swirling through the air nearby, there was no breeze. The air remained cold and still.

Dead.

The Archmage of the Green stood close to them. Two trees had grown on his shoulders and sent their roots across his body and arms. He closely resembled the green men who walked the darker parts of Elliara, though in Lyvaelan's estimation the archmage was less than half the height of the smallest green man he had seen.

As Lyvaelan stepped from the canopy, he noticed strings of dark magenta circling into the sky over the estate. Soon, everyone watched as the strings coalesced and glowed with increasing vitality, pulsing like veins around a beating heart. His breath caught and his skin prickled, although he did not understand why. The magic swirled and took a more definite form several hundred feet above the estate in the form of a skeletal head that studied them impassively.

"Attention, those who act in the name of the Council of Archmages," the head said, its voice ubiquitous and chilling, *"Know that I am the lord of these lands and you trespass on property legally procured and owned by me. Should you continue to advance, I will have no recourse but to protect my home from your intrusion. Turn away now and no blood of yours shall be spilled this night. Continue, and those who remain will live to see the pristine snow of Kazra Lo Veedra stained red from the blood of their fallen comrades."*

Lyvaelan's jaw slackened. This was a lich. Were they truly going to fight a being of such monumental power?

Garson challenged the face, his voice booming across the field, "We seek Alvaria Saccarra and her inquisitors! Surrender them and the Enda family and we shall depart for now."

The head regarded the Archmage of Dragons. *"That is quite impossible. Alvaria Saccarra is under my protection for the time being, along with those who serve her. Delay your assault but a few hours and my protection shall elapse. You have my permission to wait until that time. My terms are non-negotiable."*

Really? Is this lich telling us that Alvaria needs to be protected now, but not later? That would mean she's close to becoming a lich. How could she become one so quickly?

"I have a counteroffer," Garson Varaldan replied, his voice echoing across the expanse. "You give us the former Grand Inquisitor *now* and we won't turn your estate into a smoking pile of rubble before sunrise."

The head paused, continuing to gaze at the unflinching archmage. *"What a pity,"* it finally said, *"that we could not reach an accord. Unfortunate, but expected, given the history of your organization. Very well. Those who would fight a lord of death must not be surprised to find the end approaching. If you want war, then you shall have it, Archmage of Dragons."* The face burst and the magenta streaks of magic rained into the ground. A light throbbing sound issued from the field.

Lyvaelan scanned the expanse but saw nothing. A little way off, the snow shifted as if something beneath it tried to escape. A single hand reached from the snow, shriveled and skeletal. Then another. And another. Lyvaelan watched as tens of thousands of bodies rose from the white. Most were human, but some were other animals: deer, bears, dogs, squirrels, birds, rats, and even some lizards crawled from beneath the snow. The snow-covered plain filled with zombies, all with the faint glow of dark magenta in their eyes. They lurched toward the surrounding forces, moving from all around the perimeter of Kazra Lo Veedra, creating a wall of reanimated dead bodies.

"Finally," Lara said, cracking her knuckles, "I've been waiting to bash a few heads in."

Garo faced them. "When I first spoke with all of you together, I said that I saw greatness in each of you. I believed that each of you would one day rise above the opinions of others who might otherwise view you as monsters and become heroes. Allow me to amend my statement. You have proven beyond any doubt in my mind that you are heroes. You are not heroes because you overcame the monstrous parts of your identities. In days of old, heroes rose among humanity to fight monsters and win acclaim. Now, the monsters they face are of their own creation. What you are matters less than what you choose to do. In this hour, I ask that you fully embrace the duality of your natures." He gathered shadows into himself and grew increasingly feral. "Become the heroes you were destined to be by accepting the monsters you are." The grim's green eyes adopted a perilous glint. "For Hazel."

The uneasiness in Lyvaelan's stomach transformed into a burning heat within his heart. He looked beyond the swarm of walking, rotting corpses. A thousand undead creations separated him from Hazel. He closed his eyes. It wouldn't be enough. He opened his eyes, both pupils dilated as he strode forth without fear.

For Hazel.

The others watched him. Lara had turned into her massive lupine form, covered with dark brown fur. Alistair gripped his sword with one hand, while the nails of his other had lengthened into sharp claws. His fangs extended, and he became every inch the predatory creature he was. Lyvaelan sensed their approval. They were all monsters. They were all heroes.

When Lyvaelan's feet entered the circle of death surrounding Kazra Lo Veedra, his slow walk turned into a run, which became a full sprint as Lara's wolfish form overtook him and Alistair dashed ahead with a vampiric screech. Garo panted along beside them, many times his normal size. The Evenfall Vigil had been tasked with punching a hole in their line. They could do that.

Tonight, the four of them would give the Council of Archmages reason to know the name of the Evenfall Vigil.

Red flames blasted from Lyvaelan's hand as Lara leaped into the stinking ranks of the undead, a blur of teeth and claws shattering and scattering bodies in every direction. Alistair's sword whistled through the air as he dashed through in an intricate but frenzied display of flashing metal. Garo kicked and bit as they drove unceasingly forward.

The world slowed for Lyvaelan as the Evenfall Vigil worked in concert, cutting down zombies with precision and speed. Not one of them impeded the other as they moved, and each motion propelled the group forward, leaving no one behind. It was like a perfectly choreographed dance that none had ever rehearsed, and yet all of them knew. As Lyvaelan threw a spike of ice into a small group of approaching zombies, he realized they had trained for this moment since the day they met. They had talked together, eaten together, lived together, and fought together. They trusted each other beyond all doubts.

He risked a glance back at the Army of Selevara, who had just engaged the enemy fifty feet from the canopy. He turned back to the task before him and constructed a green whip of crackling magic he sent through the ranks of the undead. A roiling ball of flames flew toward them from the estate. He dropped the whip and threw up his hands, redirecting the fire into the horde. Psychic fingers stretched out to his allies, but he shielded them, pushing back against the sorcerous assault. Several arcane missiles flew from the top of Kazra Lo Veedra, but Lyvaelan redirected and thwarted them. Each volley they sent grew in desperation, more dangerous than the last, but each made little difference.

They pushed forward for what felt like ages, with the other three attacking and dashing forward while Lyvaelan protected them from the magic of the inquisitors. It had only been a dozen minutes before he saw the southern entrance of Kazra Lo Veedra just ahead. He gritted his teeth, trying to keep the darkness from spreading over his skin. Just a little further and they would see her.

Chapter Thirty-One
A Strange Invitation

Lysander watched as the skeleton of a stag shambled away from him and to the west. An effective preservation spell had been cast over the grounds that he hadn't expected. Many of the dead here should have decayed beyond use—especially when exposed to the elements—but the master of Kazra Lo Veedra had taken that into consideration.

He waited in silence with the Guard Unyielding for the bulk of the horde to pass. Upon further reflection, Lysander left the bulk of the elite force with the main army. Bringing a hundred soldiers covertly into the building would not have been practical. Besides, such renowned warriors among their ranks would boost morale in a way that might counteract his absence. One part to the magic of his title was the inspiration it stirred in all soldiers sworn to the allegiance of the High Archmage. The fact he could not lead them provided an unfortunate deficit in their ability to operate. Lysander also believed that the Guard Unyielding who accompanied him would primarily defeat the inquisitors more than assist him with the lich. Bringing in a huge army would alert the enemy and likely result in greater casualties because of the confined spaces within the estate. To that end, twenty would suffice to patrol and subdue the unwitting inquisitors, which would allow Lysander to concentrate on the lich without needing to watch his back.

He watched as several more undead shuffled past with slack jaws. Zombies were not known for their perceptive abilities, nor for their clever minds. If they weren't being directly manipulated, then they would continue with the last command they were issued. Lacking combative acumen, they wouldn't realize that leaving the back unguarded constituted a grievous mistake. If the lich himself remained unaware of their presence, then the zombies had no chance of detecting them. Unfortunately, zombies *were* notoriously slow, and right now, that sluggishness grated on him. They had waited nearly half an hour. The Evenfall Vigil had entered Kazra Lo Veedra almost ten minutes ago. That was part of the plan, since they would struggle to maintain stealth and the internal security of the building would focus on them and the main force rather than the relatively safe eastern flank that had seen no activity whatsoever.

Momentary panic seized him at the thought that the inquisitors inside might be *too* easy for the Evenfall Vigil to fight. If they got past and stumbled across the lich before he did...

He took a slow, deep breath to calm himself, allowing the analytical, direct part of his title to appraise the situation coolly. Garo wanted to find Hazel, not Alvaria. The black dog may have been irate with the situation, but he usually maintained a level of rationality, even in his fury. Still, the thought of them facing a lich troubled him. The Evenfall Vigil possessed formidable abilities, but a lich transcended any challenge they had previously encountered by an order of magnitude. Even a lich weakened by summoning so many undead would prove to be a lethal adversary.

The horde thinned. Most had staggered north or south around the building. There were still others, mostly small animals and human zombies, that had lost legs and moved slower as a result. He nodded to the small group behind him and put his hood on. He muttered a few words under his breath and felt the slight electricity of magic attach to his cloak. Lysander took slow steps out, unnoticed by the remaining zombies.

Invisibility could be accomplished in several ways, but this magic functioned through wizardry. The magic current surrounding him bent light around his cloak, giving the illusion he was not really present. The problem with utilizing such a spell was the magic that attached to the cloak only clung to it tenuously—move too fast, and the magic would disappear. Sorcerous invisibility and illusions had limited effectiveness on largely mindless zombies, but this effect altered actual physical appearance. A perceptive person might notice the slightest distortion in the air, but to the unquestioning undead, it was as convincing as the world itself.

The archmage crept forward, his guards close behind. They had taken many precautions to ensure the lich wouldn't know of their movements. Some measures were arguably redundant, but it was better to do too much than regret not doing enough later.

It took them over ten minutes to reach the eastern entrance to Kazra Lo Veedra. They paused many times to avoid detection as a zombie passed by ahead or close by. If only one detected them, then the others would inevitably notice as well. Fortunately, none did.

When they had finally traversed the plain, they crowded around the door. He exhaled and the fog from his breath outlined the magic across its surface. Slowly, he dismantled the spells that surrounded it. Several were simple and recent, likely placed by the inquisitors. He paused at the last one. This one was neither a lock nor a trap. It appeared to be a thin magenta cord of magic threaded into the creation of the door itself. He sighed. This was the doing of the lich. It wouldn't keep the door shut, but it would alert him that someone had entered from the east. Lysander supposed they couldn't keep up their secrecy forever, though he had hoped to have maintained it a little longer. He opened the door and stepped inside.

They entered an antechamber of sorts before moving into a short hallway which emptied into a large pentagonal room. Two hallways ran north and south at the points of the pentagon, and double doors stood just ahead. Two inquisitors stood nearby, one leaned against each hallway idly. He signaled for the group to halt. Withdrawing his marinom—a small blueish-gold dagger with black flecks—he silently advanced on the inquisitor to the left. He moved slowly to maintain his invisibility and gently insinuated sorcerous suggestions of boredom that would make him harder to detect. He pushed a little magic into the marinom and the blade sharpened as all the black flecks moved to the edge.

Lysander looked at the inquisitor. A young man with black hair, likely no older than thirty—practically a child among practitioners of magic. He could have been one of the many students at Calixford University. What promise this boy might have possessed, and yet he sided with Alvaria. Perhaps the boy had nowhere else to turn, or extenuating life circumstances had brought him to this moment. That part of Lysander, which remained the Archmage of Education, longed to question him and understand if he had chosen to do evil or if he was merely a victim of circumstances beyond his control.

The Archmage of War, however, knew only enemies and allies. Mercy was the last generosity of the victorious. The Army of Selevara had not won yet.

With a decisive motion, he drew the dagger across the inquisitor's throat. Instantly, he put another jolt of magic into his marinom and it transformed into a heavy but perfectly weighted dart. He hurled it toward the inquisitor on the other side of the room, using magic to propel it forward with perfect accuracy. The other inquisitor's eyes widened in surprise but had no time to react to her dead ally when the dart struck her in the throat with such force she was thrown off her feet. Lysander held out his hand, and the weapon returned to him. By the time his marinom reformed in his grasp, both inquisitors were dead. The soldiers wordlessly moved the bodies outside the building while Lysander cleaned his weapon and shifted it back into a small dagger. A marinom was made of finely crushed sapphire and opal mixed with orichalcum. The black flecks were ravnulium, which resisted all magic. It was useful in tactical situations against spell-casters, but because of the softness of orichalcum, it was impractical for prolonged battles against steel armaments.

They lowered their hoods when they were certain no inquisitors heard the brief encounter. Lysander watched their faces—obscured though they were by their helmets—as they stood in formation. "The lich likely knows we're here, but few others do. I want you to split up and move in groups of three. This place is a maze, so it's important we cover as many halls as possible. I will take six of you through the entrance straight ahead. Two other groups go north and two go south. Your mission is to find and neutralize as many enemies as possible. Incapacitation is preferred, but kill them if you must. Your lives mean more to me than the lives of a collection of traitors. Remember, any inquisitor you kill may return as a zombie. Prioritize rendering them unconscious, but not if it means they revive prematurely. I'd rather fight a zombie than an inquisitor. If you kill them, decapitate them. It will make them less effective if they come back as undead.

"My mission will be to find and defeat the lich. None of you are to confront the lich if you find him. I will engage him. This is not the first lich I've battled, and your skills are better applied to ensure all inquisitors behind me are neutralized. I know you're the best mages we have, but remember, the Inquisition has trained excellent spell-casters as well. Use your marinoms and it will surprise them, since they won't expect a direct physical attack. Shift the ravnulium into the edges and tips of your weapons to break through any arcane defenses. Maintain stealth as long as possible, but do not sacrifice speed. We must move quickly and quietly. The sooner the inquisitors are defeated, the sooner the main forces can flood in and reinforce us."

The group split without issue. His orders may have been superfluous, given the high level of training and competence these soldiers had, but it helped him organize his thoughts to command them.

It also bolstered his confidence.

He moved toward the door when it opened on its own. Dark magenta strands of smoke spilled out and merged before Lysander, who held his staff at the ready. It formed the same skeletal head he had seen outside.

"Ah... you must be the Archmage of War," the head said. *"I had wondered where you were. Welcome to my home. Garson Varaldan is a smart man, but leading an invading army exceeds his competence and interest. I wouldn't have expected him to adopt such a role when Lysander Relas still lived. But where are my manners? I am Zylit."*

Lysander didn't lower his stance. "What do you want?"

"To talk. Ideally, violence would be unnecessary, but I suspect our goals are such that they would not allow otherwise."

He searched the being's face for any signs of guile. "Why should I trade words with you, lord of death? You're obviously stalling."

"Because conversation can be enlightening. That, and I can make your passage through Kazra Lo Veedra swift and easy, or slow and perilous. I am the lord of this place and there are many traps I have set to activate as I desire. It could take you almost an hour to reach me, assuming you survive my home long enough. Besides that, I could also kill every soldier you've brought in here with relative ease. Agree to my terms and you can arrive here, in the heart of Kazra Lo Veedra, without shedding more blood. I will not directly interfere with your underlings within these walls. You have my word."

The soldiers awaited Lysander's response. Their expressions were hardened. They didn't fear death, and this lich couldn't be trusted. Still, he made a fair point. "What are your conditions?"

"Simple. From the time you enter the chamber where Alvaria is held, you will refrain from any violence against me or anything in the room for ten minutes while your soldiers wait in the exterior chambers. You will command your constituents to remain outside the chamber for that duration and prevent them from committing any violence as well. At the conclusion, you may take up arms against me if you choose."

Lysander's eyes narrowed. "When does Alvaria ascend?"

The head tilted. *"Soon, but she will still be minutes away from ascendance by the time our conversation concludes."*

"This deal… in order for me to agree to it, I must know all the reasons you want to make it. Explain it to my satisfaction and I will consent." Lysander hated all this talk, but he needed to understand the reasoning of this being before he agreed to anything.

"Very well. I prefer to talk in person over this informal medium. You are an interesting individual and I wish to learn from you. There is also the distant possibility you find some method of circumventing my traps and arrive before the former Grand Inquisitor's ascension, which would be inconvenient. By having you arrive on a schedule, I can control the variables to make her ascension easier to plan with less threat to myself. Furthermore…" the head leaned in closer. *"I believe I can convince you of the futility of your present course of action if we discuss it without duress."*

It was a hard offer to accept, but based on what he learned about Kazra Lo Veedra, the lich was not bluffing about the dangers of this place. If Zylit knew the movements of all these soldiers, then they would likely die. If Lysander could get close to the lich, however, then there might be some hope.

"I accept your offer."

A scroll of glowing parchment appeared from the air. "I have two amendments," he said after scanning the document, "first, change the statement from *no soldier within Kazra Lo Veedra shall be harmed until our conversation is concluded,* to *no soldier within Kazra Lo Veedra shall be harmed before, during, or after the conversation until the agreed upon time has elapsed.* Second, it says you will *allow for safe passage through Kazra Lo Veedra to the main chamber.* Alter it to state it shall be both the safest and swiftest passage through Kazra Lo Veedra and you shall guide us to the chamber yourself."

The expression on the skull was impassive. *"Done."* The words on the document shifted to accommodate the changes.

"Very well. I accept the terms of your contract."

"Then let us both be geas-bound."

"And may the gods bear witness to our pact."

The scroll rolled up and disappeared.

The head chuckled. *"I look forward to meeting you, Archmage of War."* The magenta head unraveled and shot like a ribbon back through the door, leaving a trail behind it. Lysander followed it, with the soldiers behind him. No one spoke. It was a vile thing to enter into a contract with a lich, but vile things were often how wars were won, and Lysander had no intention of losing.

Chapter Thirty-Two
Monsters at the Door

The interior of Kazra Lo Veedra remained eerily still. Alistair waited, sensing as much with his eyes as with his ears. Where were the defenders?

They had broken through the entrance thanks to the joint efforts of Lyvaelan, who dispelled the magic which sealed them and Lara, who smashed through the thick, ornate wooden doors unceremoniously. The guards on the other side had evidently expected them to break through—as evidenced by their presence in the antechamber—but had apparently not expected the werewolf to blast the doors off their hinges, as evidenced by the three dead guards who had been flattened as a result. Before Garo or Lyvaelan could do anything, Alistair and Lara had swept in and massacred the remaining five soldiers. None seemed to have been magically gifted, but neither of the two fighters wanted to wait and confirm. Lara shattered the interior door leading from the antechamber as well, and now they waited, trying to determine what foes awaited them. The stone halls echoed strangely, but Alistair could not determine why. Part of the reason might have been the strange configuration, but even so, it should have at least remained consistent. It was as if the building itself shifted occasionally to make echolocation more challenging.

"Do you hear anything?" Garo asked. The black dog's massive body blended into the surrounding walls, obscuring his form.

Alistair shook his head. "I can't explain it, but it seems like everything is simultaneously close and far away. Perhaps—"

A dark, insinuating chill passed through him. Lara glanced around and tightened her claw into a fist. The shadows surrounding Garo shrank as he braced himself. Lyvaelan remained invisible, but Alistair did not doubt that he felt it too. A vile and disturbing sensation seized him, like a decaying animal had dragged its cold, wet tongue slowly down his back.

"The lich," Lyvaelan whispered from nowhere.

A rush of frigid air brushed them from deep within the estate.

"You have entered my home without permission," that same strange voice from outside said. *"All interlopers shall suffer the same fate. Join the dead and be welcome."*

Alistair noticed it first. A series of sighs followed by scraping coming from behind them. He whipped around. "The bodies! We forgot to—"

The vampire suddenly hurtled to the ceiling without explanation. The roof had become a series of sharpened spikes, waiting for Alistair to land on them. He concentrated on his ability to fly and stopped mere feet from the spikes. Judging from his cape, gravity had inexplicably reversed.

Zombies formed from the soldiers they killed earlier clawed through to the antechamber. Garo grabbed one and thrashed it about in his jaws. Lara punched another and sent it back to the entrance. Unfortunately, neither of these actions proved sufficient to destroy either zombie.

"It would have been nice," Garo growled, "for us to have a door so we could shut them out."

Lara hefted another undead guard who had been slashed across the throat earlier by Alistair. She tossed him through the antechamber and the entrance. "How was I supposed to know we'd need to close the door again?" she asked in deeper tones than usual.

"Hmm," Lyvaelan said, still hidden. "I think more are coming in our direction. Either they noticed us in here or the lich is rerouting them to deal with us."

Alistair floated down. "Surging ahead and leaving our rear undefended could court disaster. Might I recommend—"

He dodged nimbly to the side as a series of darts whizzed past him and clattered into the wall.

"If you hadn't guessed, the lich has apparently laid traps for us," he remarked dryly. He was getting tired of being interrupted.

"One problem at a time, princeling," Lara said. She grabbed one of the massive doors and frowned at the entrance. "It's a lot easier to knock down a door than it is to put it back," she grumbled.

Lyvaelan sighed. "Put the doors horizontal along the interior of the antechamber. It's a much smaller opening and should still keep the undead from us. Lay one on top of the other and I'll do the rest."

Lara did as he instructed. The idea was simple enough, but it seemed to Alistair that the werewolf may not have been as mentally quick as usual, owing to her lupine form.

Lyvaelan stepped from the shadows and opened his hands. A dozen long nails flew from his grasp and into the wood, securing it in place.

"Will that be enough?" Garo asked.

"For our purposes, yes. It's not a permanent solution, but most of the zombies won't be able to break through."

Alistair glanced at the small aperture at the top. "Will they be able to climb through?"

"Doubtful," Lyvaelan replied. "Besides, we need a way to dump dead bodies so that they don't hinder us when they reanimate. Burning all of them would take time and energy."

Now that Alistair thought of it, he had seen little of Lyvaelan since they entered Kazra Lo Veedra. "Lyvaelan," he said, "how are you holding up?"

He hesitated before stepping closer. "Well enough, I suppose. At least under our current circumstances." His eyes were entirely black and the dark elf warlock winced occasionally as black spiderwebs appeared and disappeared across his gray skin.

Alistair nodded. "Alright, good. Just let us know if—"

The ceiling and roof rushed together. Alistair rolled out of the way as they crashed into each other.

"Lara! Drop!"

The werewolf hit the ground a moment before two stones in the wall smashed together where her head had been. Alistair leaped aside as a blast of fire erupted from the wall and singed the ground where he stood. It was then he heard it: all of Kazra Lo Veedra was moving. The building itself had been set against them.

Sections of the walls broke away and smashed together. Darts shot from hidden apertures. The whole structure appeared to flip and all of them were thrown from their feet and forced to dodge attacks coming from all directions at once.

"Damn it!" Lara slipped on the floor, suddenly slick with oil. The ground opened beneath her and it was only her swift reflexes that kept her from falling into a deep pit.

Garo disappeared into the shadows only to reappear a dozen feet from the group snarling, and shaking as if he had been covered in some itching potion.

Lyvaelan fared the best. He dodged with ease and deflected any projectile that came his way. As he continued deeper into the chamber, the same creeping feeling came over Alistair. The lich once again turned his attention to them.

The room flipped and contracted, and even Alistair could not maintain his equilibrium. Garo and Lara stumbled and intense pressure pushed in from all sides. Lyvaelan strode forward, shadows licking at his heels. A deep reverberation emanated from the dark elf warlock that grew to a crescendo.

"Enough!" Lyvaelan roared. There was the cracking of stone and the shattering of glass as all the effects around them came to an abrupt halt. "We seek to free Hazel Enda! If you stand in our way, then be prepared. I will tear Kazra Lo Veedra apart stone by stone until we find her."

"It would be interesting to see you try, warlock," the lich replied. Alistair could not be certain, but there almost seemed to be a hint of amusement in the creature's words.

They paused. The lich did not seem finished with what he had to say and yet he had not spoken. Lyvaelan waved them back and bid them wait. After nearly a full minute, the presence returned.

"Forgive the momentary interruption. Other matter temporarily dominated my attention. Alvaria Saccarra is off limits, but if you find and free Hazel Enda, then I have little interest in stopping you."

"She is our primary concern," Garo said. "If by promising we only seek to reunite with her and go our separate ways, will you guarantee us safe passage?"

"You entered the domain of a lich. There is no such safety to be found here. Regardless, I will activate no more of the building's countermeasures to slow your progress, nor will I direct spells against you. Perhaps you are a threat better faced by the highly capable members of the Inquisition." The voice gave a dark and throaty chuckle. *"Oh yes, they would be much better suited to the task."*

The presence seemed to recede but returned immediately. *"Also, you will not simply reunite with Hazel and leave, I think. Do not make promises you cannot keep. After all you've endured, it would be most unfortunate for you to miss giving your regards to the living lich of half a day."*

The lich withdrew, leaving them all to wonder what had happened and what he meant.

Alistair listened. The walls had stopped moving around them, and he could hear voices and footsteps drawing close.

He turned to his allies. "The lich may be gone but the Inquisition approaches."

"Good," Lara growled, cracking her fur-covered knuckles. "It's about time I killed some mages."

Chapter Thirty-Three
Inquisitor and Alchemist

"May I join you?"

Thomas raised an eyebrow at the spectacled alchemist before him. Paxton Averly's eyes were wide with expectation. Blueish light glowed faintly in his veins and eyes. He resembled a child, pleading with a parent for a toy.

A faint ripple in a nearby shadow caught Thomas's eye. His familiar had grown restless recently, which only added to his increasingly long list of frustrations. The creature's consciousness pawed at him, seeking attention. Its behaviors tended to increase in the presence of the spellcaster before him.

Not now, he commanded mentally. He returned his attention to the alchemist. "What?"

"May I assist in the defense of Kazra Lo Veedra? I abhor violence, but I am so terribly indebted to you and the Grand Inquisitor that I feel I should do something! I can actually be quite handy in a battle if necessary."

Thomas studied the man. Despite what Averly said, he seemed much too eager to fight and kill for someone who "abhorred" violence. The inquisitor sighed. "Look, Paxton, I appreciate the work you've done for us but, well, what is the nicest way to put this? If we needed you to defend this estate, then we would already be overrun and dead."

Paxton frowned. "But... I can be useful. I *have* been useful. Remember the battle with—"

"With the Evenfall Vigil?" Thomas interrupted. "Yes, I remember well. You clashed against four novice investigators with the aid of multiple aufhockers *I* had conjured to assist you and still had almost every bone in your body broken, while also having your mind similarly shattered. In other words, you failed. Miserably, I might add. Your research has been invaluable to the Grand Inquisitor, and we are grateful for that. We never hired you with the intent that you do any actual combat. Stick to research, Paxton. It's what you're good at."

"But..." Paxton sighed, clearly crestfallen. "I wanted to help."

Thomas pinched the bridge of his nose. *Gods, this man was annoying.* "Look, if you want to back us up, you can." Paxton's eyes lit up, but Thomas held up a hand. "Back *there*. By the stairway. We need all other soldiers and spellcasters to defend the entryways. Ensure the Endas don't escape and keep anyone but us from using this hallway." *That should keep him occupied with a meaningless task,* he thought. The Endas were confined to their rooms with guards stationed nearby. Still, if it kept Paxton out of the way, then it was a worthwhile position.

"Thank you, Thomas," Paxton said. "I won't let anyone by. The Endas certainly won't escape on my watch!"

"That's *Inquisitor Eller,*" Thomas corrected. He had no intention of getting chummy with the strange little man. His title— however incorrect it might now seem—kept that distance intact.

"Of course," Paxton replied sheepishly. "Inquisitor Eller. Sorry."

A small group has broken through the southern gate, Zylit's voice intruded into his mind. *Find and crush them. They should present no significant obstacle to you. My attention is better focused elsewhere. I have already sent inquisitors from the eastern side of the estate to investigate, but you should assess the damage and ensure the intruders are dealt with. Send a contingent of inquisitors to the western front and order them to cast spells from a distance. I will utilize ranged spells from the arcane cannons situated on the roof, but they are woefully predictable. Use conjuration to shatter their formations and my zombies will dispatch them once their ranks are broken. You have been given the chance to defeat all that the Council of Archmages stands for. Do not squander this opportunity.*

Thomas searched the faces of those around him, but no one else gave any sign of hearing the instruction. He sighed. "Inquisitor Marrow, gather all the spellcasters we have in the western side of the building and fortify the ranged assault on the army. Weigh the conditions of the battlefield before deciding who to attack. Conjuration should be your focus with some using apotropaic magic to increase the longevity of the summoned creatures. You eight, come with me. There are intruders at the southern gate and we must show them that opposing Archmage Alvaria Saccarra comes with dire consequences."

Thomas pushed aside the annoyance he felt at being given directions by the lich. At least that abomination understood that Eller was head of the inquisitors in Alvaria's absence. He strode through the circular hallway with his inquisitors in tow. Facing these intruders would likely serve no purpose. There were other spellcasters closer to the southern entrance that these insurgents would encounter first and likely die to. If they didn't fall to those, however, then they would come to wish they had. He smiled grimly at his shadow. The six glowing white eyes of his familiar stared back at him briefly before disappearing. Thomas had spent years wrapping himself and his intentions in shadows, and now he could control monsters made of them. Those who lived to see those shadows often wished they had died long before they had the opportunity. His familiar had been surly of late, owing to his shift from giving commands to taking them. No matter, the monster would soon feed and be satisfied. The insurgent mages in the south were about to be severely outclassed.

Chapter Thirty-Four
A Matter of Life and Death

Lysander entered the final circular chamber. The Guard Unyielding stood outside, ready for orders. He scanned the room, noticing the sarcophagus with the temporal container on it glowing blindingly white. It was close to full, judging by the light it exuded. Too much more and it risked shattering. He noticed several other containers, though these were dun and meant to contain magic instead of time. More than any of these things, he beheld the hovering, decrepit form of the lich.

The lich wore loose robes, the same color as the magic he used. Despite the unease Lysander felt gazing upon the being, the lich appeared placid.

"Welcome, Archmage of War," Zylit said, inclining his head. "I have eagerly awaited our meeting. Please, sit." He gestured and a cushioned chair appeared. Lysander studied the lich before sitting. The lich had promised no traps. "I understand my existence unnerves you. That is expected."

Lysander took stock of the room, noting each of the glyphs and geometric shapes engraved on every surface. "Did you want to make small talk, or did you have something important to say? It makes little difference to me, since time passes regardless."

"You are correct. I will skip to the point, then. Has it ever occurred to you that your attempts to stop Alvaria Saccarra are in vain?"

He studied the lich intently. "A wise general weighs all possibilities but should only consider defeat briefly. We stand a decent chance against her. All I have to do is defeat you to prevent her rise."

"No, that is incorrect." Zylit waved a hand, and a similarly cushioned chair appeared across from Lysander. "You fight something much stronger than me. The flow of magic itself opposes you."

"You mean the prophecy." Lysander leaned back, trying to read the lich. "Prophecies are unstable and subject to the times. Many can be altered or reinterpreted depending on their contents."

He drifted into the empty chair. "Bifurcative prophecies can, yes, but this is not one of them any longer. At a specific point, a prophecy becomes set and immutable. I suspect this one in particular was set some weeks ago. Possibly the moment you reported Hazel Enda to Alvaria Saccarra."

Without his title as Archmage of War, he would have felt guilt. "Or the prophecy can still be altered."

"No, it is set at this point. The girl has all but confirmed it. She has been at peace for the last week, at least regarding the vision. When prophecies settle, the stress leaves the prophet. Alvaria will become the living lich of half a day. There must be one, and it is she."

Lysander studied him. The creature's expression had changed little, but he could feel it pushing him to a specific conclusion. Despite the lack of emotion, there was a reason for the lich's interference.

"I think I know what you're after," Lysander said. "You don't want me to stop her because you will be forced to fight me. There's a possibility you will be destroyed if we battle, and by waiting, you will be free to let her defend herself. What oath did she place on you?"

"A geas."

"I see. She found your phylactery, I'm guessing."

"You are perceptive, Archmage of War."

"Not as much as I wish. Unfortunately for you, Zylit, I must try to stop her, even if it's a fruitless task. Even if she becomes a living lich, I will oppose her because I must."

"That is disappointingly shortsighted. Allow me to elaborate on my suggestion. I am not stating that defeating her is futile, but simply that preventing her ascension is pointless."

He raised an eyebrow. "You suggest she will be easier to destroy once she becomes a lich rather than now, while she's vulnerable?"

"Yes, actually. It may be counterintuitive, but it is the truth. Your choices are essentially two: either you decide to destroy her before her ascension and are forced to fight both me and the prophecy within a few minutes, exhausting yourself; or you chat with me until she rises and you remain fully refreshed and ready to engage her." He leaned in. "Her future may be absolute, but yours is not. You may survive your encounter with her or you may be killed. You stand a much better chance of living if you face her at full strength."

"Or I will have two liches to contend with instead of one."

Zylit leaned back. "I can see why you'd think that's a possibility, even though it is not. Alvaria and I are contractually bound to be allies until she rises. Your length of acquaintance with her is longer than mine. Do you think she would want someone such as myself working under her if it wasn't necessary?"

Lysander narrowed his eyes. "Hard to say. She fooled all of us before, so it's difficult to know what she is and is not capable of. You could be lying. Perhaps she agreed to leave your home after."

"True. Waiting for her to rise would increase my chances of survival significantly if we remained allies. I can think of no good counter to your argument."

They sat in silence for almost a minute. Lysander considered this aberration with its gemstone eyes and desiccated skin. What could drive a person to become something so abhorrently wrong?

"Why are you called 'Zylit'?" Lysander finally asked.

"You are an instructor, are you not?" the lich asked. "I am certain you know what a zylit is."

"Oh, I am aware." Lysander shifted in his seat. "A zylit is a small section of a conjuring circle. It's between the outermost and secondary circles and is unnecessary for most spells. In fact, conjuration professors advise students against using them because it takes extra time and does nothing to change the nature of the magic."

"Indeed." The lich seemed pleased. "No one has yet commented on my choice of a name. You do not disappoint me, Lysander Relas. The zylit of a conjuring circle is often overlooked, and yet it represents the conjurer himself. It is a signature informing the creature being summoned of the spellcaster's identity. An often superfluous task that does little to change the outcome of the spell.

"When I was human, I desired fame and prestige. I wanted power beyond my limits, and to be known and adored by many. That wish was to be realized as a lich, I had thought." He looked at the archmage. "As I hurtled through a hundred years of the underworld and beheld countless horrors beyond description on the edges of oblivion, I became struck by the absurdity of my quest. When I returned to this world, I was no longer the mage who desired glory. I was not Antony Larsinius. I chose the name Zylit because it signifies what I have become. The zylit represents the conjurer's identity, which is essentially useless and a waste of time. Desires for fame and glory are symptomatic of the finite view of the human condition. The conjurer's circle symbolizes the world and my part in it as Antony Larsinius was no bigger nor more important than the smallest zylit."

"Do you regret what you've become?"

"There is no regret among the dead."

"And yet your name betrays remorse."

"Not remorse, archmage, but comprehension. If all your life you had mistakenly referred to cows as dogs and you realized your error, you would not hesitate to switch. Perhaps you would be embarrassed, but ultimately it would not be a source of regret. I corrected myself. That is all." He paused, strumming his fingers on the arm of the chair. "I have great respect for you, despite what you may wish to believe. I think your continued existence would benefit the world. Are you certain I cannot dissuade you from your current course of action?"

"No. She must be stopped."

"It was worth asking, at least." He looked into Lysander's eyes with cymophane eyes. "Alvaria's ascension to lichdom and her defeat are not mutually exclusive. You can still achieve victory."

Lysander was taken aback. "Why are you telling me this?"

He cocked his head to the side. "Why do you think? I have no fondness for your Grand Inquisitor. I may be the very definition of a reluctant ally. She has forced me into servitude and stolen my home along with all my possessions. While I likely would not have cared if she had simply taken everything from me, that I must protect her until her ascension is problematic for my continued existence. I find her tenacity admirable, but recognize she will be more dangerous than most liches. She uses unstable magic. Her reasons for seeking lichdom sprout from a similar instability. The transformation may change her, but I suspect it will be categorically different for her than it was for me. So much of Antony Larsinius was destroyed as I passed through death that the name means little to me. I suspect little of her will be destroyed similarly, though the parts of her that will fall away may be those parts that made her your friend."

Lysander considered the words of the lich. "Those parts disappeared when she betrayed everything she stood for."

"Perhaps—perhaps not." Zylit steepled his fingers. "Do you think you only underestimated her and nothing else? Sure, what she has accomplished may be impressive, but there remains in humanity a tendency to ascribe complicated reasons to complex individuals. In reality, even those with convoluted designs can ultimately distill their purpose into a single primary driving force—an emotion or thought that never dies, no matter how hard one tries to smother it."

"And for what simple reason did she betray her station and friends? What could be more precious to her than that?"

"A fair question, and one you might wish to ponder further if you want to realize what makes her truly dangerous. I cannot give you all the answers, but providing you with the proper questions may eventually lead you closer to the truth than if I simply told you." The lich paused as if calculating something. "The time I have required for our conversation is over. We have both upheld our ends of the bargain." Zylit rose, and the chair disappeared. "I am most grateful that we had the opportunity to speak, even if it did not yield the results I desired. I still have no interest in fighting you. For that reason—poor thanks though it is—I must resort to subterfuge. My apologies."

Before he could react, Lysander hurtled through the air, propelled by some unseen force toward the entrance he came from. He quickly sent magic through his skin and concentrated his thoughts to countermand the sorcery. He halted in the air just outside the room. The Guard Unyielding rushed to the entrance.

"It was a pleasure talking," Zylit said, raising his hand up. "May the gods bless your efforts *after* she returns." As he spoke, a stone slab rose from the floor, blocking off the chamber with the lich inside. Lysander immediately recognized the forethought of his adversary. The entire door was plated with ravnulium. No magic could break through this wall so long as the black metal remained intact.

He turned to the Guard Unyielding. "Go to each of the other entrances and see if he has sealed himself off. If you get in, destroy the stone of this wall from the other side. If you find any others, reroute them to assist you. Two of you, help me cut through the ravnulium. We can use our marinoms. Once we reach the stone underneath, it should be a simple matter to get inside. We can't risk tearing up the floor or roof, so we have to do this the old-fashioned way." He sent magic into his marinom, which turned into a spiked war hammer. The others did likewise and hammered away at the surface.

They were close.

A loud clicking and whirring sounded from deeper in the hallway as a solid slab of rock hurtled toward them. Lysander dropped his marinom and pulled a small piece of moss from a pouch at his side.

"Spriggan!" he called.

Green and gray smoke surged from the moss and coalesced into the form of a squat gray man with a cloak of twigs and leaves.

"What d'ya want, 'Sander?" His voice was as grating as his appearance was misshapen.

"Keep the tunnel from crushing us by holding that wall!"

The spriggan glanced lazily at the oncoming rock and held out a single hand. The stone collided with the spriggan's open palm with a loud *crunch,* sending cracks along its surface. He remained unmoved and, despite the sound of straining cogs, still used only one hand to keep it back.

The fae yawned. "Is this all y'have for me to do?"

Lysander cocked a half smile. "I'd ask you to tear away the ravnulium, but I know the sidhe dislike the feel of the black metal. Your only other command is to protect us from external harm. A lich tries to destroy us using magic. Counteract what you can and I will be most grateful."

"Not a problem," the spriggan replied, "though you know the rules? I'll protect, but I've no mighty interest in fisticuffs unless I'm adequately compensated. Understand?"

"Perfectly."

With the traps of the lich handled by the conjured fae, Lysander could finally begin to destroy the barrier between him and the end of this terrible conflict. He set his jaw, picked up his marinom, and set to work chipping away at the ravnulium-coated wall.

Alvaria, we're going to stop you.

Chapter Thirty-Five
The Consuming Shadow

"How are we supposed to find Hazel in this stupid maze?" Lara roared as her claw met with the midsection of an inquisitor, splattering him against the wall. The novelty of killing inquisitors was wearing off.

"By asking the last enemy alive," Garo said as he emerged from the shadows behind another inquisitor. The black dog was double his usual size as he bit into the neck of the oblivious mage.

The surrounding scene was carnage. They had dashed through the halls, but the labyrinthian design and many doors made it difficult to fully orient. The group had traveled through a curved corridor into an oddly shaped room like a quarter of a circle, save for two adjacent circular rooms. After defeating several inquisitors there, they doubled back through a different hallway. Lara occasionally caught the faint smell of Hazel, but she had lost the scent as the stench of blood, sweat, and feces dominated Kazra Lo Veedra.

Lara examined the room. A giant triangle, and they were at one tip. The inquisitors fell faster than she expected, but then the Evenfall Vigil wasn't currently interested in exchanging pleasantries. They had consistently deposited the fallen inquisitors back behind the makeshift barricade they erected near the door, though it cost them more time than any of them wanted.

"Leaving one alive is harder than you make it sound, Ambassador Garo," Alistair said, cleaning his blade. The vampire had blood splattered over his clothes and face. His fangs remained on full display, as did his long and pointed fingernails. It was an odd sight, seeing the vampire prince so disheveled and wild. They had come a long way from their discussion on the library's rooftop. "The inquisitors seem unwilling to concede. Leaving one conscious enough to question who won't try to kill us will be challenging."

"Perhaps we can find a servant or someone similar," Lyvaelan said. "The inquisitors can't be the only ones in this place."

Lara sniffed the air. Through the putrid air she recognized a smell, somehow more noxious for who it belonged to. She bared her fangs. "Get ready, boys. There's another rat coming for us to kill."

The double doors opened as eight inquisitors walked in, led by Thomas Eller. His face flickered through surprise, confusion, and finally a dark fury not directed at them. The inquisitor quickly regained his composure. "Greetings, Evenfall Vigil," he said, "your presence is as unexpected as it is unwelcome. Leave the premises at once and we shall allow you to do so unscathed."

"You're a snake, Eller," Garo growled. "Surrender, or we will immediately execute you for treason of the highest degree."

"No, I don't think you will," he said, a dark form rising from his shadow. "The Grand Inquisitor is about to become one of the most powerful beings in existence and when she possesses the ultimate power, it shall be you who are found guilty of treason, not me." The shadow transformed into a tall, gaunt, horned form with six white eyes. It was the same final aufhocker they faced before when they fought the Alchemist. Two mages who had been chanting quietly raised their arms and two more shapes emerged from purple distortions in the air. The first monster was a tall creature with a serpentine neck and head atop a leopard body with a long, sinuous tail. A loud baying issued from its stomach as it stamped the ground with cloven hooves. Another creature, broader than the other, emerged. A humanoid face on the body of a giant red lion. In size, the creature was as big as a hippogriff, but there was a cruelty to its eyes. A long tail terminating in a plume of porcupine-like spikes wagged behind it. The creature bellowed like a chorus of trumpets as it stalked them.

Lara had no idea what the first creature was, but the second one she knew by reputation. A manticore.

Get to Eller, Lyvaelan told her mentally. *Break his concentration and we will defeat them all.* Lara nodded. Lyvaelan had disappeared. He was notoriously good at that.

Eller took a deep breath as his aufhocker grew more jagged and twisted. He smiled and opened his eyes. "Kill them."

Alistair moved first. The vampire dashed to Thomas, but the strange snake-headed beast intercepted him with surprising speed. The creature kicked at Alistair, sending him sprawling. He regained his footing just in time to dodge the monster's hooves as they came down. He placed his sword between him and the beast and parried the creature's blows as it struck with its head and whiplike tail.

Garo expanded in size again to meet the manticore. The monster was heavier than the grim, but Garo was faster. They were a blur of motion and fur as they tore at each other with the manticore, biting, clawing, and striking with its tail.

Lara looked ahead at the charging aufhocker. The strange monster Alistair fought she found almost impossible to resist chasing for some unknown reason, but Lyvaelan's psychic assistance helped her power through the temptation. She broke into a sprint toward the tall shadow. Someone attempted to invade her mind, but Lyvaelan thwarted the attack immediately. Two inquisitors threw blurs at her, but both attacks bounced away. The inquisitors gaped while Eller was annoyed. Lara grinned. Only Thomas knew Lyvaelan lurked there somewhere, and that information had come to the mages too late. She charged at the aufhocker and drew back her claw. They rushed at each other and at the moment they would clash...

She dove beneath it.

Eller's eyes widened as he cast his hands before him, creating a green translucent barrier as Lara threw a right cross directly at him with all her strength. The barrier absorbed most of the impact, but the residual force still sent him sprawling backward as his shield collapsed. One mage blasted her back with some invisible force and another sent a rolling ball of flames at her, but she smiled. She wasn't protected anymore. Lyvaelan had something more important to do.

Her fur smoked and was singed, but she barely felt it as she rolled to her feet. The aufhocker stood in almost the exact position it had been in when she dodged. After a long pause, it dissolved into the ground and disappeared.

Thomas rose to his feet with gritted teeth. The inquisitor turned toward Lara, his face contorted with hate, but something else caught his attention. Six white eyes lurked behind him.

An arm shot out from his shadow as a black hand constrained him. The aufhocker rose from his darkness and towered over him.

"No, you stupid monster, *I* control you, *me! * Obey me! You are my familiar! Listen to..." he trailed off as he met the aufhocker's eyes for the first time.

"*Shh, shh...*" the aufhocker whispered in its grating, haunting voice. "*It's been fun, but now it's time to go home. Playtime's over.*"

Tears dropped from the inquisitor's wide eyes as the aufhocker drew him closer.

"*What's the matter?*" the monster laughed. "*Afraid of the dark?*" The aufhocker opened its mouth, revealing long, dark teeth. Thomas regained his sense of self and screamed, wriggling desperately in the monster's grasp. His cries were cut short by a sickening crunch as the aufhocker bit through his upper torso. With another bite, the inquisitor was gone. So ended the life of Thomas Eller.

The aufhocker turned to the inquisitor who summoned the strange creature and disappeared into the shadows. A moment later, it reappeared behind her and brought down a giant shadowed fist. The inquisitor dropped to the ground as her shield shattered in the sudden attack. The aufhocker disappeared as quickly as it appeared and did the same thing to the inquisitor controlling the manticore. Instantly, the two creatures turned on their summoners. The sinuous creature trampled over its former master and struck several times with its serpentine head. The manticore shot spikes into its former master, trapping him against the wall as it lunged at him and tore the man apart. Lyvaelan emerged from the shadows, his eyes completely black as beads of sweat dripped from his brow. He gestured to the left and the strange creature dashed forward. He gestured to the right and the manticore shot barbs from its tail. He looked at another inquisitor, and the menacing shadow with six white eyes tore her to pieces. Lyvaelan was the conductor, the monsters were the performers, and the destruction was the music they made. The other members of the Evenfall Vigil stood aside as the inquisitors sought refuge but were cut down and devoured by these rampaging nightmares, despite all the flames and lightning the spellcasters conjured. Finally, the triangular room was empty, save for the Evenfall Vigil and the three creatures. Lyvaelan waved one hand and the manticore and strange creature disappeared. He sighed. Controlling more than one at a time was evidently taxing.

He approached the shadowy aufhocker and extended a hand as purple electricity sparked from his palm. "If I ever see you or your kind again, it will be too soon. You and all aufhockers are hereby banished from the Kingdom of Ethelian. You are greater than most of your kind—owing the greater part of your power to your association with your former master—so I command you to give others of your kind this warning: should any of you *ever* return, we will kill that one and seek others. There will be no mercy. Return to the Unseelie Court and bother us no more. Begone!"

The aufhocker bowed as it deteriorated into dust, similar to the other conjured creatures. "*Thank you,*" it said in an eerily familiar voice, "*I hope I haven't broken any trust.*" It laughed as it vanished until only its six glowing eyes remained suspended in the air before they, too, disappeared. Lyvaelan wobbled slightly but didn't collapse.

"Not bad," Lara said. She reached to take one of Lyvaelan's arms but stopped. His breaths were ragged and hungry. The darkness had spread from his eyes and covered much of his face. Shadows in the room lengthened. An electrical current crackled through her fur.

"Lyvaelan." Alistair glanced at Lara, his eyes full of emotion as he sheathed his sword and kneeled with him. "You need to calm yourself. The battle is over. We need to find Hazel. Relax."

Lyvaelan looked up at Alistair, his eyes still pure black. "Hazel?"

Yes," Alistair continued. He put one hand on his shoulder. "She's here. You don't want her to see you like this. Take a breath. We're here for you, no matter what."

"Yes," Lyvaelan said slowly. He closed his eyes and breathed. For a tense moment, nothing changed. A single, transparent tear rolled down his cheek. "You're... here for me." Gradually, the shadows of the room returned to normal and the dark lines and fissures around his eyes receded. He blinked and his eyes returned to their dark red color. "Thank you, Alistair," he panted. "I needed that."

"Whew," Lara released her held breath, "you scared us there, Lyvie. For a minute I thought we'd have to fight the lich *and* you."

He frowned up at her. "I thought I told you not to call me that."

"No, you just acted like you didn't like it."

He sighed. "I guess it's pointless to protest it now." He wobbled on his feet but had regained his composure. "I know we're in a hurry, but perhaps we could rest here, just a little?"

"Of course, a little break might be good." She looked at where Thomas had once stood. "Hey... did you tell it to eat him?"

"Not exactly." He hesitated. "I told it to kill him, but gave it permission to do what it wished. I suspect that was something the creature wanted to do for a long time. It took longer to subdue him than I expected. That aufhocker was Thomas's familiar."

Garo gaped. "A familiar's bond is nearly unbreakable. How did you do that?"

"I had a long conversation with the aufhocker. Apparently, in recent months Thomas has shown more fear than he's caused, which decreased the aufhocker's trust and respect. I provided a means to end their contract with a significant amount of magic and the aufhocker's desire. I think the creature planned to eat him from the moment they were bonded, but Thomas probably felt like he could destroy the aufhocker before that time."

"A costly miscalculation," Alistair muttered.

"Assuredly so. Regardless, we should continue on."

"Are you certain you don't need more time?" Garo asked.

"I am tired, but I can rest when we're out of here safely. Staying in one place increases our chances of being ambushed. I can catch my breath if we walk slowly. Which way should we go? I know there's only one way forward, but we don't know if that's the right way."

"I suspect it is," Alistair said. "The inquisitors came from that direction, which seems to indicate we're getting close to the interior. Let me see if I can hear anything."

Alistair moved toward the open door and stood in the hallway, still visible to the rest of the group. The vampire closed his eyes and made a clicking sound with his tongue. He nodded and looked at them. "There's a stairway somewhere in this hall. It sounds close, but there's another person there. We'll need to exercise caution."

Lyvaelan took a deep breath and walked on his own. Seeing that he was fine, Lara moved forward. The four of them continued with Alistair leading, Lara and Garo behind, and Lyvaelan trailing. As they strode through the curved hallway, they found it ended in an open door leading to a much larger triangular room. Alistair was immediately on guard as an armchair hurtled past his head.

"I abhor violence, but I make exceptions for intruders. I'm afraid you will all have to—" The Alchemist adjusted his glasses in surprise. "No, you aren't supposed to—" Lyvaelan entered finally, glaring at Paxton. The man fell to his knees, holding his hands up placatingly. "I surrender. I won't do anything, just, gods, don't hurt me!"

The others looked at Lyvaelan, who shrugged.

"That is a wise decision," Lyvaelan said coolly. "Tell us where Hazel Enda is kept and perhaps we'll let you live."

"Downstairs. I was guarding the area, but she's all yours."

"Good," Lyvaelan said, looking at the others. "Shall we go?"

"Wait," Alistair said, "we need to find her parents, too."

"That's good," Paxton said eagerly. "Her parents are there as well. Not in the same room, of course. She's in the room down the left corridor and her parents are to the right."

"Wow," Lara said, "you are the most helpful you've ever been."

The Alchemist shifted nervously, glancing between them rapidly. "Actually, I would like a favor."

Lyvaelan's countenance darkened. "You're in no position to make demands."

Paxton shrank back. "I know, I—I just want you to make them stop. Please."

Lara tilted her head. "Make who stop?"

"The monsters in the shadows. Ever since we fought, and you called those evil fae to haunt me, I haven't had a moment of peace. Please undo your curse."

Lyvaelan's expression remained neutral. "Paxton, if you stay in this room and don't escape or combat the Council of Archmages, then I will release you from the curse."

"No, please!" he pleaded. "By then, it may be too late! The Grand Inquisitor will become the living lich and you can't stop her. If she kills you, then I will be stuck like this forever!"

Lara smiled and headed toward the stairway. "Well, Paxy, you better hope we don't die, then."

The others followed her down. Garo looked over at Lyvaelan. "Exactly what curse did you put on that man?"

"I didn't, actually." Lyvaelan paused. "Or at least, I don't *think* I did. I created many dark illusions around me that he likely associated with the pain when I broke his body. What he sees now are just the phantoms of a damaged mind. It's likely nothing more than that. But then, I was making my will manifest through magic, so it's possible I actually cursed him accidentally. But I probably didn't. Probably." Lara didn't find his explanation very convincing.

Chapter Thirty-Six
The Dance of Bitter Enemies

A wyvern fell from the sky, struck by many arrows and burned by numerous spells. The monster's serpentine head screeched with pain and its long and sinuous neck flopped uselessly as armored hippogriffs and their riders slashed at its batlike wings, tearing great holes in it. A wyvern might have been a good choice against brave soldiers, but hippogriffs flew significantly faster and possessed far greater intelligence. Garson found it unlikely that a single wyvern could successfully kill a hippogriff despite its greater size. Against multiple hippogriffs, the creature had little chance.

And so it fell.

Garson glanced at Selevia Castus. Her expression only betrayed the slightest disdain for the plummeting monster.

She noticed his gaze and gave a wan smile. "Does the death of a creature like this hurt you, Archmage of Dragons?"

"Hmph." He grunted, sparks showering from his nostrils. "Hardly. I was just deciding if I should intervene to assist the riders. Do not lump wyverns in with dragons. They are so distantly related that the relationship is nearly nonexistent. Dragons are more closely related to lindworms or loong than they are to wyverns. That two-legged flying snake lacks any sort of intelligence or finesse.."

She broke into a grin. "Can't say I disagree, though a monster of that size doesn't exactly need finesse to survive."

He regarded the wyvern as it fell to the ground some distance from them, sending up a shower of snow and crushing multiple zombies. Its long and sharpened tail struck at random, seeking to skewer or poison anyone unlucky enough to touch it. It writhed on its back, screaming as it fought to right itself. Two hippogriffs landed on each of its wings, pinning it down. Their riders stabbed into the cream-colored underbelly of the beast with their swordstaffs repeatedly. The wyvern's tail whipped around, but the hippogriffs dodged and took to the air. The monster flopped over and purple blood gushed from its mouth. It attempted to walk but only succeeded in pushing itself against the ground and piling up snow. The creature could not long survive with the wounds it sustained.

It ceased struggling and panted on the ground, sending up great clouds of vapor with its breath. Slowly, the wyvern disintegrated like burning fragments of shining paper. Like all creatures summoned from elsewhere by a conjurer, the creature would return to its home to rest, drawing on the magic of its summoner to heal itself. Destroying the wyvern meant one less conjurer would be capable of challenging them. A small, but nonetheless appreciated, victory.

Garson turned his eyes to the rest of the battle. The zombies had done little to impede soldiers. The wyvern had broken the ranks and a few of the front line died, but the casualties were thankfully minimal. He peered at Kazra Lo Veedra, searching for the inquisitors. From here he observed a few lining the top of the building but partially covered behind the short parapets that crowned the structure. A flicker caught his eye.

Uh oh.

Without hesitation, he unfurled his wings and used thaumaturgy to speed him through the air. He slipped to the side of the burning salamander, who laughed as he devoured corpses, and dodged the sylph who danced as she tossed undead in unpredictable directions. The flicker atop Kazra Lo Veedra had become a steady light and intensified with each passing moment. Garson flew around to the front of the army and soared high above them, brandishing his staff. He uttered a few quick words to form a reflective shield before the light erupted. A roar of magenta energy exploded from the estate directly toward Garson. The light from the attack lit the entire battlefield as it surged toward the army. Garson channeled magic through his staff and the reflective apotropaic magic that surrounded it. The blast struck and sought to overpower him, but the Archmage of Dragons would not be easily destroyed. With overwhelming effort, he redirected the blast to the side. A huge scar rent the earth where it struck with the sound of nails on a chalkboard. The snow seemed not only to melt but to wither, and the ground bubbled and hissed with blackened, roiling tar. A small portion of the energy had been redirected toward Kazra Lo Veedra, where it sent snaking crackles of electricity along the surface of the shield that protected the estate.

Garson turned back to the army and amplified his voice a hundred times over. "The enemy uses arcane cannons! Prepare yourselves for the next attack! All spellcasters trained in magnetic apotropaic magic use it now!" Magnetic shields would attract the magic of the arcane cannon and divide it between them, dispersing it harmlessly.

With several beats of his wings, he returned to Selevia, who finished destroying a few zombies that had approached Elimerita's Chosen Conjurers from the forest. She eyed him. "Are you certain that was wise? Expending that much energy would exhaust anyone."

"Well, not me." Truth be told, he felt winded, but his draconic nature meant he would recover quickly. "Should I have let the lich decimate our forces?"

"No, but you could have told me and I would have helped shoulder half the burden."

"Your time was better served defending the elemental conjurers. Besides, it's good for the soldiers to see me leading and not sitting idly by."

She shrugged. "I wouldn't call diverting a stream of necrotic magic and then offering a single command leading, but it was nonetheless an effective way for them to recognize the power of their leader. I suppose that could help with morale."

He stuck his staff in the ground and crossed his arms. He wouldn't dignify that with an answer. Again, a flicker from a slightly different area on top of Kazra Lo Veedra appeared. He resisted rushing to divert it. They were capable and knew what they were doing. Sure enough, the blast issued from the building, but once it had gone halfway to the army, it divided into a hundred smaller streams. Each hit the arcane shield of a spellcaster with far less force than Garson experienced. He sighed and relaxed his shoulders.

"Well," Selevia said when the magenta energy disappeared, "I suppose that's one less crisis to worry about. Let's see what they throw at us next."

"I'd really prefer not to," he grumbled.

"Oh, I don't think you mean that," she replied softly. "If you don't see it, then it's likely you may never see again."

"Fair enough. What do you believe they will do next?"

Her mechanical eye flicked over the battlefield. "I think the wyvern was intended to distract from the activation of the arcane cannons. Since we've countered both, I would expect a greater emphasis on conjuration. Perhaps multiple creatures working together to break the ranks. The lich probably can't do much more beyond controlling the undead and the fortress. I imagine if we had his full attention, it would be quite another story. As it stands, we mostly have to deal with whatever magic the Inquisition uses. It's no secret one of their greatest strengths lies in conjuration. What better way to dispose of summoned undead?"

Garson nodded. "That makes sense, but I wonder what they will summon? If one had a peryton as a familiar, it is possible the others may have made deals with similarly odious beings. In fact, I suspect Alvaria encouraged them to develop rapport with monsters no moral conjurer ever would, just to disrupt our eventual confrontation." She had played the role of Grand Inquisitor for many years and developed strategies to defeat them. Alvaria Saccarra was nothing if not intelligent and thorough. Damn her.

He turned his attention to the Archmage of the Green. The man had gathered a selection of mismatched trees around himself. Bark encased him in virtually impenetrable armor. A broad rowan covered his back, while two birches formed his legs. His arms were formed from an ash and an oak. A hawthorn acted as his breastplate and a hazel served as his helm. The archmage towered above the battlefield at over sixty feet tall, and only because he hunched down. His voice occasionally rumbled across the clearing, speaking nonsense and magic. Undead flew in each direction as he swung his arms with careless power, the roots at the bottom of each trunk acting like innumerable fingers. Zombies climbed the branches but did little to harm so much as a twig. The rowan on his back fruited and tiny, glowing red berries showered the undead, causing them to swell and explode. Garson had forgotten that alchemical rowan berries could be used against black magic such as necromancy. He wondered if the trees forming his suit of armor had specific purposes beyond what Garson expected. They had never been on extremely friendly terms, despite being two of the oldest archmages alive. Perhaps that had been a mistake.

"The hawthorn that stands in the middle of a field shall not be cut down," Garson muttered.

"What was that?" Selevia asked.

"Nothing, just an old phrase I heard long ago."

She followed his eyes. "Do you think he'll be alright? He's alone out there, and I count at least sixteen undead crawling over him."

"Truth be told, I don't think he's ever alone. Bertrand is a strange sort; there is much to him none of us may ever understand. I think it is wise not to underestimate him."

A croaking scream pierced the air and sent a chill down Garson's spine. A black shape lunged from the top of Kazra Lo Veedra toward the assembled soldiers. It spread large black feathered wings, as broad as a hippogriff's, and moved with as swiftly but with a strange, erratic trajectory. The soldiers raised spears and shields to halt its descent, but right before it collided with them, the mass of black feathers shrank and condensed into a humanoid form. It was smaller than most men and Garson could not see it through the ranks, but he beheld its effects and heard the screams. Viscera and weapons flew through the air where it passed. A dense gathering of soldiers burst apart as the creature resumed its massive bird form and ripped at them with talons and beak.

"What is that?" Garson exclaimed. When he looked at Selevia, he stopped. Her eyes filled with seething fury, and her hands trembled as she gripped her spear.

"Valravn," she whispered through gritted teeth. "How could they?"

Garson stepped forward and spread his wings, but Selevia held out her spear to stop him. He opened his mouth to question her, but the words stuck when he saw her expression.

"No," she said. "I will slay this monster, and then I will have the head of the conjurer who summoned it."

Wordlessly, she donned the helm that completely hid her face. She dashed into the field of battle, cutting through zombies without worry when they crossed her path. When she stood some distance from the archmage, she reached her hand out to the creature.

"With hatred, let both be filled
Until all blood from us is spilled!"

A pulse washed over Garson as he recognized the spell of enmity she cast on the valravn. The giant bird beat its wings and scattered the surrounding soldiers. It departed from their ranks and landed thirty feet from Selevia. The giant crow with a skull seemingly attached to its face drew itself up and rapidly shrank into its shorter humanoid form. Its beak and face appeared more like a decorated white skull mask than anything real, except it moved as it breathed. Feathers covered its torso and its arms ended in hands halfway between human and raven. The feathers along its arms resembled wings, though they would be too short to fly. It moved constantly with small nods and breathed as if with its whole body. Its feet, too, possessed great talons. It stood with jerking movements and pivoted around the battlefield, its entire form constantly crouching as if prepared to attack and yet there was a chilling calm and confidence about the monster.

Its crimson eyes fixed on Selevia. "You call for enmity between us?" The creature creaked in perfect imperial common. "A vendetta, hmm? I don't recognize you, but you seem to recognize me." It sniffed the air. "I smell the loathing in your blood. Perhaps you know one of my kin."

She brandished her spear. "Have you consumed the heart of a king yet?"

The valravn chuckled. "If I had, do you think any foolish inquisitor would possess the power to control me? No, no, no. No kings, I'm afraid, but"—the valravn shifted shape into a tall man clad in ornate black armor. A shield embossed with a flying bird adorned his left arm while a cold, pale longsword occupied the right. The face remained black and feathered save for the skull mask. The valravn grinned— "do you know whose heart I had to eat to be able to assume this form? Tell me, mage, do I look like a knight to you?"

Garson understood little of what this meant. A valravn was some variety of Unseelie fae, he knew that much, but anything beyond that eluded him. Still, the words the creature spoke carried dark and malevolent undertones. From here, he sensed Selevia's rage rising uncontrollably. He reached out to her telepathically. *Don't let it get to you. It's trying to make you lose control.*

Selevia relaxed somewhat. "Tell me, valravn," she finally said, "when did mommy say you could go out and play?"

The knight's smile dropped somewhat. "What do you mean?"

She stood taller. "I'm sure your conjurer is absolutely livid that you're not doing what you were told."

"And I should care?"

"Only if you don't want to anger mommy."

The valravn gritted its teeth. "I reiterate: I don't know what you're talking about."

"Oh, I think you do. The Queen of Crows, the Lady of Ravens, the Goddess of War... the Morrigan."

The lordly form of the creature burst with the hiss of smoke and steam as it screamed at her. "She is nothing! What would a stupid human girl know of her?"

Garson could almost hear her smiling. "I know she keeps her pets on a tight leash. What do you think will happen when she discovers one of her precious birds has flown the rookery? The Morrigan won't be pleased."

"Stop saying that name!" All its feathers bristled.

"You're right to be afraid of drawing her attention." Selevia leaned forward. "The Morrigan might hear."

With lightning speed and a murderous shriek, the valravn charged. In black smoke, it sloughed its form, returning to its smaller feathered shape. It lashed out with unpredictable movements, yet the commander of the Guard Unyielding met each strike with a parry from her spear. The creature transformed into its massive raven form, but she dodged backward without losing balance. Constantly shifting to prevent her from strategizing, the valravn continued its pursuit. Despite the speed of the exchange, Garson noticed that she favored using her spear with only her right hand. Her left hand remained closed around something, though he could not see what. The archmage breathed and attuned himself to the flow of magic and sensed small pulses—barely perceptible—issuing from her left hand.

The valravn changed from bird to knight and bowled into her. She pushed against the black sword with her spear. The wood of her weapon had been specially selected and enchanted to bear such beatings, but even it strained against the large creature.

It drew close, teeth gritted. Another blast from the arcane cannon lit the sky, illuminating the hatred in those bloody eyes. "I wonder," the valravn growled, "what your heart will taste like? What power will I gain to subjugate the weak and hound the pure of heart? You are not so pure, woman, but your heart will be mine all the same."

It pushed off of her and transformed into its bird form again, but Selevia recovered quickly. The valravn swept at her with open talons, and she raced toward it. The action surprised the creature as it faltered momentarily. She sliced a long gash in its left flank and slid beneath it. With a sharp cry, it took to the sky, but Selevia's boots glowed a bright yellow. She sprang forty feet in the air to intercept it and pierced its left wing. Using the spear as an anchor, she pulled her legs up and kicked with both glowing feet as hard as possible. She dislodged her weapon and shot earthward while the bird sprawled over itself from the force of the strike and its injured wing. Selevia landed softly on the ground, her thaumaturgically empowered boots absorbing the force of her descent.

The valravn screamed in a mass of feathers as it crashed into the ground, scattering snow and undead bodies in its wake. Before the snow could settle, the creature charged from the chaos of its fall in its small, feathered form. It maintained its speed, but all its feathers were ruffled and certain patches were matted with blood. Selevia turned to meet it and slashed at its undefended midsection. It ignored the wound and wrestled with her spear.

"I am a raven of war!" the monster roared. "Do you think crude weapons of iron or ravnulium will stop me? Such metals pose nothing more than a minor inconvenience."

She stuck her helmeted face close to the valravn. "I know." She released her spear and jabbed its chest with her left hand.

The valravn dropped the weapon and stumbled back. It stared at its chest and tore at the feathers near where she had stabbed.

"Damnable human!" the valravn wheezed. It breathed heavily and staggered. "It doesn't matter... I... can still... beat you..."

Selevia picked up her spear and twirled it. "I don't think so."

In a second, she had closed the distance. The creature now dodged and avoided each blow with mounting exhaustion. A few times, it looked as if it wanted to shapeshift but now appeared to be incapable of doing so. With each step, Selevia inflicted another wound. After several seconds, the creature was entirely covered with bloody gashes, its skull face cracked. In desperation, it leaped at her with all four of its talons raised to slash at her. Selevia moved with grace and poise as she slipped to the side. She dropped her spear and drew her marinom from her side, shifting it into a shortsword. When the creature landed, she grabbed its neck with her left hand and stabbed into its back with her right. The valravn twitched as she withdrew the blade. It sunk to its knees and stared up at her as she circled around to face it.

"I... underestimated you," it whispered. "Next time I will prepare for you and then"—its eyes glowed dark red and its voice regained clarity—"I will eat your heart."

Selevia stared down at it. "You're welcome to try." With a single stroke, she slashed through its neck. Before she made it all the way through, the body dissolved into smoke and dust. The valravn had been defeated. She stooped over where its body had been and plucked something from the remains of the conjured monster.

She strode back to the archmage and doffed her helmet. Her hair stuck at different angles with sweat.

Garson snorted. "You look like you've aged ten years."

Her grin returned. "I *feel* like it. That abomination didn't give up easily."

"Or at all. What was it you did that turned the tide?"

"My secret weapon." She held up a long, golden pin. "The Seelie are hurt by the most base of metals, but the Unseelie can't abide the touch of the most precious. You couldn't see it, but when I stabbed him with that pin, the flow of magic in his body ceased functioning properly. Magic leaked out, and none of his wounds healed. Amazing what a little alchemical gold can do."

"Impressive indeed, though you made a single error."

Her smile faded slightly. "And what was that?"

"You made it personal."

She raised an eyebrow. "With all due respect, what exactly would you call volunteering to arrest one of your former best friends who betrayed your trust?"

A cold fury bubbled up, but he quashed it. She meant no harm and required instruction. He sighed. "You misunderstand. The problem is not that you took its jabs personally. The problem is that you led the creature to despise you specifically and challenged it beyond the scope of its summoning."

"Why is that a problem?"

"The darkest of creatures hold the blackest of grudges. Lysander once made such an error, though he sought to save his allies."

"Well, he survived, didn't he? Whatever he fought must not have been as strong as it needed to be. I have no problem with training for the day it comes to kill me."

"For one who sees so much"—he shook his head—"you are shortsighted. While you prepare by sparring with allies, how will the valravn prepare?"

Her quizzical expression faded as her face lost color. "No."

"Yes," Garson replied. "You assumed that because Lysander survived that he won but you never asked how many died before he reigned victorious. When the cruel are embarrassed, they seek to hurt the object of their hate in more ways than the physical."

She kneeled before him. "Forgive me, Your Eminence. I have put others in harm's way foolishly."

"Rise, Selevia Castus. My chastisement may have been too harsh. It is easy to judge proper action from the outside with the benefit of hindsight. You dispatched the creature with efficiency and skill— more than I could have, certainly. I would encourage you—once we return to Selevarian—to speak with specialists in the field of fae habits and tracking. It would be wise for you to hunt that monster before it recovers fully. While you are not responsible for its actions, it will ultimately bring you greater peace knowing it has been permanently slain. Such a being will likely bide its time, but I urge you not to wait. Hoping it will forget this defeat will only end in many dead innocents."

"Thank you, Archmage of Dragons." She rose to her feet. "At the risk of sounding rude, I did not expect such insight from you.

Whenever I've seen you or heard you speak, I never got the impression that you were quite as wise as you are."

"I'm older than the High Archmage. Even a fool can learn enough to seem wise with the weight of many centuries on his shoulders."

She smiled. "I doubt that."

Garson stared off across the battlefield to where other creatures had been summoned. Several harpies screeched across the sky, their pungent odor noticeable even from this distance. A monstrous three-legged horse galloped across the field, and another wyvern appeared. More creatures were summoned by the soldiers in the army as well, and they had the weight of numbers to aid them. For now, the two forces had returned to a near stalemate, with the army slowly gaining ground and pushing ever closer to the doors of Kazra Lo Veedra. He gazed at the menacing structure and bit his lip.

Lysander, I hope you know what you're doing.

Chapter Thirty-Seven
Tribulation and Trust

Lyvaelan descended the stone stairs and turned to the right behind the others, intent on freeing Hazel's parents. A single inquisitor blocked the way, but Alistair swiftly decapitated him. Lyvaelan wondered if they should dispose of the body, but the separation of the head from the torso would make it less dangerous for them. He considered burning it, but the last series of conflicts had exhausted him more than he cared to admit. The hungry voice within cajoled and urged him to tap more completely into his heritage, but he had resisted. Still, between fighting inquisitors and combating his dark nature, he could not recall a time he felt more depleted.

They hurried down the hallway when a door opened in front of them and to the left. Seven oddly dressed individuals approached them. They were pale and elegant, dressed in robes with white feathers. The smallest of their number carried an urn.

Alistair's muscles tightened, and Lara readied herself. The group stopped and calmly fanned out. The largest—their leader, judging by how he held himself—stepped forward. "We have no quarrel with you. Move aside or die."

"We do not yield to Moth Cultists!" Alistair said.

The larger one narrowed his eyes. "And exactly who are you?"

"I am Alistair zar Erythis, son of Venarius zar Erythis, the Lord of Noxphetalis and Sovereign of the Nosferatu."

Lyvaelan wondered if this posturing was really necessary. Could they not simply collect Hazel's parents and leave?

The smaller vampire holding the urn moved closer to the large one. "He's the youngest son. We should probably depart without engaging them."

The female vampire chuckled and crossed her arms. "Serena will be so disappointed she missed this mission."

The leader glared at her before fixing his gaze on Alistair. "Then I suppose we *cannot* let you go. A pretender sits on the abhorrent Throne of Austerity, leading the nosferatu astray. We will do our people a favor by removing one member of the false king's family from existence."

Lara lunged toward the leader with teeth bared. The leader raised his hand and Lara floated up, held aloft psychokinetically. Alistair dashed at him, but the woman confronted him instead, pushing his blade aside with her hand, despite the hiss of her palm touching it. Four of the vampires rushed at Garo and Lyvaelan, though he dodged backward as Garo moved to take up more space in the hallway and prevent the vampires from attacking Lyvaelan.

Alistair struck at the woman with a series of furious strikes, but she dodged and blocked them, occasionally slashing at Alistair with her long nails, ripping into his clothes. This woman was clearly no stranger to combat.

Lyvaelan had tired of the situation before it reached this point. He touched the mind of the leader and noticed nothing blocking his mind. The deficit that made Alistair and Lara such liabilities would finally work to his benefit. He didn't need to be subtle, or expend great effort. All he needed to do was release a psychic scream.

The vampire leader yelled and clutched the sides of his head. Lara dropped to the ground and lunged. He writhed on the ground, so she instead struck at the smaller man. The vampire's eyes widened as Lara punched directly at his chest and through the urn he carried. The vessel shattered and a spray of dust flooded the hallway.

Instantly, the vampires stopped and gaped. The woman dodged a final swing and then rushed to pick up the pieces of pottery.

The leader, now recovered from the psychic pain, scrambled to the mess. "No, no, no, no!" He muttered as he looked helplessly about and scraped the dust from the walls. The other vampires did likewise.

The Evenfall Vigil members hesitated. A moment ago, they were in a fight to the death, and now their enemies were cleaning an underground passage?

"Is this normal?" Lara mumbled to Alistair.

Alistair shook his head slowly. "Vampires can be obsessive, but this is much more than that. It isn't a ruse, though. It's too coordinated. What did you break?"

The leader glowered at them with sheer loathing. His teeth extended as he rose and advanced. The female put a hand on his shoulder. "Orson, there's no point. We could spend a year collecting the dust, but the Council of Archmages is here and we can't risk getting involved. We have to go."

Orson closed his eyes and collected himself. "We will leave." He pointed an accusatory finger at the smaller vampire Lara punched. "This is your fault, Mikhail. You will fix this, or pay for it."

Mikhail appeared calm and nodded silently.

"And all of you," Orson said, "you've made a powerful enemy this day. We shall destroy you all in time."

"You'll have to get in line," Lara growled. "We walked into a lich's fortress without giving two shits; do you really think a few vampires scare us?"

Orson hissed but dashed past them. The other vampires followed and disappeared.

They waited several moments for something else to happen, but nothing did. The conflict concluded as quickly as it started.

"Did you know them?" Lyvaelan asked.

"Only by their manner of dress," Alistair replied. "Moth Cultists. They believe all vampire governments are false because they do not adhere to the tenets of the Moth King. They rarely show themselves because their actions have led my father to order them to be executed on sight."

"Which would explain why you chose to attack people who were just trying to leave."

Alistair scratched his eyebrow with an elongated fingernail. He looked a little sheepish.

"Regardless," Garo said, "we should return to the task at hand."

"Alright," Lara said, "let's save the Enda family!"

She loped further down the hall, sniffing as she went. Lyvaelan appreciated her tracking since he disliked the idea of searching for them mentally while the lich still existed. He doubted anything bad would happen, but it was an unnecessary risk.

Finally, Lara stopped at the door. She grinned back at them with her lupine face. "Found 'em!" Before anyone could react, she punched through the door. A woman on the other side screamed, and a man swore loudly.

"No! Get back!" Kyle Enda yelled.

Lara retreated, her tail between her legs. Alistair reached toward the door but stopped when he saw his bloody fingernails. Lyvaelan looked at Garo, who also appeared more monstrous than usual and hesitated to enter the room.

I am always a monster. They can sometimes be humanlike, but I must hide myself at all times because I will always be feared.

He remembered what Hazel had said to her parents that night in the rain. She stood firm as they shrank from him. They thought he would hurt them. He was dangerous.

Danger doesn't matter; goodness does. Lyvaelan is good.

He clenched a fist and stepped into the room, despite every misgiving and alarm in his head telling him not to. There was one small voice that drowned out all the others.

I know he'll save me if I need saving.

He refused to fail her. Not now—not ever. He stepped gingerly over the shattered door. The Endas huddled in the corner. Kyle held a chair before him to ward off whatever came through the door.

Lyvaelan approached with both hands raised. A wave of doubt crossed the face of Kyle.

"Hello Mr. and Mrs. Enda," he began. "Do you remember me? I'm one of Hazel's friends. I'm—"

"Lyvaelan?" Kyle lowered the chair and rose.

He blinked several times. "Yes."

"You... came to save us?"

He nodded, suddenly feeling the need to do something with his hands.

They both walked tentatively forward. Lynn watched him warily. "How do we know this isn't some inquisitor mind trick?"

"I would hope that an inquisitor could devise something better than a werewolf breaking through your door and then remedying your fears with a dark elf."

Kyle suddenly laughed. It was a deep belly laugh which sent him back onto the bed in the corner. Lynn held her hand over her heart and breathed, but she also smiled.

"You've got to admit, the boy's got a point, Lynn." He got back up and hesitated only a moment before clapping Lyvaelan on the shoulder. "Thank you. Truly."

Lyvaelan swallowed and nodded. He glanced back to the hallway, then to the Endas. "This may come as a shock to you, but I'm not the only dangerous person your daughter works with."

"Oh, we know," Lynn said. "Lara stayed with us and told us she did competitive fighting. That handsome young man who picked her up also carried a sword, so I assumed he could handle himself if necessary."

"Well—yes," Lyvaelan replied with a frown, "but recall what Hazel told you when we visited. That's only part of the story. The werewolf who broke down the door was Lara. Alistair is a vampire.

We're all a little monstrous, but it's the only way we managed to get this far."

From their expressions, it wasn't hard to guess that they were surprised. New doubt washed over their faces as they contemplated the information.

"I trust them with my life," Lyvaelan said, "and so does Hazel. They both protected her beyond what they needed to because they cared about her."

"Of course," Kyle said, "it's just a lot to take in."

Lynn's searched Lyvaelan's face. "Have you found Hazel yet?"

He shook his head. "No, we wanted to ensure your safety first. She is surprisingly capable."

The couple shared a haunted look that said everything it needed to.

"Regardless, we should go. Just… try not to be alarmed by my friends. They might be frightening, but the only ones who need fear them are those who work for the Grand Inquisitor."

He coaxed them into the hallway. Initially, they gasped when they saw each member of the Evenfall Vigil, but they quickly recovered and thanked them. Lara still appeared downtrodden when he sent her a telepathic message.

If you hadn't broken down the door without knocking, perhaps they wouldn't have been scared witless by the presence of an eight foot tall werewolf on the other side.

She scowled at him, but what he said broke through her mood. It had the desired effect.

"Hazel is this way," Lara growled, leading them back down the hallway they came from. She looked at Lyvaelan pointedly. "This time, we can knock."

Chapter Thirty-Eight
The Immortal Struggle

After five minutes of chipping away at the surface of the wall, the ravnulium had finally cracked. Lysander jolted magic into his marinom, shifting it into a small pick. He maintained a small flow of magic to help keep its shape as he bent the ravnulium away from the stone. A few inches of stone were now visible. That was all he needed. He placed the butt of his staff against the surface and poured magic into it, picturing the stone vibrating at a microscopic level with the tiniest pieces rubbing together. The stone glowed bright orange, and soon the ravnulium did too. The black metal gradually melted. Ravnulium was easier to liquify than stone, but not when magic was directly applied. The stone behind it neared the temperature of magma. All the Guard Unyielding stepped back and put their spears—which also functioned as staves—to the ground, which they cooled rapidly. The metal, once it reached the floor, hardened almost immediately. When the magic-immune substance had melted away completely into a steaming black pile on the ground, Lysander applied a reverberating force to the wall, and the stone exploded into the room.

They were in.

Lysander absently released the spriggan from service, returning the creature to his home in Faerie. The fae bodyguard could do much, but against a lich he would be practically helpless.

Zylit floated in front of the sarcophagus in the center of the room. The Guard Unyielding fanned out around Lysander and stood at the ready. He heard banging on the other doors that had also been closed. One other door to the west had opened before Lysander's group had gotten through. The Guard Unyielding who had broken through first lie motionless on the ground. Blast marks scorched the walls as the only remnant of their struggle. The lich remained placid.

Lysander stamped his staff on the ground, and a well of righteous fury rose in him. He channeled the thaumaturgical magic into his palms and sent it into his staff, which glowed bright white. White electricity crackled across the length of the staff as it glowed. The thaumaturgy at the end of it lengthened three feet into a sharpened point of blindingly white light. This was the reason vampires feared him. He was the Spear of the Sun, Scourge of the Night.

The time for conversation had ended.

Lysander pushed magic into his legs and arms and lunged forward. His light elf heritage naturally increased his speed and agility, but the magic multiplied this many times over. In a blink, he was before the lich. Dark magenta chains appeared around the archmage moments before he struck, wrapping around him as he brought his staff down. The staff cut through much of the chain but slowed the staff enough for the other chains to throw him back against the wall before touching the lich.

Zylit observed the four members of the Guard Unyielding, and the ends of the chains sharpened into daggers. The Guard Unyielding dashed around the lich, striking with flame, staff and sword. Each chain around Zylit slithered and struck to both repel their advances and strike. The lich stood commanding the chains and created more as they were cut and destroyed. Zylit flicked his hand, effortlessly repelling the spells of the Guard Unyielding.

Lysander hit the wall where he was thrown with his feet and catapulted toward the enemy. Zylit turned as Lysander hurdled toward him. Instantly, the lich disappeared. Lysander used wizardry to slow and guide his trajectory as he hit the ground and rolled to the ready. Zylit teleported back to where Lysander had stood just behind a member of the Guard Unyielding. Dark magenta magic circled the lich as he grabbed the biceps of the soldier and ripped her arm off without resistance. The soldier didn't scream as she fell, but turned and stabbed at the lich with her glowing marinom, imbued with thaumaturgical magic. The lich dodged to each side as she struck.

"You are impressive," he said as she attempted to strike him, "I realize, now, why you are called the Guard Unyielding." He caught her forearm. "But you will yield to me, regardless." He thrust his other hand against her helmet, which corroded into dust. "Behold, the truly unyielding power of death." Black tendrils spread from his fingers and entered her eyes, ears, and mouth. She gasped.

The others rushed to help her, but the dark magenta chains had turned into serpent heads and struck with reckless aggression, holding them at bay. A great pulse from the lich repelled them. Zylit's eyes glowed as he stared into the eyes of the soldier he held. Lysander struggled forward, but there were too many of the serpents. He looked at her. She had aged decades in moments. More than that, she looked starved. Boils and cancerous growths appeared on her skin as she withered. In moments, she had dissolved into dust.

Zylit let the dust fall from his fingers. "Famine, pestilence, old age, grievous injury... these bow low before death, for death is their master, and I am master over death."

Lysander glanced at the sarcophagus. They needed a better strategy. The lich had likely used the sorcerous technique of mental division to control the undead, monitor the estate, protect Alvaria, and fight them. His resources were stretched thin. Lysander threw his marinom in dart form at the sarcophagus. The marinom glanced off a transparent shield surrounding the coffin, despite the edge of ravnulium. He nodded.

"What?" Zylit questioned. "Did you expect me to leave the tomb unguarded?"

"No, but I had to make sure." He looked at the Guard Unyielding. "Attack the sarcophagus with everything you have!" He turned back to Zylit. "The lich is mine."

"You don't expect three mages to break my shield, do you?"

"No, that's why I brought more than three."

At that moment, two of the walls placed over the arches exploded in. The rest of the Guard Unyielding had made it through. There were only four additional soldiers, but their help would be invaluable.

"Destroy the sarcophagus and the shield that surrounds it!"

Lysander advanced on the lich, his staff glowing. The lich's dark magenta serpents lunged successively, but he batted them away and sliced as he charged. The lich banished the chains and appeared to take a breath before spewing a gout of magenta flames at the archmage and his allies. Lysander put his staff before him and erected a shield that split the flame and protected the soldiers. The Guard Unyielding paid little attention to the lich as they doggedly smashed and battered the shield with weapons and spells. As the flames subsided, the archmage studied the lich, who continued to hover. The levitation faltered almost imperceptibly, now and then, like a brief stutter in the magic that kept him aloft.

Lysander walked forward. "You're running out of power, lich. Raising an army, controlling the estate, fighting all of us, and maintaining the barrier around Alvaria can't be easy. You're weakening."

"You speak true, Archmage of War," Zylit said, drawing smoky magenta energy into his hand. "But I shall show you that even a weakened lich is stronger than the mightiest of living mages." The energy solidified into a massive sword, easily six feet long and nearly a foot wide at its base. Its jagged edge resembled the curve of flames, and the mere appearance of it made Lysander shiver. Such a sword would be unwieldy were it made of metal, but this was constructed of pure magic. It would be deadlier and harder to destroy.

Zylit dropped to the ground and sprang at Lysander with alarming speed. The sudden attack surprised the archmage, who narrowly managed to raise his staff in defense. The blade felt as strong as any metal sword. Attack after attack hammered at Lysander in furious succession. The creature likely had no training in how to handle a sword, but it mattered little when the weapon was weightless and the being holding it moved like a bloodthirsty whirlwind. The lich was smaller than Lysander and used his shorter stature to avoid his counterattacks.

As they locked weapons, Zylit let out an unsettling hiss. A centipede crawled from the lich's mouth and reentered through his ear. The creature was trying to unsettle Lysander, and it would have worked, except he knew this trick. Lysander took a deep breath and energized his limbs. He stopped his defensive tactics. It was time for the final push.

He threw himself into the lich with his spear-like staff and imagined gathering thaumaturgy into his palm. He contained the energy, and—using wizardry and enchantment—bound it within glass made of light. The process took a fraction of a second and he hurled these darts at Zylit.

The lich dodged the condensed thaumaturgy while warding off the spear, but Lysander was ready for the slightest opening. He slashed with his spear as the lich destroyed one of the crystals. Zylit attempted to dodge, but the spear tip of the staff lacerated his chest and left arm.

The lich screamed and dropped the dark magenta sword, which disappeared into smoke. Zylit collapsed and scrambled backward as black shadows oozed from the injury. The lich pressed against the wall, heaving. Lysander knew the lich wasn't struggling to breathe, however. The lich was trying to keep himself from dissolving.

Lysander heard a slight crack from behind him. The shield around the sarcophagus was breaking. He looked back at Zylit. "You've lost."

The lich shook his head. "No. We've both won."

"Both?"

The earth shook, and a ubiquitous laugh filled the air. A chill ran down Lysander's spine. He recognized that voice.

The gemstones all over Zylit's body glowed. "The living lich of half a day has come."

Chapter Thirty-Nine
Fear and Trembling

Garson surveyed the battlefield. He had summoned no dragons. They weren't necessary yet. The undead army fell before their soldiers. Lysander's strategy had been effective, with some minor adaptations. The enemy mages had sent blasts of fire against the army of Selevarian, but it had done little good. The army had more than triple the number of spellcasters, and with the addition of the archmages, the defectors contributed little to their losses. Only the conjured monsters had caused any real damage to their ranks and, by Garson's estimate, numbered only in the dozens. Thousands of undead had been destroyed by comparison.

The power of the elementals also reduced the necessity for dragons. Sakirikas the salamander raged through the zombies, ripping them apart and devouring them with many mouths of flame. The gnome Darundar had created a short stone wall around the conjurers and opened a chasm between them and the enemy. Veliyana looked for all the world like she was engaged in an elegant dance, as she threw zombies in various directions. Abalia splashed through the undead, freezing their feet to the ground and tearing them apart within her.

He gazed north to the jagged wall of glass spikes. It curved around the northwestern edge of the battlefield, funneling the zombies toward the main forces. The Archmage of Crystals had performed every task with surprising efficiency. By reputation, the man was a terror to deal with, but apparently, he could work well when necessary. He now stood glowing in the north, a mass of sharpened points of thaumaturgical light. There was a vague similarity to the archmage and a porcupine, but Garson dismissed the thought on the off chance the Crystal King might hear it telepathically. It was a comical precaution, but watching him enter a frenzy on the battlefield, filled with single-minded bloodlust, made Garson feel a little more justified in his paranoia.

His scaled wings unfurled, and he flew high into the air. He studied the scene with a critical eye. It was the middle of the night, but not nearly as dark as it should have been. The glowing light exuded by the Archmage of Lights lit the snow and cast shadows back upon Kazra Lo Veedra. Intermittent blasts from the estate using arcane cannons granted additional flashes of magenta light. The undead still shambled to the battlefield from other directions. There had been tens of thousands of corpses in the area, and some zombies continued to appear from unexpected locations. He wondered when the thrill of battle would wear off for the soldiers and be replaced by the dread of fighting an endless horde of decaying monsters. They had advanced only a handful of paces since the undead engaged them. How long until this stalemate turned to panic?

He glanced to the south where the Archmage of the Green controlled the southern edge of the battle. The trees in the canopy had linked together to keep the undead from entering or exiting, and the archmage himself had grown huge and monstrous. Additional plants attached to him to create the effect that he was a walking forest. Roots burst from the plain around Kazra Lo Veedra, entangling and holding the undead. The Archmage of the Green stomped on those that wandered close but seemed content to impede their movements and draw their attention.

A flash at the corner of Garson's vision caught his eye. A light shape from the southeast dashed between the straggling undead who had not yet reached the roots of the Archmage of the Green. He flew closer and beheld a glowing and semi-translucent fox running through the zombies. As the fox touched each of the undead, they distended and exploded.

The creature noticed Garson and stopped as the archmage landed. He regarded the small creature. "And who might you be?"

"I am Confessor Paladin Anton Veruth, a kresnik of the Paladin Order of Kalendril," the fox spoke with a man's voice in cutting clarity. "I have arrived ahead of our forces to determine the direction of Kazra Lo Veedra, and it would appear I found it."

"Indeed, you did. Are there other kresniks among the paladins?"

"A few, but none are present, save myself."

"When will the rest of your army arrive?"

"Within the next few minutes. My body has already told them of the direction they need to travel in and what to expect. They ride with haste, though from appearances, you have most things under control. I assume you are in command?"

Garson looked across the melee. "For now, yes. The battle has been thankfully manageable, but I wonder—"

The ground shook violently and nearly threw Garson to the ground and the spirit fox braced itself for danger. A loud and full laugh echoed through the surrounding air. The soldiers, and even the undead, paused and listened. A huge wave crashed over everyone as a magic well of energy exploded out momentarily.

He turned to the kresnik. "Tell your order to hurry. A new lich has risen and her name is Alvaria Saccarra."

Chapter Forty
The Living Lich of Half a Day

Zylit extended his arm, and the glowing crystal temporal container flew to his hand. Lysander didn't bother stopping it as he watched green light explode from the sarcophagus, turning its stone surface to dust. Alvaria rose in the air with green magic surrounding her. She wore nothing except for the faintest wrappings. As she righted herself, she extended her arms, and the wrappings reformed into a beautiful white gown of familiar design.

It resembled the robes the High Archmage wore.

She smiled down at everyone.

Zylit withdrew a glowing diamond from his pocket. She glanced at him. "Taking some small measure of prophetic magic for yourself, Zylit? Go ahead. I have more than I could ever hope to use. And discard that vessel somewhere safe, if you would."

An amulet appeared in the air near Zylit, which he clutched eagerly. Zylit stared up at Alvaria. "Our business is concluded. You are the sole possessor of Kazra Lo Veedra and the undead that belong here." Dark magenta energy surrounded the temporal container briefly before it disappeared, teleported off to some other location.

She smiled. "Thank you. I am grateful for your help."

"The contract was merely a contract. Farewell, Alvaria Saccarra. May the crown of your success not cause you to collapse beneath its weight." He turned to Lysander. "And farewell to you also, Archmage of War. Our conversation was illuminating, however brief it may have been. May you find the victory you seek. We shall never meet again." The same dark magenta magic surrounded Zylit, and he disappeared in a plume of smoke.

Alvaria looked at her hand. "It's strange. I feel like I've lost a friend by allowing Zylit to leave, though I doubt he feels the same. I suppose I enslaved him, so I cannot blame him for departing." She turned her attention to Lysander and smiled. With arms out-stretched, she rotated. "What do you think?"

His blood boiled. "I think you've done something profoundly wrong, Alvaria. Turn yourself in."

She scoffed as she floated through the room, her hand behind her back. "You're speaking nonsensically, Lysander. I need submit to nobody's mercy. I have become the sole authority in the universe I need to obey. Self-sustaining, nearly infinite in power, and beyond the grip of death."

He gripped his staff, which once again crackled with glowing energy. "We shall see."

Chapter Forty-One
Where All Paths Converge

Hazel felt the earthquake but was unsurprised.

The living lich had risen.

She had felt it dozens of times before in her visions. She knew exactly what it meant. Alvaria had succeeded. She paced her room. Even if the prophecy had been fulfilled, they had to win.

She whispered to herself the prophecy for the last time, "In the presence of the unending shadow, a darkness shall rise. No light shall purge it from the world, and self-sustaining shall it be. The living lich of half a day shall rise with legions of undead that none can kill. Through betrayal of friends and oath, the living lich shall trample bodies and hearts. The world will quake as the impossible becomes the inevitable. The living lich of half a day may only be stopped by the slow progress of time. The time of the lich is here."

She mussed her hair in frustration. A legion of undead that none could kill? Only the slow progress of time could stop her?

Hazel felt like she was missing an important clue. When Zylit spoke to her, she got the impression he hinted at something, trying to impart some trick without being too specific. What could he have—

She jumped as a loud *whoosh* came from the corner of her room. She approached the source of the sound and wondered at what she saw. Tiny remnant plumes of dark magenta drifted off the object. She momentarily shielded her eyes from the dazzling light and stared at the object, puzzled. Then Hazel understood. All the pieces of the puzzle became entirely clear to her. She rushed to her bag and emptied her clothes. She gingerly lifted the object and stuffed it into her pack and covered it. When she felt it was sufficiently protected, she smiled and grabbed the leather pouch of seeds Lyvaelan had given her. She took out a small one and put it in the keyhole.

It was time to leave.

The seed glowed green inside the lock, and soon a yellow flower poked out from the hole. Hazel closed her eyes. *Open the lock. Twist the mechanism until it clicks,* she thought at the plant. She listened as the roots fumbled and struggled, but eventually she heard a satisfying click. She smiled at the flower. "Thank you."

She opened the door to see a very surprised werewolf on the other side. For a moment, they stood in silent shock when the werewolf tackled her to the ground.

"Whoa! Whoa Lara!" Hazel said with a laugh. "I'm happy to see you too, though you're looking a bit hairier than usual."

"Oh, right." Lara lost her fur and stood naked in the room.

Hazel glanced behind the werewolf and saw her mother looking in, followed by her father, who was swiftly beaten back, when Lynn noticed Lara's state of undress. "Hey Lara, how about we get you some clothes? Any of the ones on the floor are fine."

"Thanks, but I might need to change back soon. I don't want to rip any of your outfits."

"That's fine, I don't mind. Besides, I don't think you'll have any reason to go wolf again. Just trust me."

Lara shrugged and pulled on one of her shorter dresses. Hazel exited into the hallway and hugged both her parents. Alistair grinned and embraced her as well, forgoing his typical sense of decorum when she approached with arms wide. She then looked at Lyvaelan. His eyes were dark and dilated, but as he gazed at her, the darkness receded, revealing his red eyes. He walked to her slowly and looked her over, almost in disbelief. With a sigh, he put his arms around her and held her. It was not the warm and excited hug she got from Lara or her parents, nor the friendly and affectionate one she got from Alistair. Lyvaelan held her gingerly, almost as if he feared she might break. It was the gentle embrace of heartfelt relief. He seemed tired, but she could also feel peace radiating off of him.

Garo padded up to her with his tail wagging. "Miss Enda, I am delighted to see you again."

Hazel separated from Lyvaelan and smiled back. "Likewise."

Garo glanced back. "If you follow us, I believe we can help you and your parents escape without trouble."

She shook her head. "I can't do that."

Garo sat. "This doesn't have to be your battle. None of it was your fault."

"You might be right," Hazel said, shouldering her bag, "but that doesn't mean I'm not going to fix it, anyway."

"I agree," Lyvaelan said. "We've been fighting for others all this time. It seems arbitrary to change that now."

Alistair smiled and drew his sword. "The Evenfall Vigil has unfinished business with the Grand Inquisitor."

"Yeah." Lara grinned wolfishly and cracked her knuckles. "We still have to kick her ass."

Chapter Forty-Two
Master of Death

"When will you recognize the futility of this battle?" Alvaria dropped the last member of the Guard Unyielding to the ground, reduced to a smoking corpse. In just over a minute, she had killed them all. Lysander was all that remained. She possessed greater power than anything he had ever faced. Zylit was a challenge, but Alvaria outstripped him in every way. Lysander charged. She merely smiled. He channeled thaumaturgy into his staff, elongating the pointed protrusion of white light six feet long. She opened her arms and closed her eyes, the smile never leaving her face. The spear of light sliced through her.

Lysander gasped as he twisted around, but there was no injury. Alvaria stood utterly undamaged. His blood ran cold.

Her smile widened into a grin. "What? Surprised?"

"That shouldn't be possible," he said, collecting his thoughts. "Thaumaturgy is poison to the undead!"

"And it is, dear Lysander." Her voice was smooth and ubiquitous, full of incomprehensible power. "You must understand, however, that I am not undead. I am unliving!" Metal from the dead guards' marinoms liquidized and floated into her hand. She idly allowed it to flow through her fingers as she spoke. "I am not dead, Lysander, hence the term *living* lich. I know, I know, it's impossible—but that didn't stop me. Hazel was the key, but the prophecy certainly helped." She opened her palm, and the metal shot down at the archmage, instantly hardening around his hands. The metal blackened. He paled further, observing the change. He surged backward suddenly and landed hard against the wall.

"That should occupy you for at least a minute or two," she said. "I transmuted the orichalcum into ravnulium. Another impossibility, I know, but you'd be surprised what can be accomplished with a little eldritch magic and knowledge of alchemy and wizardry."

Lysander coughed and met her eyes. "If you're already so powerful, then you might as well call off the undead horde. You don't need their protection."

Her eyes studied the ceiling, contemplating his words. "You have a point. Thank you for the wonderful suggestion." She made a slight gesture and tiny green flames sparked out. "But there's something I need to do first, and I'd really prefer to not be distracted, so I'll create an antilife barrier around Kazra Lo Veedra to prevent creatures from coming or going. I really believe in creating a more beautiful world freed from the constraints of mortality."

She closed her eyes and swept her consciousness over the estate without attempting to conceal it. "I see," she said at last, opening her eyes. "It would seem Thomas has perished in defending me. I must confess that although his sacrifice is appreciated, he will ultimately not be missed. Your forces have dealt impressively with my inquisitors, though it seems the Evenfall Vigil may have done the heavy lifting."

She clasped her hands behind her back. "Upon the sacrifice of so many of my servants, I will dedicate the future I build. The gods are not kind, but I am. The suffering of mankind must end. I will bring my justice over the land and mete out the eternal life that all humans deserve simply by virtue of birth. My judgment shall not exclusively apply to the currently living, however. I believe this new law should be retroactive. As such, I will bring back someone who never needed to die. Someone who—of all humans—deserves to live." A small wooden box drifted to her. She dragged one of the dead bodies of the Guard Unyielding before her using psychokinesis. She opened the box and dust dropped to sprinkle the corpse.

"Alvaria," Lysander said, his face stern, "whatever you're planning, it won't work."

She pursed her lips. "I had almost forgotten that the High Archmage had bequeathed the title of Archmage of War upon you. Despicable. Little wonder you had to cut your hair. I liked it better long." A hardness entered her eyes. "I know what that title means to you, Lysander, and I will free you of it. I've always liked you better as the Archmage of Education."

Something snapped within him and again he understood the world with greater clarity and murkiness. He looked upon the dead and remembered their names. A rush of emotion threatened to overtake him, but he pushed it down. Finally, his eyes turned back to Alvaria. He no longer saw the terrible evil he had been charged to destroy. For the first time, he realized he could not reconcile what she had done with who he knew her to be. The genuine and true love they experienced as friends could not have been a lie.

"Please," he whispered, a tear dropping from his eye, "come back to me. Come back to *us.* There is still time to reconsider all of this. Zylit committed the greater crimes against us. Return to the High Archmage and I will do all I must to ensure a fair trial. I will even suffer the same sentence you do. Just... give this up. Why do you persist in this plan to rid the world of death?"

She mused on his words as a series of conflicting emotions washed over her face before settling into an expression of supreme resolution. "You see right through me, Lysander, and yet you do not truly see me." Her eyes met his. "I'm bringing my father back to life."

"No," his voice took on a frantic note, "Alvaria, you mustn't! You can't!"

"I can do whatever I like."

"Alva, please, you don't understand." He struggled against his restraints. His heartbeat pounded in his ears. "Revenants never last more than a week, and that's only the ones that are recently dead. It won't work on your father—he's been in the afterlife too long!"

She paused. The corpse covered with ashes dropped to the floor. "Do you know why liches levitate instead of walking?"

He didn't answer.

"It always struck me as curious," she continued. "For most spell-casters, levitating requires considerable concentration and a moderate sum of magic. It always seemed like such a superfluous display of arcane prowess. Now I understand." She floated toward him. "Levitation is easier than walking to a lich. It is not because walking has become any more difficult by virtue of the transformation, but levitation has become as simple as breathing to a human. Such is the power I wield." Her eyes glowed green momentarily. "I have become the queen of death herself! None can stand against me. My power has been increased beyond your comprehension. It now seems to me that my prowess as an archmage was laughable. Spells I struggled with as a high master enchantress are simplicity itself. I wish I could make you understand, Lysander, but I cannot. Our access to the stream of magic differs fundamentally from what you experience and so you will simply need to trust me. I can move mountains and level cities with a gesture. I can return my father to life."

"Alva, I hear what you're saying, but this is wrong. It isn't about the amount of magic you use, what you're attempting to do will inevitably—"

"Quiet," she commanded, cutting him off. The Archmage of Education still spoke, but his words were silenced. She turned back at the body and a few drops of blood fell from her finger onto the ashen corpse.

Alvaria straightened and looked to the side with a smile. "Hello Hazel. And friends! Welcome, one and all." She threw up a hand and a translucent barrier appeared over the archway. Lysander glanced to the side and saw the Evenfall Vigil standing close by with Hazel and her parents. "I'm glad you're here to witness this." She gestured at the tomb replete with effulgent gemstones. "I contained most of the magic from the prophecy within my body, but I had some spare diamonds on hand. I will need quite a bit of magic to perform this, though not so much that I will need to spend a single gem."

She extended her hand, and the corpse floated along with the dust and blood. Green smoke twisted and melded with the components as Alvaria concentrated.

"I call upon the soul of Telerius Saccarra. Return to the mortal world as I command!"

The green smoke muffled the shape before drifting back and revealing a middle-aged man with a graying mustache and beard. He had the same prominent cheekbones as Alvaria, but his tanned, rough skin made it clear he had previously lived as a peasant. He returned to the ground and wheeled around, bewildered by his surroundings.

Alvaria drifted to the floor. Her pompous attitude had disappeared and her eyes welled with tears. "Poppa?"

The man scrutinized her. He squinted and blinked as if trying to understand. "Allie? Allie, is that you?"

She ran and hugged him. "I've missed you so much." There was complete silence in the room as they embraced. The universe fell still as if balancing on the edge of a knife. A sickening pit formed in Lysander's stomach. This was wrong. With her shifted attention, he concentrated on self-transmutative wizardry and carefully shrank ever so slightly. The magic Alvaria used was dangerous in more ways than one.

"Allie, I don't understand, how"—Telerius Saccarra noticed his surroundings and paled—"This... this isn't right. Allie, what have you done?"

She held his hand. "Don't worry, everything is fine—"

"No." His eyes widened as he gripped the sides of his head, shaking violently. "No, no, no, no, no! This isn't right! I shouldn't be here!" He buried his face in his hands, taking faltering breaths. After several moments, he stared up at her as blood dripped from his eyes. "What have you done to me?"

"Poppa!" her voice took on a tone of alarm. "I can fix this! I have the magic, the power! I can—"

A bloodcurdling scream interrupted her as her father tore his own ears off.

"Poppa! Stop!" she cried. In that moment, Lysander saw the young girl who lost her father trying desperately to hold on to the one thing she loved that was slipping from her grasp.

Telerius bent to the floor and repeatedly bashed his head on the ground, spreading blood onto every surface he touched. Alvaria raised her hand, and he levitated off the floor, writhing in the air. She searched wildly around for help, but there was none.

"Poppa! Please, I can *help* you!" She drifted closer to him, green magic flowing through her fingers as she began to cast a spell.

He spasmed in the air as she held him. He stared at Alvaria through bloodied eyes, and she paused halfway through her spell to meet his eyes with horror. "You're not my girl. She would never cause this pain. You're... a monster." A series of loud pops exploded from his body and dark stains spread from within the clothing Alvaria created for him. His eyes darkened, drowned beyond sight in his own blood. Multiple ruptured organs. Telerius Saccarra no longer writhed in agony. The dead wished to remain dead. Semeleme regained the soul that belonged to her.

Alvaria collapsed to the floor, hair covering her face as she cradled her father's bloody corpse. Lysander stood. He had freed himself of the restraints. The room was silent but for her quiet sobs and whispered nothings to her deceased father.

"I'm sorry, Alva," Lysander said. "I know how much you wanted this. Your father has been dead too long. No one can bring him back, not even someone as talented and powerful as you. I miss my mother too and if I thought I could see her again, I would do almost anything. Please, don't take what he said to heart. I know you care for others and wouldn't want anyone else to die if you could prevent it.

Come with us peacefully, I beg of you. There has been enough blood-shed today."

She raised a finger. The antilife walls she erected around the estate collapsed. There were no more walls and no more undead defending Kazra Lo Veedra. A relief flooded him.

"Thank you, Alvaria. Come back with me. Come back with *us*. We can take your father and lay him at peace in Selevarian."

"At peace?" she whispered. "No. There is no peace."

"Alvaria..." he trailed off. He looked around the room and noticed dust suspended in the air. There was an electricity in the room he hadn't noticed building.

She stood and dropped the body. Blood stained her white gown as she faced him. Her eyes glowed green, but other colors swirled as well. Blood and tears smeared across her face, yet she did not care. "There shall be no peace. For me, or for anyone." Her voice was hoarse and resigned. She glanced in Hazel's direction. "I had thought to maintain the green magic to honor the one who made it possible, but I now see I should instead take the color that was provided by my father." The dark purple-red of her father's blood spread across her white gown and the magic in her eyes changed to match. "I shall be red, for my father who died before me. Red for all those I killed to get where I am. Red for the throat of Hazel's father that I cut. Red for all those outside who oppose me. And red for the blood I will drown the world in. I rename myself. No longer am I the Archmage of the Inquisition. I renounce the title and all its magics. I am Alvaria the Unliving, the Living Lich of Half a Day, the Queen in Red."

Lysander sensed the magic take hold. True to her words, she had revoked the title of Archmage of the Inquisition and adopted the name of the Living Lich of Half a Day. As he noticed the designations take hold, unspeakable panic rose in his chest. "Alvaria, don't do—"

Alvaria extended a hand to her crypt, and three brightly glowing diamonds flew to her hand. They instantly dulled as a red shockwave erupted from her. Conjuration magic, but... stronger. Much stronger. Staggeringly powerful.

"Alvaria, what have you done?"

She looked down at him and turned away, leaving the body of Telerius Saccarra where it fell. The stone of the sarcophagus shifted and melted into a throne, set with various glowing gemstones. She dropped the diamonds to the ground.

"Alvaria! What have you done?" He repeated. An overwhelming dread filled his heart.

"I have fulfilled prophecy," she said, stepping slowly to the throne. "Hazel herself said I would raise an army of undead who no one could kill, and so I have. The zombies are gone. In their place, I have created a horde of invincible draugr."

Lysander caught himself as he nearly fell back. *No,* he thought, *it can't be.* "How?"

She dropped into her throne and slouched. She regarded the dead body of her father. "I have a massive quantity of magic at my disposal. I could have created a few liches with the power I possess, but I prefer empowered underlings. They're less subversive."

"Let the soldiers go! None of this is their fault. Blame me, if you must, but they are innocent!"

"There is no innocence, just more blood," she muttered, staring at her hand. "Nothing but blood."

Lysander banged the butt of his staff to the ground and made several motions in the air with his other hand. He weaved a net of magic around himself. A dark purple cube spun in his hand as he muttered rapid incantations under his breath. He thrust the cube into the staff, and it disappeared. Pointing the weapon at Alvaria, he lunged. Purple light erupted from the head of his staff and encircled her, becoming an opaque cube of the same color. He put his staff against the cube and willed as much magic into it as he could. This box was designed to kill liches and powerful spellcasters. It should imprison her if it did not outright destroy—

The box shattered and hurled Lysander back, though he landed on his feet. Alvaria watched him with weary eyes. "You shall live to see others die before you. I'm sorry."

Gritting his teeth, he sprang with energy against the wall. He leaped across, seeking to prevent her from predicting his movements. A black sphere gathered around his hand as he jumped from wall to wall, sucking magic from the air. When the oblivion sphere reached critical power, he hurled it. It would expand and obliterate anything that required vast quantities of magic to function.

Alvaria waved a tired finger, and the sphere dissolved into harmless smoke. Lysander's eyes widened, but he redoubled his assault, throwing spell after spell. He moved with such speed that he doubted even a vampire could track him and cast every spell he knew. Each one, she countered with ease, never leaving her throne. Finally, he dropped to the floor, drew his marinom, and rushed at her. Before he could blink, she was in front of him, one hand holding his wrist. In a split instant, he saw in her eyes tears, pain, and regret.

Snap. He quickly used sorcery to block the pain from his broken wrist.

An unseen force lifted him from the ground and drew him away, beyond his power to resist. His legs mangled beneath him, accompanied by several sharp cracks. He screamed in pain and frustration as she discarded him. He failed—he couldn't defeat her.

She returned to her throne and spoke, but it wasn't to the people within the estate, it was to the soldiers outside.

They were all going to die.

Chapter Forty-Three
None Can Kill

Garson looked in bewilderment at the battlefield. The zombies had simply... stopped. More than pausing, the creations had collapsed. Their control spirits had been released. The soldiers noticed and pressed forward tentatively over the corpses, but Garson remained uneasy. He focused on the building, but it offered no ready clues beyond a green shield placed over the entrances.

"Something is off." Selevia Castus stood close by. Her hair was stained reddish brown from the conflict.

"Does your eye tell you that?"

"I can see the green light blocking entry is an antilife field, but that isn't what I meant. Soldier's intuition tells me something is amiss. This is like a deep breath before a piercing scream."

A dark red light washed over the battlefield emanating from the estate. It spread far beyond the clearing and into the earth.

Commander Castus looked at Garson. "What was that? It looked like some kind of conjuration magic."

The blood-red face of Alvaria Saccarra appeared above Kazra Lo Veedra in the same manner as the lich before. As Garson watched her, he noticed her pain, even if it was but a monochromatic illusion. He shivered and sensed that her name had changed. She was Alvaria the Unliving now. She had truly ascended to lichdom.

"Hear me, Army of Selevara," her voice echoed across the plain, *"And hear me, Paladin Order of Kalendril."* She paused, her face sad. Then she looked up and her sorrow deepened into an expression of blank resignation. *"This is the end. There is no surrender, and no escape. The world will run fresh with blood until it drowns and you are the beginning. There is no hope, and no god who will save you. You are all going to die."*

A gurgling laugh, harsh and unnerving, arose from the plains when Alvaria's image disappeared. A zombie stood and smiled at them, its eyes glowing with the same color red.

Garson's blood ran cold. "Defensive positions, now!" he roared. "Pull away from Kazra Lo Veedra!"

The same laugh echoed from all over the battlefield as the zombies rose again. Garson watched as one staggered in his direction. The creature's eyes blazed as beams of fiery heat burst in a concentrated blast. Garson spread his wings and created a shield with his staff big enough to protect him and Selevia. When the light disappeared, the creature had closed more than half the distance and had broken into a full sprint. Garson growled and lowered the shield, dropping his staff to the ground and assuming a fighting stance. The undead leaped from over a dozen feet away with fangs and claws extended. Garson grabbed the creature by its shoulders and unleashed a torrent of blue flames from his mouth, utterly incinerating the creature's head. He tossed the withered husk away, but as it landed, it contorted in the air. Blue flame took the place of its head and a skeletal grin appeared amidst the fire. It scuttled away on all fours.

Garson turned back to the commander with a haunted expression. "These aren't zombies. They're draugr." He picked up his staff and drew several images in the air, and a giant conjuring portal appeared in the sky. Three dragons, one after the other, dropped from the portal.

Mighty batlike wings held aloft the gargantuan bodies of the creatures. A long serpentine neck and tail extended out in almost equal length. Each was a different shade of green, with various patterns and markings. These were not the biggest dragons. The largest was only sixty feet long, but right now Garson needed numbers.

Selevia had already shouted the order down the line that draugr were attacking. She didn't question the veracity of the claim. It was becoming increasingly clear. A single draugr had greater physical strength than a dozen zombies and possessed intelligence equal to that of any human. Many possessed uncanny magical abilities that were virtually impossible to predict. Some were even mistaken as liches.

Garson saw the draugr across the field growing and shrinking. Some hurled fire from their hands, while others created and threw icicles like spears. One of the front soldiers hurtled back. They ran with coordinated attacks, like a pack of wolves, dismembering and then disappearing.

Some of the dead bodies amid the army had risen and sent spellcasters soaring as they tossed them aside. One courageous soldier leveled a glowing spear, but the draugr dodged and ripped him to shreds in moments.

Garson looked south and saw the gleaming weapons of the Paladin Order of Kalendril weave between the monsters. Some of the draugr met them and rushed forward. The paladins crashed into the draugr astride their horses. A small cluster of draugr fled into the trees and away from the paladins. A loud moan rumbled from that side of the forest as a branch crushed one rider. Trees bent down and walked. The bark was black and diseased, and the notches formed a twisted semblance of a face. The draugr were creating monsters of their own.

The Archmage of the Green attempted to slow them by rooting them to the ground, but several draugr caused the roots to decay by touch, spreading blight through the living trees. Bertrand disconnected from the diseased branches and struck the draugr with monumental swings of his tree-covered arms. He stomped and slashed, but his branches kept dying and the draugr had adapted to his fighting style and surrounded him.

The other archmages fared similarly. The Archmage of Lights deflected their ranged attacks as she continued to exude light that flickered. Nearby draugr belched noxious smoke, obscuring the surrounding effulgence and impeding the thaumaturgical magic. They raced through the umbral fumes, tearing screaming soldiers apart.

The Archmage of Crystals had several chunks of glass broken from his body, but pressed on. He fought with vigor, but the draugr lifted massive clods of earth from the ground and hurled them onto the archmage, slowing him down. The glass wall hemming in the draugr had broken in countless places and several escaped through the apertures or crawled over the vertical surface.

The elementals battled furiously to protect their conjurers. The flaming salamander leaped and slashed through the undead, but some of the draugr touched him and tore at his flames. The mighty rock gnome smashed the draugr and erected walls, but the monsters relentlessly attacked and either scaled the fortifications or smashed through them. The sylph tossed the draugr in all directions, but some grew twisted wings and returned. While the undine fared best, her waters had turned murky, and she now resembled a slurry of blood and detritus.

Garson beheld the chaos and felt very small. There were more draugr every moment. Soldiers were dying. Paladins had leaped from their horses and struck out at them with better luck, but their numbers were too few and many had died. From what he could see, not a single one of these new undead had been permanently destroyed and more were being made every second. The ranks of the army had been broken.

Escape.

Panic filled his heart. They had to escape.

He rushed to Selevia, who had driven off a draugr with some difficulty. "Selevia! Sound the retreat. Everyone must get through the amethyst gate immediately."

She turned to reply but stopped. Her magic eye glanced at the forest. They both gazed into the dark and saw red eyes approaching. First just two, but then more, until the woods were filled with the menacing gaze of many.

"You are clever, Archmage of Dragons," said one of the draugr in a grating and mocking voice, "but none of you are leaving. None of you. The Queen in Red has spoken, and we follow her command."

The draugr who addressed him emerged from the shadows with its comrades carrying large chunks of purple stone, which they tossed at Garson's feet before falling into raucous laughter.

Amethyst. The gate had been destroyed.

There was no escape.

Chapter Forty-Four
The Slow Progress of Time

Lyvaelan watched as Alvaria the Unliving tossed the Archmage of Education aside. The spells he used should've worked.

But they didn't.

"Lara, Alistair, get him and bring him into the hallway!" Hazel said when the barrier fell. "Garo, Lyvaelan, stay here and keep my family here. I need to talk to her."

Lyvaelan wanted to protest, but found he couldn't. The others appeared similarly conflicted and hadn't moved. What could be done against a being of virtually infinite power?

"Lyvaelan." She grabbed his shoulder. "Can you shield my mind subtly? I can do what I need to do mostly on my own, but I need your help. She must not know what I'm thinking." He nodded. Subtlety in magic was a definite strength of his. "Lara, Alistair, hurry and help the archmage after I start talking with her and get back here as soon as possible." There was a firmness to her voice. "I know what I'm doing."

She walked out before they could object. "Alvaria! We need to talk."

Alvaria didn't even glance at Hazel as she reclined on her throne. "Let me guess: you want to persuade me to stop? This little dance grows tiresome. My draugr have their commands and I will not alter them—not for anyone." Her voice was dejected.

"No," Hazel said, stepping into the chamber. She put her clothing bag on the ground and walked closer. "I'm not going to convince you to stop. I don't think you *can* be convinced to stop."

"Well, at least you have some sense."

"That's why I'm going to stop you." Lara and Alistair had pulled Lysander back into the hallway as Hazel spoke.

A humorless smile twisted the lich's face, but her eyes burned with loathing. "Perhaps I spoke too soon. Do you think you and your friends can stop me?"

"No," Hazel said, taking a seed from her pouch and dropping it. "That's why I'm going to do it myself." The seed instantly grew into a tangled mass of jasmine that snaked back to her friends and wove across the arch, blocking them from accessing her. The vines continued to grow over the walls and the ground until every surface but the throne had been covered.

"Hazel!" Lyvaelan shouted through the vines.

"Stay back! Trust me, like I've trusted you." She stared at her. The jasmine flooded the floor, layering over itself many times. The floor couldn't be seen through the dense mesh of greenery and white flowers.

Alvaria reclined. "You actually want to fight me? Didn't you see what I did to Lysander? I broke him. What do you think you can accomplish that he couldn't?" There was no more bravado in her voice. No pride or confidence. Only bitterness.

"I can defeat you."

"You are still so much a child. You have no idea what you're saying."

"I think you're actually talking about yourself."

Lyvaelan watched as Alvaria's eyes met Hazel's. There was hate in them, but it wasn't directed at Hazel.

"I think the hardest thing about facing you is I understand," Hazel said. The jasmine bunched together before her into the semblance of two giant fists. "I love my family, and you love yours. We both don't want the people we love to die, and we'll do anything we can to keep that from happening. Unfortunately, there isn't anybody alive who you love anymore. Not even yourself."

"Shut up!" Alvaria spat as she slammed her fist down. A blast of red energy would have knocked Hazel over if she hadn't rooted herself to the spot with her vines. Several red blades sliced across her face, but the lacerations healed as she returned her gaze to the former Grand Inquisitor.

"Your father called you a monster, but you're not. You're just human, like the rest of us. Even after every terrible thing you've put me through, I don't hate you, I just... pity you. All you have left is your pain. You're one of the most powerful people to ever live, but even that isn't enough to get you what you want. I'm sorry." There was genuine regret in Hazel's voice. "I don't know what I would do if my father called me a monster, but I know you're not one. I've seen what you've done, and you've hurt me and people I care about more than anyone else, but that doesn't make you a monster. You're just a person who made a series of bad decisions and is too hurt to come to terms with her own weaknesses. You never got the chance to mourn him, and now you don't know how to. I know you miss him."

Alvaria's eyes glowed red with fury, and tears streamed down her cheeks. "I don't need your pity, *child*. I will kill everyone in this Mirnak-damned world and then I will have peace from idiots who presume to understand me!"

"Fine," Hazel said, the two green fists of vines rising, "but you'll have to go through me first, and I'm notoriously hard to kill."

"We shall see!" Blood red flames exploded from Alvaria's hands as Hazel reformed the fists into a wall and pushed them forward. The fire ripped apart the vines and almost reached Hazel when a loud shattering sound accompanied a blast of white light from where Alvaria's power struck the vines. The flames near Hazel had stopped.

She stood in the same position, transfixed. Alvaria's face was contorted with immutable hatred. All within was frozen and silent.

"What in Stezelra's name happened?" Lara whispered.

Lyvaelan put his hand against the vines and burned them away. He tried to enter but was blocked by what felt like a solid wall. The others examined it as Hazel's parents watched in worry.

"I've seen this before," Lyvaelan said. He touched the wall and pressed as hard as he could, but it budged less than a fraction of an inch. "This is time. A temporal distortion. Everything inside the room is moving much slower than everything outside of it."

Lysander used thaumaturgy and medical wizardry to heal both legs, but only enough to set the bones and repair some of the biggest breaks. The archmage had expended a vast quantity of magic. He looked exhausted and astounded. "Lyvaelan is right. I recognize it as well. Hazel must have known the room acted as a containment vessel, which was why Alvaria could capture so much of the magic from fulfilling the prophecy. I don't know how she found a time container, but her plan worked." He shook his head. "She said that only the slow progress of time could stop her. The prophecy becomes clearer by the moment."

"That's good news," Alistair said, "but how do we extricate her from the trap?"

Lysander winced. "I don't think we can. That time is much too dense to move through, and I don't have the strength to help. I've heard of others moving time, but it's outside my area of expertise. I might be able to do it if I had any magic left to use."

"Then we'll do it ourselves," Lyvaelan said.

Lysander frowned. "How?"

Lyvaelan looked back, his eyes entirely black. "By demanding it." He turned to Alistair and Lara. "I need you two to grab her as fast as you can. Speed is important. I suspect the temporal distortion will seek to keep her stationary." The other two nodded and readied themselves. The power swelled within him, almost overwhelmingly intoxicating, but as he watched Hazel, his resolve hardened. She would not be made into a sacrificial captive. He wouldn't allow it. Mentally, he reached out to her and sensed through the magic the dense temporal space before him. He extended both hands and forced the wall apart. The effort he exerted was tremendous, and he struggled against the dizziness, but refused to give in. The slowed time opened before him as Lara and Alistair pushed forward through the tunnel he created. It nearly reached Hazel, but the time was densest there. Alistair dashed into the area with Hazel at great speed, although to others, it looked exceedingly slow and exaggerated. He pulled Hazel behind him and reached out to Lara, who took his hand and pulled them further. Bits of time leaked into the tunnel, slowing them down despite his best efforts. Sweat beaded on his brow and his arms trembled from the exertion. The pressure was almost too much for Lyvaelan to bear as the tunnel collapsed behind the three.

He watched them nearing with Hazel and strained to keep it open, but they moved ever slower until, with a final surge of power, he pushed the time aside and the three tumbled out. Lyvaelan sank to the ground, exhausted. He panted as the excitement drained from his body and his eyes resumed their natural color. Lysander stared at him.

Hazel gasped loudly. "You saved me. Again!"

"That's... what we do." Lara panted. "How did you... stop time?"

"I was given that glowing glass container just before you found my room. I think it was a parting gift from Zylit, the lich. It's possible he wanted to get revenge on Alvaria the Unliving, even though he claimed to have no emotions."

Lysander shook his head and leaned back. "Hazel, that's amazing. You outwitted the archmage who outwitted other archmages."

"Indeed," Garo said, "she fulfilled the prophecy. Only time could stop Alvaria, and now she is stopped. For a while, at least."

"Do you really think so? Should we be concerned she will find a way out?" Alistair asked.

"Not for the moment, no," Lysander said, rising unsteadily to his feet. "By my estimates she is probably experiencing approximately one hundred and twenty years in probably"—he extended his hand, testing the barrier—"three months, our time. I can't tell you the exact mathematical breakdown of what that means for us, but I suspect it will take her some time to realize she's stuck. Hopefully longer. For the moment, we don't need to worry about her. I should get outside to the soldiers."

The group moved through the halls unimpeded. Hazel had healed the worst of Lysander's wounds, but he was still exhausted. They walked through the triangular room where the Alchemist sat idly and gestured for the criminal to join them when several of the Guard Unyielding entered. They informed the archmage that all the inquisitors in the north, south, and east had been dealt with. Lysander commanded all the other guards to move ahead and neutralize the inquisitors to the west.

He turned to Hazel. "Did you truly mean what you said to her?"

"I did," she replied quietly. "I knew she would never stop, but I still had to try."

The archmage bit his lip and nodded as they continued forward. He wished to say more, but emotion choked him.

The walk to the western side of Kazra Lo Veedra was easy. The sight they beheld upon exiting was not.

The snow was red with blood and the cold air reeked of death. Undead ran through ranks of men who shouted in fear as the monsters with glowing red eyes attacked. A dragon struggled on the ground, pinned by five undead, each over twenty feet tall. A wall of spiked crystals hemmed in the battlefield partially, but the undead still crawled over it and had shattered most of it. The Crystal King swung madly with a giant glowing sword of diamond, slicing into the monsters, who maintained their distance. In fact, each of the archmages appeared to be doing the best, from what Lyvaelan could see, though each was nonetheless harried by draugr.

The soldiers fell. Some men begged for mercy, but there was none. Those who died returned with red eyes of their own. More draugr to vent the bitterness of their master.

Flames and lightning shot from the undead at random intervals, and many used spells in the way spellcasters did. A skeletal deer tore through several soldiers spitting acid, while another draugr transformed into a small, undead dragon. The creatures moved unpredictably and were powerful beyond belief.

Lysander sank down shakily on the steps a hand covering his mouth. "I don't know what to do."

"Do?" Lara yelled. "How are these things still moving? Didn't we just defeat their maker?"

"We did," Lysander said, "but they are still tied to her will and power. Time doesn't sever the bond."

"How do we stop them?" Alistair said, appraising the field, "There are at least another eighteen thousand draugr. Even if we kill most of them, a dozen can be enough to raze a city. We might survive, but..."

"The soldiers won't." Lysander completed, covering his face. "Thousands dead, and I can do nothing."

Chapter Forty-Five
That Which Cannot Die

Hazel beheld the scene. Men and women screamed as they fell at the hands of horrifying monsters. Alvaria intended for them all to die. She had failed to save her father, and ceased to care about anything else. Her only consolation was the knowledge that she deprived others of what she could never have. She had given up.

Hazel hadn't.

They want to live. A small voice in the back of her head said. *Remember why you live.*

She looked back at her parents. They raised her, cared for her, and gave her everything she needed in life. They loved her enough to let her make her own decisions, even if it might mean losing her again. Throughout this second life, they supported and joined her even in captivity. So many of their sacrifices had been for her.

She looked at Alistair. He was the one who loved to read as much as she did. He was normally polite and dashing, but could be delightfully awkward at unexpected moments. Her parents made him promise to protect her and had been the first to defend her from the Cult of Semeleme. He was smart, and genuine, and warm.

She looked at Lara. This woman was the strongest person she'd ever met. She could be rough, but she cared deeply about Hazel and the others. She never tried to act smart, but was a brilliant tactician. Lara had always joked with Hazel and had even given her a nickname. The werewolf could be sloppy and carefree, but there was no doubt in Hazel's mind that she would do anything to help her friends.

Finally, she looked at Lyvaelan, who held her gaze. Through him, she learned how to use her powers. He had been with her as a confidant and helped her to the best of his abilities. He could be dark and moody, but was also funny and sarcastic. More than anything, he had never once doubted that Hazel was good. When she wasn't sure if she would do evil, he firmly denied it. He had taught her many things, but she felt she had taught him as well. He had brought so much joy to her life and found herself thinking of him often.

With a deep breath, she stepped out and thought of everyone else important to her. Garo. King Aldric. Tommy. Claire. Commander Comrear. Even Hickory. Something stirred deep inside her. She remembered when she first woke from death, how she couldn't feel emotion. It took months before she could smile genuinely. She felt dead inside. No joy, sorrow, anger, or fear. Now she knew that in trying to help others, she helped herself. She loved them. All of them.

She cherished them. They had helped to awaken something in her. Something beautiful.

She held her arms out and felt the green energy swirling inside her. She dropped the bag of seeds Lyvaelan gave her. The others spoke to her, but she couldn't hear them. She had to do this. The world slowed as the seeds scattered.

She concentrated on that green energy and poured every piece of herself into it. Every thought and experience, every hope and dream fed this interior power. She felt anger and sadness, embarrassment and joy. Every memory—both good and bad—she fed to the swirling green. Each one was like tinder on a fire, and it grew. The power didn't destroy her experiences; she simply told it her story. Last, she put herself into it and all that she knew she meant to others and experienced the magic. It was a pure and sweet contentment, a light joy tinged with melancholy, sorrowful tears in the midst of innocent laughter.

It was the feeling of being alive.

Green light exploded from her body and expanded across the battlefield and trees in every direction. The seeds at her feet scattered across the plain and grew in all directions, becoming trees, bushes, flowers, and vines. The draugr turned and inhaled the green light, their eyes filled with the sensation of life for but a moment before slumping to the ground forever as vines and moss overtook them, their power destroyed. She kept the surge growing far and wide as she listened to the trees sing to her in relief that the darkness of Kazra Lo Veedra was finally over. A shattering sound like tinkling glass echoed across the plain, but she disregarded it. She followed the call of the living things to find the undead and give them life, unmaking them in the process. Soldiers on the brink of death gasped and rose with renewed vigor and hope. In the dark of the night, Hazel had become a radiant green sun of life that utterly purified the corruption of Kazra Lo Veedra.

Gradually the light faded from her even as it lingered through the trees. Hazel stood on the steps in silence. She took one last breath and crumpled to the ground.

Chapter Forty-Six
Spring Within Winter

Lyvaelan ran to Hazel's side where she dropped. She fell softly with such otherworldly grace that the Archmage of Education barely registered that it had happened.

His eyes brimmed with tears of wonder as he gazed across the battlefield.

She had made the world new.

Spreading out from the entryway, a wide expanse of foliage had pierced the snow and connected to the forest. The edges where they had camped no longer existed as trees, grass, and flowers invaded the grounds of Kazra Lo Veedra.

He rose to his feet and staggered down the steps. The soldiers appeared similarly perplexed and awed by what had occurred. Gradually, the realization sank in and they laughed and cried. Lysander could not determine which action was the more appropriate.

With the flap of mighty wings, Garson landed beside him.

"What happened here, Lysander? What magic is this?"

"I don't know if we have a right to call this miracle 'magic,' but it was all Hazel Enda."

"Is the battle truly over?"

"Yes, thank the gods."

Garson's eyes welled, and he embraced Lysander. "I was so afraid we'd lost you. When I noticed your title had disappeared, I feared the worst. I couldn't bear to lose two friends to this madness."

Lysander sniffed. "I know."

They separated, and Gar looked behind him. "Whatever she did used life magic purer than any I've encountered. We owe her much. Will the girl be alright?"

"I don't know. Gar, I'm almost completely spent. Can you summon your scry mirror for me?"

"Of course." The archmage held out his golden scaled hand and from across the field the mirror flew to his hand. "Do you need me to activate it for you?"

"No, I should be able to manage at least that much." He pushed a trickle of magic into it and its surface shimmered. He glanced up at his friend. "You may want to listen to this debriefing."

The mirror cleared, revealing the face of the High Archmage.

"Lysander! Selevara be praised. I am overjoyed that you live!"

"Only barely, High Eminence," he replied. "We have won the battle, but I must request that you send for the Archmage of Time immediately. I do not wish to assume victory before everything has been secured. Gar, can you tell the Archmage of Crystals to create another amethyst gate right here?"

Garson nodded and flew off. The High Archmage concentrated momentarily and then nodded. Lysander relayed all that had occurred along with the fulfillment of the prophecy. Garson returned when Lysander's story neared the present.

"Although I cannot confirm it myself," he said, "I suspect that Hazel Enda shattered the spells surrounding Kazra Lo Veedra. I feel no more undead influence, yet that should not be possible."

The High Archmage stroked his beard. "On the contrary, it makes the most sense. Recall the concept of arcane oppositional overload. A pin with an ice enchantment can have the enchantment dispelled purely by using a fire spell against it in vast quantities. While the exact mechanisms are poorly understood, opposites tend to destroy each other when enough force is applied. Miss Enda used life magic in such a vast quantity that the necromantic spells binding the estate were destroyed utterly, although it was likely not her intent."

Lysander had heard of this idea, but the amount of magic necessary to break a series of spells so old and powerful bordered on the impossible.

"How could she have accomplished this?" Garson asked. "She's just a girl with no training in magic."

The High Archmage nodded. "An interesting question indeed."

The Crystal King approached and built the amethyst gate without protest, which surprised Lysander. Garson assisted the Archmage of Crystals in laying the enchantment upon the gate.

"One more thing, Lysander," the High Archmage said. "I notice that your title is missing. Allow me to reinstate your position."

"Actually, Grand Eminence," Lysander said, "I would prefer to go without it. Garson did more leading than I did and the soldiers know that I have seniority by reputation. Besides, as painful as it is, I need to face reality."

He nodded sadly. "You are wise, my Archmage of Education. I will forgo the appointment of the title. I must go. Additional supplies will be sent to your location and the authorities will be alerted. Be at peace, Lysander."

There is no peace, he remembered Alvaria saying, but he merely bowed as the mirror returned to its normal reflective surface.

He returned to the group that huddled around Hazel. He was about to speak when a loud stomping sound approached from the south. The Archmage of the Green ran to them, shrugging off trees and bushes from his body which fell to the ground and swiftly took root. By the time he reached them, he had returned to his usual self. Hazel's parents stared at him with wide eyes.

The archmage clapped his hands together happily. "Oh, joyous night that brought the seeds to rest within the inhospitable earth of winter and yet found root! Gladly do we bloom, for the maiden has flowered and the scent she releases perfumes the air with the sweet odor of life!"

"Excuse me?" Kyle Enda exclaimed.

"Ah," Lysander cut in, "he means that she has brought life to the world around us. This is Bertrand Rollodore, the Archmage of the Green. He is a master of plant life and... other magic."

"Can he fix Hazel?" Lynn asked. "What's wrong with her?"

Bertrand stepped forward and stooped over her with an unreadable expression. He reached into his beard and dislodged a small seed, which he dropped onto Hazel.

Lysander's eyebrows raised as the seed sprouted and flowerless thorns spread over her.

The Archmage of the Green looked at her parents. "She does not die, but only sleeps the sleep of the restful folk beneath the hills. Briarsleep is upon her until her power returns many days hence."

"A briarsleep?" Lysander said. "Are you certain?"

"As certain as the taproot of an aged, thirsty hornbeam."

Lysander turned to the others, who clearly did not share his understanding. "Essentially, Hazel is in a state of unchanging rest. Certain fae can enter a briarsleep when grievously injured, and it stops their condition from worsening while also improving their strength. Ambient magic causes a natural protective barrier to form in the presence of certain seeds. In time, entire homes may be covered with brambles designed to protect the one asleep. What makes this curious is this is almost exclusively fae magic. How she has placed herself in such a state eludes me."

"Does it not bear to reason," Bertrand said, "that she is one of the sidhe herself? Indeed, the plants welcome her like one of the people beneath the mounds."

"Well, it certainly wouldn't be the strangest revelation of the day," Lysander conceded. From the south, weaving between the plants the Archmage of the Green had left behind, a small troop of cavalry trotted toward them. Their armor gleamed silvery white beneath tabards of black and red, with a prominent coat of arms depicting a winged sword suspended between a golden chalice and a green shield.

Garson joined Lysander, and they both met the incoming group of paladins.

"Hail!" called the paladin at their head. The man was clean shaven and although he had long passed his prime, his hair grew long and dark green, like seaweed. "I am Justiciar Calman Zedonia. I am joined by Confessor Anton Veruth"—a young and tired looking man inclined his head—"who spoke with the Archmage of Dragons."

"Well met, Grand Judge," Garson said. "Your assistance in the battle cannot be understated. Had you not arrived when you did, I fear our army might have been encircled and utterly destroyed. I also commend the good work of Confessor Veruth, who aided us in the battle first with his kresnik abilities."

"We do all that we must," Justiciar Zedonia replied. "Tell me truly: is Alvaria Saccarra destroyed?"

"I'm afraid not," Lysander said. "She is, however, contained. I fear her current state may be temporary, but we have already been in contact with Selevarian, which sends reinforcements and can hopefully offer a more permanent solution."

"Troubling though it is that she survived, I suppose containment must suffice. I have sent a score of paladins through the woods to determine if any draugr escaped or if any members of the Inquisition have fled. I have brought as many paladins as Mountainhome could muster, as well as my own diligentia. With your cooperation, we will question those members of the Inquisition now in custody. We will also maintain a presence here until further notice."

"Your aid is appreciated, but we would not wish to impose on your goodwill."

"You misunderstand," the justiciar said as his eyes swept the area. "It is not a courtesy we extend, but necessity. The Grand Master spoke with the High Archmage and clarified that Kazra Lo Veedra should be administered by both the Council of Archmages and the

Paladin Order of Kalendril. Given that the Inquisition is incapable of performing a proper inquiry, for obvious reasons, we will act as investigators and execute justice on behalf of the people of the Gray Empire." His horse plodded forward, and he handed Lysander a small scroll. "By order of the Gray Emperor, executive administration over Kazra Lo Veedra has been granted to the Paladin Order of Kalendril, specifically to Justiciar Calman Zedonia. We would like to work alongside the Council of Archmages to ensure the safety of the public, but understand that our presence here is a requirement while yours is not."

Lysander read through the scroll, his eyebrows lifting. "The emperor himself signed this? How was it done so quickly?"

"He sent his swiftest griffin riders to deliver it while we were en route. We received the edict not a full day ago, although I was aware of the situation before we left Mountainhome."

Lysander handed the scroll back. "We will gladly work with you for the foreseeable future. Additional accountability may help prevent such disasters in the future."

"One can hope."

"I would ask you to be careful within the building, at least for the next few hours. The method through which she is contained is tenuous at best. We would prefer to secure the central chamber before admitting others."

"That is acceptable. I defer to your best judgment. Alert me when it is done and perhaps you can give me a tour of the interior of Kazra Lo Veedra. I will return to my brothers and sisters to assess what must be done." He turned to his soldiers. "Confessor Veruth, take three paladins of your choice and Squire Soraya to check on the injured within the Army of Selevarian. When you have finished, return south. We will make camp there for the rest of the night."

"Grand Judge," Squire Soraya said, "might I not join the others in hunting for inquisitors?" Lysander was unaware the slight individual was a woman, and yet the voice was impossible to mistake. She wore a blank silver mask over her face and a cowl prevented any other part of her from being visible. Lysander guessed she must have been around fifteen years old.

Confessor Veruth frowned at her. "Until you learn how to heal, you shall not begin to hunt."

"He speaks truly, child," Justiciar Zedonia said. "Besides, your brethren likely toil in futility. Few inquisitors would have abandoned Kazra Lo Veedra and escaped notice."

The confessor and his group rode off, and the justiciar watched them go. Finally, he turned back to Lysander. "Forgive the girl her occasional impertinence. Young minds are too easily swayed by songs of glorious battle."

"I would not deign to question your methods," Lysander began carefully, "but what benefit is there to bringing a child into battle?"

"She is young, but must learn. Before we took her in, she was no stranger to pain and hardship. Now, she will see the life she chooses before she must take her vows in the next year. We do not force children into our ranks, but we do raise them according to the philosophy of our founder. If it's her safety that concerns you, the squires take up the center of our formation and are the least likely to succumb to danger."

"I thank you for indulging my questions." Lysander bowed.

"Indeed. I shall return and order a camp to be made. Keep me informed." With a curt nod, he departed with the rest of his cavalry.

Garson watched as the paladin departed. "What do you think?"

"I think," Lysander said, walking back to the others, "that the Inquisition's services will be heavily complemented by other organizations for the foreseeable future."

The Archmage of Dragons nodded. "I should return to the soldiers to let them know you're still alive. I'm sure Selevia will be thrilled as well." With a flap of his wings, he took to the air and flew over the newly grown trees.

Lysander took a breath and glanced at the amethyst gate which had begun to glow.

"May I join you?" Lyvaelan asked.

The archmage studied him and smiled. "Certainly. We never did have any formal lessons. Maybe now is a good time to start."

The space between the two pillars that formed the gate glowed and out stepped the Archmage of Time, flanked by a dozen attendants. Gabrielle Sesturnia blinked at her surroundings through rectangular spectacles. She kept her graying brown hair tied behind her in a tight ponytail and the rest of her appearance reflected a similar exacting diligence. There was an almost birdlike manner to her behavior as she studied the area, which was only exacerbated by the presence of two brown wings, since she was one of the few non-human archmages who were volarim. In one hand she held a gold and silver staff topped with an ever-moving armillary sphere with etched sigils along its surface. She wore simple blue and red robes with a shifting sequence of numbers along the fringes of the fabric.

"Archmage of Time," Lysander said, "you arrived more swiftly than I expected."

She turned her small brown eyes up to meet his. "Well, hmm, yes, it would be rather strange for the Archmage of Time to be late." She spoke with odd precision and a fixed tempo.

He smiled. "A joke?"

"No, Lysander, you know I hate jokes. The High Archmage impressed upon me the, hmm, urgency of my arrival. What, exactly, are we doing here?" Her emotions rarely extended beyond this calm inquisitiveness. He also recognized that, true enough, she genuinely hated jokes of almost any kind.

"Well, we are out on the field of battle. Alvaria became the Living Lich of Half a Day and—"

"How does this, hmm, concern me?" she asked. The question stemmed from pure curiosity, not from impatience. She remained unperturbed by the blood that surrounded her. Truly, the Archmage of Time was one of a kind.

"It might be best if I showed you. It's within the estate." He turned to leave when he thought better. "Also, this is my student, Lyvaelan. He will join us."

She blinked at Lyvaelan. "Hmm, you do, of course, realize this boy is half dark elf and half warlock, correct?"

Lysander gave a half smile. "I do, yes."

"Hmm. Very well. Proceed."

The Archmage of Education led them back into Kazra Lo Veedra but noticed Lyvaelan's expression of confusion. It had taken Lysander time to understand Gabrielle, but he now possessed a basic understanding of how she functioned. If it had to do with time, she cared. If it didn't, then she didn't. Recognizing this small and yet pivotal truth made interactions with her substantially easier.

They returned to the spot where Hazel had blocked them from intervening. Alvaria still stood with her expression of pain and hate. Hazel had friends who would save her, but who would save Alvaria?

"Hmm, yes, I see the issue." The Archmage of Time examined the wall of time. "I assume you want to, hmm, get her out?"

"No!" Lysander exclaimed. "She's the cause of these problems. We want to keep her contained in slow time."

"Ah, I see." She peered at Alvaria within. "The former Archmage of the Inquisition looks displeased. I wouldn't mind, hmm, keeping her trapped for some years. Her parties never started on time. Really it's, hmm, inexcusable." She glanced over at Lysander. "Unfortunately, she will be free within the next few days."

"What!" Lysander gasped. "But that much time should have kept her contained for weeks or months!"

Her brow knit together. "Hmm. You simply aren't seeing the, hmm, bigger picture." She removed her glasses and handed them to Lysander. Through the enchanted spectacles, the area within the room was a swirl of blue waves that seeped through areas of the roof and one of the corridors. It leaked slowly, but like a bucket filled with holes, it could not fully contain what it had.

"As you can see," she said, "the man who designed this chamber made some, hmm, conspicuous miscalculations. In most cases, it would not adversely affect any of the normal spells cast from within but, hmm, for holding tempecules it is no good."

Lysander handed the glasses back. His head swam for a moment. He felt ill.

"Isn't there anything you can do?" Lyvaelan asked.

She looked at the dark elf warlock with surprise, as if she had forgotten he was there. "Well, hmm, of course. Now that I know what is desired, it should be simple to fix."

"Why didn't you lead with that?" Lysander groaned.

"I thought it was, hmm, self-explanatory. I only needed to know the problem and what you wanted to do with it. You are sure you want her contained, not freed, correct?"

"Yes, very correct."

"Hmm. Good." She turned to her attendants. "Seal the holes in the containment chamber. I will obtain the requisite materials from the High Archmage." She looked back at Lysander. "How long do you want her imprisoned?"

"Forever would be nice," he said. He realized he shouldn't speak so casually with her, since she would likely take it literally, but he was tired.

She frowned. "Hmm, well, forever is not really a possibility. I'm afraid it will need to be much less than that. I can keep her reliably contained for, hmm, only nineteen thousand years, if we round the number down."

He gaped. "*Nineteen thousand years*? How is that possible? The containment vessel that shattered couldn't have contained that much."

"It didn't," she replied as she walked back toward the entrance to Kazra Lo Veedra. "We don't need time to, hmm, slow her down. We just need magic. When she was slowed, she released magic, opening her arcane conduits to lash out at some kind of plant. We can transform Alvaria's power into tempecules, which will slow her even further. I will also have my assistants build a smaller, hmm, container for her. The smaller area will condense the temporal magic and increase its duration."

"You can use her as a power source? Is that really possible?"

She blinked in confusion. "I thought I already said that it was. If she had the mental capacity to resist, then it would fail, but since she is mired she will, hmm, not even notice her absence of power until several thousand years have elapsed. There is much magic in that room besides her, so we can siphon that as well."

Lysander sighed with relief. "Gabrielle, you have saved us all. Thank you."

She shook her head. "I diagnosed a problem and offered the best, hmm, solution. Saving others never entered the equation."

The Archmage of Time scuttled back to the entrance while they lingered behind.

"Will that plan really work?" Lyvaelan asked.

"If she says she can do it, then she can," Lysander replied. "She may be the most reliable archmage in Selevarian, though she might argue that she isn't currently in the city, which I suppose would be a fair point."

Lyvaelan stood silently for a moment. Eventually, he met Lysander's eyes. "We need to take Hazel home. She doesn't belong in Selevarian."

He sighed and nodded. "I know. I will accompany you back to Coruvaine, along with a detachment of soldiers. Only the Inquisition would disagree, but their perspective is currently moot." He rubbed a hand through his short, blond hair. "I'm sorry, Lyvaelan. Truly."

The young man glanced back at the chamber where Alvaria lashed out for all eternity. "It isn't your fault. Good people sometimes do the wrong thing by accident. If she had been dangerous, then your caution would have been justified."

"You give me more credit than I deserve, but thank you for understanding."

Lyvaelan narrowed his eyes. "I do have a question for you, though."

"Ask."

"When you trapped Hazel in the library, you used a spell of nine bindings. What were the nine bindings?"

Lysander couldn't help smiling. "I suppose if you're to be my student that I ought to teach you something. Tell me, how many of the bindings did you identify?"

Lyvaelan cast his eyes to the side. "By the time the Grand Inquisitor arrived, I found five of them."

"I'm impressed! Most would struggle to find two in the time you had. You should be proud. The nine bindings are location, nation, shape, memory, cognizance, and power."

Lyvaelan frowned. "That's only six."

"Indeed." The archmage chuckled.

The dark elf warlock crossed his arms. "So there really were no nine bindings at all, only six?"

"Well, yes, and no." Lysander leaned back against a pillar. "The last three are just as powerful as the others but not magically so. The seventh binding was the doubt you experienced over how many you needed to find and untangle. The eighth binding was the fear you had at attempting something that could backfire. And the ninth binding was the love you had for Hazel, which kept you from doing anything that might hurt her. Uncertainty, fear, and love may possess as much power as any spell. Never underestimate them."

"It's a little disappointing to learn that the nine bindings are essentially a trick."

"Only in part. It is a convention among spellcasters to give a numeric value to the spells they cast in order to misdirect those who seek to undo them. You need to be aware of the problem in order to fix it, after all."

"I suppose that makes sense." He looked toward the exit. "We should head back."

"You go along first. I need to rest a moment and then I'll join you."

Lyvaelan nodded and left the archmage alone.

Lysander gazed at the woman stuck in time—the blood on her face, the anguish in her eyes. He remembered the night they spent on the roof of Chateau Zarielle, laughing, drinking, and enjoying the time they had together. None of that merriment remained for either of them. There would be no more pleasant days of leisure or jokes shared between them. The friendship they cultivated over decades had ended in pain and betrayal. Her face now remained twisted with loathing as she hurled immense destructive power at a teen girl whose only crime was expressing a desire to help her. How had she gotten to the point where she sought to kill a child who wished only to understand her? He approached the wall of time and put his hand against its solid surface. A few tears fell from his eyes, but he wiped them away. With effort, he withdrew his hand.

He took one last look at her and turned away with a heavy sigh.

Goodbye, Alvaria. I'm sorry.

Chapter Forty-Seven
The Lord of Life

Hazel opened her eyes to the sound of singing birds. She wore her white dress but was barefoot. This place tickled at the edges of her memory. Green grass and the light babble of a creek greeted her. With the soft rustle of a warm wind, she recognized these trees.

"I'll bet that you've never climbed this high in a tree before."

Above her sat a young man, only a few years older than her, in a high branch of an ash tree. She studied it more closely and its proximity to the murmuring stream.

It was the tree she had once fallen from.

She shook her head and climbed, feeling excitement at scaling a tree again. It had been too long. She reached a high branch; one she had once taunted a dear friend from. The young man sat just a few feet higher on another sturdy branch she had never seen before. He wore a loose white shirt and brown breeches. He was barefoot, like she was, and softly hummed a tune. His dark brown hair had the tousled look of a bird's nest but perfectly matched him. From this angle, he was handsome, but there was something strange about him as he faced away from her.

Hazel frowned. Her mind felt equal parts clear and clouded. A dawning realization came, and her pensive expression faded. "You only climbed higher because you cheated."

He smiled from the side. "How did I cheat?"

She studied him seriously and felt a chill. "You made another branch."

He chuckled softly. "Looks like you caught me. Here, I'll make a little room for you so we can sit together." He patted the branch, and it extended out to accommodate her. She climbed up next to him. He watched the distant beginning of the sunset contentedly. His eyes were a bright, verdant green. The same color green as—

"I'm sure you have questions," he said, swinging his feet, "ask away."

"Who are you?"

He leaned against the trunk of the tree and looked into her eyes. "I am the one who called you from the dark of the abyss into the light of day. I am the one who gave you life. I am the whisper you sometimes heard, encouraging you in difficult times."

Her brow furrowed. She knew her guess was wrong but ventured it, anyway. "Hickory?"

Silence ruled as he turned to her. Time slowed to a near stop as she held her breath. His response was little more than a whisper, and yet it filled the entire world.

"Hemericanth."

A gust of wind blew through the trees. His eyes glowed with a familiar power and a staggering rush filled her heart. Green light wafted from his hand and transformed into two green butterflies. They flitted away and changed into other brilliant colors as they became living creatures.

"I have many names and I look different depending on who sees me, but Hemericanth, the Lord of Life, would be the most familiar to you."

She nodded. She realized she should feel surprised, but somehow it just felt... right.

"Any other questions?" he asked, manipulating the light with his hands to create more living things. A squirrel ran up to him from another tree and he formed a chestnut. He handed it to the creature, who scurried off. "It's not every day you get to commune with a god and have him directly answer."

"I *do* have a lot of questions"—she watched his movements, almost entranced—"but I don't know where to start."

"The beginning is usually best."

She squinted at him. "Snarky remarks aren't helpful, Hemericanth."

He laughed merrily. "My apologies, Hazel Enda."

"Why am I here? Where *is* here? What even happened?"

"All good questions." He swung his legs absently. "You are here because you used a high quantity of my power but were unprepared for how much it actually was. Your body needs rest and so you entered a briarsleep, which just means you do not age or require sustenance for as long as you remain asleep. As for our location, we are currently in your unconscious mind, but with some divine changes. Finally, regarding what happened, you saved a great many people and destroyed a great many undead."

Hazel nodded. That sounded familiar. "Am I also undead?"

"Ha! No. You, my dear Hazel, are very much alive."

"How?"

He gazed deep into her eyes. His expression was kind but serious. "It's complicated. More than you realize."

"Okay, so explain it to me. Why am I alive when Alvaria's father exploded from the inside?"

Hemericanth used the green magic to show images as he spoke. "Even eldritch magic cannot wrest a soul away from my sister for long. Alvaria tried to steal something that was not hers, whereas you were a gift."

"What do you mean?"

"It means..." he hesitated, "that I made a bargain with the one you call Semeleme. You were never supposed to die. Not like that."

He gazed wistfully at the sunset. "Of the billions of sentient life forms on this continent, you were the one I most enjoyed. Every time you ran through my grass, or climbed my trees, or splashed in my waters, I sensed the life within you. I am known as the Lord of Life, but the title is not the entire truth. I give life to things, yes, but also the *feeling* of being alive. When the joy of living meets life itself, it is the most beautiful music imaginable, as meaning and matter coalesce. Every time you went outside, you exuded a supreme love of life. The plants noticed it too, I might add.

"When you died, I was bereft. I may be a god, but my ability to intervene is limited by my sphere of influence. There was nothing I could do to prevent your death. Before you traveled fully into the land of the dead, I stopped you. I requested that you be allowed to return to the land of the living. Semeleme is... stubborn, though fair. She allowed you to return on two conditions. The first was that you would only remain living for as long as your soul desired for you to live. The second was that for as long as you did, you would be my beloved high priestess.

"The process of choosing the ones mortals refer to as the 'beloved' is challenging because all gods are limited to only a handful. Choosing you meant I would be incapable of choosing another."

This was more complicated that Hazel realized. "Why did she care? Why would she want me to become your high priestess?"

"Because the power I grant is the power to infuse all things with life and, by extension, to heal. It is toxic to the undead, as Zylit told you. Semeleme knows this and knew also that undead would rise eventually with the ambitions of Alvaria Saccarra. Expecting this, she wanted someone who could destroy the undead quickly where her high priestess could not."

"Hmph." Hazel crossed her arms. "It would've been nice if she could have told the high priestess about that."

He chuckled. "My sister isn't the most communicative. It's rare to talk to even the chattiest of us, so it's little wonder Caeli Relinon thought you were an undead abomination."

"What will happen if she touches me with her power?"

He lifted his eyebrows mysteriously. "Perhaps you should find out—the sooner, the better. You have nothing to fear, but it's better to have that cult with you than against you."

"Believe me, I know that better than anyone." She looked him up and down. "Is this what you really look like? You don't seem like a god."

He shrugged noncommittally. "This both is and isn't what I look like. The gods are a collection of traits and interests that are interpreted by humans. What you see before you is how you would interpret my true nature to the best of your abilities. I appear somewhat different to others, but the unified experience of seeing me would be largely the same. Many would likely think I didn't seem like a god, although few would actually say it." He gave her a meaningful look. "Present company excluded."

"Anything else I should know?"

He gazed into the distance. "That is a very subjective question. What I might find essential may not matter to you, and vice versa."

She sighed. "Okay, let me see if I understand. You gave me the power to put life into things, talk to trees, and tell prophecies, right?"

"No, not really, or even mostly." He faced her and gestured in mock grandeur. "I grant you my own infinite power, channeled through your own finite body. That power manifests as the green light you see. Talking to plants and telling prophecies had nothing to do with me whatsoever. Oh"—he seemed to remember something else and wrinkled his nose—"and also, your current green complexion wasn't me either, just in case you felt upset about it."

Her eyebrows shot up. "Really? Hmm. What can you tell me about Hickory? What did he do, and how does he fit in?"

"Hickory provided me with the mortal means to revive you. He had strange ideas I helped along. Mostly, I needed someone crazy enough to exhume you. You actually live quite close to him, so he knew of your passing because he saw you often. It wasn't challenging to guide his thoughts in a specific direction to get what I wanted. He had some unnecessarily complicated formulas to bring you back, but I ultimately did that. The rest of the magic he used on you was"—he shifted his hands back and forth in the air—"questionable. It certainly did something to you, but I won't tell you precisely. You should probably ask him."

"Is he well?"

He nodded reassuringly. "Alvaria Saccarra scrambled his mind, but he was pretty scrambled to begin with. He has returned to his normal self, if that's what you're wondering."

She thought hard for a moment. "I don't think I have any other questions, at least not that I can think of."

"Very well," he said, rubbing his hands together, "there are a couple more points we need to go over before you can be reunited with everyone. The first regards the limits of your power."

She nodded. "The exhaustion, right?"

"That's only a small part of it. There are two limitations you should know of. The first is you cannot bring life to one who truly does not wish to live. If the central spark of life—that is, desire—is gone from the person, then you can do nothing to excite it into healing. The second limitation is you are incapable of killing anyone. You can hurt, attack, and apprehend, but you cannot kill. You are literally incapable of it. Should you kill a creature with sentience and do so with full weight of intention and knowledge, then the power I have granted you will disappear and you will die for rejecting my gift."

"Huh. I don't think I've ever tried to kill someone, so I don't know if that's really such a big deal."

His face grew somber for a moment. "It may be, as you progress. Regardless, it is not for you. With that in mind"—he stood on the branch which expanded to accommodate him, suddenly regal despite his common appearance—"Hazel Enda, you are my high priestess and my beloved. I have chosen you from among countless others with the sacred task of bringing life to all. Spread my light to desolate places and be the joy of my forests." He closed his eyes and took a deep breath. When he opened them, he smiled crookedly at her. "I should also mention my followers are mostly a relaxed group, but they may give you a rather embarrassing title. Try not to read too much into it. I think they take the idea of me being the Lord of Life a little too seriously."

"Why? What's the title?"

"Consort of Hemericanth."

She scowled at him.

"It isn't my fault! Humans are just... humans." He waved dismissively. "You'll be glad to know you don't have many proper duties in a temple or anything, so at least there's that."

She crossed her arms. "I suppose it's something." She acted annoyed with him, but secretly she tried not to laugh. There was something wonderful about him and this place. She felt alive around him. Hemericanth was like the older brother she had never had.

He suddenly hugged her. It was a warm, energizing embrace. The smell of flowers and growing things filled her senses. He pulled away from her after several seconds, still holding her shoulders, and smiled down at her. "Keep being full of life, Hazel. You make the world a better place by simply being part of it." He sighed. "It's time for you to go. The others will miss you."

"But... what am I supposed to do with this power now? What do you want from me?"

His expression softened. He leaned down and kissed her forehead with a lingering gentleness. His eyes again met hers. "I want to see the world you will create by breathing life into it." He brushed a few strands of hair behind her ear. "I want to see how you grow as a person, and, more than anything"—Hemericanth closed his eyes and put his forehead against hers—"I want you to live."

Her heart fluttered. "When will I see you again?"

He smiled mysteriously and separated from her with a small shrug. "Perhaps soon, perhaps never. Who knows? That's life."

He touched her, and she fell into the sky. As she rose, the colors of the world shifted across a rainbow palette before turning light green and finally fading into a soft, comforting black.

Chapter Forty-Eight
A World Made New

Hazel felt herself waking from a deep sleep. She was more comfortable than she had been in a long time. As she woke, she noticed exactly how relaxed she was. She rested on her side and blinked her eyes open. The curtains were drawn on her window, allowing only the smallest sliver of sunlight through. For a moment, she experienced disorientation. Was she back at Kazra Lo Veedra? No, there were no windows in her room. Was she at her parents' home? She rolled onto her back and studied the room. Finally, her eyes settled to her left. Slumped in a chair, eyes shut, sat Lyvaelan.

He slowly blinked and gazed at her. Her heart skipped a beat as their eyes met. He jolted and closed his eyes briefly before coming to her side.

He kneeled before her bed and looked at her in wonder. "Hazel, you have to stop doing things like this."

She grinned. "Sorry, but I somehow doubt I can do that."

He smiled back and was about to respond when footsteps come from the hallway and both her parents burst in. They embraced her with tears and kisses. Lyvaelan shifted uncomfortably and muttered something about getting tea before leaving the room.

Her father watched as he left. "You know, Hazel, you've been asleep for some time. Your mom and I have been living at the library until you got better, but despite that, I would have to say there's only one person who watched over you as much as us and it's Lyvaelan. I see why you wanted us to meet him. He seems nice." Lynn glared at him. "What?" he exclaimed. "He *does!*"

Hazel wondered briefly if a blush showed up on green skin.

Lara, Alistair, Garo, and King Aldric entered after another minute. Lyvaelan had telepathically alerted them and each rushed in.

Lara leaned against the foot of the bed with a grin. "You gave us a bit of scare, kid. It almost seemed like you were going to pull a fairytale princess on us and never wake up."

"Why? How long was I out?"

"From the moment you collapsed," Alistair said, joining Lara, "it has been three weeks and two days. It's the first of Verathia, the beginning of spring." He grinned. "Happy New Year."

"I *have* been asleep for a while. What did I miss?"

"Mostly boring business stuff," Lara said.

"Actually," Garo said, walking to the opposite side of the bed, "you missed some very *interesting* 'business stuff.' Your burst of healing magic annihilated the undead in the area surrounding Kazra Lo Veedra. We studied the prophecy you left and realized that the statement that none could kill her horde was a riddle. That which is dead cannot die and therefore cannot be killed. You instead gave them life, which ended their undead existence. You saved many soldiers. Lives were lost, but you prevented the deaths of thousands, which is something the Council of Archmages will not soon forget. By decree of the High Archmage, Lyvaelan is to be tutored further in magic by the Archmage of Education. Furthermore, the Council feels it owes us a debt it cannot readily repay. They have agreed to give us access to their libraries and facilities at Calixford University and at any other establishment run by the Council. They have also given us permission to use their amethyst gates and will build a small one in the library's basement, so you can come and go from the city as you please.

"Alvaria Saccarra remains at Kazra Lo Veedra, suspended in that room. The Archmage of Time has stationed additional guards to ensure she remains in temporal stasis indefinitely. They are using the magic from the diamonds she filled with prophetic energy and from Alvaria herself to fuel the magic, keeping her confined. The estate is currently being dismantled and reformed while the dead bodies are being laid to final rest with the assistance of the Paladin Order of Kalendril. Thanks to you, life grows around the estate once again.

"Paxton Averly was captured without effort and placed in a cell within Arcanathema Prison. He is currently undergoing psychological treatment for the ghosts and shadows that he claims haunt him.

"The Gray Emperor himself has commended you and the other Watchers of the Evenfall Vigil for your success and labors. He has, by his rights, made you all Guardians of the Gray Empire, which gives you permission to function beyond Ethelian in an authoritative capacity, similar to what paladin orders enjoy.

"All of that aside, you did something truly incredible. You are full of surprises, Hazel Enda."

She smiled at everyone. "Oh, I think I have a few more surprises for all of you."

The others looked at her in bemusement as she sat upright in her bed. Her mother was the first to speak, "What do you mean, Hazel?"

Hazel looked at King Aldric. "Can I ask you for a couple of favors, Your Majesty?"

He cocked his head and smiled quizzically. "Of course, Hazel. Whatever you'd like."

"Thank you. The first favor I want is to see the high priestess of Semeleme, Caeli Relinon."

More than a couple of jaws dropped in the room. Alistair was the first to regain composure. "Hazel, are you really sure?"

"Positive." She nodded.

"It's confirmed," Kyle Enda said. "My daughter is crazy."

Hazel smirked. "Like you didn't think that already."

Lynn jabbed his side. "She gets that crazy streak from *you*."

King Aldric scratched his stubble. "You don't truly need my permission for that, but I wouldn't advise confronting her. That said, if you wish to see her, you are welcome to do so."

"Thank you," she said. "My second request—"

"—is to see Hickory," he said with a sigh. "I understand little of everything that's happened, but at this point I'm willing to trust he won't be able to control you." He smiled. "It seems nobody is capable of that."

"Isn't *that* the truth," her father muttered.

"You can come by the castle whenever you'd like. I will set up a room for you two to talk in that is less dreary than the jail."

"Thank you, Your Majesty. I think I'll get ready now. First, I'll see the priestess, then the mage tomorrow." She threw off the bedcovers. "Now everybody, go! I need to change."

The group shuffled out with Lyvaelan leaving last. He turned and looked like he was going to say something but stopped. He smiled at her and closed the door.

She desperately wanted to talk to him. She wanted to sit down and laugh with her friends, but she had burning questions to ask, and she knew only one person who could answer them.

Chapter Forty-Nine
Sisters In Life and Death

"Are you certain you want to do this?" Lyvaelan asked as they faced the Veiled Chapel.

Hazel nodded. "Things will get worse before they get better if I do nothing. She may still hate me, but she needs to know that I am not what she thinks."

"Do you really think she'll listen?" Kyle asked as he examined the building distrustfully. Her parents refused to be separated from her so soon after awakening. Garo joined them along with Alistair and Lara, despite their lack of powers due to the daylight. Hazel declined an escort of additional guards. This group already made her stand out more than she wished.

"She might not," Hazel said, "but I doubt she'll be able to resist the opportunity to destroy me."

"That's not exactly comforting, Haze," Lara mumbled.

"It wasn't supposed to be."

She led them to the large wooden doors of the building. True to its name, dark drapes hung on the exterior between windows and beneath alcoves to avoid the extremes of the weather. It was crafted from dark stone and rose high and pointed. The architecture alone demanded a certain respect and reverence from any who passed beneath its shadow.

An old man, clean shaven with a dark brown cloak, sat at the entrance smoking a pipe. He eyed them but said nothing until they approached. "May I help you?"

"I'm here to see the High Priestess of Semeleme."

He puffed out a cloud of smoke. "Well, you found the right place, but she's praying inside and not to be disturbed. Tell me your name and I'll let her know when she's done."

Hazel recognized the way the man looked at her. He knew exactly who she was.

"This is taking too long," Lyvaelan said. He raised his eyebrows at him but said nothing else.

The man stood and fumbled for something in his pocket. "Apologies for keeping you waiting," he said and opened the door.

Hazel would need to get Lyvaelan to teach her that trick.

They entered the building, which smelled of incense. A few wooden pews stood close to them, but besides that the floors were bare save for standing candelabrum positioned between the interior pillars. Statues stood beneath arches along the side, covered with a thin black linen which concealed them just enough to lead one to question who—or what—they were. Further in and above several steps of polished marble kneeled the High Priestess. Before her stood an altar and above it loomed the dark visage of Semeleme.

"I ordered that I was not to be disturbed," she said, her voice echoing through the chapel.

Hazel led them forward. "We thought you might make an exception for me."

Her head whipped around and she rose from her place. The edges of her black dress grew into a murky mass of tendrils. She recovered her calm and studied the intruders warily as the smoke dissipated.

"You show an alarming lack of good sense for a draugr or whatever you are," she said slowly, stepping forward, "or perhaps an excess of cunning. How did you escape the Inquisition?"

Hazel shrugged and smiled. "Me and the Inquisition parted ways with the compliments of the Council of Archmages."

Caeli's eyes narrowed. "Did they find you lacking in power?"

Hazel had to giggle at that. "No, not at all. I'm not entirely at liberty to say, but it generally amounts to a big misunderstanding."

"Indeed." The High Priestess crossed her arms. "And the reason you came here after obtaining your freedom is...?"

"Because I want you to use your power on me."

Despite the echoing interior, the chapel fell completely silent. The High Priestess mused on this for some time before responding. "Really?" She walked a little closer. "You want to experience my power even though it will destroy you?"

Hazel beamed. "It won't." She held out her hand.

Caeli looked from her hand to Hazel and approached. The High Priestess had her suspicions, but her trust in Semeleme overrode her distrust for Hazel. Dark tendrils of black smoke swirled around Caeli. A sinister buzz surrounded her as she stretched her hand out and touched Hazel's fingers. Without intending to, the smoky green light emanated from Hazel and twisted around the black smoke from the priestess. A sound came from Hazel as well and melded with Caeli's, producing two separate tones that blended into a bright and beautiful harmony.

Hazel sensed the power in her touch. A chill ran through her as if the power itself spoke to her. That coiling magic invited her to one day embrace the end of herself and all things, but not yet. She recalled all those who had died and the bittersweet melancholy of knowing that all things must eventually conclude. In many ways she experienced the same flood of emotions she did when she purged Kazra Lo Veedra of the undead, but tempered with a certain sobriety, silence, and peace. Where her power expressed the vigor of holding on, this power voiced the serenity of finally letting go.

The priestess staggered back and put a hand to her mouth, eyes wide. Tears trickled down her cheeks and a series of emotions overtook her. The others may not have comprehended this transition, but Hazel did. For the first time since Hazel had returned, the High Priestess truly saw her for who she was and not what she believed her to be. Caeli threw off the veil that covered her face and she grasped Hazel's hand as the magic receded. She searched her eyes, seeking the words to express what she experienced. "Hazel, I am so sorry."

Everyone else was perplexed.

Hazel smiled gently. "You were wrong, but for the right reasons. I forgive you."

"She doesn't speak for all of us," Lara interrupted. "What's going on? Why the sudden change of heart?"

"I experienced her power," she replied softly. "The gentle warmth of being alive and the joy of knowing every day brings new flowers into bloom flowed through me. Too often I have forgotten such simple joys, but I see now that our powers are complementary, not oppositional. We are different and yet have more in common than any other two women. Put simply"—Caeli put an arm around Hazel's shoulder and smiled more brightly than ever—"we're sisters, though it may take me some time to overcome all my previous antipathies."

The room was silent.

"What?" Lara shouted, her voice echoing off the high ceiling.

"Hold on," Kyle said, "I think if I had another child, I would know about it." He looked at Lynn, who raised an eyebrow. "I mean, I would *definitely* know about it, so I don't."

Caeli shook her head. "We are not sisters by blood. We are sisters by the gods."

"What she means," Hazel said, "is we are both beloved by gods. She is beloved by Semeleme and I am beloved by Hemericanth."

"You're—what?" Lynn said. Everyone else was stunned.

"Priestess," Hazel asked with a grin, "did everyone act this surprised when you were chosen by Semeleme?"

"No, not quite this surprised." She smiled. "But fairly close. Also, call me Caeli. We are sisters, after all."

"Does this mean," Alistair said, collecting himself, "that you will call off your followers who seek to hurt Hazel?"

"Of course," she replied, "and I am sorry for what happened, though the problem could have been easily rectified if you'd just let me use my power on her to begin with."

"Now hold on—" Lara said, pointing an accusatory finger.

"You fought undead, did you not?" Caeli stared at Lara unflinchingly. "I can see it in your faces. After fighting abominations, can you say my concern was unjustified?"

"She has a point," Hazel said, keeping Lara from responding, "but the greater fault lies with me. I should have submitted myself."

"All that is behind us," Caeli said, separating from her. "I will spread the word a new high priestess of Hemericanth has been chosen. He must have bargained to get you back from Semeleme, which means you are special to both. If you ever need any support, I am happy to help. Even if I was right to be worried, some terrible things happened to you that go beyond my ability to justify or amend. I would make it up to you, if possible. All you need to do is ask."

Hazel looked at the ceiling as a slow smile crept across her face. "Actually, I can think of at least *one* favor."

"Very well. Ask and it will be yours."

"I want the Cult of Semeleme to drop their charges and grudge against Hickory Allkirk."

Caeli's eyebrows shot up. "What?"

"I know he'll still be imprisoned for what he's done, but he shouldn't have to be persecuted by the cult afterward. He robbed my grave and tried to raise me from the dead, but that was partly Hemericanth guiding him to do it."

She sighed and shook her head. "Your wish is granted. We will pursue no legal or extrajudicial punishment for him. He must swear to never attempt such a thing again."

"Deal."

She pursed her lips doubtfully. "Do you think he'll agree to it?"

"I'll persuade him." Hazel shrugged. Truthfully, she had no idea whether or not he would do as she asked but there was no sense in worrying the priestess with the specifics.

"Very well," she sighed, but there was a whisper of a smile on her face. "You do not ask for much, admittedly. Perhaps I can be of use to you in other ways as well. We both occupy the ranks of a small group of the divinely chosen. While our gods differ, I would gladly assist you with navigating your newfound abilities, connection, and your new position, High Priestess of Hemericanth. You have a cult to lead, and I know more than a little about such things."

Hazel frowned. "I know almost nothing about leading others."

"Oh, but that's not true at all," Garo said, his tail wagged slowly on the ground. "You are a leader by example, not by command. Where you go, others will follow. It will be the support you provide that brings them to you."

Hazel looked behind her at all the people who joined her. They supported her through harrowing experiences and crossed vast distances to save her. Despite the threat of losing their lives, they followed after her. She hadn't intended to lead them, but she started to suspect Garo might be right.

"The grim speaks true," Caeli said, "but some may desire greater structure than your friends and family. The Cult of Hemericanth has never been as rigid or demanding as others, but they have not had a high priestess who was beloved before. Soon, many will desire your blessing."

"Blessing?"

"We'll work it out, Hazel. Don't worry." Caeli squeezed her hand once more and walked back to the entrance of the chapel. "I now need all of you to leave. I have a sermon to prepare for my Undertakers and congregants. They should hear of this immediately."

As they left, Hazel looked back at Caeli, who smiled before she turned away and closed the doors.

I have a sister. Wow.

Chapter Fifty
Life and What it Means

Hazel sat alone in a small but comfortable study. A tapestry hung on the wall, depicting flying griffins and an attacking army. A thick rug quieted the room. The fireplace was lit and tall windows provided excellent light. She resisted the temptation to look through the books displayed on several shelves.

Despite her friends' insistence they join her, she needed to come here alone. For the first time in what seemed like ages, she walked by herself without concealing her identity. She knew some people stared at her, but after Caeli had spoken with her followers, the most Hazel had experienced from them were fervent apologies. Others had heard there was a girl who returned from the dead, and after the arrival of the Inquisition and the disappearance of the Enda family, it wasn't hard to guess who they suspected the undead girl might be. Many still regarded her fearfully, but others just seemed curious.

The door opened, and a guard entered, followed by the shabbily dressed form of Hickory. His gray hair was as disheveled as she remembered, but now he had a disheveled beard to match. Despite his threadbare clothing, it appeared clean and there was a wetness to his hair that Hazel guessed meant the guards had insisted on bathing him prior to their meeting. He glanced around the room nervously before his gaze settled on Hazel and his mouth worked noiselessly.

She grinned. "Hi Hickory."

"Oh!" He shuffled forward and stopped. He appeared torn between hugging her and keeping his distance out of respect. She chuckled and hugged him quickly before showing him to his seat.

"Hazel, I—this is tremendous!" he exclaimed. "I have wanted to see you for months now! Oh, but it seems so much longer than that! How have you been? I was worried the Inquisition was going to destroy you."

"We don't have to worry about that. I have some things I need to tell you." Hazel explained what had happened in the past months. Of the betrayal of the Inquisition, and their victory over the undead. She left out the details of where the battle had taken place and of Alvaria Saccarra's ascension. Those details—she had been told by Garo and Aldric—were confidential. If others believed they could use Hazel to become a powerful lich, then it would spell disaster for many, herself included. Finally, she concluded with Hemericanth's revelation.

Hickory shook his head. "I must confess, I am both disappointed and relieved I didn't find some alternative way to raise the dead. I appreciate that you interceded with the Cult of Semeleme for me. You didn't have to."

"But I wanted to," Hazel said emphatically. "You mean a lot to me. I don't think anyone understands why, but for a long time I thought you were the only reason I came back. You did your best to bring me back to life and back to my family. It may not have been by your power that I returned, but you still tried, and I appreciate that."

He smiled. "You talk a lot more than when we first spoke. It's a nice change."

"I've had some practice." Her smile shifted into an expression of interest. "I do have questions for you, though."

"Like what?"

"Hemericanth essentially gave me immortality and the ability to infuse life into living things. Everything else came from you. He said I should ask what you did to make me."

"Oh, that." He scratched his head. "It's honestly a little difficult to remember *exactly* what components I used. Some happened to simply be whatever was readily available and seemed reasonable..."

Hazel gave him a look of disbelief.

"I'm sorry! It *was* half a year ago! Besides, I had my mind tousled by that icy witch of the Inquisition. Still, I remember I tried to use different components from magic creatures, hoping to imbue you with life. I used some bark from a tree inhabited by a melia, that I know for sure." He paused. "Actually, that is likely why you can communicate with trees and why fire hurts you more than other things. I also used some hair and a hazel wand from an aloja. They are supposed to live a long time and are quite magical fae, so I thought that would help. Plus, they are associated with life-giving properties. It's probably why you heal so much faster in water. I also used some tears from a banshee, hoping their relationship with death would help in bringing you back, but I suppose all it did was give you pre-cognitive abilities. There might have been some other aspects, but I honestly can't remember. I wanted to use phoenix feathers or ashes, but those aren't easy components to find, and the market price is absolutely absurd."

She didn't know what most of those creatures were, but she could find out later. "Is the hazel wand the reason I can use magic?"

His eyes widened. "You can use magic?"

"Yes, or at least that's what I was told. I heard that my ability to talk to plants and my affinity for sorcery were separate."

He blinked several times at what she said. "Well, my girl, you should get tested! Go to the college and demand it. They can tell you what schools of magic you might be able to use."

She nodded. It was worth trying.

"In the meantime..." he hesitated, "would you mind terribly if you came to visit me again?"

"Of course not." She smiled. "You still have another few months for your sentence since the cult agreed to not press charges, and I put in a friendly word with the king. Just stay on your best behavior and maybe he'll let you out early."

He grinned. "I will do just that, though I don't know what I'll do when I get out. Jail hasn't been as bad as I expected. I've managed to catch up on reading while I've been here."

She pondered the question and a small smile spread over her lips. "You should probably avoid using magic, but do you think you could organize books?"

"Well, hmm." He frowned thoughtfully. "Perhaps. My own home was not overly organized, but my shelves were generally pretty well sorted."

"Well," Hazel ventured, "we work in a library but don't have time to catalogue everything. Since you know about magic but aren't supposed to use it, you could sort the books better than me or Alistair. Would you be interested in becoming our librarian?"

"A librarian," he mused. "I had never even considered the idea."

"Well, you might give it some more thought, then. I can always put in a good word with my boss and I doubt he'll object to having you work where others can make sure you're not getting into trouble. Also"—she touched his hand—"it would be nice to see more of you."

He patted her hand and smiled. "You are too kind, child. I will consider your proposition. For now, though, I must return to my cell. I'm reading the second book of a series and very close to the end. Everything is coming to an end, and it's a little sad, but I have hope there may be sequels in the future." He rose and took one last look at Hazel before exiting the room with the waiting guards. Hazel walked out shortly after.

She left the room and skipped a couple of paces. Talking to Hickory somehow seemed right. It was like something that had been nagging at her had finally stopped. She sauntered through the halls of the castle with a lightness in her step. After departing, she closed her eyes and took a deep breath. The air was chilly, but the sun shined.

Spring had just started. As she breathed in the cold air, she realized there was still a little nagging, like she was forgetting something. She crossed her arms. Who else was she supposed to talk to?

She walked toward the gate and absently overheard a guard and woman talking on a stone bench. The woman held out a small basket for him.

"Aw, you shouldn't have!" she overheard the palace guard say placatingly. "You are *just* the best."

"I know both of those things," the woman said. "Don't forget your lunch again, or I might just forget to bring it to you."

Hazel froze. She recognized those voices. She turned and walked toward them. It had been months since she heard them, but she knew that banter anywhere.

"It isn't my fault," Tommy said. "The captain requires us to remember—" he stopped mid-sentence when he saw Hazel approach. His mouth dropped open.

Claire turned around and her eyes widened as she covered her mouth. Hazel noticed she wore a small gold ring.

Hazel's heart beat faster. She didn't know what to say. Hello? Hi? A pithy remark? Nothing seemed to—

Claire and Tommy jumped up and embraced Hazel. They held her and started crying. As they cried, Hazel realized she was crying too. Gradually, their tears turned into laughter. Tommy separated first, wiping his eyes and ushered the two girls away from the gate.

Hazel looked both of them over and smiled through the tears. "I missed you." They all fell back into tears that intermingled with joyous laughter.

"Hazel," Claire said, "how is this possible? We heard rumors, but we didn't listen to them, we"—she looked away—"didn't want to listen to them."

"It was really hard after you... left," Tommy said, averting his eyes. "Really hard. I didn't know what to do. I felt so"—he breathed slowly, keeping himself from weeping again—"I felt like I was responsible. I shouldn't have left you. I'm—"

"It wasn't your fault," Hazel interrupted. "You couldn't have stopped the tree branch from breaking and we had done things like that hundreds of times before and nothing bad ever happened."

"I know, but—"

"Tommy," Hazel said, locking eyes with him, "it isn't your fault. I don't blame you, and you shouldn't blame yourself."

He nodded but couldn't speak.

"I felt bad too," Claire said. "I wanted to visit your parents. I wanted to see them and tell them how sorry I was, but I couldn't do it. Each time I got to their door, it hurt too much to see them. I wanted to take care of them, but I didn't. I'm sorry."

"I love you both," Hazel said, holding both of their hands, "and there is nothing I blame or fault you for. I would have probably done the same. It doesn't matter anymore. I'm alive. And it looks like"— she smiled mischievously—"you two don't have a problem with kissing anymore."

They both immediately blushed. Claire cleared her throat. "Well, Tommy isn't as bad as I thought he was, I guess."

Hazel raised an eyebrow. "Or at least good enough to marry, hmm?"

Tommy grinned. "That's the way it looks."

Hazel breathed in and felt something between them. She pushed her mind out to sense the living things around them, and she grinned. "I'm happy for you. All *three* of you."

Their jaws dropped.

Hazel shrugged, trying to contain her joy but failing. "I guess you two really didn't mind kissing after all." She tried to maintain a straight face as both of them turned even redder. She burst out laughing. The other two eventually joined her.

"Yeah," Tommy said, "Claire is going to have a baby. We only found out earlier this week. I'm confused. She isn't *that* big." Claire elbowed his side. "Ow! I mean, how could you tell?"

Hazel shrugged. "I just have a good sense about these things."

"Is that why... you're green?" Tommy ventured.

Claire made a face at him.

"What?"

Hazel chuckled. "Kind of, yes, but also no. It's a little complicated. Truthfully, even I'm not sure why I'm green."

Claire looked at Hazel, suddenly serious. "Me and Tommy agreed that if we had a girl, we would name her after you."

Hazel swallowed the emotion bubbling up and laughed. "What about if the baby is a boy?"

"Oh, I don't know," Claire said. "We'd probably name him Robert or something."

"Well," Hazel said, reaching out mentally again, "it's a good thing it won't come to that."

"Yeah, it's—what?" His eyes widened. "Do you mean—"

Hazel nodded and both her friends laughed.

Claire looked at Tommy. "We'll have to make an offering to Hemericanth that she grows up happy and healthy."

"I think I can put in a good word or two for you," Hazel said. They both looked at her quizzically. "Don't worry about it. What are you two doing for dinner tonight? I would love to have you over so we can really catch up. I have a very long story to tell both of you."

"I'll bet you do," Claire said. "Should we come to your parents' house?"

"No, come to the old Calixford University Library."

Their confusion grew.

"Like I said, I've got a lot to tell you. I also have some friends I want you to meet."

"We would be happy to!" Tommy said. "Are they as weird as you?"

Hazel thought for a moment. "No, they're weirder."

"Then I'm sure we'll get along." Tommy grinned.

Hazel bade her friends farewell. She would see them again that night. As she strode into the city, she took a deep and refreshing breath of cold air. She grinned as she went, a spring in her step.

It was good to be alive.

Epilogue
Ending At the Beginning

"I told you I could do it!" Hazel yelled down from her high perch. She dangled her bare feet off the highest branch of the tree.

"Not too bad, Hazel," Lara called back. "At least for a human."

"I think it's pretty amazing she reached that height without using any special powers," Alistair said, leaning against another tree.

Hazel breathed in the cool night air. It was late. It was so late it could even be classified as early. She looked at the view that was so familiar to her. She had seen it many months ago with a different group of friends gathered around the base in the few minutes before sunset.

"It's nice that she can climb a tree, but"—Lara raced to the tree and jumped from branch to branch, rapidly ascending to just below where Hazel was—"I can still do it faster."

"Oh yes, impressive with your immense werewolf strength," Alistair said. The vampire floated off the ground and rose until he alighted on a nearby branch. "But if we're just going to use powers, I would say flying is much more remarkable."

"Yeah, it would be, if you could actually do it well."

"I'm better than I was!"

"Not by that much, Al."

A memory of similar circumstances and a flutter of mischief entered Hazel's heart. "Why don't you two just kiss already?"

"Don't be gross," Lara said without thinking.

Alistair's brow knit together. "I believe that's the most patently absurd thing I've ever heard you say, Hazel."

"She may have a point," Lyvaelan said. The dark elf sat on a branch near Hazel but a little lower than Lara. "Your bantering could be a precursor to potential romance."

"You mean like an '*opposites attract*,' kinda thing?" Lara said.

"Hmm." Alistair mused. "I've heard such human couplings are common but rarely work."

"They work *some*times," Hazel said defensively.

"Well, don't hold your breath, Haze. I respect the prince, but he's not exactly my type. I prefer guys who are more substantial. You know, big, meaty, someone I can really sink my teeth into."

Alistair raised an eyebrow. "Are you sure you're describing a man and not a cut of beef?"

Lara grinned. "What's the difference?"

Hazel sighed contentedly. The stars were still out, but a few had faded in the approaching light of the sun. Pretty soon, the night would be over and morning would be here. Part of her wished the night would never end. The trees rustled occasionally with the wind. Animals moved in the dark, but she had nothing to fear.

"By the way," Hazel said, "have you decided if you're going to stay with us, Lara, or did Aldric lose the bet?"

She stretched. "I think I'll stay with the Evenfall Vigil for a little while longer, so I guess I lost the bet. Still, I get as many gold nobles as if I had been winning fights every week, so I don't think I lost the bet *too* badly."

"How will you spend your winnings?" Lyvaelan asked.

"Not sure. How much do you think a hippogriff carriage costs?"

Alistair half smiled. "With, or without, the attached hippogriff?"

She didn't have to think for long. "With."

"Probably worth more than triple that."

"Even with the whole *'you owe us for screwing up'* discount?"

Alistair scratched his head. "Hard to say. They *did* seem sincere about aiding us in the future, but I'm not sure how far we should test that."

"As far as we can, Al. Use it while you have it. Also—unrelated—I've come up with a good name for your sword."

Alistair chuckled. "Oh, really?"

"Yeah, I think you should call it Silvertongue. You're good with words and persuasion, plus your sword has actual silver in it."

"That's... actually not a terrible name," he said slowly, nodding his head. "Silvertongue. I like it. I've never cared much for names anyhow, and that name *does* make sense. Sure. Silvertongue it is."

The two continued talking while Hazel and Lyvaelan remained silent. She looked over at the dark elf warlock. His eyes were closed as he leaned against the tree. This was as peaceful as she had seen him. He seemed content. Still, Hazel dreamed about the day he would be happy.

"The sun will be up in a little over an hour," Alistair said, looking eastward. He drifted down from his spot. "We should return to the library before sunrise."

Lara jumped out of the tree to land on the ground. "Yeah, I guess so." She looked up. "You coming, Hazel?"

"Yeah, you can get started if you want to."

"No," Lyvaelan said. He had descended the tree with effortless grace. "We'd prefer to wait for you."

Hazel grinned and scurried down the tree. Her hands and feet knew the way. The tree told her where to go. Soon she had reached the bottom. She crossed her arms and looked at them.

"Coming, Hazel?" Lyvaelan asked.

"I have an idea," she said. "Let's have a race to the third wall, starting with our hands on the base of this ash tree."

"A race?" Alistair said. "I think a race—"

"I'm in," Lara interrupted. She jeered at Alistair. "What, afraid of losing, princeling?"

Alistair grumbled something under his breath and plodded over.

"Okay," Hazel said, "Let's start with one hand on the tree." The others put their hands on the trunk. "On the count of three, we run. One"—a slight green glow emanated from the girl—"two"—she grinned—"three!" She darted away from the tree and glanced back as Lara yelped in surprise.

The tree trunk had grown around their hands and kept all three attached to the spot.

"Hazel, you cheater!" Lara yelled, struggling against the thick trunk. "Get back here!"

"Nope! I'll see you all back at the third wall." She looked at Lyvaelan, who cocked his head at her.

You know I can break out of this whenever I want, right? He asked telepathically.

I know, she answered back. *I want you to keep them here so I can win!*

He stared blankly and then chuckled. The others looked at him in amazement.

Alright, get going. I suppose I can keep them here for a while with a little sorcery.

She grinned wider and sprinted back to Coruvaine. The wind in her hair, the loud protestations of her friends, and the exhilaration of her imminent victory filled her with invigorating joy. The sun would rise soon. It was a shame, since it was such a beautiful night, but there would be others. For Hazel, there would be many beautiful nights like this, beneath the stars, within the trees, and among good friends. She laughed as she ran through the dark.

And that was how Hazel Enda lived.

Appendix A: Glossary and Pronunciation Guide

Abalia (uh-BALL-ee-uh): An undine.

Alchemy: One of the seven arcane arts practiced by human spell-casters. It requires a high level of memorization but little magic. It is known for creating potions that cause a variety of potent effects.

Aldric Valmore (ALL-drik VAL-mohr): King of Ethelian, he rules from the capital city of Coruvaine.

Algendis (al-JEN-diss): The name of the world.

Alistair zar Erythis (AL-iss-tur ZAR air-ITH-iss): Youngest son and child of the vampire royal family of Noxphetalis and member of the Evenfall Vigil.

Almar Galesti (AL-mahr guh-LESS-tee): The creator of the Inquisition, first Archmage of the Inquisition, and member of the Seven Companions.

Aloja (uh-LOY-uh): A fae creature known for its regenerative properties and affinity to water.

Alvaria Saccarra (AL-VAR-ee-uh suh-CAR-uh): Archmage of the Inquisition and Grand Inquisitor of the Council of Archmages.

Alza'varathede (AL-zuh VAIR-uh-THEED): A famous dragon.

Amphisbaena (am-fiss-BAY-nuh): A small serpentine creature with an identical head at the end of its tail. They are venomous but generally skittish. They use their four small legs to aid in locomotion as they roll along the ground similar to a wheel.

Anton Veruth (ver-OOTH): A confessor of the Paladin Order of Kalendril and a kresnik.

Antony Larsinius (lar-SIN-ee-us): A mage who tried to become a lich and was master of Kazra Lo Veedra before his death.

Apotheotic Magic: The alleged perfected form of each magical art, or the hypothesized summit of their capabilities.

Arcanathema Prison (ar-can-ATH-em-uh): A penitentiary containing those who used or abused magic to commit crime. The prison is run by the Council of Archmages and directly overseen by a warden.

Arcane Arts: The seven methods used by humans to manipulate magic. These seven arts are Alchemy, Conjuration, Enchantment, Lesser Magic, Sorcery, Thaumaturgy, and Wizardry.

Arcane Cataclysm: An immense release of magic causing unpredictable and dangerous changes in the vicinity. This can occur when a warlock loses control of magic and emotions.

Archmage (ARCH-MAYJ): An individual with high mastery in two of the seven arcane arts and mastery in the others may become an archmage. Once this minimum requirement is met, the candidate must be recommended by a current archmage. The entire Council of Archmages then votes, and the individual becomes an archmage with either a two-thirds positive vote, or a one-half positive vote with the express blessing of the High Archmage.

Arlith Kovak (ARR-lith KOE-vak): Chamberlain of Chateau Zarielle, he is a mage and confidant of Alvaria Saccarra.

Athelea: See Appendix C.

Aufhocker (OWF-hawk-er): A generally malevolent shapeshifting fae of shadow, known for leaping on the back of its victims.

Aviana za Serus (ah-vee-AH-nuh zuh SAIR-uss): A vampire.

Avrael (AV-ray-el): Archmage of Nullification, he is also the Warden of Arcanathema Prison. He is half dark elf and maintains a neutral affect.

Bertrand Rollodore (ROLL-uh-dohr): Archmage of the Green.

Black Dog: A variety of fae which may be malevolent or benevolent, depending on the specific kind. They generally appear to be black dogs of greater size, intelligence, and power than normal.

Blood Wine: A human invention designed for vampire consumption. It uses a few drops of human blood and a gallon of wine to create a drink that provides substantial nutrition for vampires.

Bloodcurse: A spell found in vampires, therianthropes, and other nocturnal monsters which increased aggression and predation against humans. Those afflicted exhibited a loss of conscience, decreased intelligence, increased strength, and feral tendencies.

Bluecap: A generally benevolent fae that usually appears in the form of a flickering blue flame and is known for mining.

Briarsleep: A state of suspended animation used by some fae to regenerate expended magic.

Caeli Relinon (KAY-lee RELL-ih-non): High priestess of Semeleme and also the beloved of the same goddess.

Caleptis: See Appendix C.

Calixford University (CAL-icks-furd): An institution for higher learning regarding magic. It is one of the chief magic universities on the western coast and is located in Coruvaine. Lysander Relas acts as chancellor.

Calman Zedonia (CAL-men zeh-DON-yuh): A justiciar of the Paladin Order of Kalendril.

Canneva (CAN-eh-vuh): A silky working for King Aldric.

Cassiana Sommura (cass-ee-AH-nuh soe-MOOR-uh): A mage working within Elimerita's Chosen Conjurers wielding the elemental of water, the undine.

Claire Pernault (per-NALT): One of Hazel's childhood best friends.

Centaur (SEN-tar): A species of daimon, they appear as a human from the waist up with a horse's body and four legs. They are known for their strength and speed. Centaurs are also notoriously dangerous when they consume alcohol.

Chaldra (CHAL-druh): The name of a massive tree and the city that surrounds it in the heart of Elliara. The surrounding area is inhabited by fae and elves. It is also the regular meeting place of the Council of Light.

Charlie: The redcap cook who lives in the Calixford University Library and prepares meals for the Watchers of the Evenfall.

Chateau Zarielle (ZAR-ee-EL): The home of the Grand Inquisitor.

Conjuration: One of the seven arcane arts practiced by human spellcasters. It uses a variable amount of magic depending on the rapport the conjurer has with the creature being summoned. It is known for controlling monsters, casting spirits from those possessed, and for creating summoning circles.

Corbin Parstasia (CORE-bihn pahr-STAY-shuh): Better known as the Warlord of Sarth, his name is used as a byword for the authoritarian and cruel.

Corrim Kalsidere (CORE-ihm KAL-sih-deer): The Archmage of Crystals, also called the Crystal King.

Coruvaine (cor-uh-VAEN): The capital city of the country of Ethelian. It is the location of the primary garrison of the Watchers of the Evenfall.

Council of Liches: A quasi-mythical organization composed of numerous powerful undead beings.

Cult of Semeleme: A religious group dedicated to the proper treatment of the dead. They perform the majority of funerary rites within any given city. Their priests are also known as Undertakers.

Daimon (DIE-mon): Any of a class of beings with a range of special abilities and ties to nature that are not classed with fae. Nymphs, satyrs, centaurs, and minotaurs are examples.

Dark Order: A group of spellcasters known for practicing magic illegally. They orchestrated the destruction of the Light Order and the Gray Order.

Darundar (DAHR-oon-DARH): A gnome.

Diligentia (dill-ih-JEN-see-uh): A collection of confessor paladins led by a justiciar within the Paladin Order of Kalendril.

Dragon: A giant flying reptilian creature possessed of great intelligence, magic, and strength.

Dranderis (dran-DARE-iss): A powerful lich who attempted to destroy the country of Salverno but was stopped by the Seven Companions.

Draugr (DRAW-gur): A form of undead stronger than a zombie but weaker than a lich. They possess intelligence and a myriad of special abilities unique to each.

Drovir (DROE-veer): A dwarf high master alchemist and dean of the

College of Alchemy within Calixford University.

Elchoran: Historical Archmage of Sound who devised a special spell bubble that prevented sound from entering or exiting it.

Elimerita's Chosen Conjurers: A collection of high master conjurers dedicated to the four primary elementals.

Elimia: See Appendix B.

Ellen Honrick (HON-rik): A mage working for the Evenfall Vigil, she reports directly to Commander Marcus Comrear.

Elliara (EL-ee-AR-uh): The vast forest region bordering the Vernal Sea and the Noxphetalis Mountain Range north of Ethelian. It is a place of great magic and home to many fae and elves.

Elliavenra Sivenna (ell-ee-uh-VEN-ruh sih-VEN-uh): The Archmage of Lights.

Elves: A race subdivided into phylogenetically different subspecies and cultures, they share some core traits which separate them from fae, humans, and daimon. While they possess the pointed ears common to many fae, their culture exists independently of other fae and has little interest in humans. They are related to the fae but their exact relationship is unclear. Wars have been fought between light elves and dark elves for millennia and only came to a tipping point when humans aided light elves and pushed the dark elves further north and into the mountains. Elves are generally known for their capriciousness.

Elves, Dark: Generally feared by humans, they are the darkest in complexion and disposition of all elves. Their magic tends to involve illusion and stealth.

Elves, Light: Since they allied with humans during the War of the Night, they are generally viewed positively, even if their behaviors are poorly understood. Their magic tends to involve healing and light.

Elves, Wood: Humans regard them with healthy suspicion and fear. They maintain forests and the balance between flora and fauna. Their magic tends to involve speaking with beasts and plants.

Enchantment: One of the seven arcane arts practiced by human spellcasters. It uses generally large quantities of magic, depending on the enchantment. It is known for imbuing objects and creatures with magic effects which may be beneficial or detrimental.

Ethelian (eh-THEL-ee-uhn): A kingdom on the western coast of the continent, governed from the capital city of Coruvaine by King Aldric Valmore.

Eustace Skilliven: A friendly barkeep and owner of Skilliven Tavern.

Evenfall Vigil: A subset of the Ethelian city guards which handles nocturnal and supernatural threats.

Fae: A class of beings gifted with considerable magic and in possession of rational thought. They are broadly divided into the Seelie Court—for generally benevolent fae—and the Unseelie Court, for malevolent or hostile fae. They generally dislike use of the term "fae" and prefer to be called "sidhe," "the good neighbors," or "the fair folk."

Faelsday: See Appendix B.

Faerie: A world connected to Algendis that is home to the fae.

Felicia Durhost (DUR-hawst): A mage working within Elimerita's Chosen Conjurers wielding the elemental of earth, the gnome.

Gabrielle Sesturnia (ses-TUR-nee-uh): Archmage of Time, she is also a volarim.

Garo (GARE-oh): A grim, he works as an ambassador for the Seelie Court and advisor to the Watchers of the Evenfall Vigil.

Garson Varaldan (GAR-son vuh-RAL-dun): Archmage of Dragons. He used to study them and now he resembles them.

Garvey: A bluecap.

Gazrilan (GAZ-rih-lihn): A dragon little known by others. He is considered lazy by some and is given the epithet of "the Indolent," as a result.

Geas (gesh): A form of contractual magic binding one or more people to a specific course of action to achieve a desired end.

Gharazan'nar'rakesh (gah-rah-ZAHN NAHR ruh-KESH): A famous dragon, known for his cruelty.

Glamour: Magic used primarily by fae to disguise their appearance and influence the attitude humans hold toward them.

Gnome: One of the great prime elemental races representing earth.

Gnostrevaine: See Appendix C.

Gray Empire: The largest human governing body on the continent. It is a confederacy of countries overseen by the emperor. Each country maintains considerable autonomy but must obey rules, laws, and standards put forth by the empire.

Griffin: A large creature with the head, wings, and forelimbs of an eagle with the hindquarters of a lion.

Grim: Also called "church grim," they are mostly benevolent fae who guard particular areas or individuals. Garo is an example.

Guard Unyielding: The elite warrior mages whose primary duty is protecting the High Archmage.

Hazel Enda (HAY-zuhl EHN-duh): Only child of Kyle and Lynn Enda. She died when she fell from a tree. She returned from death and became a member of the Evenfall Vigil.

Hemericanth: See Appendix C.

Hickory Allkirk (HIK-or-ee AHL-kerk): A mage illegally experimenting in Coruvaine. He brings Hazel back from the dead.

Hippogriff: A large creature with the head, wings, and forelimbs of an eagle with the hindquarters of a horse.

Irid (EER-id): A diminutive daimon closely related to nymphs, known for their speed and proclivity to gossip.

Kazra Lo Veedra (KAZ-ruh loe-VEE-druh): The estate belonging to Antony Larsinius.

Kelsyn (KELL-sin): A human master sorcerer working as secretary to Archmage Lysander Relas at Calixford University.

Kiran (KEER-ihn): Lyvaelan's deceased teacher and father figure. He was a human mage.

Kistra: See Appendix C.

Komora: See Appendix C.

Kresnik (KREZ-nihk): A person who can send out a magical manifestation of their consciousness in the form of an animal that deters and destroys creatures of malicious intent or black magic.

Kyle Enda: A blacksmith by trade. He is the father of Hazel Enda.

Kythis (KI-thiss): The small pink moon orbiting retrograde around the planet. In poetry and colloquially, it is referred to as either the sister or the lover of the larger moon, Progon, and is occasionally regarded as feminine. Children born under the full moon of Kythis are believed to be of cheerful disposition.

Lara (LAH-ruh): A werewolf, previously famous for power fighting. She now works for the Evenfall Vigil.

Lesser Magic: One of the seven arcane arts practiced by human spellcasters. It uses generally variable quantities of magic depending on the type of ability being used. It is known for its practical application of the other arcane arts, including pest control, medical potions, healing, and agriculture but eschews complex theories and spells with a narrow range of uses.

Lexia: An irid.

Lich: The most powerful variety of undead, capable of summoning great undead armies and wielding massive amounts of magic with ease.

Living Conduit: A former mage who experimented on himself. He is an inmate of Arcanathema Prison.

Loong (LONG): A close relative of dragons, it has a serpentine body and possesses the ability to fly without wings and can control the weather.

Luthain River (LOO-THANE): A river that passes through Coruvaine.

Lynn Enda: A midwife by trade. She is the mother of Hazel Enda.

Lysander Relas (lih-SAN-dur RELL-us): Archmage of Education and former Archmage of War. He is the chancellor of Calixford University.

Lyvaelan (lih-VAY-luhn): A half dark elf, half warlock young man who lived in Elliara until he joined the Evenfall Vigil.

Mael Stromm (MAY-ELL STROM): The ruler of Salverno and subject of a prophecy.

Mage: A human spellcaster who has attained proficiency in two or more arcane arts.

Magelamp: A magical construct that emits light.

Magomechanics: A field of magical experimentation that combines mundane technological advances with magical advances.

Malvex Sorrelle (MAHL-vex sur-EL): Archmage of Sorcery, and half dark elf. He was the previous Grand Inquisitor before Alvaria Saccarra.

Manticore (MAN-tih-cohr): A large creature similar in shape to a lion but possessing a humanoid face and innumerable venomous quills at the end of its tail.

Marcus Comrear (COM-reer): Human commander of the Evenfall Vigil. He appears gruff to most people.

Marinom (MARE-ih-nom): A weapon that can change shape and is used by spellcasters.

Mark Annokest (ANN-o-kest): A mage working within Elimerita's Chosen Conjurers wielding the elemental of fire, the salamander.

Melantria: See Appendix B.

Melantros: See Appendix C.

Melia (MELL-ee-uh): A daimon and nymph of ash trees similar to a dryad.

Mellius Concornus (MELL-ee-us cun-COR-nuss): A satyr working for the Evenfall Vigil. He possesses the rank of sergeant.

Mikhail zar Alacris (uh-LACK-riss): A vampire.

Minotaur (MIN-uh-tar): A monstrous daimon that appears to be a combination of human and bull. They are known for their strength and ferocity.

Naiad (NI-ad): A nymph with the ability to control water. Usually found in areas of fresh water, such as rivers and lakes. They appear as generally beautiful humans with blue skin.

Necromancy: The illegal use of magic to resuscitate, control, or speak with the dead.

Nosferatu (NOS-fehr-AH-too): A particular kind of vampire known for aversion to sunlight, close resemblance to humanity, and social allure. Alistair is an example.

Noxphetalis (NOCKS-feh-TAL-iss): A mountain range known for harboring vampires and Unseelie fae.

Nymph: A particular subspecies of daimon, known for their beauty and generally positive disposition toward humanity. Nymphs are either all female or only the females of species are known.

Oleisia (uh-LEE-see-uh): A naiad who works for the Evenfall Vigil.

Orichalcum (or-ee-KAL-cum): A rare coppery-gold metal derived from ore found in areas of high magic. Its physical properties as a metal are most similar to copper but with a slightly lower melting point. It is valued by spellcasters for its magic conductivity that even exceeds gold.

Orson zar Aeneus (uh-NAY-uss): A vampire.

Palace Valsidan (VAL-SIH-DAN): The headquarters of the Council of Archmages and the home of the High Archmage. It is located in Selevarian.

Paladin Order of Kalendril (cuh-LEHN-dril): A group of warriors possessing magic skill in thaumaturgy dedicated to the mission of their founder, Kalendril, and guided by the triune worship of Veratheragan, Melantros, and Caleptis.

Paxton Averly (PACKS-tun AE-ver-lee): An alchemist living in Coruvaine, he occasionally works as a consultant for the Evenfall Vigil.

Pegasus (plural: pegasi): A winged horse known for its speed.

Peryton (PAIR-ih-ton): A hybrid monster of deer and bird parts with a savage temperament.

Petrim (PEH-trim): A country to the south of Ethelian and bordering Selevarian. It is governed by an aristocracy of knights. The country is known for the chivalry of its ruling class and the high magic that permeates the land.

Pixie: A diminutive fae of the Seelie Court.

Power Fighting: A recreational sport where nonhuman creatures and magically enhanced humans fight one-on-one in a minimally regulated brawl. It is a popular event among gamblers.

Progon (PRO-GON): The large white moon that orbits prograde around the planet. In poetry and colloquially, Progon is referred to as the brother or lover of Kythis, the smaller moon, and is occasionally regarded as masculine. Children born under the full moon of Progon are said to be more serious or ambitious than others.

Ravnulium (rav-NULL-ee-um): A black metal that is noted for its anti-magical properties.

Raynard: A werefox.

Redcap: A generally malevolent fae, it is known for its talonlike claws, short stature, and eponymous red cap. Charlie is an example.

Revenant: A human returned to life through necromancy. The creature shows signs of mental and physical deterioration within a few weeks before dying again.

Riglin Carstaff (RIHG-lihn CAHR-staff): A dwarf living in Coruvaine, he works as the chief foreman of the fourth wall and oversees his bluecap workers.

Ryxiv (RICKS-ihv): The underworld, or an area of the underworld often considered the darkest place filled with torment and fear.

Sakirikas (suh-KEER-uh-kiss): A salamander.

Salamander: One of the great prime elemental races representing fire.

Sapphire Guard: Coruvaine's city guard that confines and interrogates criminals with magical abilities, consisting of normal humans and spellcasters. They operate from within the palace.

Satyr (SAY-tur): A specific species of daimon known for their halfway appearance between human and goat. They are known for their agility, exuberance, and magic.

Scry Mirror: A device used to communicate over vast distances quickly, but expensive to create and requires magic to operate.

Selevara: See Appendix C.

Selevarian (SEL-uh-VAR-ee-uhn): The city-country of spellcasters. It is ruled by the High Archmage and Council of Archmages. The city is noteworthy for its size, high population, and prevalence of magic.

Selevia Castus (sell-EE-vee-uh CASS-tus): A commander of the Guard

Unyielding, she possesses a mechanical eye created by the Archmage of Magomechanics.

Semeleme: See Appendix C.

Shadarqiir (SHAH-DAHR-KEER): A lithe monster that lurks in the dark and possesses intelligence. He is utterly unique.

Shadow World: A partially formed realm that runs parallel to Algendis, showing reflections of the world in the form of shadows. Some creatures pass through it to travel great distances in a short time.

Shadowseer: An individual who uses the images of the Shadow World to predict the future or interpret the past.

Sidhe (SHEE): See Fae.

Silky: A household fae similar to a brownie but it governs larger estates and wears silk.

Skilliven Tavern: A bar and inn operated and owned by Eustace Skilliven.

Soraya: A squire of the Paladin Order of Kalendril.

Sorcery: One of the seven arcane arts practiced by human spellcasters. It uses little magic but requires significant creativity and mental fortitude. It is known for reading the thoughts of others, moving objects without touching them, and creating illusions.

Spellcaster: A human who uses magic.

Spellweaver: One who uses magic to create garments or cloth, which gives the item an innate magic that differs from a normal enchantment. Such artisans are rare and expensive to hire.

Spheres of Elchoran: A spell devised by an archmage to aid with studies. It creates a spherical area of silence. The spellcaster can choose whether it blocks sound from entering, exiting, or both.

Spriggan (SPRIG-in): A fae bodyguard known for possessing incredible strength.

Squareball: An athletic game played by spellcasters. It consists of four teams vying for control over a ball. Each group uses magic to maintain possession over several timed rounds.

Succubus: A generally malevolent spirit who seduces others in the guise of a woman but drains their life force.

Susan Telemica (tel-EM-ik-uh): An alchemist practicing in Coruvaine.

Sylph: One of the great prime elemental races representing air.

Talva (TAL-vuh): A human enchantress and alchemist who pioneered literary cuisine. She runs her own shop called Talva's Cookbook.

Tavek: See Appendix C.

Telerius Saccarra (tell-AIR-ee-uss suh-CAHR-uh): Deceased father of Alvaria Saccarra.

Terekmalamae: See Appendix C.

Thaumaturgy (THAW-mat-erj-ee): One of the seven arcane arts practiced by human spellcasters. It uses little magic but requires a specific spiritual alignment to function properly. It is known for healing and enhancing physical traits.

Therianthrope (THER-ee-an-thrope): A being formerly human but now capable of assuming the appearance or abilities of specific animals at night. A werewolf is an example.

Thomas Eller: Chief Inquisitor of Coruvaine.

Throne of Austerity: A magic seat given to the vampires upon which the lord of Noxphetalis sits.

Tommy Beckinger (BECK-in-jerr): A childhood friend of Hazel Enda.

Thyrsus: A staff topped with a pinecone, used by certain daimon to induce a state of extreme intoxication.

Transcendent Society of the Moth: A group of vampires dedicated to the tenets of their legendary deceased leader, the Moth King.

Treland (TREH-lehnd): A city along the northern border of Ethelian known for its amphitheater and power fighting.

Umbravelle: See Appendix C.

Undine (UHN-DEEN): One of the great elemental races representing water.

Valravn (VAL-rawn): A raven which becomes imbued with fae magic and the ability to shapeshift after consuming the heart of a human. Additional hearts increase its power.

Vampire: A class of being with nocturnal habits, pained by thaumaturgical healing, and generally human appearance. Camazotz and nosferatu are examples of different species of vampire.

Veiled Chapel: The home of High Priestess Caeli Relinon and the primary place of worship for the Cult of Semeleme.

Veliyana (vell-ee-AW-nuh): A sylph.

Venarius zar Erythis (veh-NAR-ee-us ZAR air-ITH-iss): The King of Nosferatu, located in Noxphetalis. He is the father of Alistair.

Veratheragan: See Appendix C.

Volarim/Volar (voe-LAHR-ihm, VOE-lahr): Humanoids with bird-like wings, they come from the far north.

War of the Night: A conflict between humanity and vampires, therianthropes, and Unseelie fae, spanning several centuries and ended with the removal of a curse from vampires which stripped them of reason and morals.

Warlock: A human who broke the oath of Selevara in order to cast in the manner of the fae. They possess magical prowess far exceeding the majority of humans but limited ability to control it.

Werefox: A therianthrope with the ability to transform into a fox.

Wizardry: One of the seven arcane arts practiced by human spellcasters. It uses generally large quantities of magic and requires significant education and knowledge to function. It is known for altering the physical world in dramatic ways.

Wyvern (WI-vurn): A draconic creature bearing wings and two legs.

Yokai (YO-KI): Strange beings from another continent.

Zelim Thain (ZEL-im THAYN): A mage working within Elimerita's Chosen Conjurers wielding the elemental of air, the sylph.

Zigglepet (ZIG-uhl-peht): A bluecap working on the fourth wall.

Zylit (ZI-liht): A small portion of a conjuring circle indicating the summoner's identity.

Zombie: An undead creature possessed of no will of its own except for what its creator desires. It is an animated dead body manipulated by an obedient control spirit.

Appendix B: The Imperial Calendar

The imperial calendar was devised early in the formation of the empire to assist with commerce between nations. Before the unification, each country had widely varying measurements for the year, with a new year starting at different times, weeks of differing lengths, and months devised regardless of season. Scholars collaborated to create a calendar that was reasonable, accurate, and incorporated the cultures of the countries within the empire.

There are twelve months, which are composed of four weeks each. The first day of the year is also the first day of spring on the first of Verathia. Each season lasts for three months. The months in order are: Verathia (vare-ATH-ee-uh), Hemeria (hem-AIR-ee-uh), Rylith (RI-lith), Faerake (FAE-rayk), Kryvsta (KRIV-stuh), Kistria (KISS-tree-uh), Caleptia (cuh-LEPT-ee-uh), Reapwell (REEP-well), Elimia (el-IHM-ee-uh), Melantria (mell-AHN-tree-uh), Athelia (ath-EL-ee-uh), and Venamor (VEN-uh-mohr).

A week has eight days, each named after a different god. The first five days are named after gods of order whose months were renamed (with the exception of Versday which honors Veratheragan and recognizes his primacy among the gods), while the last three days—or "weekend"—are named after the first three Gods of Chaos to unite with the Gods of Order (see Appendix C for additional details). In order, the days are: Versday, Kalsday, Faelsday, Kaesday, Selsday, Komsday, Talsday, and Semsday.

Appendix C: The Pantheon

While there are regional deities and beings worshipped by those in the countryside, the Gray Empire recognizes twenty-two "true" gods whose existence is known through history and direct revelation.

The general understanding of the first age is that a conflict arose between the gods. Eleven gods held that it was best to create new things (these are now referred to as *Gods of Order*) and the eleven remaining gods disagreed, claiming that the nothingness of the beginning was beautiful and ought to remain unspoiled (these are now referred to as *Gods of Chaos*).

The powers on each side were equal until an accord was reached by Veratheragan and Semeleme, who represented the greatest of the gods of order and chaos, respectively. After Semeleme agreed to join with the Gods of Order, Komora abandoned the mission of her fellow Gods of Chaos, as did Skizivik Tal. With three Gods of Chaos adopting their cause, the Gods of Order quickly forced surrender or defeated the remaining deities.

In the ensuing peace, it is believed the gods collaborated on the fundamental structure of the universe, with each God of Order creating the rule and a matching God of Chaos providing a limitation to the rule.

Below are listed the Gods of Order followed by the Gods of Chaos. Some believe the order they are traditionally presented in correlates to their order of importance in the pantheon, since Veratheragan and Semeleme appear first on both lists. This is questionable to some scholars since various cultures and texts refer to gods as varying in strength, while others think discussing relative "power" to be a purely human invention and one as inappropriate to the gods as discussing the relative intelligence of stones. While each god is attributed a specific domain of influence, the listed qualities are only those most acknowledged throughout the Gray Empire.

Gods of Order

Veratheragan (VAIR-uh-THAIR-uh-gin): Ruler of the gods, Lord of Peace (but considered a god of war). Usually depicted and referred to as male.

Selevara (SEL-uh-VAHR-uh): Lady of Magic, patron of spellcasters. Usually depicted and referred to as female.

Caleptis (cuhl-EHP-tiss): Lord of Healing, the Lifebringer, usual patron of doctors and thaumaturgists. Usually depicted as male, though some cultures see the deity as female.

Athelea (ATH-uh-LAY-uh): Lady of Earned Knowledge, said to favor those who toil for knowledge, including scientists and students. Usually depicted as female.

Melantros (mel-AN-trose): Lord of Hospitality, said to protect the household and guests. Usually depicted as male.

Faelvirma (FALE-VEER-muh): Goddess of Freedom, it is said the god favors those who are ambitious. Usually depicted as female.

Kalignus (kuhl-IG-nuss): Shepherd of Many Herds, considered the god of animals, specifically those domesticated. Usually depicted as male.

Hemericanth (hem-AIR-ih-canth): Lord of Life, traditionally considered the guardian of plants but also of life itself. Usually depicted as male.

Kistra (KISS-truh): Lord of Stars, considered to be the one who designed constellations and placed the moons into orbit. Generally depicted as male or genderless.

Elimerita (el-ih-MARE-ih-tuh): Lady of Elements, considered to be the creator of weather and the elementals. Usually depicted as female.

Kaerestra (KAY-RESS-truh): Lady of Reality, considered to be the patroness of philosophers and those seeking the truth. Usually depicted as female.

Gods of Chaos

Semeleme (seh-MELL-ehm-ee): Lady of Death, the Veiled Maiden, ruler of the Gods of Chaos. Usually depicted as female.

Terekmalamae (TAIR-ek-MAL-uh-may): Lord of Magic, considered the patron of fae and those who use magic innately. Some attribute Arcane Madness to him. Usually depicted as male.

Mirnak (MEER-nak): God of Destruction and Violence. No cult exists that worships this god officially, though some invoke his name as an extreme malediction. Usually depicted as male.

Gnostrevaine (NOES-treh-VAIN): Lord of Secrets and Forbidden Knowledge. This god favors those who wish to know what should not be known. Usually depicted as male or genderless.

Komora (KOE-MORE-uh): Lady of Lonely Paths, she is the goddess of wanderers, travelers, and those who are metaphorically alone. Usually depicted as female.

Fal Inderva (FAL ihn-DERV-uh): Lord of Fate and Prophecy. Usually depicted as male.

Stezelra (STEZ-EL-ruh): The Wild Lady, she is the goddess of the wilderness and untamable animals and monsters. Usually depicted as female.

Zerkendra (zuhr-KEHN-druh): The Inexorable One, this goddess is considered to cause all physical laws to function without regard for human desires. Usually depicted as female.

Umbravelle (um-bruh-vell): The Dark Lady, she is the goddess of night and all nocturnal creatures. Usually depicted as female.

Tavek (TAH-vihk): Lord of Inevitable Motion, he is thought to power the hands of smiths and craftsmen beyond their control. Usually depicted as male.

Skizivik Tal (SKIZ-ih-vihk TAHL): Lord of Madness and Poetry, he is considered the patron of those obsessed with their work. Often thought to be the most colloquially chaotic of the gods. Usually depicted as male.

Acknowledgements

All those who helped me during the release of the first book deserve similar praise here. Mary, for being the first reader, deserves great thanks, as do William and Peter. My parents, my sister, and all other friends who supported me I also thank.

To everyone who bought the first book, thank you! Your support is extremely meaningful and I love that we can enjoy the world I made together. Very special thanks is due to those who read it *and reviewed it.* I cannot stress enough how important reviews are to authors. If you think your opinion doesn't matter, you're wrong. It matters very, very much. If you ever want to make an indie author happy, just write a review.

My third thank you goes to Rachel, who drew what she imagined many of my characters looked like. I admire people with artistic talent as it is not a skill I have cultivated. Seeing my creativity directly inspire creativity in others is an experience for which there are no words. Thank you for your art.

Finally, I want to thank everyone I talked to who finished my book. I get passionate about my work and tend to interrogate and probe to see how certain aspects of the story landed. If you are one of these people, I appreciate your honesty and patience. Thank you.

About the Author

Joe Field is the author of all books set in the world of Algendis, and *Watchers of the Evenfall* is his debut novel. After submitting his manuscript to numerous literary agents, Joe decided to self-publish so he could be rejected by a much wider audience. Realizing his first book was not disappointing enough, he opted to publish its sequel. He is a student of psychology and an amateur YouTuber. He loves world folklore and mythology and wished to see a greater range of monsters in fantasy than dragons and unicorns, which is one of the inspirations for his work. He lives with his two cats in north Texas. If you have questions, or would like to learn more, you can visit his website at www.joefieldwriter.com.